TRAP AND TRACE

BY

MEGAN CARNEY

Learn more about Megan Carney at megancarney.com.
ISBN-13: 978-1734759044

To anyone who thinks resilience can't be learned.
You're wrong. I know I was.

PROLOGUE

AS FAR AS Jackson could tell, the spiky green mold on his left-overs posed more of a national security risk than the targets of his current assignment.

From the driver's seat, he stared at the glass and steel sculpture that was Schiphol, the Amsterdam airport. It did not spit out his quarry. Jackson Fletcher tapped his finger impatiently near the door lock. Even on a quiet afternoon, he would keep the car locked until he had to get out. He'd learned more than once not to let his guard down. The car idled. He'd chosen the Renault because it was one of the most common in the city. The anonymity suited his business for the day, picking up an undercover CIA agent ten years his junior.

A gray Peugeot 206 pulled up in front of him. Doors swooshed open for a man in his fifties and a young girl. They both wore New York T-shirts. A father and a daughter, Jackson guessed. The woman at the wheel jumped out to hug them. Excited voices in Dutch drifted through the car window; he translated out of habit. They'd eaten pizza, visited Times Square, seen the Natural History Museum. They hugged for a second time. Jackson looked away, feeling like an intruder.

He wondered again why he'd agreed to spend his vacation

chasing ghosts in Amsterdam when he could have been skiing Mount Bohemia with his family instead. No, he knew why. Because Erin wouldn't be talked out of going on this assignment. And he was tired of dinners at his parent's cabin, lying to his family about what he did.

Perhaps he had been in the agency too long. He knew two analysts who had quit in the past year. One had been asked to change his report to exaggerate the threat posed by a splinter Taliban group. The other had been asked to amend her report with information she had already dismissed as unreliable. A lawyer he knew had quietly been asked to resign after objecting to a new surveillance program.

There were unhappy employees everywhere, even in the best of times. But recently, Langley had more than usual. A paranoid man might say the trouble at headquarters had something to do with the president's fading poll numbers. President Orway had swept into office on promises of transparency, honesty, and straight talk. What landed him in the news lately was the unpopular military presence in Afghanistan and the new surveillance powers he was requesting from Congress. Last time Jackson had been stateside, he'd overheard rumors that the president was getting desperate to salvage the last two years of his term. A desperate man in a high office was a dangerous thing.

Jackson had to wonder if any of his operations had been tainted by the president's political problems. Jackson's normal stomping ground was Afghanistan, tracking terrorist training camps. This time he had been assigned to follow a group from Afghanistan to Amsterdam. Frankly, he would have preferred to leave them alone. The only one in the group with any intelligence was the leader. He had proved himself to be cruel and calculating, but without much in the way of management skills. The rest of the band could charitably be called amateurs. Their ham-handed plan was to kidnap the loved ones of public figures with high-level security clearances and demand information as ransom. For reasons unknown to Jackson, his superiors had decided this terrorist cell was part of a larger ring with the same intentions.

Now he was going along with his orders only because of Erin Brody, a colleague and an old friend. She had agreed to play the niece of a senator and let herself be kidnapped by the group. An extreme version of reverse interrogation.

Jackson hated the plan.

Getting her kidnapped might be the quickest way to find the base of operations, but it was also the most risky. It made more sense to give Roy, the agent Jackson was picking up, time to earn their trust. To get inside the cell as a participant rather than a victim.

He scanned the sparse crowd again. Roy should have arrived by now. There he was. He carried a backpack and pulled a bulging roller bag behind him. First sign of a novice: he had overpacked.

Jackson unlocked the car so Roy could open the hatchback. The roller bag thumped against the upholstery when Roy threw it in. He kept the backpack with him, hugging it to his chest.

When Roy slipped into the passenger seat, his nerves were written on his face. "Good afternoon." Roy had forgotten to use the sign/countersign agreed on earlier.

A reprimand on the importance of good tradecraft could wait. "Afternoon. How was the flight?"

Still clutching his backpack, Roy scanned the panorama of faces waiting for rides.

"Being a little anxious is normal," Jackson said. "You'll do fine."

"This is my first operation undercover." Roy's fingers twisted the strap on his backpack.

Jackson knew it was Roy's first time. He also knew other agents who had the right experience were available.

"I mean, I'm honored and all," Roy continued. His expression was a cross between a grimace and a smile. "To be picked for an operation as sensitive and high profile as this means they really trust me."

Or they need a fall guy, thought Jackson. Roy's assignment was not an easy one. A rookie was an odd choice. It was just one of many things about this operation that didn't add up. Jackson didn't normally resort to scare tactics, but everyone would be better off if he could frighten Roy into backing out.

"Yeah, it's certainly a vote of confidence in your skills," Jackson said. "The leader of this cell was a doctor, you know. Around the camps, he was known as the human lie detector because he could read people's vital signs so well from across a table. They used him for a lot of interrogations."

Roy's eyes widened. Then he pasted that nervous, overconfident grin back on his face. "I play a good game of poker."

A good game of poker? Jesus. What exactly did Roy think was at stake here?

"I'll only be a few yards away the whole time," Jackson said. "And since you're meeting him inside the Van Gogh Museum, he'll have to go through the metal detector, so he probably won't have a gun or a knife." The meeting was actually at a restaurant near the museum.

"No, the meeting is at the restaurant a block away."

"Oh, that's right."

Jackson let Roy ponder what a doctor with a knife could do to him in the sixty seconds it would take before his backup arrived. The slightly nauseous expression on Roy's face told Jackson his comments were working. He wouldn't be able to talk Roy out of this operation in one car ride, but overnight he might have a chance.

"You know, we can always delay this meeting. Pretend your plane was late. It would give you some time to scout the location.

Maybe get a bit more comfortable." A veteran agent would have insisted on such precautions.

"No," Roy said. "I want to do this."

Inwardly, Jackson sighed. "Let's go over the plan again." He pulled the Renault into traffic on the A4, trying to ignore the whining sound the clutch made every time he pressed the pedal.

"I'm meeting the group at a—"

"They don't go out in public as a group. You're just meeting one of them, right?"

"Yeah, that's what I meant."

Be nice, Jackson told himself. "And which one of them are you meeting?"

"The Londoner, the guy in charge."

"He's not from London, he's from Manchester."

Roy looked a little carsick. Maybe I should lower my expectations, Jackson thought. Jackson had been a soldier before he'd been a spy. He'd smiled at the devil long before he went undercover.

"Repeat your cover story," Jackson said.

"I just finished grad school in California. I found the American Jihadist's videos online—"

"Only government agents call him that. What's his name?"

"O-omar Hammami."

Jackson checked his mirrors to hide his expression. Had he been this bad on his first operation? "Good. That's right. So you found his videos online and . . ."

"Then I started reading and posting on message boards. My girlfriend, Jackie Pierce—"

"Your ex-girlfriend."

"Right. My ex-girlfriend, Jackie Pierce—"

"Do you normally refer to ex-girlfriends by their full names?"

"Oh, right, no. My ex-girlfriend, Jackie, got angry at me. She said I was starting to sound like a terrorist. I realized that I needed to change my direction in life, ditch my old ties to the imperialist, capitalist system and the infidels running it." That sounded a little better.

"And you saw Neil Logan's kidnapping plans on a message board and you thought of your now ex-girlfriend because . . . ?" The fact that the sleeper cell had posted their plans publicly was just another hint they weren't much of a threat. In Jackson's experience, the boastful ones enjoyed imagining their cruel fantasies more than acting on them.

"Who's Neil Logan?" Roy asked.

Jackson hoped Roy would be less of an idiot when the nerves wore off. "The one from Manchester. The guy you're meeting." He pulled onto the A10, the ring road surrounding the city center. "Your cover would only know him by his handle, liverpoolsucks."

Roy looked carsick again.

"I'm sure you'll do fine." Jackson wasn't sure at all. Honestly, it would be better for everyone if Roy failed to impress Neil Logan. That bit about the knife and the gun had been an exaggeration. With Jackson as backup, it was unlikely Roy would be hurt. And with Neil scared off, maybe Jackson could move on to higher-value targets. "You thought Neil might be interested in your ex because . . . ?"

"Because her uncle is a senator with top secret clearance."

Jackson turned off the ring road onto one of the main arteries into the city. He kept one foot near the brake. The cyclists in Amsterdam were fearless. And with so many of them, Amsterdam was one of the few cities in the world that had bicycle traffic jams.

"Okay, so your goal for this meeting?" Jackson asked.

"Convince Neil that the fictional Jackie Pierce would make a good kidnapping target."

Erin would be Jackie Pierce when the time came. It was a stupid plan. A stupid, stupid plan. Jackson pulled the car into Parking Museumplein, one of the large parking areas inside the city center. They were six blocks from where Roy was supposed to meet Neil. "And if everything goes well today?"

"I send him Erin's—I mean Jackie's—itinerary and a description of the traveling party. Jackie, five foot six, with blond hair and hazel eyes. A female friend with dark hair and green eyes and a male friend with red hair and brown eyes."

Jackson wanted to hit his head against the steering wheel. "You have the wrong description. The other two undercover agents getting kidnapped are both male."

"But I was sure—"

"Never mind," Jackson said. "We can fix that later. All you have to do today is convince him Jackie Pierce is a good target."

Roy clutched his backpack and nodded. "Can I ask you something?"

Jackson pulled into an empty spot next to a gardener's truck that had seen better days. "Sure."

"Were you nervous your first time undercover?"

He hadn't been.

"It's like sex," Jackson said. "The first time is always awkward, but you won't regret the experience."

Roy looked more scandalized than relieved.

"That was a joke," Jackson said.

The laugh Roy forced sounded more like a hiccup.

Jackson wondered how he was going to keep Erin alive.

Erin eyed the box of chocolates she could see through the peephole. It was rare for Byron to be in DC after five on a Friday night. He had said more than she wanted to hear during their phone call. She wasn't his daughter; she didn't need a lecture. He should go home to his manicured lawn and neighborhood watch group.

Byron looked up and down the hallway, then lifted the lid of the chocolates. There was no candy in the box, just a pistol. He held it up so she could get a better look. The Black model made by Cerberus Tactical. Her favorite.

Like Erin, the pistol cared more about utility than beauty. Its lines weren't sleek, but it was reliable and accurate. Unlike some prettier guns, the grip worked well with gloves when she didn't want to leave fingerprints. Which was pretty much always. If she didn't let Byron in, the pistol would probably just sit in Byron's gun safe for the rest of its life.

That would be a crime.

She opened the door and Byron pushed through, as if he was afraid she would change her mind. Jackson had probably put him up to this.

"It's an early birthday present from Jackson and me," Byron said.

The trio had been friends for a long time, but they rarely exchanged gifts. "My birthday is two months from now."

"I said early."

She took the box from him and weighed the gun in her hand. It felt just right. She'd lost her Black on her last operation, but she still had plenty of spare ammunition. Tomorrow afternoon she could visit the gun range and get reacquainted. She set her present on the coffee table where she could admire it.

"You only get to keep it if we talk," Byron said.

"Jackson can't dictate to me all the way from Amsterdam."

"It's my condition too."

She gestured toward the couch. "You might as well sit while I pretend to listen."

Byron didn't sit so much as perch on the edge of the cushions. He leaned toward her with an earnest, intent expression. "There's something off about Operation Critical Mass. You shouldn't go."

She settled into the cushions and put on her best listening face. "All of my operations are dangerous."

"Not like this. You're making yourself a target for a kidnapping ring. When they take you from the airport they're going to drug you. It'll be an hour before you're even able to defend yourself."

She'd been home for three weeks now and was itching to get back in the field. This operation wasn't her first choice, but her handler had been firm: take this operation or be benched for an undetermined period. Byron hadn't been in the field for years. He had retired to a desk job to be closer to his wife and daughter. Of course he wouldn't understand.

"So if you're acting like my mother, does that make Jackson my father?" she asked.

Byron glared at her. "I might not have your combat skills but I've been in the background of a lot of operations. There's something very wrong with this one. We should wait for Roy to earn the trust of the kidnapping ring. You don't have to play the victim." He launched into the same list of objections he'd bored her with on the phone.

She tried not to yawn.

"And I have a new reason. Today some guy from ops comes to me asking about an image search he did for Operation Critical Mass. Looking for women who are five-six, weigh one hundred fifty-five pounds, and have hazel eyes."

"Operations does that routinely to find photographs of me that might have been posted online." It was half-true. Normally image searches were limited to pictures that had been posted publically, and only to facial recognition. She'd never heard of a search that included height and weight.

"He was asked to search the passport and driver's license database. For five-foot-six *blonde* women who have hazel eyes."

Her hair was jet-black. Soon she would dye it blond for the operation. She fingered a lock before she could stop herself. "So they're looking for pictures of me as a blonde woman to prevent cases of mistaken identity."

"If they wanted to make sure no one else gets kidnapped they'd give the kidnappers a better way to identify you."

It was odd that Willy, the operations manager, hadn't given the kidnappers a definite signal—like a distinctive suitcase or temporary tattoo. But she didn't want Byron to see that she was concerned. "Maybe the image search was one of Willy's stupid ideas."

"I asked him and he didn't know a thing about it. He also didn't know why ops was ordered to run credit reports through one of our shell corporations for anyone who's a close match."

That was definitely not routine. "I've been in plenty of dicey situations. I'll be fine."

He hesitantly put a hand over hers. "Jackson's your friend. I'm your friend. We're just trying—"

Erin punched Byron's shoulder "Ow!"

"I'm touched, but it's none of your fucking business," she said. He should know better than to interfere.

Byron looked hurt.

"You know I'd kill for you," she said. It was her way of declaring friendship. "Jackson, too. But you two are being paranoid."

"Jackson's a field agent. He's supposed to be paranoid."

"What's your excuse?" she asked.

"Old habits die hard." Byron had never been an enthusiastic field agent. He hadn't taken pride in his work, like she did.

"You can leave my gun and take your advice with you."

CHAPTER 1

NAVY TRENT ALWAYS thought about the ex while she was climbing. Not her last ex-boyfriend, but *the ex*. Look at me now, she wanted to tell him. Sixty feet in the air, clinging to a waterfall of ice. *I am not afraid. You did not break me.* Even now, she could see the text of the police report. Victim found unconscious. Five-foot-six blonde female. Approximately one hundred fifty-five pounds.

Her open-mouthed breath condensed on the ice just in front of her nose. She wasn't cold; the exertion of her muscles wouldn't allow it. Her adrenaline and, yes, anger helped too.

A quickdraw, two carabiners connected by a short strap, dangled from the ice screw near her shoulder. The rope connecting Navy to her climbing partner, Sara, ran through it and up to the belay station where Sara waited and watched. Sara was anchored to the ice for Navy's safety. Navy disconnected the rope from the carabiner. She removed the ice screw, with the quickdraw attached, and attached the quickdraw to a loop on her harness.

Navy found the next anchor five feet up and to her left. She extended her left leg, enjoying the strength of her muscles. Tap, tap, crunch. The blade at the tip of her crampons dug into the ice. She brought her right leg up to her left leg. Tap, tap, crunch.

Set the other foot. Now anchor. She swung the wicked point of the ice axe against the glittering surface. On the third time she felt the point dig in to steady her. Ting, ting, ting. Chips of ice dislodged by her axe, no larger than snowflakes, kissed her nose.

Technically they were trespassing, but judging by the rust around the hole in the fence, no one cared.

Three more feet to reach the belay station. Climbing, her first instructor had told her, should be as simple as walking up a ladder. Legs used for lifting. Arms used for steadying. Listen to the rhythm. Tap, tap, crunch. One foot set, and she stepped up. Tap, tap crunch. Second foot set. Ting, ting, ting.

Navy reached the ledge where Sara waited. The belay station was three ice screws, spaced over a foot, with a triangle of rope that led to a carabiner. Above them, an overhang protected the belayer from anything the lead climber might dislodge. They didn't speak as they swapped leads and checked each other's harnesses. Climbing was as close to church as either of them came.

"Belay on," Navy said. Now Sara would continue the climb while Navy belayed. As lead climber, Sara's job was to set a good route. Navy's job was to catch Sara if she fell from the hundred-foot sandstone cliffs of the abandoned quarry. Someday they hoped to do Mount Ranier.

"Climbing." Sara's long braids swung as she stepped off the ledge and kicked one crampon into the ice to anchor herself. Tap, tap, crunch. Tap, tap, crunch. Ting, ting, ting. Sara's movements echoed Navy's. Ten feet left to reach the top. Sara set another ice screw and attached herself with a quickdraw. Seven. Sara climbed toward the triangle of sunlight stabbing into the bowl of the quarry. Tap, tap, crunch. Tap, tap, crunch. Ting, ting—

"Navy?" Sara shouted.

"Yeah."

"This ice is soft."

A south-facing wall. A sunny day. Enough to weaken the ice, despite the freezing temperatures of the previous week and their deliberately early start. Even careful climbers were subject to the whims of nature. "Can you make it to the top? Or down to the ledge below you?"

"I'll try for the top. This could be an ice dam. I don't want to be underneath it," Sara said.

Let the ice hold, Navy thought. Just until Sara is safe. Until we're both safe.

Sara held her axe out from the wall, hesitated, then struck. The familiar ting was overshadowed by the sound of Velcro ripping. A crack starting in the ice. Navy tightened her grip on the rope and focused her prayers.

The fracture started on Sara's right and spread like an X toward the overhang, running in a jagged line above the rope. Navy looked between the spreading crack and Sara. *No, no, no.* Then the ice exploded, shattering into large chunks that sparkled as they fell. Navy couldn't see Sara through the dissolving ice dam. A sudden weight pulled Navy up and toward the slick wall. Sara must be falling. Navy reacted as she had practiced a thousand times, yanking the rope down to put the brakes on as she bent her knees to absorb the impact as she hit the wall. The rope was stretched tight. Navy dug in. She was Sara's counterbalance. She could not fail.

"Release! Release!" Sara's scream was barely audible over the crashing ice.

Let go? Let her fall?

The white cloud shifted. The thunder subsided. Navy saw Sara again, on the ledge that had been five feet below her. Only a stub of rope was connected to Sara's harness; she was anchoring herself to a quickdraw.

If it wasn't Sara's weight pulling on Navy . . . Navy looked down. Except for the three anchor points at the belay station, the avalanche had taken all their ice screws, and the rope too. The ice holding Navy's crampons protested under the weight of winter's beauty. The rope was stretched to its limit. The tension would prevent Navy from unhooking cleanly. She scraped the blade of her ice axe against the rope and the rope vanished. Nylon under tension didn't require much.

Between Sara and Navy the cliff was wet where the ice had fallen away, like a glistening wound. Navy couldn't tell who was in the worse position. Sara was closer to safety; she was only ten feet from the top. Navy was ten feet below her. On the other hand, the ice near Sara was obviously not stable. The ice near Navy had held.

"My axe cut the rope when I fell." Sara looked at the pile of ice below her, the same ice that could have buried her or knocked her unconscious. "Lucky, I guess." Even with the distance, Sara's voice betrayed a tremor. "Can you get down safely?"

"Easy. Just get comfortable, and I'll come get you."

Concern for Sara made Navy want to rush, but she could not afford mistakes. Navy set an ice screw to hang her gear. Her axe would get in the way while she prepared to belay down. She held one strap of her backpack as she released her arm from the other. Using another quickdraw, she hung the pack in front of the ice axe.

With deliberate movements, she removed her gloves and stowed them in the pack The cold would stiffen her fingers if she didn't move quickly. But her hands knew the movements better than her mind did, and her spare rope was soon set in the belay device attached to her harness. She would belay on double ropes so she could recover the rope at the bottom. She slipped her hands back into the protection of her gloves. Then retrieved her bag, which held her first aid kit.

Simple, she told herself. Now put your feet on the wall and lower yourself down. *I am not afraid.*

She pulled with her left hand to put slack on the rope, then braked with both hands by pushing the rope against the ridges in the belay device. Two feet down. Fifty-eight more to go. Pull, brake, repeat. She didn't risk thinking too much.

The sweet release of climbing was in moments like this; she was forced to exist where instinct met intellect. The ground came before she expected. She allowed herself one breath of congratulations before coiling the rope.

"Hold on," Navy yelled. "I'm coming." She threw the spare coil of rope over her shoulder and tore off her crampons.

Navy watched her feet as she ran up the path. She knew the direction well, but the path was littered with hazards. Rocks that would twist her ankle, chunks of ice that would make her slip.

At the top, she wished she had brought her crampons. A sheet of smooth ice covered the flat ground. She took a carabiner from her harness and knotted one end of the rope around it. She walked as quickly as she dared to the edge, then dropped to her hands and knees. Sara was only five feet down, but it might as well have been fifty. Her cheeks were red with exertion, and her eyes bright with fear. Thankfully, the anchor she had set in the sandstone was holding.

"Hook this to your harness," Navy said, lowering the carabiner. "Don't let go until I say."

Sara nodded.

There was a solid tree ten feet from the edge Navy could use as a winch, but it was surrounded by smooth ice. The anemic tree three feet from the edge would have to do. There was a rock between the tree and the edge of the cliff that she could brace against. She walked around the tree so the rope was looped, then sat behind the rock and pushed her feet against it. The slack came up easily. Navy's pulse sped up when she felt the weight of her friend at the other end of the line.

"Now!" Navy shouted.

Sara's weight slammed Navy's soles against the rock, and the rope fought to escape her grip. Sweat ran into Navy's eyes. Concentrate on the rhythm, she told herself. Left hand over right hand. Right hand over left hand. Keep the rope taut. The tree bent but held. And again, left hand over right hand, right hand over left. Her vision narrowed to the rope and her hands around it. Finally, the rope went slack again.

"I'm up," Sara called. "I'm." A soft pant. "Up."

Navy released the rope and let her arms drop. Her legs shook when she stood, worn out from holding herself away from the rock. She followed the line of the rope to Sara.

Sara unclipped the rescue rope from her harness and threw the carabiner down on the ice. She was shaking too.

"We've climbed in these conditions a hundred times and never had a problem," Navy said. "You couldn't have known. Neither of us could have."

Sara's musical laugh startled Navy. She wondered if the shock of the close call had unbalanced her friend.

"Don't look at me like that," Sara said. "I was just thinking that we're even now. I convinced you to leave that rat bastard, and now *you've* saved *my* life."

Navy would have preferred to forget about the room filled with gray, rickety metal bunks where she met Sara. Navy had been a temporary resident; Sara had been a volunteer.

The buzzing of Navy's phone was a welcome distraction. She glanced at the caller ID. For once Navy was glad to get called into work on a weekend. "Our prod server is paging me. We need to head back."

"Just don't let work make you miss our flight tomorrow,"

Sara said. Her voice was steady. "A safari is worth more than a job any day."

Six thousand dollars an hour in lost shoe sales. Sales that Navy's company needed to close the venture capital deal that would keep the company growing—and keep her in a job. She glanced at her watch again; it was almost midnight. Five hours until her flight.

She peered into the corners of the dissected server. She had to steady the wobbly folding table in the data center. Fluorescent light fixtures buzzed above her head. On either side of the aisle, racks of servers rose to meet tangles of networking equipment and cables. Each server and router had its own fan; the combined hum made it sound as if she were in a bee hive. Her ankle brushed the metal cover balanced against one of the table legs as she leaned in for a closer look.

Along the bottom of the opened box was a perfectly level miniature city paved in green and gold. Tips of her hair skimmed the fat, round capacitors in all colors perched on tiny wire feet and connected by precisely etched golden lines. Among them, square chips planted their many legs into plastic sockets, like geometric spiders. All roads led to the large silver box in the corner, the place where two power cords emerged from the outside. Smaller versions of the city were turned sideways and stuck into plastic slots along the back.

Her eyes teared with the effort of examining the server. She had been here for hours. There was nothing wrong that the naked eye could see.

The phone rang, and she hit the speakerphone button before the ring finished.

"Navy." Amber's impatience was audible even over the noise in the data center.

"Amber."

"The CIO wants to know when the server will be back up. He wants me to remind you that we lose a thousand dollars in shoe orders for every ten minutes it's down."

"No new questions? That's exactly what you asked me an hour ago."

"Navy."

"Maybe you should ask him why he cut our budget for virtualization, cloud infrastructure, support contracts, and on-call personnel."

"Just tell me when you can have it fixed."

"I don't know." Navy was too tired to yell. "I don't have any spare parts to swap in. No retail stores are open this late. We let our support contracts expire. Jarrod is the only sysadmin. And this is the first night he hasn't been on call in three weeks."

"Then call him."

"It's date night. He won't answer his phone. I wouldn't."

"Oh! That's him calling me back now. I'll conference him in."

Navy sighed and stood to lift the handset. "Just remember that a celibate sysadmin is a cranky sysadmin."

"Amber?" Jarrod's voice.

"Navy needs your help." Navy could hear a smirk in Amber's tone.

"Shit. The e-commerce server again?"

"Yes," Navy said. "Just for the record, I refused to call you."

"Six thousand dollars an hour!" Amber piped up, starting to sound a little hysterical.

"We know," Navy and Jarrod said in unison.

There was a rustling sound as Jarrod adjusted his cell phone. "So what's happening?"

"It's not working," Amber offered.

Jarrod sighed. In the background, Navy heard the clink of

glasses and the low roar of a busy night at the bar. Probably McGuire's, where Jarrod and Carlie liked to play trivia games. Jarrod would be in the dark hallway that led to the bathrooms, leaning against the dirty wall and scratching at his beard.

"Intermittent shutdowns," Navy said before Amber could jump in again. "Sometimes it runs for ten minutes, sometimes for five, but it won't stay powered on."

"Sounds like a hardware problem."

"That was my guess." Navy turned a screw over in her fingers and felt the sharp edges bite into the tip of her pinkie.

"Did you run a memory check?"

"Passed."

"Reseated all the network and RAID cards?"

"Done."

"Dusted the fans on the CPU and the power supplies?"

"Twice on every one."

"How do the capacitors look?"

"Nothing obviously bulging or leaking."

"Checked all the cables?"

"Yep."

"How are all the other machines?" he asked. "Maybe we have a power problem."

"This is the only server having issues."

"And we have no spare parts," Jarrod said, more to himself than to Navy.

"Nope."

"Do you want to break the news to Amber or should I?"

"She didn't believe me, maybe she'll believe you."

"We have to get this server back up," Amber insisted. "I show the books to the venture capital people in two weeks. They're nervous about our server architecture already."

"It's a hardware failure," Jarrod said. "Probably needs a new power supply or motherboard. Remember last month? When I told you the server needed replacing?"

"Oh."

Navy pressed her fingers to her temple. "How long does the average sale take from start to finish?"

"Three minutes?"

Navy couldn't tell if Amber was embarrassed or unsure. "I could put it back together and set it to automatically reboot every time it shuts down," Navy said. "It would be unreliable and slow, but it would be up. Sort of."

Amber huffed into the phone. "Can't you run out to a twenty-four-hour Walmart or something?"

"Why didn't I think of that?" Jarrod snapped. "Dell server parts are on rollback this week right between the fake Oreos and fake Chips Ahoy."

"Not necessary, Jarrod," Amber said.

"It'll be a full day to get a new server bought and installed—if there's a local supplier that has one in stock. Otherwise, it'll be two days. Navy's idea is the best we can do for now."

"Two days!" Amber squeaked.

"I'll get this put together," Navy said. "By the time I get back from Africa, Jarrod'll have it fixed for real."

"By the time you get back," Jarrod said, "the new hardware will be old."

CHAPTER 2

BYRON SCOWLED AGAIN at the mission plans for Operation Critical Mass. His half-eaten ham sandwich from the deli had wilted next to his keyboard. Lunch was four hours ago; the mayo was past safe. He tossed the sandwich in the garbage can. Too bad worrying didn't burn more calories, he thought, feeling his stomach push against the edge of the desk.

The phone rang from underneath a pile of papers. He cleared them off, glanced at the caller ID. There was only one person who would be calling from Amsterdam. Byron looked at his watch. It was 2200 there.

"Evening, Jackson."

"The mission briefing is soon, right?" Jackson asked.

Byron stared at the pictures of his daughter that cluttered his desk. She was nearly seventeen now, but he couldn't quite make himself take down the picture of her first day of school. "Yeah, at sixteen hundred. In five minutes."

"You know this operation is a bad idea. Give Roy a few more months and the kidnapping ring will trust him enough to give us something useful. We don't need to get our own agents kidnapped."

"You don't need to convince *me*." Byron's patience was wearing thin. He knew Jackson was right, but there wasn't much

Byron could do. There wasn't much either of them could do. Jackson was a field agent for the CIA and Byron was an intelligence analyst. It would take someone far above their heads to abort the operation.

"You talked to Erin again?" Jackson asked.

"You have a PhD in psychology and you couldn't talk her out of it. Why did you think I'd have better luck?"

"She has to know this is risky, even for her. She knows the kidnappers are planning to use halothane to knock them out. She could be unconscious for an hour. That's more than enough time for the kidnappers to find the GPS trackers, figure out she's an agent and—"

"Telling her something is risky is not a way to talk Erin out of anything. And yes, I tried. She told me to butt out."

"Those were her exact words?"

"Well, there was more profanity. And some hitting."

"You know there's only one way this operation makes sense," Jackson said.

Jackson was being cautious about what he said on the agency phone line. Byron understood. If anything went wrong it would take a quasi-military operation to rescue the three kidnapped agents. A perfect news story to bolster the president's fading poll numbers—three Americans heroically rescued from terrorists. "Yeah, I know."

"I should never have agreed to support this operation," Jackson said.

"She would have gone ahead anyway, you know how she is." Spiny was the best word to describe Erin, but she was their friend. "I have to go to the briefing. It's my last chance."

"Good luck," said Jackson flatly.

Time for Byron to go to the conference room and make himself the least popular man in the office.

When Byron wasn't sitting in a cubicle, he was in a meeting room like this one, scratching at the wood-grain pattern with the tip of his pen. A few dim bulbs in a cheap light fixture lit the gray walls badly in need of a fresh coat of paint. The scratched brown laminate table cast a shadow that swallowed the legs of the men and women surrounding it. Some leaned back, some rested their elbows on the table, some sat at attention with backs stiff as rods.

Most of the men and women here were like him: middle-aged, graying at the temple, and a little pudgy near the belt. Too often, petty loyalties and external politics overrode common sense and decency. Some days it took a lot of effort to remind himself his agency was saving the free world, or as close to it as anyone could claim.

Operation Critical Mass was going to fail. He was sure of it. He'd heard other analysts quietly complaining about the unnecessary risks. But, despite objections from several well-respected colleagues, the operation was going forward anyway. Willy, the operations manager, was droning on about the importance of the mission, and therefore himself.

"So our plan is to have the terrorists kidnap the agents in Amsterdam," Byron said. Willy looked shocked that someone had cut him off. Good. Willy the Grand—or William, as he liked to be called—was a prick. "And then what? The terrorists use some car stereo parts to find the transmitters while our agents are passed out from the halothane and we have three more dead Americans."

Erin looked at Byron with piercing eyes. "The kidnappers are amateurs. We can take care of ourselves." Her relaxed posture didn't fool him. She was the fastest and meanest fighter he knew.

Willy nodded too eagerly. "Erin and her team are highly trained, experienced agents."

Erin had experience. But the two agents that had been chosen to go with her were rookies.

"They can rescue themselves even if the transmitters . . . malfunction." William looked around the room to make sure everyone he had bullied into agreeing with him was still sitting at attention.

"And if they can't? We should have a better backup plan," Byron said.

Erin's eyes were daggers now. Byron would hear about this later.

William coughed and cleared his throat. "There's risk in any operation."

"What about the risk to us? If the operation springs a leak, it will look like the CIA created a kidnapping plot to foster support for the war in Afghanistan." There, Byron had said it. What everyone was thinking but no one wanted to admit.

"This is an intelligence gathering operation, not psy ops."

"But if a miracle rescue by the military happens to take place, and the media happen to hear about it, you wouldn't be upset." The hard toe of a dress shoe kicked Byron's shin. Carl was always good about warning him when he was about to get into trouble. "Fine." Byron held his hands up. "I've made my feelings about this operation clear."

Chairs and feet and paper shuffled. The room emptied except for Byron, Carl, and Erin.

"You've been talking to Jackson too much," Erin said. "Come down to the gym and spar with me, then you'll see who needs rescuing."

"In your mood? I'll pass."

Erin glared at him again and left the room.

Carl followed Byron out of the room, practically stepping on his heels.

"You shouldn't push William so hard," Carl said softly. Willy was only halfway to his office.

"Oh, you mean Willy the Grand." Byron didn't bother to keep his voice low.

"That's the sort of stuff I mean, Macalester. We're just analysts."

"I've been here too long for them to fire me for being ornery."

Carl ground the toe of his cheap dress shoe into the carpet. "They could bury you at the drop of a hat if they thought you were a security risk."

"Do you think I'm a security risk, Carl?"

He paused for too long before answering. "No. But Willy—William—might. You need to be more diplomatic."

"Diplomatic?" Byron snorted and shook his head. "Operation Critical Mass is going to blow up in our faces and you know it. It's propaganda, not intelligence gathering."

"Maybe."

Carl turned to walk away, but Byron stepped in front of him. Carl looked down at the floor, and Byron found himself talking to the sallow spots on top of Carl's balding head. "We gather evidence. We make predictions. We find out things about foreign governments that foreign governments would rather us not know. That's the way it's supposed to work. We don't do psy ops against our own civilians"

"You don't know that Operation Critical Mass is psy ops."

"You just don't want to admit it."

It was just another argument on just another day in an office building in the DC area. He and Carl walked silently back to their cubes and their screens and their paperwork.

CHAPTER 3

ERIN TWIRLED A pencil around her thumb, catching it in time to write down her next entry on the internal passport request form. Around her, keyboards clicked, phones rang, footsteps hurried, and hushed conversations passed over cubicle walls. She might as well be stuck in a row of cages.

Jackie. Her name for this operation was Jackie Pierce. A respectable name for a senator's niece on vacation in Europe. Her eye color would have to stay the same; she would be too close to her captors for colored contacts. She filled in hazel as the eye color for the passport. Blond for her hair. That had been settled since the kidnapping plot had been planted by the double agent weeks earlier.

Operation Critical Mass had been in the planning stages for long enough. Erin was eager to be walking through Schiphol airport, with her overstuffed bags and her two companions, also undercover agents. When the kidnappers had lured her to a quiet place, they would pull a bag over her head, hold a halothane-soaked cloth over her mouth, and carry her to the rest of the sleeper cell. The ride would be the most dangerous part. Even though she would have held her breath, she would be woozy, disoriented.

When the halothane wore off, she and the other two agents

would escape whatever weak security the kidnappers had in place. And then her team would take the ones that didn't fight too much into custody and use them to unravel the rest of the network. The ones that did fight would be granted their wish for martyrdom.

She savored the trill of fear that passed through her. Byron worried too much. She didn't need anyone's help.

And she didn't need anyone delaying her mission.

Of course Byron didn't understand. She liked him, respected him even, but he had gone soft from spending too many years stateside. And anyway, he had never loved his undercover work as much as she did. He was a reluctant soldier turned spy and then desk jockey.

For her, joining the reserves had just been a way to pay for college, and her job as a programmer had just been a way to pay the bills. But she discovered she liked the feel of a gun in her hand, the adrenaline of a good fight, and the shape of her body after weeks of training. And then one dusty day during the first Iraq war the CIA had needed a computer tech to go on a small undercover mission, and she fell in love—with a job. Undercover work meant leaving herself behind.

She thought of the vault room where all of her still-active identities were stored with the identities of all the other undercover agents based at this office. Rows of metal shelves with white cardboard boxes labeled in black marker. Mary Parker, intrepid reporter following the war in Afghanistan for a little-known paper. Nellie Best, sous chef at a restaurant in Germany who had been well placed to overhear the plans of a money laundering ring. She could be any of them again in a heartbeat. Or someone completely different.

Not all of her identities were in the vault. Passports were lost sometimes. Or erased from the records. Or her expense reports were padded just enough to pay a shady expert in a back alley to make her a citizen of anywhere she wanted. An untraceable passport was always good to have on hand.

"How are the preparations going?" The shoulder of a well-cut black suit peppered with dandruff leaned close to her. William Grand. She had never liked William. He had floated up the ranks to middle management purely by seniority. He wasn't good at reading people. He wasn't good at analyzing reports from agents in the field. He wasn't good at managing operations. He wasn't good at his job. Despite that, he could be useful because he was easily manipulated. An asset was an asset, foreign or domestic.

"Fine." She smiled to put him at ease.

"You shouldn't worry about Byron," William said, more to himself than to her. "The kidnappers won't be looking for tracking devices. And Jackson and your support team will be close the whole time." Byron's objections must have shaken William's confidence.

She didn't care if they found the tracking devices. The kidnappers wouldn't kill them until they had interrogated them. "I expect we'll rescue ourselves before the cavalry even mounts their horses," she assured him.

William nodded, disturbing the wispy strands of his thinning gray hair.

Another overpaid bureaucrat, Kyle Pierson, walked past Erin's row of cubes. Kyle was William's political rival, opposite in politics but similar in lack of conscience. His suit was more expensive than William's and his belly stuck out more over the waistband. More rich dinners at fancy restaurants with important people. Kyle was here to check up on William's projects—it was the main reason he ever spent any time at the office. Kyle was an asset too, of sorts. Kyle was trickier to manage because he was always looking for a way to get one more rung up the ladder.

Keeping mental dossiers on everyone was part of her job.

Every manager Erin had ever worked for was an asset. Every agent she worked with was an asset. Even the ones who were old friends, like Byron. She had to remember who owed her favors, whether they preferred rooftops or windows when sniping, what mistresses they kept hidden.

Any good agent was gathering the same information on her.

"Great, great." William's forehead was beaded with sweat. His eyes followed Kyle's path down the hall. How William had ever passed the polygraph was a mystery to her. "Call me right away if you need anything," he said. By the time he finished the sentence he was rushing to catch up with Kyle.

William stopped Kyle in the hall with false friendliness. They exchanged barbed, wide smiles. Erin looked down at her desk, pretending to stare at her paperwork. The key to eavesdropping wasn't superhuman hearing. It was focus. The page blurred in front of her. She could almost feel her ear adjusting to the perfect position to catch their tense conversation.

Still, she could only catch every other word. Kyle was repeating Byron's concerns about the tracking devices being found, about how the operation would look if it were leaked. William was trying to plead for noninterference without appearing like he was asking. Asking would mean admitting weakness.

Kyle's voice rose, rich with sarcasm. "The only thing that could make Operation Critical Mass any better for you would be if the agents died."

"What?" William seemed genuinely confused. Erin was confused too. Public arguments weren't Kyle's normal tactic. For some reason, Kyle wanted witnesses.

"No senator would dare vote against a war-funding bill if three American citizens were kidnapped and killed by terrorists."

The gauntlet had been thrown. The whole floor listened for

William's response. Erin abandoned her pretense and looked up. The rest of the floor was watching, so she might as well.

"That's not what this operation is about. And anyway, you can't stop it." A nervous tic in William's left heel shook the hem of his dress pants.

"Your funeral." Kyle turned and walked away.

Erin twirled her pencil around her thumb again. Nothing about the argument made sense. Kyle could stop the whole operation if he wanted to; he was on the internal review board that approved joint NSA/CIA operations. The shuffling of positions following the midterm elections had pushed many of William's congressional allies into the cold and put Kyle's allies in place. He was playing to William's ego, letting William think that Kyle had been intimidated into backing down. So did Kyle believe the operation was going to succeed or fail? And what outcome was he hoping for?

Erin filed the mystery away for later review. Jackie Pierce. From Alabama. She wouldn't have to practice the dialect much. Her kidnappers wouldn't know Alabama from Louisiana. What would Jackie Pierce from Alabama wear when passing through the Amsterdam airport? Skinny jeans, tight at the hips. And a T-shirt with cropped sleeves. Trendy sneakers—definitely not white. Gold hoop earrings and a messy updo. She dialed the hair salon in the basement.

"I need an appointment to have my hair dyed . . . Yes, two this afternoon will be fine."

She needed to make sure the smell of dye wore off before the operation started.

CHAPTER 4

THE ALARM JANGLED Navy's nerves. She felt like there was sand in her eyes. She forced herself to swing her clumsy legs out of bed until her feet landed on the carpet. Three weeks in Africa. Her dream vacation. She wouldn't let Amber's late-night tantrums at the data center ruin it. Her bags, one daypack and one duffel, were packed and by the bedroom door. A list of last-minute tasks sat on top of the daypack, written just before she had collapsed into bed last night.

The mirror above the vanity showed the dark bags under her hazel eyes. Navy splashed her face with cold water until her fingers protested. Sara and Moss would be here in thirty minutes.

Navy grimaced when she saw the first item on her list and decided to leave it until last. She gathered the last of her toiletries—toothpaste, mouthwash, deodorant—and put them into a clear plastic bag for airport security. She ate one slice of the barbecue chicken pizza in the fridge, then threw the rest away, along with the leftover Chinese. She emptied all of the trash cans in the apartment into the one in the kitchen and walked the bag of trash down to the chute in the hallway. There was nothing left to do but the first item on the list.

She picked up her cell phone and took a deep breath.

"Hi, Mom."

"Navy! I was worried sick. You said you'd call before you left. I was just watching this Dateline about kidnapped women in the international sex trade—"

"I'm still at my apartment."

"You aren't still packing, are you? You know, if you don't pack the night before you might leave something important behind. Like your malaria pills. You packed the malaria pills, right?"

"Yes. I packed the malaria pills."

"And you finished your shots?"

"Three weeks ago. You asked me the same thing last week."

"What about that thing you found on your credit report last week? The inquiry from that California company. . ."

"Rainbow Tree Funding, Inc." Navy regretted even mentioning it. She'd been trying to distract her mom from worrying about the trip by impressing her with how carefully Navy had reviewed her credit report.

"I did a business search for them on the California Secretary of State site, and I couldn't find anything," Mom said.

Navy wouldn't admit that she had done the same thing, or that she was worried. She had done her own research. Rainbow Tree Funding, Inc. had a bare website that didn't even list their services. There were no other hits on Google. According to several Internet archives, the site had only appeared two months ago. "It's probably just some company that's going to send me junk mail."

"Identity theft is real thing, honey. I've been reading all about it online. Someone could do a lot of damage while you're gone."

Patience, Navy told herself. Her mom always meant well. "I froze my credit report, and I'm going to carry extra cash in case there's an in issue with my cards. That's all I can do."

"Just be careful, okay. Call me during your layover in Amsterdam."

"I'm not calling until I get back. Nothing's going to happen."

"I'll carry my phone to dinner so I'll get your call."

"Oh, that's Sara and Moss," Navy lied. "I have to go. I'll call you when I get back to Iowa. In three weeks." She hung up the phone before her mom could protest.

Ten minutes later she heard a rapid knock on the door. Through the peephole, Navy saw Sara's petite form framed by her long, dark hair and Moss with his mound of red curly hair. When Navy opened the door Sara jumped into the apartment and hugged Navy.

"Africa!" she squealed.

"She's been like this since we got up this morning," Moss said, stifling a yawn. "Sorry."

Navy returned Sara's hug. "No more caffeine for you."

"Call your mom yet?" Sara asked.

"Yes. She's worried I'm going to be kidnapped and sold into the international sex trade."

"Huh. Well, if Moss and I run out of money . . ."

"Funny girl."

"Need help with your bags?" Moss asked.

Navy shook her head and pulled the duffel bag across one shoulder until it landed on her back. The daypack she slung over one arm.

"That's all you have?"

"I offered to teach you how to pack light . . ."

"I'm not cutting my toothbrush in half."

Moss and Sara held hands as they walked down the hallway in front of Navy. They made a comical pair. He was tall, gangly in the arms, doughy in the middle, and rarely raised his voice, even when telling a joke. She was petite, with a round but taut body that never seemed to stand still. Like now, when she flicked her hair over her shoulder, then twirled another section around two fingers.

"Victoria Falls! We have to see Victoria Falls. They have these gliders—you can float right over it."

"That'd be worth it just for the picture to send my mom," Navy said.

"Quiet for a second," Sara said. "I have to change my voice mail." She picked up her cell phone and dialed through the menus. "You've reached Sara Farmington. I'll be out of the country until March third. I'll return all messages at that time."

"You're not worried about someone trying to break into your house after they hear that?" Navy asked.

"I'll take that risk over someone getting angry because I haven't returned their call. Moss, honey, you changed your voice mail too, right?"

Moss nodded. "Yes, dear."

Winter still had a firm grip on Des Moines. Dirty snow lined the roads and patches of gray ice filled the cracks in the sidewalks. Navy checked, again, that she had remembered all the important items: phone, passport, wallet. Her mother was always worried when Navy traveled. Navy was just tired, that's why she felt anxious. The credit inquiry meant nothing.

Getting from Pier B of Schiphol to Pier G required crossing the whole airport. They wouldn't make their connecting flight unless they ran—past other crowded gates, past the stores selling over-priced luggage and scarves, past restaurants that made Navy's stomach growl. Thanks to her late-night adventures at work, she had slept through the meal on the plane. In the past twenty-four hours she had eaten one slice of barbecue chicken pizza. The strap of her duffel bag dug into her sweaty shoulder and the backpack bounced against her forearms.

Moss was pulling two overstuffed roller bags behind him, one in each hand. Another rushing passenger bumped Moss and the two bags collided with each other and flipped. Navy stopped and tapped her foot impatiently while Sara helped him right the bags.

When Navy looked up, she noticed a small circle had cleared around them. An electric cart had pulled up next to Moss. In the driver's seat was an olive-skinned man with a skewed, wrinkled blue vest. An airport ID badge with a faded picture was clipped to the pocket. His left eyelid drooped a little lower than the right. He seemed eager to offer them help. Navy tried to remember if this was a scam she had read about in any of her travel books.

"Need a lift?"

Moss' expression changed from grumpy to hopeful.

"Thanks, but no thanks," Sara told the driver. "I think we can run faster."

"I'll take a ride," said a voice on the other side of the cart. Navy couldn't tell if the cart driver was ignoring the other traveler or hadn't heard him.

"There are some service hallways I can use," the cart driver said. "How soon do you need to be at your gate?"

"Ten minutes ago," Navy said.

"No problem, hop on."

Moss was sitting on the back seat before Navy could object. Sara shrugged and sat in front, patting the seat next to her. Navy climbed on reluctantly. The duffel bag crowded her feet and she hugged her pack tightly in her lap. The cart began to clear the way in front of them. Was it her mother's silly warnings tensing her shoulders? She was so tired that the world around her seemed to be moving very fast.

She didn't feel any better when they left the lit, busy terminal for a concrete hallway sparsely populated by airport employees who watched the passing cart. Their vests were a slightly different color. Navy's exhausted brain finally managed to form the thought that had been bothering her—they had never told the driver what gate they needed. He had taken off without asking and no one had said a word since.

The light fixtures in this part of the tunnel had missing and burned out bulbs and greasy dust gathered in the corners. They turned into what looked like a small loading dock. Navy was leaning over to whisper a warning to Sara when three dark shapes leapt from the shadows toward the cart. Her anxiety flashed into fear. A rough bag was pulled over her head. The fabric of the bag scratched at her cheeks and made her eyes water. She felt a hand come up from underneath her chin. She smelled something like paint thinner, but sweet. A wet cloth was pressed over her nose and screaming mouth.

No one was going to hear them, she realized, and making noise would only waste precious air. She held her breath and pretended to go limp. Her lungs were burning by the time the hand disappeared and the bag was pulled tight around her neck. She felt groggy even though her heart was beating fast. The stale air inside the bag felt like water being forced down her lungs. The fumes had already gone to her head. Someone's fingers searched her pockets and pulled out her cell phone. She heard the cheerful, familiar beep as it turned off. Then she heard the snap of the battery being removed. A lifeline being cut off.

"Load them into the van," said a voice, deep and gravelly. The accent was high-class British—the kind of person she imagined would be seen in an expensive suit on a London street. He was obviously the leader.

She would call him the Brit. It helped to give her attackers names.

She wondered if she should run. No, when she was lifted from the cart she felt her legs swing like rubber over her abductor's arms. Scream? No, they would dose her again and she'd be completely helpless. She was loaded roughly onto a cold, corrugated metal floor that pressed its pattern into her arm. A van? She could hear an engine running. Two heavy things were thrown in after her. She couldn't tell if the large objects were Sara and Moss or luggage. What could anyone want with her? Or her friends?

Footsteps shook the floor in the back of the van. Benches on either side of her protested at the weight of the men belonging to the voices. Doors slammed near her ear and in the front, where the driver must be.

"Their flight was two weeks earlier than we had planned." It was the Brit again. "It was a good thing you checked with our contact." It was not the same man who had driven the cart. The cart driver had a higher-pitched voice and an American accent.

"Which one is related to the senator?" This voice was younger than the leader's, with the squeaky, unsettled tone of puberty underneath it.

"The blonde one."

The ride was long and bumpy. Exhaust fumes from the van and other cars on the road seeped in through the cracks in the doors and settled on the floor. Navy needed to know if Sara and Moss were with her. Navy was lying on her side so maybe . . . yes, that might work. Her thoughts were clearing. At the next turn she rolled over, throwing out her arm as if it had fallen that way. She felt a warm, downy arm. Not hairy like a man's. Sara was in the truck with her.

Her momentary relief changed to guilt. She didn't want to be alone, but part of her had hoped Sara and Moss were still back at the airport. Unless their abductors wouldn't have left them alive.

"The halothane will wear off soon," said the younger one nervously. "Are we almost there?"

Navy felt Sara stirring and used the next abrupt stop to slide her arm away. Waking Sara would draw attention to her. Would it matter if Sara and Moss woke up? Was this a van with windows? Would someone hear if they screamed for help?

Navy's hope faded as they left the busy, noisy road for a quieter one. The combination of fatigue and the exhaust fumes and the halothane threatened to pull her into a deep sleep. She counted the turns to stay awake. Left, right, left, left. The smooth pavement underneath the wheels changed to rutted surface with potholes that bounced her shoulders painfully against the metal floor. Right, right, left. Small rocks kicked up by the tires started to ping the undercarriage just below her head as they left the badly paved road for a gravel road. The van stopped. Her ears were ringing from the sound of the gravel.

A door in the front of the van opened and someone climbed out. The nervous one in the back of the van took two noisy breaths before the door closed. They pulled forward a short distance and someone got out of the front again before the van continued, driving slowly this time.

They had traveled a highway to a major thoroughfare to a local road to an unmaintained road to a gravel road to a gate. It was quiet here. They were at least a forty-minute drive from Amsterdam. No one would be looking for them for three weeks. Navy wished she had promised to call her mom from the airport.

CHAPTER 5

THE DINGING OF the elevator was the only sound on the floor. The eerie quiet reminded Byron of the silence just after a gunfight, when everyone kept their heads down. Of course, it had been awhile since he had raised a gun anywhere but the range. Now he fought his battles with snide words and internal memos. Near Willy's office, yelling erupted, muted by a closed door. Carl walked by with his head down, eyes focused on his empty coffee cup. Carl's tie was crooked and he had the jittery walk of a man powered more by caffeine than sleep.

In the break room, Byron cornered Carl near the coffee machine.

"I can't talk about it," Carl muttered, clumsily pushing a filter into the basket.

"Can't talk about what?"

"You're not on the operation anymore. If you wanted to be involved, you shouldn't have pissed off William last week."

"Erin hasn't even left yet, what could have gone wrong this early?"

Carl pressed his fingers against the speckled blue counter. His wrinkled, tanned skin went white from the pressure.

"The inside agent was compromised? Someone in the press

got wind of the operation? The sleeper cell got spooked and went back to Yemen?”

Carl shook his head at each possibility.

“They kidnapped the wrong people. Three civilians.” Byron could barely believe his own words. Not the disaster Byron had predicted, but he wasn’t entirely surprised. It wouldn’t be the first operation Willy had screwed up. A heroic rescue of three agents who had sworn oaths to protect state secrets was one thing. A rescue of three civilians—one of whom might wonder why she was mistaken for a senator’s niece—was another.

“I really can’t talk about it.”

“When’s the team meeting?” No one else would speak up on behalf of the civilians if he didn’t show up—Erin was too cold and everyone else would be too afraid.

Dark liquid was starting to fill the carafe drip by drip. Carl’s eyes followed every drop.

“Carl.”

“You’ll be crucified if you make trouble over this. They could take your security clearance.”

“There’s a fifty-fifty chance between them doing the right thing or trying to cover this fuck-up by making the civilians disappear.”

“I know,” Carl whispered.

“If they were your kids. . .”

“Don’t bring my family into this.”

“Let me be the bad guy. Just tell me when the meeting is.” I’ll do what you’re not willing to do, thought Byron.

“Five minutes.”

“I won’t tell him you told me.” As if Carl deserved Byron’s protection. Byron’s diplomatic skills might be weak, but at least he knew when to stand up.

Byron walked past conference room 350 and feigned surprise at the familiar gathering of faces. Erin’s face was a thundercloud.

Her mood probably had more to do with her mission being scuttled than humanitarian concerns for the three unlucky tourists in Amsterdam. Her detachment made her a good undercover agent—and a frightening human being.

Willy the Grand entered last, choreographed as always. His composed expression faltered when he saw Byron. A scowl contorted his lips before he recomposed himself. Byron lifted his right hand to his forehead and gave Willy a mock salute, then leaned back in his chair. The scowl appeared again and disappeared just as quickly. Carl looked between them and shook his head.

"We're here to talk about how to rescue this mission," Willy said. Byron hoped that it was guilt tensing Willy's jaw.

"Why don't we go over exactly what happened," snapped Erin.

"The kidnappers spotted someone in the airport they thought was the senator's niece and her party. They kidnapped the wrong group. Roy, our inside agent, says the kidnappers don't know they have the wrong people yet."

"That's not everything," Erin said.

Willy cleared his throat. "Our inside agent sent the kidnappers the wrong date and the physical descriptions weren't, um, specific enough. There was some confusion."

"And who wrote the message?" Erin was letting her temper get the better of her. She knew just as well as Byron that Willy micromanaged every operation he ran. The words that were sent to identify the kidnap victims had been exactly whatever Willy had written. Erin wanted to humiliate Willy for his incompetence. In front of the entire team. Willy would never forgive her for it.

It was time for Byron to throw himself under the bus. "So in other words, I was ri—"

Willy swung around and slammed his hand on the table. His eyes were wild and vicious, clouded with guilt and anger. "Don't even say it."

The second hand of the clock on the wall made one full rotation before anyone spoke.

"Can we even find them?" another analyst asked.

"Video surveillance footage from the airport shows a stolen white delivery van leaving the loading dock area at thirteen twenty." The junior agent was fresh-faced and uncomfortable under the intense focus of everyone's eyes. "It hasn't been found and the company's GPS is not responding."

"What about traffic cameras?" Willy asked.

"It's possible a traffic camera on the south end of the city saw them."

"Possible?" Willy asked the question with a sneer.

The junior agent slumped and tried to disappear into his chair. "The plates were different, sir. But the dents on the rear door matched."

The young agent couldn't be faulted. Finding that van would have required hours of review, and getting any footage was difficult without starting an official investigation.

Willy paced the width of the room, pulling at the tip of his aristocratic nose. "I need ideas. *Now*." The man must drink Pepto Bismol by the gallon, Byron thought.

"We figure out who was kidnapped," Byron said. "We find them and we rescue them. We have a few agents at Valkenburg who can start as soon as we call."

"It's not that simple." Willy looked so upset that for a second Byron actually felt a little sympathy for him.

"It *is* that simple. Not easy, but simple. We drop everything else and we find them."

Willy looked unconvinced.

"The kidnappers are planning to use the niece to blackmail the senator, right? So we find the senator and ask him to go along with it and use that to buy us some time."

"What language do the kidnappers speak again?" Willy asked, turning to Carl.

"The leader is from Manchester," answered Carl. "English and some Arabic."

"So anything the captives happen to overhear they're likely to understand?"

Carl paused and Byron gave him a sharp look. "Yes."

A sinking feeling was forming in the pit of Byron's stomach. He'd given the agency fifty-fifty odds this morning, but those odds were shifting. "Not rescuing them is not an option," Byron said.

"It's unlikely we can find them and rescue them in forty-eight hours. And if we explain this to the senator, there's a good chance it will leak. " Willy looked like a mannequin posed as a leader. "The inside agent on this mission is too important. We can't allow this agent to be compromised."

"You didn't brief the senator?" Even the cold-blooded Erin looked shocked as she said it. "What were you going to do when I was kidnapped?"

"You were supposed to escape before the kidnappers managed to contact the senator."

Byron put a hand on Erin's arm, wincing at the glare he got for holding her back. "There's only one right thing to do here," he said. "We rescue them. If our agent is compromised we take our lumps and move on."

"Our resources are limited," Willy said unconvincingly. "We can't afford to waste them on a Hail Mary."

Willy didn't know an end zone from a free throw line. Those were someone else's words, Byron was sure of it. Someone who frightened Willy enough that he was telling a conference room full of people to let three United States citizens die.

The quiet whine of the electric motor in the clock and the shuffling of feet were audible in the room. Carl's face was a cross between horrified and nauseous. The junior agent who had found the van fidgeted with his laptop.

"You can't let this happen, William," Byron said. "I'm going back to my desk and I'm going to try to find them. Are you going to stop me?"

Willy shook his head. "I can't get the senator's cooperation for you. I'm sorry. It's not my call."

Byron stood and swept the eyes of everyone in the room. "We have forty-eight hours. Carl, I want you to call Valkenburg and tell them to shake every branch they can. New guy, I want you back on video and satellite surveillance in that part of the world. And the security footage from the airport. Anyone finds anything, let me or Erin know."

Byron's power would only last as long as William felt guilty about this operation. And his guilt would wear off soon enough.

CHAPTER 6

THE BLANKETS SCRATCHING at Navy's skin had small pills of cotton from being washed too many times. A drooping canopy hung from the tips of the bedposts. The mattress beneath her was soft and sagging, almost swallowing her. A dusty window filtered pale, yellow light from a sun that hung low in the sky. Dawn or dusk? How long had she slept? Where had they taken Sara and Moss? She wasn't related to any senator, like she'd heard the men talking about in the van. Was the whole kidnapping a horrible case of mistaken identity?

The last thing she remembered was the bright stab of sunlight as the van doors opened, and the cart driver's voice whispering obscenities in her ear as he carried her inside.

Her wrist was bare—only a white band showed where her watch had been. The cash in her back pocket was missing too. Navy didn't remember the cart driver's hands in her pocket. The thought made her shiver.

Navy sat up and found herself facing the door to the room. She wanted to throw it open, but thought better of it. Even trying the doorknob might be enough to bring a guard running. No, she needed to find something that could be used as a weapon.

And the view out the window would give her a hint of the best direction to run if she got outside. She had to escape and get help.

The bed creaked with every small movement she made. Dust stirred as she slowly moved to the edge. She held her breath and pressed a finger underneath her nose to keep from sneezing.

A mahogany armoire, decorated with carved whorls that resembled eyes, looked down on the bed. Was there a camera watching her? She took a sharp breath, wanting suddenly to crawl back into the sagging bed and nurse the growing fear in her belly. She forced herself to walk to the window and look outside. The worn carpet scratched against the soles of her feet; her shoes and socks had been taken.

The room was getting lighter. Morning, then. It was morning and the window faced east. She pushed open the translucent curtains overlooking a brown lawn dotted with bare trees that swayed in the wind. No, not a lawn. The grounds were large enough to call it an estate. A black wrought iron fence bordered the grounds. Hard to tell from this distance, but it seemed the fence could easily be climbed over. If she could get to it. Navy could see two rows of windows below her. Beyond the fence was another estate, almost hidden by a stand of trees.

A man in khakis and a heavy coat walked across the lawn, his right fingers curled around a trigger that wasn't there. He walked jerkily, as if he was trying to transform his soldier's gait into a nonchalant stroll. No one watching would be fooled. She turned back to the room.

The wall facing the window had a door in the center with two waist-high dressers, one on each side. Each dresser held a silver vase filled with silk flowers. The dressers were centered beneath old-fashioned oil paintings. She searched the first dresser; the drawers were empty. She weighed the vase in her hand. It was too light for a weapon.

One painting pictured what could have been a modern family of four. They were dressed in formal attire—the man and a somber toddler in tuxedos, the woman and a girl in gowns. The second painting was of just the boy. The chubby fingers of one hand clutched at a red ball. The painter had made the child's face serious, and it seemed out of place with his playful pose. She lifted the corner to look behind it. Some paper lined the back and a length of clear string hung the painting on a nail. A nail and string might be useful. As she released the painting, a glint near the floor caught her eye. A handheld mirror had fallen between the dresser and the wall. She held it up to her face, eager to ground herself with something familiar.

There were bags underneath her eyes and small scratches on her face. A small round bruise just above her jawline brought back the memory of the hairy hand pressing the handkerchief against her mouth. She gently pressed her finger on the bruise and winced. The image in the mirror began to shake. Yes, she was afraid. She set the mirror down. Deep breaths, Navy thought.

For a second she was in the gym at her elementary school, staring up at the balance beam that seemed higher and narrower than in practice. Navy remembered how her stomach had turned over, threatening to leave her retching on the floor in front of the sparse audience. Her mom had come out to the floor and held Navy's palm against her belly button. Navy remembered the smooth, slick fabric of her new leotard.

"Push your hand out when you exhale and pull it in when you inhale," her mom said. "Five deep breaths and you'll feel better."

It did help.

She faced the wall with the window again. The sun was above the horizon. East. She turned to the left to face the wall with no furniture. North. She turned left again to face the eyes of the paintings. West. She turned to face the wall with the dominating armoire. South. She needed to give herself questions to answer—tasks to keep her mind focused. First question: was she being watched? She sat down on the bed and studied where the ceiling met the wall. Nothing obvious was attached to the crown molding. Her study of the ceiling was blocked by the canopy so she turned her attention to the furniture and the walls. The mauve rosettes on the yellow wallpaper seemed to shift, mocking her, as she stared at them.

All she found was an outlet on each wall. A modern old-fashioned mansion, then. When she had exhausted the nooks and crannies of the furniture, she stood up and pretended to stretch. Nothing but cobwebs on the ceiling. No cameras that she could see.

A microphone then? It didn't matter, there was no one to talk to anyway. She felt her focus slipping and searched for another question to continue the game. Was there anything in the room she could use to escape?

She opened the drawers in the dresser underneath the portrait of the small boy. There were handwritten letters in a language she didn't understand, probably Dutch. Some rubber bands and paperclips. She could make a spitball slingshot, she thought sorely.

There were also some old computer speakers and a few audio cables. Strangulation tools. If she could get close enough. If she was strong enough. Or she could use the wires to start a fire with the electricity in the outlet. A diversion while she escaped out of the window on a rope made of bedsheets? Right. If she were in a Nancy Drew novel.

The mirror. Shards of the glass might work for a weapon.

Navy heard the doorknob turn. She set the mirror down just as the door opened. It was the cart driver with the droopy eyelid. His hair was dark and curly and oily, and he had only a dusting of a beard. A machine gun on a leather strap swung at his side. He wore a dark green uniform of some sort, like the fatigues she'd seen at army surplus stores. A handgun was holstered on a black leather belt at his waist.

He looked her up and down, and his leering smile made her stumble back. "Come with me."

Her heart beat as fast as a hummingbird's. A scream stopped in her throat. This nightmare was real. Very real.

He stepped into the room and motioned for her to follow. Somehow she unlocked her muscles and moved toward the door.

"Good," he said. "It'll be easier if you listen."

CHAPTER 7

JACKSON FROWNED AT the computer screen that lit his small, monk-like room in the barracks at Valkenburg Air Base in Amsterdam. The room had a bed, a desk, a mirror, and one narrow shelf. Normally it felt utilitarian. Today it felt claustrophobic.

He had been staring at the screen since Byron had called to say that three tourists had been kidnapped. Jackson was following the only lead he had. Not really a lead even, just a stab in the dark.

The local police had sent him a list of panicked-parent calls received in the past twenty-four hours about travelers passing through the Amsterdam airport. The police politely took down the name and description of the "missing" person and then filed the report. In most cases, the son or daughter had simply forgotten to call. Or decided not to. Most of the panicked-parent calls were about people between eighteen and twenty-five, so if the kidnapped tourists were much older it was unlikely anyone would call.

He'd used this tactic once in Kabul to attach a name to an American student seduced into going to a training camp. Of course, back then he'd only been trying to find a name, not mount a rescue operation.

But sifting through the surveillance video at the airport would take too long without knowing who they were looking for. And interviewing airport employees about "something odd" would attract too much attention.

Jackson heard a light knock at the door. Before he could say anything, the door opened, taking up a good chunk of the room. Roy looked down the hallway, then closed the door quickly.

"Any progress?" Roy asked, scratching at the beard necessary for his cover.

"Still sifting. You?"

Roy tapped a folded square of paper against his leg. "Byron said we were doing a rescue operation."

"Yes."

"This is the message I've been ordered to send to the kidnappers. I need your head-shrinking skills."

"Your respect for my profession is overwhelming." Jackson took the piece of paper Roy held out. The crease ran through the center of the message. *Wrong package picked up at airport. Disposal requested.*

"What will they do when they get this?" Roy asked.

Jackson wouldn't grant Roy absolution for executing three American citizens. "You already know what they'll do. Why ask me?"

"I don't want to send it," Roy said.

"Then don't."

Roy shifted his weight and glanced toward the closed door. "How I handle this operation determines my career."

Jackson knew Roy wasn't wrong.

"If I disobey a direct order . . ." The strain of Roy's dilemma pulled his face into a mask of tragedy. He shook his head, then recomposed himself. "It's like this sometimes, right? We're given orders that are difficult to follow. We don't get explanations. We have to trust that we're doing the right thing." Roy looked to Jackson for confirmation.

No, you have to stop being a fucking coward. "Your handler needs to earn your trust, just like you need to earn his."

Now Roy looked like he was having stomach cramps. "These orders weren't from my handler."

"That's not normal, you know." Jackson didn't believe that Roy's temporary crisis of confidence would last. If Jackson spoke too honestly, Roy might betray him later.

"It isn't?"

"If you tell me who, I can help you."

Roy shook his head. "If he found out I told you . . ."

Fucking coward. "Can you delay by twenty hours?"

Roy shook his head again. "Ten hours is the best I can do."

"Fine." Jackson had made sure his voice was even, but inside he was seething. Being green was no excuse for caving. Jackson had ten years of experience, though. Would he have done the right thing on his first operation?

"Look, I don't know if this helps or not, but the kidnappers said they used an electric cart," Roy said.

Jackson stared at him blankly.

"At the airport. When they picked up the victims. They offered the tourists a ride to the gate." Roy's hand was twitching on the doorknob.

The information would have helped several hours ago.

"Tell Byron . . . tell him I'm sorry."

"Go. Get lost before someone sees you."

Jackson had his headphones on before the door shut. He was already exhausted, but there was no time to sleep. He flipped through the reports for another hour before his hand paused on a scrawled report from thirty-six hours ago. An older subject than the typical missing person. The subject was a thirty-year-old blonde—just like the fictitious niece, Erin's cover. The number of companions was right; Erin was supposed to have two agents with her. Jackson went into another database and pulled up the driver's license photo for the blonde. Navy Trent from Des Moines, Iowa. She could have been Erin's sister. The same round face with a pointed chin. The same almond-shaped hazel eyes. The same impertinent, turned-up nose.

Dumb luck on the blonde's part. Two other people were on the same itinerary, Moss Warwick and Sara Farmington. Jackson picked up the phone with one hand. With the other he pulled up Navy Trent's flight plans to confirm the nervous mother's report.

"Byron, I think I've found them. I'm sending the information to you now."

"First good news I've heard this morning. When did they land in Amsterdam?"

"Thirteen hundred. They didn't make their second flight and they haven't been rebooked."

"I'll cross my fingers and get started on the cell phone records. Hopefully they had contracts and not prepaid plans."

"I'm going to the airport to see if I can find any employees that saw them get picked up by an electric cart," Jackson said.

"How do you know they were—"

"I'll tell you later." Jackson suspected Roy hadn't told anyone because he'd been ordered to make the rescue more difficult. Naming Roy would only get him in trouble.

"Service corridors," Byron said.

"What?"

"Surveillance shows the kidnappers left from a loading dock. That means they had to go through the service corridors. Passengers aren't normally there. If they weren't hidden, they should have stuck out like a sore thumb."

"I'll check it out. My watch is running a bit fast here."

"How fast?"

They should have had twenty hours before the kidnappers'

deadline to rescue the tourists. Because of Roy's cowardice, they would only have ten. "Seems to count two seconds for every one."

"They don't make them like they used to." There was a click on the other end of the line.

Jackson reached the door in two strides, then realized what he was wearing. Green shirt and army fatigues wouldn't do for the airport. He changed into civilian clothes and ran to the garage.

CHAPTER 8

THE CART DRIVER used the butt of the machine gun to push Navy out of the bedroom. They were walking south. Ten paces and she passed a closed door. Were Sara and Moss behind it? Were they in separate rooms? He pushed her roughly forward again and she stumbled, feeling her toes dig in to the thin carpet as she fell. As she stood up, she noticed the eight-inch blade snug in a sheath around the cart driver's ankle.

Ten paces more, another closed room and the hallway turned west. Soft lights were mounted on the walls. At the end of the hallway an open door spilled a cone of light into the hall.

"Where are my friends?" she asked weakly. She wondered what fresh torture waited in the lit room.

"Go in the office." The cart driver angled his head and leaned down so his face was in front of hers. He had clean breath and bright white teeth. His eyes were full of fury and purpose.

Navy obeyed.

She noticed his boots first—black, heavy and scratched. Where the heels met the carpet, dirt scattered on the floor. They made her think of broken jaws and bruised ribs. She followed the lines of his stiff green pants—the same pants as Cart Driver wore—interrupted once by the horizontal line of the desk. A lamp illuminated papers scattered in front of him. He was leaning back, fingers interlaced, hands resting on his chest. His uniform was starched and pressed. He had a full beard and a black skullcap that was only distinguished from his hair by strands of gray.

"Good morning, Jackie," he said. He leaned forward until the chair rested flat on the floor again. His voice was familiar. The British man who had been in the back on the ride here.

The cart driver waved his gun at the chair in front of the desk. She sat.

The Brit reached into a drawer and pulled out a small camcorder. "If you cooperate, you have a chance at getting home."

"Cooperate?" Navy remembered what she had overheard on the drive. They thought she was related to a senator. How exactly? What kind of ransom were they planning? "What about my friends?"

"Your friends are nobody. We have other plans for them."

Telling them she wasn't Jackie would just make her expendable. But how could she pretend to be someone when she only knew a first name? Her eyes darted around the room, trying to take in all the details. To distract herself from the panic rising in her throat. There were bright rectangles on the wallpaper where frames had been. A prayer mat rolled up in the corner with a machine gun next to it. A gray filing cabinet that probably belonged to the real owner of the house.

She felt the light but firm touch of a finger on her chin. This wasn't the barely controlled fury of the cart driver. This was the touch of a man who knew his own power.

He turned her face toward him and tipped her chin up until her eyes were forced to meet his.

"You're going to record a message for your dear uncle. And if your uncle responds correctly, you just might make it back." He had the gaze of a crocodile, coldly calculating and violent by instinct.

"I'll cooperate." She tried to sound calm. "But I want to see my friends."

He laughed and a wide smile split his face. "You can't save them."

She could play the desperately naïve, hopeful socialite. Was Jackie a socialite? But she had a feeling he would see through any elaborate performance she offered. Perhaps she could use his ego against him. "They got away and you don't want me to know."

"No," he said sharply. Then he paused, considering. "It will be good for you to see what happens. If you try."

She swallowed the tears threatening to spill into her eyes and looked directly into his cold stare. They had to be alive, or he wouldn't have said he had other plans for them.

"Take her to see her friends for a few minutes," he instructed the cart driver. "Then bring her back to me."

With any luck, Sara and Moss were in a different area of the house. The cart driver would take her through the rest of the mansion and Navy could get a better feel for the layout. She counted her paces. They continued west, past more closed doors. Through some closed doors, Navy could hear men snoring. Behind other doors, men laughed. It was sixty paces before they turned north. Then twenty paces and they turned east. She tried to build the layout of the mansion in her head—roughly, a rectangle. Thirty paces east and she was staring down a grand staircase that curved gracefully to the ground floor. The sudden expansiveness made her dizzy and breathless.

Navy followed the cart driver down two flights of stairs, past a second floor that looked very much like the third. The staircase widened as they descended toward the front door, opening into a marble foyer covered with men's boot prints. The front doors had large windows fitted with glass cut into diamond shapes. Even the meager morning sun left a brilliant kaleidoscope of colors over the muddy prints. She wasn't more than twenty feet from the door. She wondered how fast the cart driver could run.

"Don't even think about it," the cart driver said.

"I wasn't." Her voice came out more belligerent than she intended.

"This way," he barked.

They followed the ornately carved handrail down and around to a narrow door under the main staircase. He gestured for her to open the door. This flight of stairs was lit by only two bare bulbs. The stairs led to a utilitarian hallway. The fixtures were simple frosted glass, spaced widely. Servants' quarters, she supposed. She caught a whiff of gasoline and spotted a door to her right, facing east. As they passed the door, she shivered from the cold air. A garage. Several sets of keys hung on hooks next to the door.

He prodded her forward. Five paces took them past a room with threadbare couches and clothes thrown haphazardly around the room. A man lounged in one of the couches, watching television, legs propped up on the dirty armrest. He looked up as she passed, then shrugged when he saw the cart driver follow her. Ten more paces took them past a small room with gray sheets hung to cover every wall. There was one table in the back and a tripod set up facing the table.

Five more paces and she found herself staring through a small glass window in a closet door. At two people she barely recognized.

"Two minutes," Cart Driver said.

She opened the door and ran to the two bodies huddled against the wall. Moss had a nasty bruise on one side of his face. Blood had caked under Sara's nose. The room was as cold as a meat locker. How were they asleep? And with that smell, like an outhouse. Her nose wrinkled as she searched for the source. The bucket in the corner.

"Moss, Sara." Navy put a hand on Sara's shoulder and gently shook it.

"N—" Sara started. Navy leaned in as if to hug them and covered Sara's mouth.

"If they ask, my name is Jackie," she whispered.

"What's going on?" Moss asked, as he stirred.

Navy heard the cart driver shifting his weight outside the door. "Act like you're crying and put your head down."

Sara didn't need to act.

"Most unlucky case of mistaken identity ever," Navy whispered. She was hovering on the edge of panic, like standing on the edge of a chasm, her toes hanging in thin air. If she gave in, she knew she would never find her way back.

"I already tried to escape. They have guards," whispered Moss. He coughed, wincing, and put a hand on his side. "I think they broke some ribs."

"Oh, Moss." Navy leaned her forehead against Sara's. "Just hang on. I'll be back as soon as I can."

When had Navy started crying? She couldn't see through her tears, couldn't breathe through the sobs. Hysteria was a luxury she couldn't afford.

The cart driver pulled her away and locked the door. Navy forced herself back to the game. She counted how many sets of keys were hanging by the door to the garage—five. She counted the paces back to the door at the bottom of the stairs—fifteen. She studied the guards' room while Cart Driver pushed her forward. She walked as slowly as the cart driver would allow, to give herself time to think.

The second floor was eerily empty. What was she expecting? How many men did it take to kidnap three tourists? Thirty paces headed east from the landing on the third floor, past her room, around the corner, and back to the office of the man with the British accent and the crocodile smile.

"Satisfied?" he asked.

Her eyes stung. "Yes." She wanted to leap over the desk and grab the machine gun in the corner. She would die in the attempt, but the thought of his perforated head almost made the idea worth it.

He pushed a typed sheet of paper toward her and picked up the camcorder. "Now we're going to record that message for the senator, your uncle. When I start recording, say your name and read this."

Her name. He flipped open the view screen and pressed the large black button on top of the camcorder. A red light came on near the lens. She left the piece of paper on the desk. If she tried to hold it in her hands, he would see her hands shaking.

"My name is Jackie." The words were wrong. She was Navy Trent. She was on a tour bus on her way to a wildlife refuge. "My name is Jackie. This is a message—"

He stopped the recording and set the camcorder down on the desk. "Your full name. Use your full name."

She let one of the sobs she had been holding back escape from her throat in a low moan. Jackie would be scared. Maybe scared enough to forget her own name.

The cruel smile that spread on his face told her the ruse had worked. "Pierce," he said. "Your last name is Pierce."

She had run out of fear. There was only a dull ache left in her stomach. "My name is Jackie Pierce. This is a message from my captors. We know you have a top secret security clearance. Send us the names and pictures of all the CIA agents operating in Yemen or we will kill your niece. You have thirty-six hours."

He stopped the recording for a second time. "Good. Take her back to her room."

Cart Driver closed his hand around Navy's arm. "What happens now?" she asked.

"Pray that your uncle feels like a traitor. I wouldn't think about your friends too much."

A room with a tripod and sheets covering the walls. Sheets

to cover the walls so no one would know where the filming was done. An execution. Like Daniel Pearl. She dropped her gaze to her lap so he wouldn't see her anger or desperation. The Brit's machine gun still sat in the corner, tempting her. No, if she had any chance of saving them she had to pretend compliance. The thought itself was poison. She promised herself that if she could not escape, she would dig her nails into his face deep enough to leave a scar.

The cart driver yanked her out of the chair. His other hand was on the machine gun, flicking a small lever above the trigger up and down in an irregular rhythm. The safety? As if she would ever get close enough to the gun for it to matter. She was pushed into the hallway and led back to the room with the sagging mattress. He didn't lock the door when he closed it. The guards Moss had mentioned would keep her here if she tried to leave. She sat on the bed until Cart Driver's footsteps faded.

The game. The questions. She went over to the armoire to finish her search. It was empty, not even a speck of dust inside. She had some stereo cables, a few paperclips, two rubber bands, one mirror, and thirty-six hours to escape. Moss and Sara had a filthy bucket and an unknown amount of time to live.

The sun was directly above the house now; the sparse landscaping in the yard cast no shadows. Soon it would pass to the other side of the house. Tonight she would be afraid of the dark.

CHAPTER 9

JACKSON TOOK A badge from one of the lockers in the employee break room at the airport. His accented Dutch would be good enough to pass as an employee trying to locate a missing cart. The police had already written off the missing persons report filed by Navy Trent's mother; at least he didn't need to dodge them. It only took thirty minutes of interviews to locate the loading dock where the tourists had been kidnapped. Several people remembered seeing a scruffy cart driver with three passengers driving through the service corridors. The kidnappers had chosen a loading dock whose outside entrance was partially blocked by construction—one they knew wouldn't be used for a while.

The loading dock was at the end of a long hallway. Greasy spots on the concrete floor had gathered coatings of dust. The only recent signs of activity were from the electric cart still sitting near the concrete edge marked with yellow and black warning stripes. There was no sign of blood and little sign of struggle. Two roller bags sat in the back of the cart, tipped over haphazardly as if kicked. On the front bench were two backpacks, one large and one small, and a duffel bag. He picked up the smaller pack and spread the contents out on the seat.

Two outfits for a woman. A plastic bag with toiletries, including a toothbrush that had been cut in half to fit. No wallet or phone. He searched the pockets to see if he had missed anything. Something crinkled when he pressed against the bottom. He turned the bag over and unzipped the pocket that held the rain fly. Stuffed in with the rain fly was a gallon plastic bag with folded photocopies of a passport, a driver's license and two credit cards. The photocopied passport belonged to Navy Trent.

He went through the other bags and found two wallets: Sara Farmington's and Navy Trent's. In Sara's pack he also found a camera. There were only two pictures: one of a red-haired man who had just woken up and another of Navy in the backseat of a car, smiling and holding up a guidebook titled *Lonely Planet Africa*. The red-haired man matched the driver's license photo of Moss Warwick that Jackson had looked at earlier.

He flipped open his phone and called Byron.

"The kidnappers left their luggage at the loading dock. There's ID for Navy and Sara. Looks like we found our lucky party of three."

"Are their phones with their luggage?" Byron asked.

"There are two here still powered on."

"I'm guessing those belong to Sara and Moss. Navy's phone has been off the network since the kidnapping. The kidnappers must have taken the battery out. We won't be able to trace them that way."

"The kidnappers probably had phones, right?"

"Disposables," Byron said. "What are you thinking?"

"Could we cross-reference the phones that were in the proximity of the victims' phones here with the phones that were near the intersection where the van was caught on camera?"

"We don't even know for sure that's the right van."

"The tracks here are consistent with that make and model," Jackson said.

"That's all you've got."

"That's all I've got."

"It's going to take a few hours, maybe longer than we have."

Jackson leaned against the cart, trying to imagine the person who would animate the clothes scattered on the white plastic seat. "Yeah, I know."

He scoured the grimy corners of the loading docks for more clues, but the kidnappers had been careful. To be thorough, he pulled out a portable fingerprint kit and pulled the prints from the steering wheel. There were probably prints from half of the airport employees on the wheel too, but it might be useful later. The fingerprint dust turned his handkerchief black when he wiped the knobby surface clean.

He put everything back in Navy's bag and loaded all the bags in the front seat with him. If he and Byron pulled off a miracle and managed to rescue them, he could return their luggage. It needed to be collected anyway, before too many people started asking questions.

If he dared to hope for a second miracle, it was that this whole episode could stay under the radar. The lives of Navy and her friends depended on it.

CHAPTER 10

WITH EACH PASSING hour the shadow of the fence grew longer, extending around the house like a mouthful of teeth. Navy's stomach growled. She had managed to slurp water from the tap when they let her use the bathroom, but that was the only liquid she'd had since being brought to the mansion. Would they bring food for her later? She didn't want to feel grateful if they did.

Don't think about it. Find a weapon. She would attempt to escape tonight out the window, using the sheets from the bed to lower herself down. The blanket was a dark color and if the moon wasn't bright she could use it as a sort of camouflage and maybe get across the lawn without being seen. If she managed to get across the lawn and over the fence she would walk barefoot until she found help.

She went to the dresser and picked up the mirror. Broken glass could work as a weapon. Navy put the mirror under two layers of blankets to muffle the noise and used the speaker to smash the glass. The mirror shattered into small, thin pieces— none larger than a quarter. Nothing that could be used as a knife.

The handle of the mirror might break off; the plastic was old and brittle. She would need something to sharpen the edges. The screws from the handles of the armoire? No, too difficult to remove. Outlets, she remembered. If they had used metal boxes when installing the outlets, she might be able to use the edge of the box. But she needed a way to get the screws off the outlet cover.

In the meager daylight remaining, she searched through the shards until she found one with an edge that could work as a screwdriver. The rest of the shards she pushed under the armoire. She chose the outlet in the shadow of the bed frame; it wasn't visible from the door. Her fingertips were red and sore by the time the faceplate hung loose. She said a quick prayer before pulling the faceplate off. Bits of sheetrock crumbled onto the carpet. The wires were nestled in a plastic box.

As she leaned down to examine the box more closely, she saw a glint of metal underneath the bed. L-shaped metal braces were reinforcing the wooden frame of the bed. She scooted herself underneath the bed. The gray cover on the bottom of the box spring sprinkled dust in her face every time she moved. She closed her eyes and felt for the brace. It wiggled under her inspection. The screws were loose. No wonder the bed squeaked and the mattress sagged.

Blind, she worked at it for ten minutes, twenty, it was hard to tell. It seemed like all she had managed to do was strip the head of the screw. But then something small and metal fell against her cheekbone. She set to work on the other screw, glad she couldn't see the room getting darker as the sun dipped lower. When the brace finally fell off, she wiped at her face with her hands, trying not to cough. She opened her eyes to find it was late afternoon. Time was passing too quickly.

Break the handle of the mirror. That was the next step. It would be trickier than breaking the glass. And louder. There was no way she could hide the sound with a couple of blankets. She stood on the oval portion of the mirror, watching the door. Then she grabbed the handle and pulled until her shoulder burned. It was hard not to grunt as she struggled with it. When it gave way, it snapped loudly and she fell against the side of the bed, hitting her elbow on the edge of the wood. She bit her lip to keep from cursing. She cradled her stinging elbow and leaned her head against the mattress. Count to one hundred. Breathe.

Nobody came.

She pushed the mirror frame underneath the armoire with the glass shards. The mirror handle and the metal brace she took with her when she climbed back into the bed. In the dim light that filtered through the sheets, she began to whittle away at the curved edge of the mirror handle. The sun's angle told her hours had passed. Plastic shavings itched at her wrists. Cramps made claws of her hands. But she could feel a bevel forming on one edge.

The doorknob turned with a soft click.

She slipped her knife below the edge of the blanket, and closed her eyes as if sleeping.

"Sit up." It was the man with the British accent and the crocodile smile.

The shavings on her hands were gritty like sandpaper as she pushed herself up. She wiped her palms on her sheets before pulling her hands out from underneath the covers. He was holding a tray with a glass of water and a bowl of beige mush that she couldn't identify. He set it down on the bed and leaned toward her.

"Aren't you going to ask me about your friends?"

"No." She wondered if that was the wrong answer; she didn't want to allow him to torture her.

His smile didn't change. "Eat. You'll need your strength."

She cursed her stomach for growling at the sight of food. She cursed him as he left.

Navy didn't realize she'd been holding her breath until he

shut the door. She devoured the tasteless mush in the bowl. She drank the water too, then considered that she might have been drugged. Why would they bother? They didn't think she had any chance of escaping. She needed to eat. She was dangerously low on energy.

Her knife attempt seemed pathetic when she lay down again. One edge was barely sharpened. She wanted to fall asleep and work on it later. Instead, she closed her hands around the dull, one-edged blade and pulled it toward her. Counting kept her calm. A mansion twenty paces deep and sixty paces wide and three stories tall. A garage with five sets of keys by the door. A hallway downstairs where Sara and Moss were in the third room on the left. Four men she had seen.

She repeated the counts until it seemed like a song in her head, and she scraped plastic to the rhythm. When the door opened again, she almost cut herself hiding the knife.

The cart driver picked up the tray and gestured impatiently toward the door. "Bathroom, if you want it." She followed, feeling naked without her makeshift knife. It took all of her willpower not to look back at where it lay hidden. After she used the toilet and washed her hands, she gulped water from the tap until he pounded at the door.

After the cart driver deposited her in the bedroom and shut the door, she started the second edge of her knife. The sun went down and she finished in the dark. Now she needed a way to carry it. She couldn't hear anyone close to her door. It might be safe to move around the room. There were no sounds from the office down the hall. She gathered the plastic shavings and pushed them under the armoire with the broken glass and what was left of the mirror.

She looked out the window and saw the guard walking the grounds. In the light of day, she should have timed him to see how long it took him to circle the house. Now she could barely see to the corners of the mansion. She crept slowly to the dresser with the speaker wire in the drawer, her knife sharp and precious in her hand. If someone walked in now, she'd be caught.

She yanked the wire from the back of the speaker and used it to tie the knife to her arm, just above her elbow. This left the knife resting against her left forearm. She pulled her sleeve down and passed her hand lightly over her forearm to see if it was obvious. It was passable if no one looked closely.

As dark as it was, it wasn't dark enough to escape yet. She crept back to the bed. It creaked as she climbed in and slipped under the covers. When her head hit the pillow she realized she was exhausted. Her eyelids felt heavy and she started to drift in the warmth of the bed, despite the plastic shavings that scratched at her ankles and arms. She couldn't let herself fall asleep. But she had to stay in the bed in case anyone checked in on her. She threw off the top blanket—the warm, dark one—and let her shivering keep her awake. The knife shivered with her. She tried to imagine stabbing a man with it, and failed. She tried again, this time imagining stabbing the cart driver, and succeeded.

She waited for the stars to come out as it grew darker but it was a cloudy night. Better for her, she supposed, but it left her with nothing to think about but the knife that pressed urgently at her arm and fatigue that threatened to pull her under.

"Bitch!" The door flew open and slammed against the wall, rattling the paintings. The Brit stomped into the room. This time, he was not smiling. Cart Driver followed him, leering again, this time with impunity. She wasn't special anymore. "You lied."

He pulled her off the right side of the bed onto the floor, holding her arm painfully hard, wrenching something in her shoulder. At least he grabbed the arm without the knife. She huddled against the wall, feeling the corners of a hard rectangle underneath her. The outlet plate. She'd forgotten to put it back on.

"You're not Jackie," the Brit said, glaring at her. "Who are you?" He shook her arm and the pain was intense.

She couldn't help but smile a little. It felt good to have him know there was one small battle she had won. "Not Jackie Pierce."

"Well, it doesn't matter. If you were important enough to ransom, you would have told us by now." He stood up and adjusted his uniform, back in control. He pulled the knife out of the holster around his ankle even though there was a gun at his waist. "Get up."

Her knife bounced against her forearm as she stood. She briefly considered using it, but she needed time to release it and the element of surprise. She hadn't been expecting to need her knife until she was on the lawn.

"Take her downstairs to her friends," he ordered the cart driver. "She'll be executed with them."

She held his eyes until the cart driver pushed her shoulder to turn her around. He pointed down the hallway toward the large staircase they had walked down that morning.

The grand entrance to the mansion was dark now. The stairs down to the basement were darker. She wondered how they knew she wasn't Jackie Pierce. Her wallet had been in her duffel bag and she hadn't heard them load their luggage. Unless they grabbed the luggage and loaded it in the front? They had taken her phone at the loading dock, but she had a PIN set on the SIM card. They wouldn't have been able to turn on her phone without the code. Or pull the data from the SIM card without forensics equipment.

Don't think about why. Think about a new escape plan. She was in the basement hallway now and Cart Driver's machine gun was against her spine. Passing the room with the TV and the couch. Passing the room staged for her execution. *Think.* Now at the door of Sara and Moss' prison. Sara and Moss barely reacted when the cart driver shoved Navy into the room. They were pale and their eyes were glazed over, from pain or dehydration or hunger she didn't know. The knife swung against her forearm and she clenched her fists.

The image came with frightening clarity—her hand closed over her knife, the blade buried in the cart driver's stomach, her hand red and slippery with his blood. But the door shut, locked, and then he was out of her reach. She went to the corner where her friends were fading, trying to hug both of them at once. They were cold, almost shivering. Her warmth was all she could offer.

"They found out you weren't Jackie," Sara whispered.

Navy nodded.

Sara's eyes closed, hope of escape fading, and she fell into a restless sleep.

CHAPTER 11

THE DOOR WITH the tiny window, the metal rack with the orange basketballs, the bench against the wall, the weights lined up neatly in their slots, the plastic chest that held the boxing gloves and headgear. And again he passed the door with the window, the metal rack, the weight bench, the plastic chest. Jackson ran the small rectangle around the gym until the repetition made him dizzy. Soon he would have to begin the distasteful task of monitoring the militants' video sites for news of three infidels murdered to avenge the misdeeds of the Great Satan.

He checked his phone, the third time in the last five minutes. Roy's message to dispose of the package had been sent to the kidnappers an hour ago, and there was still no word from Byron. Jackson had run all the queries he could think of against all the databases he could access. He had looked over the entire file on the operation again. Finally he had come to the gym to keep from pacing his room like a caged rat.

His phone rang and he grabbed for it eagerly, almost letting it slip out of his hands.

"What have you got for me?"

"A location, I think," Byron said. "An old estate forty minutes east of Valkenburg. Your idea worked. We tracked some disposable cell phones to the estate. The family doesn't use it in the winter but satellite pictures have picked up recent activity."

"And the caretaker hasn't been seen for a few days," Jackson guessed.

"You're psychic. Ten or fifteen men were at the mansion, but satellite footage shows most of them are gone."

"I'll go check it out."

"You might be too late."

"I know."

The sweat dried cold on his arms as he raced out of the garage, glancing at his phone for directions. They had been close the whole time. He sent the location to Roy, but he didn't expect anyone else to get there in time. Hell, he wasn't expecting to get there in time.

Men moved back and forth in the hallway, ignoring Navy's face in the window of the door to the janitor's closet. They carried what looked liked bags full of hockey equipment that weighed down their shoulders. Guns? She heard engines starting in the garage and the sound of doors opening, then being slammed shut. Were they were packing to leave?

"The three of you will stay to help me." Navy recognized the Brit's voice in the hallway. "The rest can go."

Any escape would be entirely up to Navy. Sara and Moss were almost delirious. They had likely had no food or water for at least twenty-four hours. Navy's new plan seemed even less likely than the old one. But she couldn't give up. The possibility of escape was the only thing that kept her from curling up in the corner and waiting to die. *I am not afraid.* A few wooden crates were carried past the door, another engine started, then the grinding of a garage door opening.

The man with the British accent peered through the window. She shrunk back against the wall and slid down until she sat next to Sara. He had the cart driver and two others with him.

"It's time for your film debut," the Brit said.

She shivered; her hidden knife brushed her forearm. No, it was too soon. And the wrong place. There were four of them and no room for her to move. Cart Driver hoisted her up and trailed one hand up the inside of her leg. He pressed his knuckles into her spine and when she arched her back to squirm away, he grabbed her wrists, tying them together behind her back with a rope that scratched at her skin.

Another man pulled Sara to her feet, and the third kicked Moss until he stood. The guards tied their hands too. Navy's muscles were rubber bands pulled too tight against her bones. She tried to breathe deeply but her stomach threatened to spasm into sobs. They were led in a line—Moss, then Sara, then Navy—to the room next door with the tripod. The camcorder was mounted on the tripod, facing away from the door. Her captors pushed Sara and Moss into seats in front of the camcorder. The cart driver was pushing her in the same direction. Resisting seemed useless. Her plan was silly. Stupid. The ravings of a dehydrated mind.

No. Focus.

At least Sara and Moss were facing the door. She might be able to warn them to duck before she shot their guards. If she could get the Brit to send her to the other room with fewer people guarding her. If her knife worked well enough to get a gun.

"Wait," she said. Her dry throat made the syllable crackle. "I have money." She didn't have any amount that would impress them. But the desperation would make her next offer more credible.

"Money?" The Brit laughed. "Your blood is more valuable." He pointed at the chairs and the cart driver pushed her toward them.

Navy swallowed hard. "Then take me." She craned her neck

to look at the cart driver, with his leering lopsided gaze. "I'll do whatever you want. In exchange for their lives."

A deceitful smile flicked across the leader's face. "All right." He pointed to Cart Driver. "Have your fun, but take a guard." Cart driver nodded and grabbed her arm, pulling her toward the door. One of the guards led the way out the door.

"No!" Sara and Moss cried out at the same time, finding some strength to struggle at their bonds.

She hated to let the Brit think she believed him, but there were other things to worry about. She hadn't planned on releasing the knife without having a hand free. It wasn't budging. A fall might jar it. When the cart driver pushed her forward she tripped herself. The hard floor slammed into her shoulder and she cried out. But the fall had dislodged the knife. She clamped her hands together to keep the knife between the tender skin of her wrists.

The cart driver pulled her up. "No tricks!" She felt each knuckle of his fist as it hit her jaw.

The hallway was short, just five paces to cut through the rope. She stared down at the floor, trying to concentrate on the awkward motion of sliding the knife between her wrists. She could feel a warm, slow drip where the edge of the knife caught the flesh of her hand. Her blood made her wrists slide against each other smoothly. The rope was old and frayed and gave in quickly. Two more paces and they were in the room with the couches and the television, still on. A tourism commercial filled the screen with red tulips on top of bright green stems on a sunny summer day.

"Hold her," said Cart Driver.

The guard did as ordered, holding her arm halfway between her shoulder and her elbow loosely, not expecting any resistance, not bothering to check if her hands were still bound. The barrel of the guard's machine gun, hanging from a strap across his chest, brushed her fingers. The cart driver pulled his machine gun off his shoulder and laid it on top of the television. He undid the holster at his waist that held the handgun and draped the worn black leather across the flickering tulips.

I am not afraid. But she was. She was afraid of the way his tongue circled his lips as he took three strides to the couch. She was afraid of the way he unbuttoned his uniform jacket with ceremony and laid it on the couch, as if she were his lover instead of his prisoner.

Underneath his jacket, he wore a dirty tanktop, yellowed at the armpits. Small, but defined, muscles clung to his frame like vines. He reached for the bottom edge of his shirt, pulling it over his head. For one crucial second, he would be blinded by the fabric. It was now or never.

She released the pressure between her wrists and let the knife fall into her right hand. It cut her palm. She turned easily in the guard's loose grip and plunged the knife with all her strength into his stomach. If he cried out, she didn't hear it. The stuff of life, ligaments and muscles and the yellow fat over them, tangled around her blade, resisting her stroke from right to left. She stifled a sob that was as much disgust as fear. His blood poured down her wrists, soaked her pants, coated her hands, mixed with her own.

Something clattered behind her. The cart driver, his undershirt hanging around his neck, was reaching for the machine gun on top of the TV. The knife to get a gun, she reminded herself. Her guard was still standing, dying but not dead. Alive enough that he wouldn't give up his machine gun. She circled behind him, wrapping her arms around his waist to keep him upright. Her knife dropped between his feet. She grabbed for the trigger of his machine gun. But the body was heavy and her fingers slipped along the smooth metal, still wet with blood. She found the trigger, finally, and squeezed. Nothing happened. The safety.

She felt for the lever and pushed it up. Suddenly the gun was spitting bullets, slamming the guard's midsection into her.

The cart driver fell to the floor. She dropped the guard and his head hit the floor with a crack, his gun trapped underneath him. She needed the cart driver's uniform. She left the guard moaning behind her and turned away. But a hand closed around her ankle. The guard's. She tried to kick him loose but he held on tight. Her knife was still between his feet, beyond her reach and his weakened one. His moans got louder and he opened his mouth wide to yell. His cry was cut off when she kicked her free heel into his nose. She leaped toward her knife, knees jarring against the thin carpet. She spun around and stabbed at the first soft spot she saw. The point where his artery pulsed in his throat. He crumpled, gurgled, then sighed into silence.

Her heart was beating too fast, too loud. She breathed in deeply, once, twice. She figured she had two minutes—maybe three—before the Brit started to doubt that it was she who had been shot. She went to the cart driver; blood was just beginning to pool around him.

She tossed his boots aside. Too big, and bare feet would be quieter. The knife sheath was harder to release. She looked away as she yanked his pants off. His butt fell against the floor with a soft slap. Her jeans were soaked, heavy with blood. She peeled them off and left them in a pile on the floor. The uniform was too big for her. She had to cinch up the belt on the pants and roll up the sleeves on the jacket like a kid playing soldier. Which she was, really.

Navy picked up the cart driver's machine gun and hung the strap across her chest. This time she found the safety easily.

The hallway was empty. A language she didn't understand was coming from the room with the camcorder. She went down to her hands and knees and crept along the hallway until she reached the open doorway. She peered in, worried one of her captors would be facing the door. Only Sara and Moss were facing the door, sitting at the table. The man with the British accent was speaking, his back was to her to keep his face off the camera. The fourth man was standing with his machine gun ready, pointing at Sara and Moss.

Still on her hands and knees, Navy leaned forward into the opening. She caught her friends' eyes and pressed a finger to her lips to warn her friends to stay quiet. She motioned for them to duck and then counted down with one hand. Five. Four. Three. Two. Hopefully they understood. One.

When her pinky bent down, she stood up. She was counting on the microsecond of surprise wearing the guard's uniform would give her. She aimed high with the machine gun to avoid where Sara and Moss had thrown themselves on the floor. The gun seemed to have a mind of its own, slamming into her midsection over and over as she fired. The guard fell first. By the time the Brit fell, she was fighting dry heaves. Despite the holes in his gut, the Brit was struggling to unsnap the holster at his waist, almost smiling. She stepped into the pool of his blood and felt it rise between her toes. Her stomach calmed. *You did not break me.* She pointed the machine gun at his head and squeezed the trigger. His head bounced from the impact of the bullets.

She let go of the machine gun and its strap cut at her neck, the barrel hot on her thigh. She tried to take the gun off but the canvas strap caught on her ear, tangled in her hair. Finally she tore the gun free and threw it to the ground.

Sara stood up slowly, wide-eyed. Moss sat, too tired to move. Navy reached into her pocket—Cart Driver's pocket—for his knife and went over to them. Navy's hands were weak and shaking, still feeling the vibrations of the gun. Somehow she managed to cut Sara's hands free without cutting Sara. She gave the knife to Sara to cut Moss free.

"Are you two okay?" Navy asked.

"Are you okay?" asked Sara incredulously.

Navy looked down at her stolen outfit, spattered with blood. The cuts on her hand were oozing and suddenly stung. She had just killed four men, and all she felt was numb. Sara's hug surprised her. Then Moss was hugging both of them. Their tears threatened to unhinge her.

Navy untangled herself and pushed them away. "We have to go. In case someone is coming back."

❧

The estate was dark, a shadow on the horizon across a wide expanse of brown field. Jackson flicked the headlights and running lights off and sped up. A pair of headlights emerged from the side of the house—the only lights on the property—and drove down the driveway, exiting via an open gate. They didn't bother to close the gate after they passed through. They were clearing out. Was there anyone left to save? Or was he just rushing to recover a few bodies? He pressed the accelerator down further. The irregular, staccato rhythm of pebbles against the bottom of the car increased but the car didn't seem to move any faster.

The car he'd watched leave was long gone when he finally swerved into the long driveway. The mansion was a quarter mile away. He was the first one here, as expected. Without backup, he needed to scout. He turned off the car to survey the scene. It was eerily silent. He picked up his night vision monocular and scanned the grounds. No warm bodies outside. No sounds of humans. So the execution was done.

A small motor rumbled on the side of the house. Like the kind of motor used to run a garage door. A white van with lights on emerged from the garage Byron had mentioned. Anybody in the van would have spotted him already. He looked through his monocular, night vision turned off, with his left hand and grabbed his gun with his right. He focused on the driver, quickly, to get a visual before the headlights turned toward him and blinded him.

Three people with familiar faces were in the front seat—the tourists. Navy Trent wore a militant's uniform. What the hell were they doing driving a van? Had they escaped? It hardly seemed possible. But if they had, and he left his lights off, they might assume he was one of their kidnappers and try to run him down. If he turned his lights on, and there were militants in the van, he'd be making himself a target. He'd only seen their faces for a split second but they'd seemed more tired than scared. He decided to bet on escape. The van was slowing anyway; they had already seen him. If he had to die, he'd rather die an optimist.

He flipped the switch to turn the running lights on to let them know he wasn't hiding. He left the gun and the monocular in the car when he got out. The chill night air, damp from the ocean, raised bumps on his arms. He held up his hands as if he were being arrested, to show he had no weapons. Hopefully the army uniform he was wearing would vouch for him. He still had his army ID with him from the base. Better not to tell them he was a CIA field agent. The van slowed further as it got close.

He pointed to the flag patch stitched on his uniform. The van approached cautiously, crunching to a stop five yards from him.

It was Navy who stepped out of the driver's seat, leaving the van running. The headlights of the van lit the space around him like a spotlight. When she stepped into the light, Jackson could see the suspicion on Navy's face. The uniform pants she wore were covered in the fine spray of blood from gunfire. Even bunched, the waist hung at her hips. The top, an inch too long in the arms and too wide in the torso, was spattered with blood as well. A nasty purple bruise, still forming, was on her left cheek. Her hair was oily and tinted with red flakes. White strips of someone's T-shirt were tied around her palms as hasty bandages.

One of her bandaged hands held a six-inch knife. She was holding it wrong, like a beginner. He should try to get it from her—it wasn't unheard of for victims to hurt their rescuers in a panic.

"Navy Trent?" he asked.

"Who are you?" she demanded.

"Jackson Fletcher, U.S. Army psychologist."

Her eyes flicked to the gun lying on the passenger seat.

"Psychologist and assorted duties."

"A rescue party of one?"

"I was the closest."

"Do you have ID?"

"In my pocket." He reached one hand slowly into his back pocket and pulled out his white identification card. She held the knife out as she walked toward him. Ten feet. Eight feet. Six feet. He planned the moves in his head, sweep her arm, grip her wrist, spin her backwards and knock the knife from her hand. But the odd calm in her hazel eyes stopped him. She wasn't anywhere close to panic. She reached for his card and backed away to examine it in the headlights of the van. When she returned it to him, her touch was dry and cold. Dehydration, he guessed, and fatigue.

Her fingers released the knife so quickly that it seemed her ligaments had snapped. It left an impression in the gravel where it fell and for a long second, she watched the knife and its shadow in the glare of the car's headlights.

"Thanks. It was sweet of you not to take the knife from me."

"Anytime."

"My friends are hurt. Moss has some broken ribs. They need food and water and medical attention."

"There's a hospital at the base. Are you okay?" Her eyes darted around the lawn, chasing shadows, looking for attackers. The fading adrenaline rush was letting her use the last of her energy to stand. He knew the feeling from his worst days in the field. Adrenaline was better than morphine, but the crash came hard.

She still hadn't answered him.

"I have some water in the car," he said. "We should take my car anyway. It'll be faster."

Jackson turned off the van. He carried Moss to the backseat of the car while Navy helped Sara. Navy was right. They were listless, dehydrated, and bruised. He knew the creak of a broken rib too well, and he could hear it when he buckled Moss' seat belt. But both Sara and Moss were able to gulp down water—they finished two bottles each.

He handed a bottle to Navy but she shook her head.

Moss' eyes managed to focus on Navy briefly. His voice was between a whisper and a croak. "Drink."

"When we're on the way," she said. Moss' eyes closed. It was a bad sign.

"Let's go," Jackson said.

Navy paused with her hand on the handle of the passenger door, staring at the gun on the seat. She didn't move until Jackson put the gun in the glove compartment.

"It's not far," he promised.

"Okay," Navy said. She turned toward the dark horizon, hand resting on the door lock as if she still needed a way to escape.

CHAPTER 12

BYRON RAPPED HIS knuckles on the wall just above the nameplate that read "William Grand, Manager." He was glad the Americans had been found alive, but loath to give Willy the Grand any sort of relief with the news. Willy waved him in, cradling a phone on his shoulder while he searched the top drawer of his desk.

"I promise you'll know something when I know something," Willy said. "Just talking to him now." He hung up the phone and rubbed at his receding hairline. He didn't offer Byron a chair. "What's the word from Amsterdam?"

"Jackson found the tourists alive. Clean-up crew found four of the kidnappers dead—the rest were gone. A forensics team is at the mansion now, but there's not much to find."

"Thank God."

Willy's relief seemed genuine. Byron was trained to look for signs of people lying but he had learned in the field that it was hard to know for sure. Nobody was ever exactly what they seemed to be. "I'd like to go out there with Erin to supervise the debriefing," Byron said. Try and stop me, he thought.

"Fine. The most important thing is to find out what the tourists know."

"There was halothane in the back of the van. I think they were unconscious the whole time they were transported."

"Make sure the mansion is cleared of anything that might tie us to this operation."

"Understood. After I get back from Amsterdam, I'd like to never think about this operation again." Good intentions didn't mean much in Byron's line of work. Willy deserved a little credit for allowing Byron to attempt an impossible rescue. And for genuinely caring that the kidnap victims were found alive. But it was Willy's incompetence that had blown the operation in the first place.

He left Willy's office and walked over to Erin's cube. Erin turned when she heard him. She leaned back in her chair, and chewed on the end of her pen. The cube walls were empty except for an internal phone list. Nothing cluttered the desk but her computer and a half-filled-out report. No pictures, no knick-knacks, no calendar, no coffee cup or box of tissues.

"How do you feel about wooden shoes and tulip bulbs?" he asked.

"I was just about to cancel my tickets," Erin said.

"Willy wants you to fly out with me to debrief the kidnap victims."

One side of Erin's mouth curled into a calculating smile. "You mean, you suggested to him that the two of us should fly out there."

"It'll be like old times—you, me, and Jackson working together again."

"I'm not the nostalgic type," she said.

"I need a female agent to bunk with Navy at Valkenburg. Gain her confidence. Find out what she knows."

"Are you sure I'm the right one? She'll start asking questions about our resemblance."

"I don't have a choice. Bringing someone new in would be . . . dangerous. You're the only female agent already on the operation."

"Have you lost your faith, Byron?"

"Come as a favor to me?"

"I keep track, you know."

"I know."

He booked a ticket on Erin's flight and sent the schedule to Jackson. Then he drove home in the chill of the early evening, through the remains of rush hour traffic. He would have time for dinner, a little bit of packing, and a two-hour nap before boarding the plane. In Amsterdam, it was almost dawn.

CHAPTER 13

ERIN SPREAD THE papers from the operation file in a semi-circle around her on Jackson's cot at Valkenburg Air Force Base in Amsterdam. The quarters were gray and spartan, comforting in their simplicity. She was glad to be in the field, where she could finally figure out how things had gone so wrong. Someone would pay. She would make sure of that.

No one fucked with her operations.

If Willy thought a corner office and a fancy nameplate could protect him from her, he was sorely wrong. Byron's well-intentioned warnings had been echoing in her head the entire flight. There were plenty of undercover agents who could have played a senator's niece. Her specialized skills were in high demand; no one hunted lies or humans better than she did. So why had her handler threatened her career unless she played along?

She ignored the layouts of the mansion, statements to the owners reporting a break-in and possible robbery. After all the evidence was collected, all traces of Navy and her friends would be erased. She reread the records of the messages sent to the kidnappers.

Packages arriving in six weeks. Three dolls total, two boys, one girl. Girl is blond with gray eyes. One boy is dark-haired, blue eyes. The other, brown hair with blue eyes.

And then, four weeks later this message:

Packages arriving tomorrow. Two girl dolls, one boy. One girl doll with blond hair and gray eyes. One girl doll with dark hair, green eyes. Boy doll has red hair, brown eyes.

No explanation for why the target had changed from two men and one woman to two women and one man. No mention of why the timing had changed. And yet, the kidnappers had accepted the change without question. As if only one of those messages had actually been sent.

Jackson walked through the open door to his room and dropped a leather satchel on the desk. "Feel free to make yourself at home."

"Someone's cranky," she said. "I came to warn you. Willy's here."

"I thought it was just you and Byron."

"Yeah. Me too. He showed up at the last minute."

"Do you know who sent him?"

"He probably sent himself."

Jackson shook his head. "Seems suspicious."

"You and Byron are getting paranoid." She held up the autopsy report. "Have you read this? I think I like my doppelganger."

He leaned down to read the report, blinked at it tiredly then straightened. "Why don't you fill me in."

"She made a shiv out of a plastic mirror handle, disemboweled and stabbed one in the throat, then used a machine gun to shoot the other three. The leader was finished off at close range."

"Messy first kills. That explains some things. She seems to have more than her share of survivor's guilt."

Erin shrugged. "Did you just get up or something? You look like shit."

He turned the chair at his desk to face her and sat down, pushing the chair back with one toe of his boots until he could lean against the wall. His eyes closed of their own accord. "I never went to bed."

She put the autopsy report down and folded her hands in her lap with mock seriousness. "Tell me what's bothering you."

"Funny." He opened his eyes to glare at her. "Are the messages we sent to the kidnappers in your file?"

"Yes."

"See if they match these." The legs of the chair landed with a hard thump. Jackson pulled his satchel toward him and handed her a small stack of papers from it.

Erin took a sharp breath as she read them. "So it wasn't Willy's fault. Where did you get these?"

"Better if you don't know." He paused and rubbed at his eyes. "Navy looks like you, no doubt. But she arrived two weeks before you were supposed to. And with one male companion and one female companion. You were supposed to be traveling with two males. It doesn't seem like a simple case of mistaken identity."

"Roy was taking orders from someone else. Most of these messages don't match what's in the file. Where did you get these?"

"Like I said, better if you don't know." He grabbed the papers before she finished reading them and put them face down on the desk. "Someone sabotaged this operation. They found an American that looked like you and was traveling through Schipol. Then they made sure the kidnappers targeted her party of three instead of yours."

Kyle, Erin thought immediately. Maybe that's why he let the operation go forward with mock protests.

"You know something," Jackson said. Her expression must have betrayed her thoughts.

"You know better than to head-shrink me." She tapped him playfully on the nose. "Best not to try or you'll get lost."

"Would you mind?" He pointed toward his bunk. "I need some sleep."

"I should go meet my new bunkmate."

"She'll see right through you."

"I think you have a crush on this one, thinking she's so smart."

He shrugged. "She's still sleeping. I'd wait. It's probably better if I do the first debriefing anyway."

"How are the other two?"

"In the base hospital recovering from severe beatings. Moss had internal bleeding."

She gathered up the files on the bed and walked to the door. "Sweet dreams."

"I'm going to lock the door after you leave. In case you were thinking of picking up those papers on the desk."

"I'd never."

He pointed toward the hallway. "Out." But the second after the door shut he opened it again. "Erin?"

"Yeah."

"Wake me up if you see Navy around. I need to make sure she doesn't tell Willy anything he shouldn't know."

"Sure thing."

CHAPTER 14

JACKSON WOKE UP to see Erin's/Navy's face hovering above his own.

"Rise and shine, sleeping beauty." It was Erin's voice, mocking and sarcastic. He looked at the clock—he'd slept the whole day. "Navy's in the kitchen, digging around in the cabinets. You said you wanted first contact. Willy's sniffing around so I'd hurry."

"I locked the door to my room," he said.

"Yes. And you hid the copies of those messages. That wasn't nice of you. I'll find them eventually, you know."

He shook his head and rubbed the sleep out of his eyes. His left hand reached down to the floor where he had thrown his T-shirt. He sat up and pulled the shirt over his head in one motion. "Thanks for waking me." He took a small bottle of mouthwash off a shelf in the closet and swished a capful in his mouth until the stinging cleared his head. He spit the green liquid into a coffee cup he kept on the shelf.

At the door, he paused and studied Erin's figure, sitting in his desk chair. "I don't suppose it would buy me anything if I ordered you out of here and locked the door." If Erin found the messages she would figure out Jackson had copied them from the safe in

Roy's room. Jackson wanted to make sure Roy was out of Erin's reach before that happened.

"It might delay me by a couple minutes."

"In that case, good luck."

Jackson hurried through the corridors toward the kitchen area. Technically, Valkenburg was a Dutch military base. They had a small self-contained corner of it. He passed the room Navy had—the one she would share with Erin—and then the room Byron had claimed. Four other tiny rooms lined both sides of the hallway. All were empty. Willy would stay in the officer's quarters, on other side of the kitchen. Each of the two officer's quarters had its own ridiculously small bathroom.

At the end of the hallway there was a small gym and a kitchen area just across from it. One entrance to the kitchen was from the hallway next to the gym, the other was from the officer's quarters on the other side.

He entered the kitchen just as Willy's face peeked in. A curt shake of Jackson's head warned him off. Navy sat at the circular table, flipping through an old copy of *Dutch People*. She was wearing the clothes he had found for her, jeans and a button-up cotton shirt. The tourists' luggage was still being processed. Her hair was wet and curled into a bun at the back of her head.

"Evening," he said.

"Is it? On what day?"

"Tuesday. One day after you escaped."

"Tuesday." She smiled a little, hand poised to turn a page. "What a normal word."

"Would you like coffee? Or dinner?" He opened the fridge. All he found was a couple of takeout boxes and a moldy package of cheese.

"Food, actually. There doesn't seem to be any here."

"Only ramen, I think." He heard Willy shuffling on the other side of the wall. It would be easier to talk without him around. "We could go off-base. If you're up to it."

She flipped past two more pages with images of glamorous couples on a red carpet. "A noisy place. With lots of people."

"I know a place like that."

He picked his coat off one of the hooks on the wall and slipped it on. He looked through the rest of the coats and picked one that looked close to her size and held it open for her. She took the coat from his hands and put it on herself. The exam at the hospital had showed no injuries other than the nasty bruise on her face and a few minor cuts on her hands. Her treatment had been a peanut butter sandwich from the nurse's desk and orders to drink plenty of water.

Jackson led the way to the garage, two wide aisles lined with nondescript sedans and military humvees. She was hunched over, her hands stuffed deep into the coat pockets. "So this is what CIA spies take to work. Not flashy sports cars."

"Why do you—" He looked at her face to see if he could get away with denying it. No, she wasn't fishing. She just wanted him to know she knew. He pulled the key out of his pocket and unlocked the doors.

A different car than yesterday. Moss' blood was still being cleaned from the backseat of the other one.

She opened the passenger door and sat down before he could think of anything else to say. "No denials?" she asked as they pulled out of the garage.

"Would you believe me?" It was a chilly early evening. Small wisps of heat came out of the vents as the engine warmed. The clouds had cleared and stars were appearing.

"No."

"Just out of curiosity. How do you know?"

"You arrived alone in street clothes in a family sedan. No

lights and sirens. You have a U.S. Army ID but your hair is longer than regulation. And the only other person I've seen on base wasn't wearing fatigues."

"I do have a psychology degree. And I was in the army."

"Okay." She smiled, relaxed, as if there was a joke in the statement somewhere. When she spotted the sunroof she pulled back the felt cover and reclined the seat until she was looking up through the glass. She was silent for the rest of the ride.

⁕

The restaurant smelled of soy sauce and fried dough. The hostess behind the podium glanced at Navy's purple and green bruise and then at Jackson.

"An ex-boyfriend," she told the hostess. "Not him."

"Could we have that little room in back?" Jackson asked.

The hostess nodded and picked up two large laminated menus. She led them to a room lined with glass windows, mostly occupied by a rectangular table surrounded with chairs at odd angles. Navy ordered a large plate of orange beef with a side of noodles, cream cheese puffs for appetizers, hot tea, and a pitcher of water. Jackson ordered shrimp chow mein.

When the cream cheese puffs arrived her eyes lit up and she slathered one in sweet and sour sauce before bringing it to her mouth. She looked nauseous after the first bite. "I'm sorry. I was just so hungry . . . but now. I don't know if I can eat."

"It's all right." He resisted the urge to cover her agitated hand. "We can sit here as long as you want. We need fresh take-out anyway." It was the first time he'd seen her show any typical signs of distress. He'd interviewed victims in seven countries, and none had prepared him for her.

The small tea cup was swallowed in her hands. His was still

burning hot. She took three small sips before setting it down, but she didn't let the cup go.

Dinner rush at the restaurant had filled most of the tables. Waiters with heavy trays were bringing steaming dishes to families on the other side of the glass. The noise of the restaurant was dulled, but not muted, by the glass surrounding them.

"This is perfect," she said. "Thank you."

He nodded, uncertain of what to say. He was impatient to hear her story, to see how much Navy knew about what had happened. Someone in the agency had made the decision to kill Navy and her friends to cover up the sabotage. Jackson didn't doubt that the decision could be made again.

The waiter arrived with the last of the food and left with a sympathetic glance that Navy ignored.

"Do you want to tell me about what happened?" he asked.

She focused on the tips of her chopsticks as she stirred her orange beef. Then she pushed the plate away and pulled her legs into a cross-legged position on her chair. "I don't have much of a choice, do I?"

"Of course you do." She didn't, but he didn't want to be the one to tell her.

"Well, I can talk to you now and you can give whatever version you like to that agency bureaucrat at the base." Her stare was disconcerting and intense. "Or he hangs around when I talk to someone else later."

"So you met William."

"Yes. Maybe you can tell him I have PTSD and talking to nervous bureaucrats makes me suicidal."

He laughed, despite himself. "I'll think about it."

She stabbed her chopsticks into the lo mein noodles on her plate. "We were going to Johannesburg. But you probably know that already. We were going to wander around southern Africa for three weeks—see the sights—do a safari. My dream trip." A sad smile turned down the corners of her mouth and she looked up at the ceiling. "Anyway, the flight from Des Moines to Amsterdam was late. We were rushing to make our connection when the cart pulled up next to us."

"How did he get you into the service corridor?"

"He offered us a ride. I didn't want to. But Moss jumped right on, then Sara. And I thought, what the hell. I was tired. We were all hungry. It was stupid to get on, I know."

"No, not stupid."

She studied him for a long second. Her eyes were stars of blue surrounded by gray. Not like Erin's at all. Her face was impassive.

"Okay, a little stupid," he admitted. The mask on her face dropped for a moment. He had said the right thing. She was testing him to see if he was being honest.

"I didn't realize until we were almost to the loading dock that we hadn't even told the driver our gate. I was going to warn Sara but before I got to it—"

She stopped to take a sip of tea, as if something were caught in her throat. "Before I got to it we were in the loading dock and these men jumped out at us. They held something over my mouth. So hard I thought maybe he just wanted to suffocate me." She touched her chin and took a hesitant breath.

"The cloth was soaked in halothane. Similar to chloroform, but easier to steal. They found the bottle in the van."

"I tried to hold my breath but I was still woozy. And then we drove for a long time—about forty minutes, I think. There were two of them with us in back. One man I named the Brit and another guy. Not the cart driver."

"How many people were in front?"

"I don't know. The cart driver must have been, but we couldn't hear what was happening in front."

"Did you ever hear them use names?"

"No. There was Cart Driver, the Brit, and a younger one. Like his voice was still in puberty. But there might have been more."

"Go on."

"You do have a psychology degree."

"Forgive me?"

She smiled a little and put a small piece of beef in her mouth, chewing it slowly. "They were talking about me—I heard them say they thought I was related to some senator."

He tried to keep his expression neutral to hide his disappointment. Knowing that she had been mistaken for the fictional senator's niece was enough to make the situation dangerous for her.

"Aren't you going to eat?" Navy pointed at his untouched food with her chopsticks.

Jackson had to do a better job of hiding his concerns. "Just letting it cool down. So you heard them talking about a senator. And then?" He broke apart his chopsticks and took a bite of his meal.

"I was mostly awake when we came to the driveway. They stopped to open the gate and then we drove to the house. Mansion, I saw later. They carried us in separately, so I didn't know where they took Sara and Moss until the next morning."

"And they didn't say anything this whole time?"

"The cart driver was whispering in my ear." Her lips tightened and her eyes narrowed. "Dirty things. I passed out. I woke up in a room upstairs by myself. It was dusty." She ran her hands down her sleeves, as if she needed to brush herself off. "Everywhere but the basement was dusty. I could tell the sun was rising, but I didn't know the time. They took my watch." She stopped, pressed her lips tighter, censoring herself.

"What is it you want to tell me?"

"Useless stuff." The tips of her chopsticks tapped against the wide brim of her plate, her fingers seeming disconnected from her body, which she held perfectly still.

"We'll figure out what's useful later."

"I was afraid. I thought I'd go crazy with fear."

Most people wore fear like a wet blanket. It made them shiver, hunch over, swing between tears and anger. She had an eerie sense of calm.

"I made myself keep track of things as a distraction. Like what direction each of the walls faced. What was in the room. I had to pretend that I might be able to escape."

"You did escape."

"It wasn't likely."

If he lied, he would lose her trust. "Doesn't matter. What happened then?"

"Cart Driver showed up at some point. He took me to an office. The Brit said that if I cooperated I might survive." She put another piece of beef in her mouth and chewed slowly, continuing only after she swallowed. Her eyes drifted to the corner of the room. She was drifting too. Part of her had gone back to that office, back to her enemies. "I told him I'd cooperate if he took me to see my friends."

She pinned him with an intense glare meant for someone else. "He laughed at me. He had this smile, big and wide and cruel. He was—" She shivered. "He was cold. None of this is helping you, is it?"

"This isn't just about me."

"Will I be getting a bill for this session then?" Her voice caught at the end, and the joke fell flat. She took another bite of her meal. "They had Moss and Sara in this little closet downstairs. They hadn't even let them use the bathroom."

He waited. She was eating larger bites now.

"Moss said they tried to escape. That's why they got beat up. I told Sara and Moss to call me Jackie."

"How did you know the name Jackie?" Another thing she shouldn't know.

"The British man used the name earlier. After I saw Sara and Moss, they made me record a video. Saying I was Jackie Pierce and that if my uncle didn't deliver the names of all the CIA agents in Yemen in thirty-six hours they'd kill me."

"So it wasn't just your intuition that told you I'm a spy."

She smiled briefly. "No. Does that make you feel better?"

Strangely, it did. She didn't wait for his answer before continuing.

"They put me back in the room upstairs after I recorded the statement. I started making this knife from the mirror handle. I made up this ridiculous escape plan. I was still waiting for it to get dark when the Brit came into the room cursing at me—saying I wasn't Jackie."

"How did they know that you weren't?" Knowing that she had been inadvertently swept up in a CIA operation was dangerous but manageable—knowing that the operation had been sabotaged would mark her for death. The saboteurs hadn't intended for her to survive.

"I don't know. My wallet was in my luggage, so it wasn't that. I guess they had my phone—but it has a PIN on the SIM card. I don't know how tech-savvy they were or if they had equipment to get around that. Sara and Moss could have let it slip, I guess. They were pretty out of it." She took one shaky breath in and out, tried to sip her tea but the cup was empty. She refilled it.

"What happened next?"

"The leader told me I was going to be executed with Sara and Moss. People were carrying things out, I heard cars leaving. I still had the knife I made, but I didn't have a way to release it quickly." He saw her tongue probe the edge of the bruise on her cheek and she winced.

This was the part he was most interested in, though it was the least useful tactically. He'd been over her history on paper again and again and nothing suggested she had combat or fighting skills. Not even so much as a karate club in college. The person he'd met was strong, brave, and smart. But there was nothing in her that seemed to suggest the viciousness necessary to kill four men who were stronger and better armed.

"Cart Driver had been eyeing me since I got there. As long as I was Jackie and getting special treatment it didn't matter. But I thought maybe—" She took another shaky breath. "Maybe if I could separate him from the rest I could use the knife if he got close. And if I could get his machine gun, maybe I could take out the rest of them. I knew Sara and Moss couldn't help—they could barely stand."

Jackson found himself holding his breath.

"They took us to a room with a tripod. To film the execution." She was no longer hesitating. Her voice was firm and distant. "I told the leader I would do whatever they wanted. In exchange for Sara and Moss." She hugged her arms to her chest. "He pretended to accept the deal. I had to fall to get the knife free so I tripped and it made the cart driver angry. He hit me."

"That's where the bruise came from."

"Yes. You're looking at me strangely."

"Most people wouldn't react like you did."

"Survival's a strong instinct."

"Panic is too."

She tilted her head to study him again. Not testing him anymore, just curious. "He sent me to the next room with the cart driver and one of the guards. I cut my hands free in the hallway."

"The blood trails in the hallway were from you."

"Yes." She focused on a spot of soy sauce on the table, hugging herself tighter. "I waited until the cart driver had taken off all his guns before I stabbed the one guarding me. I used the guard's gun to shoot the cart driver."

He thought back to the autopsy report. "The one guarding you, he was stabbed twice."

She looked up, surprised. "He grabbed me. So I had to—I had to stab him in the neck. I stole the cart driver's uniform. It was the least bloody. I thought it would give me a split second before they started shooting back."

"What were they saying when you got back to the room with the tripod?"

"I couldn't understand it. Arabic, I suppose. I tried to use hand signals to tell Sara and Moss to duck. And then I counted down from five to one. And then I shot them."

The first time he shot a machine gun it had felt like a bucking bronco in his arms. At close range, the bullets clustered so tightly the target was shredded, not just killed. The leader—the one she called the Brit—was the one who had been shot at close range. He wondered if she had seen the leader's mangled face, more meat than flesh, in her dreams last night.

"And then you showed up."

"You were smart," he said.

Her short laugh had no joy in it. "I was lucky. If the Brit had grabbed my left arm instead of my right he would have found the knife. If they had faced Sara and Moss away from the door I wouldn't have been able to tell them to duck. If whoever was supposed to clean out my room upstairs had finished the job, I wouldn't have had any weapon at all."

"Smart and lucky. That's how it goes most of the time."

"That's how you got the scar," she said.

It was a long curved line that ran from below his ear, down his neck and past his collarbone. A close call. "Yes."

"Tell me about it?" An order and a request. Her retelling had exhausted and exposed her. She needed him to offer something that would leave him as vulnerable.

"India. A few years ago. There's a religious sect there that carries around a special sword as part of their daily devotion."

"The kirpan." She twirled a greasy lo mein noodle with bits of carrot around her chopsticks.

"You've been to India?"

"I read about them once, an article in the *Times*."

"I was waiting to catch a cab to the airport. I guess I'd been followed. I'd been watching for tails, but you don't always see them. I was pretty much alone, it was late, but one guy started walking down the street toward me. Sikh, I thought, since he had the costume down well. But just as he's passing me I see his other hand reflected in a store window, reaching for his sword." It was easy to travel back to the dark street where litter rattled in the wind along the sidewalks. The colors came back distinctly. Orange turban, white tunic and pants, silver kirpan, and a black strap to hold it. "I didn't sidestep fast enough and I saw the blade right next to my face. There was a nick in it, no larger than the width of a dime." The bright moon had caught the edge and made it sparkle.

"But you're here?"

"It takes practice to learn how to tie a turban well. This guy hadn't practiced his disguise. His turban fell off his head and started to unravel when he lunged at me. It gave me enough time to step behind him. But he did manage to get me first. From here," he put his finger below his right ear, at the corner of his jaw, where the pulse of the carotid artery could vaguely be felt. When Jackson traced the line of the scar with his finger he felt the edge of the knife again, so sharp he felt the triangle of the edge slip underneath his skin. The line finished near his heart, just past the thick cartilage at the center of his ribcage.

"And you killed him?"

Jackson nodded slowly. "I strangled him with the turban."

"Did it—I mean—was it—"

He waited while she searched for the words.

"It felt wrong, killing them," she said. "I mean, I know I had to in order to get away. They would have killed us without thinking about it. But it still felt wrong."

"Because part of you enjoyed it."

She looked at him, startled, about to deny it. "Yes."

The waiter interrupted them.

"A box, please," Navy said. She pushed the half-eaten plate of beef and noodles toward the waiter, a perfectly normal gesture. As if they'd been discussing a movie they'd seen.

The waiter took Jackson's empty plate and her half-empty one and left again.

"When we go back," he said, "William will want to know what you know."

"Isn't that what you're going to tell him?"

"Not everything. It will be easier for you . . . if there are certain things we don't tell him."

"So if he asks?"

Until he could review the evidence found at the mansion, and interview Sara and Moss, he wouldn't know how much she could credibly deny. "Let me handle it for now."

"I don't think he'll be satisfied with that."

"Not forever, no. I just need to figure some things out. When I know more, we'll figure out what to tell William and how."

"So it's dinner and a show." If the thought frightened her, he couldn't tell.

"Eventually, yes."

"Just tell me when." Her trust was humbling. She had no particular reason to believe that he had her best interests at heart. The waiter returned with their food. "Are you ready?" Jackson asked reluctantly. The base and all its problems seemed far away.

She nodded. "Can we see Sara and Moss when we get back?"

Jackson twirled a take-out box by its handle. "I can take you there. But—"

"Don't tell them anything they don't already know," Navy guessed.

Jackson dropped his eyes to the table and nodded. She would need her friends to recover. What he had asked her to do would put a wedge between Navy and her friends.

He sat with her in comfortable silence until the check arrived. He pulled out his wallet—with the Army badge that hadn't fooled Navy—and dropped some bills on the table. She stifled a yawn and stared out at the dim, cheerful restaurant. He wasn't eager to leave either. But she needed sleep and he needed to get back to talk to Erin and Byron. It wouldn't be as simple as he had hoped, but at least she didn't know her government had tried to kill her.

CHAPTER 15

THE INFIRMARY WAS smaller than Navy had expected—eight beds lined up in two rows with a nurse's desk near the door. Tall, gleaming IV stands guarded the beds. Moss and Sara seemed doll-like, surrounded by crisp, white sheets. The nurse looked at Jackson for approval before letting Navy pass.

"Moss! Sara!" She ran to their beds.

Navy tried to hug them both at once, then settled for hugging Moss first. "Easy," cautioned the nurse. "His rib is broken."

"I think I've slept for twenty-four hours straight," Sara said.

"It's Tuesday," Navy said. "For a little bit longer."

Moss winced as he struggled to sit up. "What I want to know is what you're going to tell your mom."

Navy found a perch on Sara's bed. "We'll say I lost my camera and Africa was awesome."

"Moss and I were wondering . . ." Sara touched Navy's hand. "Where were you before they threw you in the closet with us?"

"Upstairs."

"Did they—I mean, were you kept separately because—"

"It's not what you think," Navy couldn't think of what to say to her friends. If Jackson were to be trusted, she should say nothing at all. "Really, it's not."

"Anytime you're ready," Sara said, misreading the reason for Navy's evasiveness. "Never's all right too."

"Don't worry about me until you guys get better."

Moss ran his hand across the white bandage wrapped around his bare chest. "I'm sorry, I tried to stop them."

"Oh, baby," Sara said. "It's not your fault."

The room shrunk to the size of the space between Sara and Moss—Navy was invisible to them. She looked back at Jackson. He had one shoulder against the wall by the door, watching but keeping his distance. A small frown pressed his lips together. He was a strange man. He spoke mostly with his intense emerald eyes and his lean body, as if words were a luxury. He was keeping things from her, and yet she looked to him for comfort. The thought jarred her, and she looked back at Sara.

"What happened?" Navy asked.

"The beating was a punishment for trying to escape." Sara pulled her legs together, the fabric puckering in her lap. Not just a beating, then. A worse sort of violence. Sara looked at Moss, the dark experience hanging in the air between them. Moss had tried to protect her and they had punished Sara to punish him. "And then they pretty much left us alone. Until they put you in the closet with us."

"I'm so sorry," Navy said. The wrong words were the only ones that came to mind.

"Why is everybody apologizing?" demanded Sara, wiping tears from her eyes with the shoulder of her hospital gown. Navy couldn't look away from the dark, wet spots. "It was bad luck, that's all."

"Yes. Bad luck." Bad luck and what, Navy wondered. Even before Jackson had warned her she had started trying to calculate the odds. The kidnappers had been waiting for them. Like they knew their flight schedule. What were the chances that Jackie

Pierce's kidnappers would be at the airport on the same day that Navy happened to pass through? What were the chances of Navy looking exactly like the senator's niece? What were the chances that Jackie Pierce was also traveling with two companions: one tall, redheaded male and one petite brunette?

The odds were a million to one, if she were generous. Something else was going on. She could ask Sara how their captors had figured out Navy wasn't Jackie Pierce. But what would that gain Navy? The answer didn't matter anyway. She wasn't interested in disturbing the nest of snakes they'd stepped into. They were safe now. In a few days they could go home and never think about the nightmare again.

"Get well," Navy said. The end of the IV scratched the center of her palm when she patted Sara's hand. "Rest. I'll see you later."

She left the infirmary with Jackson and followed him through a labyrinth of gray corridors. "How badly were they hurt?" Navy kept her eyes focused on the end of the hallway.

"Are you sure you want to know?"

"Yes." Another answer that didn't matter. But this one she had to know. They were hurt because of her.

"Sara was—" he paused. "Sara was mostly just bruised and dehydrated. Moss was lucky to make it. He was bleeding internally."

"Was she—" Navy stopped. Did I get my best friend raped? She wanted to ask, but she couldn't even finish the question.

"Was she raped, you mean?" Jackson kept his distance.

She closed her eyes. "Yes."

His answer was a second too long in coming. "The doctor didn't check for that." For the first time that evening, she was grateful he was trying to lie. Or maybe he knew that he was giving the lie away and wanted Navy to know he was sheltering her. She gave up trying to untangle his intentions, instead stepping through the door he opened for her into their corner of the base.

"We finished processing your luggage. I had it put in your room."

"You found our bags?"

"They left everything at the loading dock."

Jackson stopped at the door to her room. Her room. The phrase seemed odd to her now. A week ago it had meant her almost empty bedroom in her apartment in Des Moines. Two days ago it had meant a room in a historic mansion that was also a prison. Now her room was a gray square that held two cots in the barracks of a military base.

He reached past her to knock on the door, his face close to hers. He hadn't shaved recently and dark circles hung below his eyes.

"Come in."

"You have a roommate," Jackson said.

The narrow door opened and Navy's own face greeted her. She stumbled back and felt Jackson catch her.

"Hello," said her twin.

"Well, that's interesting," Navy said, brushing Jackson's arms away. She walked past the woman. Her bags were, as promised, on her cot.

"I'm Erin." The woman held out her hand.

Navy ignored it. "Good to meet you."

"And you are?"

"Let's not pretend." She was suddenly exhausted and short on patience. Was this Jackson's doing? William's? It was another piece of the puzzle she didn't want to see. Erin, annoyed, looked at Jackson. Jackson held his hands up in protest. "No, he didn't tell me," Navy said. "But you know who I am."

"Direct." Erin circled her, sharklike, studied Navy from head to toe. "Rude, even." Navy felt like she was being examined by her own reflection. "Navy Trent, I knew I was going to like you the moment I read the autopsy report."

Navy wondered how many other people had read the report and what judgments they would make. "Thanks, I think."

"Be nice," Jackson chided Erin.

Erin plopped down on her cot, the springs protesting at the sudden weight. "For you, Jackson, anything."

He looked away, fed up or disgusted, Navy couldn't tell. "We'll talk more tomorrow, Navy," he said.

"Wednesday." She wasn't sure she trusted the floors to hold her anymore. Or the walls not to fall down. Or that there were twenty-four hours in day and a Tuesday night would be followed by the sun rising on a Wednesday morning.

"Yes, Wednesday." His smile was slight but his eyes were kind. He shut the door behind him and his footsteps echoed down the hallway.

Navy's eyelids were heavy, and her limbs felt weak. She had only been up a few hours and already she could sleep for another twelve. She dug through her bag and found her pajamas. They smelled like her detergent, freshly washed just before the trip. The floral pattern was overly playful and wrong next to the drab blanket still rumpled from her restless sleep last night.

"My first kill was a coyote," Erin said.

Navy turned to find Erin staring at her. Again. At least she was no longer mocking her. "The animal?" Navy asked. She sat on her cot and scooted back until she could rest her head against the wall.

"A people smuggler. I was supposed to be a crooked INS agent. But I did something stupid and I blew my cover." The memory didn't seem to upset Erin. It was simply an object that existed—like the dust motes that swirled in the air. "I was stuck in this little trailer that got as hot as an oven in the middle of the day. He took my gun, put a knife to my throat. I had an alarm clock set for noon, and the radio started blaring. The noise distracted him, and I managed to get the knife. But I didn't have long enough to get a clean kill. I had to stab him in the stomach and hold him in a one-handed hug until he bled out. He didn't go quietly. He kneed me in the ribs. Kicked me in the shin so hard I had a hairline fracture. He scratched my chest with his dirty nails. Took weeks for the scratches to fade."

Navy swallowed hard. She wasn't ready for the emotions flooding to the surface. She didn't want to deal with them in front of this odd imp of a woman.

"I didn't deserve to survive. I made the mistake. I wasn't watching him carefully and that's how he got my gun. There were a thousand ways that fight could have gone differently and I wouldn't have made it. You get over that."

If there hadn't been a mirror to make a knife. If the Brit hadn't fallen for her ruse. Yes, things could have gone differently. "I don't understand." Navy lied.

"Now who's pretending?"

Navy searched the featureless white ceiling for a place where she could avoid Erin's gaze.

"What you had to do was messy. You don't need to feel guilty about it. You don't need to go over all the ways things could have gone worse. You don't need to know why you made it out in better condition than your friends."

"Then what do I need to know?" Navy didn't trust Erin. She wanted this little lesson to end. She wanted to sleep until she forgot everything she knew.

"That you're willing to fight." Erin got up and stood over Navy. "Nothing else matters."

Navy found herself appreciating Erin's clumsy attempt at comfort. In Navy's mind, even after they escaped, she had been fighting her way out of that mansion in every possible scenario. There were scenarios she wouldn't have survived. Her life in this universe was optional.

It had always been true, she supposed. But the truth hadn't confronted her until she had shoved her knife into a man's stomach and felt the warm, thick gush of his blood mixing with hers in the cuts on her palms.

CHAPTER 16

THE CONCRETE WALLS of the kitchen at Valkenburg were devoid of windows. Their corner of the base was underground. Some days the barrier felt like protection. Some days it felt like confinement. Right now, Jackson would have liked to see dawn rising.

Three cups of instant coffee steamed on the small table.

Byron sipped his and grimaced. "This is terrible."

Erin seemed to enjoy his discomfort. "Some of us don't have offices near Starbucks."

Jackson watched the hallway where William's room was, hoping William would sleep in. The discussion Jackson needed to have with Byron and Erin required privacy, but he couldn't risk going off-base and leaving Navy alone with William.

"How much does she know?" Byron asked.

Jackson glanced toward the officer's quarters again.

"Jackson?" Byron asked.

"Willy's still asleep," Erin assured him.

"How do you know?" Jackson asked.

"Have you ever had the pleasure of traveling with Willy?" Erin asked. "He's about as subtle as a buffalo."

"How much does she know?" Byron asked again, in a quieter voice.

"She knows the kidnappers thought she was Jackie Pierce, the senator's niece. That's it, as far as I can tell. She doesn't know that Roy sent a message telling the kidnappers to kill her."

"You're telling me she's not wondering about how she was picked out? How the kidnappers figured out she wasn't Jackie Pierce?" Erin asked. "She seems too smart for that."

"I don't know if she wants to pursue those questions. She had a chance in the infirmary to quiz Sara and she didn't take advantage of it."

"Maybe she didn't want to ask those questions in front of you."

Jackson couldn't deny the point, but he didn't believe that was the reason. Navy trusted him. How he knew that, he couldn't say exactly, but he was sure of that one thing. "I think she'd rather not know."

"So it's not a complete catastrophe," Byron said.

"Let me have a crack at her first," Erin said.

Jackson bristled at the phrasing, but understood. In their place, he wouldn't have believed Navy's lack of curiosity either. Byron's decision to bring Erin to Amsterdam certainly didn't help set Navy's questions to rest. Jackson would have made the same decision despite the risk. He wouldn't have trusted anyone else. "Well, regardless of what she knows we need to keep her here for a little bit."

A cot banged against a wall and something clattered to the floor. Then a faucet came on and a cupboard door slammed. "Told you," Erin said. "Like a buffalo."

William's hair was still wet and disheveled when he came into the kitchen. His suit, however, was pressed and spotless, even after the long international flight. He took the fourth chair at the table without asking, eyes taking in the papers and photographs scattered on the table. William turned a little green when he looked at the glassy eyes of the man with a jagged hole in his carotid artery.

"We need to keep Navy here for a couple of weeks," William announced. "Find out what she knows."

"That's what we were thinking," Jackson said. Dealing with William's ego made the situation delicate. "How should we convince her to stay a couple weeks?" Jackson would have to gracefully redirect whatever ham-handed suggestion William came up with, but the offer had to be made to keep him mollified.

"I thought we'd just tell her she has to. PATRIOT Act and all that."

Erin put a hand over her mouth, and coughed to cover her laughter.

"She might not react well to that," Jackson said. "I think she'll say yes if we can offer her something."

The conversation ended when Navy entered the kitchen. She was barefoot—that's why they hadn't heard her. Floral cotton pajamas pooled at her feet and a tank top left the bruise on her upper arm exposed.

"Sorry to interrupt." Navy's body language said she wasn't sorry at all. She walked straight to the fridge and her face lit up when she opened the door. "Someone bought groceries."

Byron stood up and offered his hand to Navy. "Byron. The good host."

"Thanks. Now I don't need to have orange beef for breakfast. I'm starving."

Jackson picked up the photos, then quickly gathered the papers scattered over the table. At some point he would have to walk Navy through the reports of the scene. Seeing the pictures would trigger new memories—new details that would help them track down the rest of the kidnapping ring. But it was too soon.

Byron helped Jackson clean off the table while Navy dug through drawers looking for a spoon to go with the yogurt she'd pulled from the fridge.

When Jackson looked up, William was standing behind Navy, reaching out to put a hand on her shoulder. A mistake Jackson didn't have time to stop. Navy stiffened at Williams's touch; her hand froze in the silverware drawer. "How are you feeling today? Did you sleep well?" William asked.

Navy turned to face him, holding the spoon in a white-knuckled hand. Her other hand was clenched around the container. William stood too close, crowding her. A muscle in her jaw twitched and her eyes narrowed. This was exactly the interaction Jackson had been hoping to avoid: William's tone-deaf people skills antagonizing Navy and possibly leading to Navy antagonizing William. Jackson caught Navy's eye. Careful, he mouthed. She swallowed whatever she had been about to say. "I slept very well."

"We're all very glad that you and your friends are all right," William said. The statement seemed genuine. Was it true what Byron had said? That William was growing a conscience?

Navy's hostility softened to wariness. "Thank you."

"We've decided that you should stay with us for a bit," William said.

"Oh?" The sharpness had returned to Navy's voice. She set the yogurt on the counter.

Erin turned in her chair, a hint of a smile on her face. Of course Erin would want to see the show.

Jackson knew he should get between William and Navy, but he was transfixed by the change in her. In a split second she had gone from wary to aggressive. Her athleticism was evident in the well-formed muscles of her arms.

"And if I wanted to leave?" Navy asked William. William stepped back. So this is what had carried her through the mansion, Jackson thought. There was something in her eyes that Jackson hadn't seen the first night he met her, or the second night while she calmly explained how she'd been kidnapped and almost raped. Today she had the eyes of a cornered animal.

"It—it would be better if you cooperated."

Shit. William was really going to be this dumb.

"What if I don't?" Navy's voice was soft and dangerous. Most kidnap victims would have reacted with tears. Pleas. Panic. Navy was using her fear, turning it into anger. "Will you lock me up in some dusty mansion? Throw me in a closet with a shit bucket?"

William took another step back, looking toward the table for support. Jackson stood up, crossed his arms, and watched William flounder.

"Or maybe you'd like to give me away as a party favor to a homicidal flunkie?" She tilted her head, predatory, a bitter smile twisting the corners of her lips as she leaned in closer. William had his back against the wall. "Do you really think anything you're capable of could break me?"

"Your duty as a United States citizen . . ."

Jackson stepped between William and Navy, pushing them apart. "William, I need you to get lost for a while." William was predictable; Jackson focused on Navy. Her hazel eyes were stormy. He wondered what she was capable of.

"Fine." William sounded like a small child who had been denied a toy. He turned toward his room.

"I meant off the base," Jackson said.

Navy hadn't backed down. Only his hand on her chest kept her away from William. He could feel the rapid, strong beats of her heart, her energy against his palm like a live wire.

Navy didn't relax until William's clomping footsteps were inaudible.

"Good strategy," Erin said to Navy. "A taller opponent won't have the advantage of reach if you get in close."

"Not helpful," Jackson snapped.

"I wasn't going to attack him." Navy stretched her face toward the ceiling and took two deep breaths before she looked back at the table. "Well, probably not."

"Think of him like an untrained puppy," Byron advised. "He's well meaning but not too bright."

Navy sat down at the table with the opened yogurt. Her eyes jumped to the unmarked manila folders neatly piled in front of Jackson.

"Are those the files on the kidnapping?"

The kidnapping. Not *my kidnapping*. "Yes," Jackson said.

"Can we—"

"Not today."

"First things first," Byron said.

"Okay. What's first?" Navy asked.

Thanks to William, Jackson thought, they had to make this plan up on the fly. Navy had to feel like she had participated or they would lose her cooperation.

"What William meant to say is that it would be helpful to us if you and Sara and Moss could spend a couple weeks here," Jackson said.

Navy tensed again, the spoon poised between the container and her mouth. "Would be helpful or is required?"

"We won't force you." Would they? Jackson wondered. If it came to that. He watched her consider the offer, the micro-expressions flicking by like a high-speed filmstrip. She was worried, anxious, scared, angry.

"I'm listening."

"It's probably best if no one at home knows what happened to you and your friends. You'd get a lot of media attention. Maybe become a target again." That wasn't the real reason, but hopefully it would be convincing enough.

"You mean they might go after us again?" A sliver of fear creased her forehead.

"It's a possibility." Jackson reminded himself he was lying to her for her own protection.

"Would they track us back to Iowa?"

"Unlikely. They don't know who you are. It would be a long search and you're not a high-value target. Assuming it doesn't make the news, of course."

"So what do we do?"

"Your flight to Africa was booked as part of the tour package. Maybe you had a change of plans."

"Like the tour company messed up our reservation and we couldn't make the last leg of our trip."

"And you spent three weeks in Amsterdam instead," Jackson said. "Do you think Sara and Moss will go for it?"

She nodded slowly. "There's something else you want from me."

Byron arched his eyebrows. *She's smart*, he was saying to Jackson.

"We need your help in figuring out more about this sleeper cell," Jackson said. And your help in getting the three of you out of this alive, he thought.

She shook her head. "I already told you everything I know."

"It's surprising what you can remember over time."

"Will they be looking for us here?"

"No. The four you killed won't be expected back for a while." Actually, Roy was going to make it look like the four men Navy had killed died while traveling home. "We think the rest of the cell has already left Amsterdam."

"What about the video of the execution? Isn't someone going to notice it was never released?" Navy didn't flinch when she asked the question.

"It's not unusual for execution videos to be delayed by a few weeks before they're released." Jackson didn't want to explain the reasons why. Delaying the release extended the search for the victim, good for creating news, and made the final crime harder to track.

"Think of it as a vacation paid for by the U.S. government," Byron said. "Jackson and I will take you around to some of the sights, get you a few pictures to show off at home."

"And we'll spend a couple of hours each day seeing what you can remember," Jackson added. He left out Erin's role. Navy might figure out that Erin was there to spy on her. She might not. But Erin was right. They needed confirmation about what Navy knew. Based on Navy's reaction yesterday, she had already figured out the kidnapper's had mistaken Navy for Erin. If they were lucky, Navy would just think Erin was in Amsterdam because of the original operation.

"Do you know when Sara and Moss will be out of the infirmary?"

"Today or tomorrow, the doctor said."

Navy nodded slowly, her fingers tapping lightly on the table. "Okay. I'll talk to Sara and Moss when they get out. Is it all right if I use the gym?"

"I was just going to invite you to gym therapy," Erin said.

"Therapy?" Jackson was afraid to ask.

"Oh, it's a lot like what you do," Erin said. "Except with less talking and more hitting things."

⁓

Navy followed Erin down a set of steps off the main hallway of the base. The gym was half the size of a basketball court and twice as tall as any of the other rooms in the compound. Windows along the top of the gym looked into the hallway that led into the kitchen. At one end of the gym a basketball hoop with a torn net hung over faint markings for the out-of-bounds lines. A small padded bench and a set of weights stood at the other.

Erin unwound a tight loop of rope around a metal brace on a wall. There were several punching bags suspended from the white girders. Erin lowered a large cylindrical bag. Others were human in size and shape, arms and legs stuck permanently in aggressive stances. From a plastic chest, Erin pulled out two pairs of boxing gloves, creased with wear.

"Hold your hands out," Erin said.

"I was thinking maybe running. Or—" Navy spotted the basketballs. "A game of one-on-one or something."

"Trust me," Erin said.

Navy didn't. But she presented her hands to Erin, palms down.

"Palms up," Erin said. Navy obeyed. The gloves smelled like old sweat. Erin tightly laced one around each of Navy's wrists. "In a fight, you won't have gloves, of course. So here's what to remember when you make a fist: keep your thumb out, your fingers tight, and your wrist straight." Erin held up a hand to demonstrate, pulling each finger down one at a time and wrapping her thumb around the corner formed by her knuckles. Erin's nails were short, some bitten down to the skin. The knuckle of her middle finger had a thick, white scar running across it.

"Thumb out, wrist straight," Navy repeated. "What happens if you don't?"

"A broken thumb or a broken wrist."

"Ouch."

"Yeah, they never show that in the movies." Erin took Navy by the shoulders and turned her toward the punching bag. "Show me how you punch."

Navy looked at the bag and then at her hands, comically large, like one big black soft knuckle hanging off each arm. "I don't really."

"Don't really what?"

"Punch things. It doesn't come up a lot."

"Who's the one that used you like a party favor?" Erin asked the question in the same tone she might have asked about the guy with the long mustache or the guy with the loud tie.

"The Brit." Navy heard his laughter when she had asked to see her friends.

"Punch that bag like it's the Brit."

Navy's shoulder was jarred by the impact of her fist against the bag and she stumbled back. She had put all of her strength into it and the heavy bag had barely moved.

"Not bad for a first time."

"That's generous of you."

"A lot of people think a good punch comes from strong biceps. Your strength doesn't come from there."

"For men it's different?"

Erin shook her head. "It's the same for men. Good rotation is what gives you strength." She pulled a glove onto her right hand, letting the laces hang. "See?" She raised her forearm until it was level with her shoulder, her arm bent almost at a right angle, and she rotated her whole torso. She moved so fast Navy barely saw her turn before the bag was swaying from the force of the blow. "Core strength. Think of a hammer—the head of the hammer only delivers the force. The power comes from the swing. Your fist is the head of the hammer." Erin stopped the swinging of the bag with her ungloved hand and stepped back.

Navy tried again, ignoring the ache in her shoulder. This time the bag swung a quarter inch, tapping her outstretched fist as it swung back.

"Better. Stick with that hook for now. Straight-on punches look good but they're harder to land well. Second lesson."

"Already?"

"Can't let sloppy form become habit. Recoil immediately

after you punch. Leaving your arm out there makes it vulnerable to attack."

Navy hit the bag with her right hand again, then her left, then her right. She liked the rhythm of the movement, the slap of leather against leather, the swing of the bag and whoosh of air as she recoiled. Navy saw the British man's face on the bag with his mocking dark eyes and scruffy beard. Slap, swing, whoosh, slap, swing, whoosh. Her blood was boiling. She wanted to punch through the bag and watch it empty its sand in piles on the floor.

"Whoa, girl."

A hand grabbed Navy's right arm and held it to her side. She whirled, left arm raised to punch, before her vision cleared. It was Erin, with what might have been a sympathetic expression. Navy could hear the rope scraping against the metal girder as the bag swung. "I'm not done."

"You're holding your arm a little low. You'll hurt your shoulder that way and it's less powerful. Arm up, level to your shoulder, like I showed you."

Navy returned to the bag. The face was a composite now. Cart Driver's lopsided, leering eyes with the Brit's hawk nose and the high-pitched voice that had scraped at her nerves while the metal floor of the truck imprinted itself on her arm.

'Hold her.'

She hit the leather over and over again, not waiting for the bag to settle before the next punch. Her knuckles ached despite gloves. Her arms burned. Exhaustion finally forced her arms to drop to her side. She felt the warmth of her sweaty armpits clinging to her T-shirt, the trail of sweat traveling down her back.

"Now I'll teach you how to kick," Erin said.

Good. Because no matter how many times Navy hit the bag, the face was still there.

Jackson watched Navy kick the bag like her life depended on it. Her form was sloppy but getting better with each tip Erin gave her. Maybe this was what Navy needed right now—a physical release for the tension of the last few days. But he wasn't here to watch Navy. He was here to intercept William. Well-meaning or not, William had just about blown the whole operation with his threat to detain Navy against her will.

The compound door opened and shut. Jackson looked away from Erin showing Navy how to flex her foot for a sidekick.

"William, just the man I was waiting for."

"I don't really have time to talk right now." William rolled his shoulders back and puffed his chest out. He was taller than Jackson, but spindly in the arms and legs.

Jackson stood in the center of the hallway. When William tried to walk around him, Jackson stuck his arm out, fingers spread against the wall, his wrist at the level of William's throat. He'd had enough of trying to cater to Willy the Grand's ego. "I need you to avoid Navy."

"I think you're forgetting that this isn't your operation. I'm in charge. We need to know what she knows. I intend to find out."

"If she knows nothing, you're just going to make her suspicious with stunts like this morning."

"We need—"

"We'll find out," Jackson growled. "I'm making progress with her already. But you're not helping. If you're going to stay, I need you to avoid her."

"I was just trying to make her understand how important it is that she cooperate."

"You threatened a kidnap victim with kidnapping. Are you

going to threaten Sara with rape to get her to tell us what happened?" Jackson waited for the realization to sink in.

"Oh."

"I think we can make this go away. I think we can convince Navy and Sara and Moss to go back to Iowa and not say anything at all."

"That would be ideal," William said.

"But if that's going to work, I need Navy to cooperate with us. And I need her to go home acting like a tourist, not a PTSD patient."

"Her therapy isn't our concern," William snapped. "She's an asset."

"Her cover story is our concern. Re-traumatizing her isn't in our interest."

"She was threatening me this morning." A small drop of spittle hung from his lower lip. "She would have hurt me."

"She was complimenting you," Jackson said. "She doesn't think you're a soulless terrorist."

"Great." William stepped back and licked the spittle from his lip.

"Just let us do our job. Erin's bunking with her, Byron and I will be with her during the day. We've got it covered. We'll keep you updated."

"I want daily reports."

"If you—"

"Stay out of her way." William rolled his eyes. "I got it."

CHAPTER 17

SECRETS WERE ERIN'S favorite thing to collect. She waited until she was alone before picking the lock on Roy's quarters. William had gone off base, babbling about a very important meeting. Navy was out with Jackson and Byron on the first day of her fake vacation. Roy was out too, but Erin was confident he would appear soon. She knew Roy had been ordered back to headquarters. That meant he had to come back and get his things today.

Roy had been the one to dangle the fictional senator's niece in front of the kidnappers as a target. Roy had been the one communicating with them. He would know what they had been told and, more important, why. Roy was the key.

Erin easily found the safe hidden under Roy's cot. She couldn't decide whether it was a sign of idiocy or ignorance. A safe this cheap was barely good enough to protect costume jewelry.

Inside was the set of messages Jackson had showed her, the ones sent to the kidnappers. Jackson had probably returned them to Roy's room after making copies. Erin took pictures of all the messages with her phone, then returned them to the safe. She studied the pictures carefully while she waited.

Erin's mission had clearly been sabotaged. Under someone's

orders, Roy had been setting Navy up as Jackie Pierce ever since Roy had arrived in Amsterdam. William's orders had been ignored.

She heard footsteps in the hallway and tucked her phone in her pocket. Sara and Moss were still in the infirmary. It could only be Roy. The door opened.

"Hello, Roy," she said.

He jumped, surprised, his hand reaching for his gun. She often had that effect on men. "Erin. What are you doing here? I thought—"

"That everyone was gone." She rearranged his pillows so she could lean against the wall in relative comfort.

"Navy shouldn't see me," he said, as he closed the door. "William said so."

"It would be awkward," Erin said. "Since you're the one who planned her execution."

"I had to," he mumbled. "Orders."

"Of course. One should always follow orders."

Erin watched as Roy's eyes measured the distance between Erin and him, then between her and the door. He went to his locker, then pulled out a suitcase and started to neatly stack his clothes in it. "I fly back today."

Erin crossed her arms and continued to stare at him. Roy wasn't quite nervous enough yet.

"I really am sorry," he said. "You have to believe me. I didn't want to send that last message."

"What you mean to say is you didn't want to kill three American citizens."

Roy winced. "It was—"

"Orders. So you said." Erin put on her best shark smile. "What I want to know is from whom."

He picked up the rest of the clothes in his locker and shoved them in a messy pile into the suitcase. "I can't say."

"Sure you can. Just use your words."

"I really c—shouldn't." She was scaring him, no doubt. But someone else had scared him first. He zipped the suitcase shut and picked it up. She closed the distance between them in two strides and slammed the suitcase onto the desk.

"We haven't had much of a chance to talk, you and I."

Roy backed away.

"There are two things you should know about me. I don't like people fucking with my operations. And I always protect my friends."

He backed away farther, stumbling into the door with a thud.

"I kind of like Navy. And I was supposed to be in her place. So you're going to answer a couple questions for me."

Roy's hand was poised on the doorknob, but he would have to step closer to Erin to open the door. "You w—wouldn't hurt me. Not here."

"You're thinking too small," she said. "A promising young agent such as yourself, I could really move your career forward. There are plenty of armpit assignments that would be perfect for you."

"Armpit assignments?"

Now he was exactly where she wanted him. "There's a horse farm in Israel favored by some top generals. The agency needs someone to clear stalls there for six months or so. Or, if that doesn't suit you, there's an operation hiking through jungles in Africa with some unbalanced militants. You'd need to get your yellow fever shots, of course. And malaria pills."

Roy slumped against the door.

"If it helps, just think of my questions as orders." She paused to let him squirm a bit. "Tell me who ordered Navy's execution."

"William, sort of."

"What do you mean, sort of?"

"I heard someone in the background. Forcing him."

"Name," she said.

"I don't kn—"

"I hope you're a better liar in the field."

"Andrew," Roy said. "I only heard the first name."

She patted his cheek. "See how easy that was? Just one more question. William was supposed to be managing this operation. William's orders were to tell the kidnappers about a group of two men and one woman. But the messages you sent to the kidnappers identified the targets as two women and one man. Tell me whose orders you were following."

Roy shied away from her, as if he thought wishing hard enough would let him walk through walls.

"You're more scared of them than you are of William. Interesting."

"Please don't make me tell you." The poor boy really was upset.

"How about I guess and you just let me know if I'm right. His first name starts with *K* and rhymes with *pile*. And his biggest rival is William Grand."

Roy nodded. Kyle Pierson had sabotaged her operation, hoping it would fail. Probably to embarass William. But that didn't explain who Andrew was. There was no one by that name on the support team, either in Amsterdam or DC. She handed Roy his suitcase. "Have a nice vacation. I'll tell Navy you said hi."

CHAPTER 18

DAY FIVE OF the fake vacation, and Byron was already sick of museums. He scanned the displays behind the glass. Hemp clothes. Hemp medicine. Hemp building materials. According to the marijuana museum, hemp was the solution to world peace. Ah, for the optimism of youth. He wandered into the next room, where a collection of marijuana plants grew behind a glass wall.

"This must be weird for you," Navy said, appearing beside him.

"Weird?"

"I mean, aren't you usually arresting people for this?"

"Wrong three-letter agency," Byron said. "Half the time these days we're choosing whose poppy plants to leave alone." He cleared his throat. "That's off the record."

Navy smiled. "Of course."

Byron should be more guarded around Navy. She had earned his respect through her escape, but she already knew more than was safe for her to know. He glanced around them, and located Sara and Moss in the corner by another display, out of earshot. "How are you?"

The question seemed to surprise her. "Fine. Good, I guess."

He hadn't meant to pry. "Forget I asked. My wife always tells me I don't know when to shut up."

"The truth is, I don't know." She shoved her hands in the pockets of her coat. "I should know, but I don't."

Byron shook his head. "Forget about should. We should be giving you a commendation, but instead we're playing these games. I hate this business sometimes." He had surprised her again.

"A commendation for what?"

"When we didn't find you before the deadline, I was sure we'd be collecting bodies. You pulled off a fucking miracle."

"I don't feel like a saint." She looked ahead, through the glass wall, where a man was giving out samples to customers of the neighboring marijuana shop. "I feel like I shouldn't be here. Look at them. Their biggest worry is what they're going to eat for lunch."

Byron wished Jackson had come on this outing instead of him. Jackson would know what to say.

"I worry that I'll never sleep without a nightmare again. That I can't go back to being a normal person worrying about normal things because I'm not like them anymore."

"I've had to do . . . things I wasn't proud of." The memories of his years in the field were littered with encounters he'd rather forget. "You just have to remind yourself what you would have lost. Who you were protecting."

"That sounds like something Jackson would say."

Byron smiled. "Jackson did say it."

At the mention of Jackson's name, Navy's posture relaxed. "He's helping."

Inwardly, Byron sighed. He had suspected romantic feelings were developing between Navy and Jackson. Their therapy sessions had gotten longer each night. Jackson should know better than to get attached. Byron should too.

CHAPTER 19

THE SCENT OF fresh flowers struggled to cover the musk of dead fish at the neighboring market stand. Jackson dodged a camera shot from a tourist admiring the daily catch. Hard to avoid being photographed these days, but Jackson tried.

The market had just opened, better for Navy, he thought. She seemed hesitant in crowds. In front of Jackson, Byron led Navy and her friends along the wide center aisle between the stands. Jackson kept behind them. He hadn't decided how to break the bad news to Navy. William had called for a meeting tomorrow with Jackson and Navy. Not that Jackson wanted to leave Navy alone with William for even a minute, but the choice of company was odd. Like William wanted to see how Jackson reacted to Navy being questioned as much as William wanted to hear her answers.

His phone buzzed in his pocket. It was Kevin, his handler. Dodging the call would only make Kevin cranky.

"Isn't it three a.m. where you are?" Jackson asked.

"Not even a hello? And here I was, having trouble sleeping without you." Kevin's voice was rough, but it often sounded that way. Caffeine was his solution to sleep. "Seriously, I need you back here. Not visiting cheesy tourist attractions in Amsterdam. I can't delay your next operation much longer."

The market wasn't Jackson's idea of a good time either—that was Sara's choice. But he had suggested adding Oude Kerk to their itinerary for the day. When Jackson needed peace, that's where he went. He wanted to share that with Navy. "Just a couple more days. We're almost done cleaning up here."

"You should have left after you found them." Jackson's handler wasn't known for his kinder and gentler side. "Erin stepped in something with this operation."

The aroma of sweet almonds and butter replaced the scent of fish. Bankets, the traditional Dutch pastry made with almond paste. "Those questions I had, did you get a chance to ask around?" Jackson wanted to know who had been giving Roy orders from Langley. It wasn't William, even though William thought it was.

"Best to leave it alone."

For something less important, Jackson wouldn't have challenged that tone of voice. But he wanted to be sure Navy and her friends would be safe when they returned home. "You mean you know, and you won't tell me."

Kevin sighed. "I called in several favors. I couldn't find out anything. Like I said, Erin stepped in something with this one. Try to be nice to William, and get out of there while you still have a job."

Jackson wasn't surprised by Kevin's lack of compassion. Kevin's warnings, however, were unexpected. Not much rattled him.

Navy and Sara were examining a rack of designer silk blouses. Sara held up one to show the right sleeve was six inches shorter than the left. The two laughed. He could count on one hand the times he'd seen Navy laugh.

"I told you, it's like a flea market," Jackson heard Sara say.

"Jackson?" Kevin barked in his ear. "Still there?"

"Yeah, I'm here."

"There's a lot of talk around here about Amsterdam. William's likely to lose his next promotion for fucking this up. He's not above sacrificing you to buy his way back into good graces. He's already spreading rumors about you and the blonde."

"You mean Navy."

"Whatever her name is, he says you've been spending too much time with her. He thinks you and Byron and Erin are covering for her."

That would explain why William wanted Jackson and Navy together tomorrow. "I'm trying to protect the operation and make sure she adjusts to going home. They're counseling sessions."

"Is that what the kids are calling it these days?"

He set the bankets back on the vendor's table. "We just talk." After their conversations, it was hard to remember exactly how the hours had passed. All he knew is that being with her felt like sitting on the dock at his parent's cabin in the calm twilight, when the comforting weight of Lake Superior was the same deep blue as the sky. "It doesn't matter. Once she goes home, I'll never see her again."

"I'm glad you understand that."

Jackson felt the edges of his phone digging into the palm of his hand. "Are we done here?"

"Yeah, we're done."

When he caught up to the group, Moss was trying on a fitted Armani leather jacket with crooked seams. He put his hands in the pockets, turned to see his profile in the mirror, left and right.

Navy stifled a laugh. "You look like a leather pencil."

"I do not." Moss strutted away from the mirror, then back. "I think it suits me."

"Sorry, sweetie, she's right." On her tiptoes, Sara pulled the jacket off his shoulders, handed him another one. "Try this."

Byron nudged Jackson, pulled them just out of earshot. "Who called? Everything okay?"

"Yeah, it was just Kevin being Kevin. Everything's fine." Everything would be fine. Jackson would make sure of it.

❧

A flock of black birds rose behind the imposing Gothic church like a column of smoke against the gray sky, swirling up and away until each pair of wings became a pinprick on the horizon. Tourists milled around in the cobblestone rectangle between Oude Kerk and the frozen canal. Navy reminded herself she was a tourist too. A tourist who traveled with escorts who never appeared in the photos. Beneath the sounds of rushing cars and honking horns, Navy could hear organ music bleeding through the church doors. Sara held a guidebook open with one gloved hand while they walked.

"Oude Kerk was originally a wooden church in the thirteenth century, but it was replaced in the fourteenth century with a single-aisled Gothic church. Eventually the church became a basilica. It is the oldest church in Amsterdam."

"I s'pose they couldn't have known how much the neighborhood would change." Moss pointed toward a rectangular brass paving stone in the sidewalk. It pictured a woman's bare torso with a hand cupping one of her breasts.

Sara smiled, flipped the page and continued reading. "It says here that sailors used the octagonal bell tower to get their bearings."

Navy turned up the collar of her new wool coat and tried to bury her neck in its warmth. The long, black coat swallowed her form. Men's eyes skipped right over her, exactly as she intended. Today was the first day she and Sara had left the base without heavy makeup. The bruises had finally faded. With pain medication, Moss could breathe without wincing. Two weeks after the day an electric cart had pulled up to them in Schiphol, there was no outward trace left of their ordeal.

The days had a blissful regularity. Each morning Jackson or Byron took them to a tourist attraction in the city. Like Dam Square. Or the Van Gogh Museum. The paintings from this morning had slipped through her mind as easily as a breath; she couldn't tell one from another.

By noon they were always back on the base. While Sara and Moss rested, Navy trained with Erin. Navy's body felt different now, always hungry for a fight. She could make the bag swing a full inch. But she still tensed before every move—Erin said it made her slower. After resting, Sara and Moss would each have a session with Jackson. By the time Navy had showered, it was time for her session with Jackson.

Her sessions lasted hours, sometimes through dinner. She had seen parts of the case file now. She could look through the pictures of men she had killed—even the autopsy photos—without flinching. She and Jackson had talked through the experience over and over again, until she thought there was nothing new to say. But often she remembered new details. The face of the man she had seen once in passing in the guardroom. The exact sequence of turns on the route to the mansion. The logo on the vest the cart driver wore. Words and phrases from the papers on the leader's desk—the ones in English anyway.

It was therapy, too. They talked about the difficulties of returning to her apartment, her job, her life. How to cope with the anger that flared as unpredictably and suddenly as thunderclouds on a sunny afternoon. In just two days, Navy would be home. Her apartment shimmered like a mirage when she imagined putting the key in the door. Her old life was waiting for her. The life without terrorists and guns and secrets. And without Jackson.

"Space cadet." A hand waved in front of Navy's face. "Back to earth." Sara pulled Navy toward the front of the church and handed the camera to Jackson. "Picture."

Navy stood next to Sara and Moss in front of the variegated stone column and pasted a smile on her face. The pretending wasn't so hard. The truth was, Navy wasn't unhappy or happy. Their purgatory in Amsterdam was the only thing that felt solid and real. She felt out of place in her body—as if fear had driven Navy out of her own form and rearranged the molecules before she had stepped back inside herself. Navy felt out of place in her life, too. A new phone had been delivered to her room this morning. She had started to dial her parents' number but never finished. The words were easy enough. *You didn't need to worry about Africa after all—we had a change of plans.* Dad would pick up the other line. *I went to a marijuana museum. We visited the Begijnhof garden.* Navy could share all sorts of innocuous, true stories. Cover stories. But she couldn't make herself dial.

Navy had left the phone in her room. The phone would stay in the box, she decided, until she left Amsterdam.

Jackson handed the camera back to Sara and held the wooden door open for everyone.

Sara and Moss strolled to an alcove on the other side of the church. Byron, feeling around in his coat pocket, held back. "Phone call," he said. "I'll wait out here."

"This is one of my favorite places," Jackson said.

"You're allowed confession?" Navy found it easy to relax around Jackson. She had no secrets from him. She sat down in the kaleidoscope of a stained glass window and turned her face toward the sun trapped by colored glass. The rays warmed her coat and she hugged it around her to drive away what was left of the chill from outside.

Jackson sat next to her. His knee brushed her leg. She didn't shy away from the touch or move toward it.

"I come here to see how the light changes. See that pattern on the floor?" He pointed at the shimmering, distorted rainbow of colors on the uneven stone. "It's a cloud passing by the window. You'd never guess a gray cloud could make something like that."

Navy pulled off her gloves. "I think I might have been religious in a different century. It's easy to believe in God in a place like this."

Jackson glanced at Sara and Moss, who were making their way slowly toward them, stopping at every nook along the way, then turned back to Navy. "William wants to meet with you and me tomorrow."

"Sounds like fun."

"I held him off as long as I could."

Navy was surprised by the guilty expression on Jackson's face. "I didn't mean—you've done so much for us already." The hard wood of the chair pressed against her back. Her apology didn't appear to relieve him. "What should I do?"

"There are a few details he shouldn't know. Details that would make life . . . difficult . . . for you."

"Difficult how?" she asked. So far, all she had managed to figure out was that someone had mistaken her for Erin.

"Except for those details, you need to tell the truth as much as you can." Jackson hadn't answered her question.

"It's easier to lie that way," Navy said, repeating something Erin had told her. "What parts do I leave out?"

"Anything about Jackie."

"So I never heard the name. What about being related to the senator?" she asked.

He shook his head.

"But it'll be on the memory card from the camcorder."

"The card never made it into evidence," Jackson said. "It's been destroyed."

"Oh. What about Moss and Sara? I told them to call me Jackie."

"It's taken care of."

"What did you do?" The sudden volume in her voice attracted the attention of a man admiring a statue.

Jackson was silent until the admirer moved away. "I used the power of suggestion."

"You can change memories that way?"

He looked uncomfortable. "There was a case once of a girl who had memories 'recovered' by her therapist. The girl claimed her father had conducted elaborate satanic rituals in an abandoned barn and sexually abused her. None of it was true. The barn was torn down before she was born. But before the police figured that out they brought the father in. Interrogated him for days. And he confessed to everything."

"But you said it wasn't true."

"A well-meaning therapist was searching for explanations of the girl's trauma. A couple well-meaning detectives repeated a story enough times their suspect believed them. That's how the power of suggestion works."

"Simple as that? There was no hypnosis involved?"

"No hypnosis. It's an extreme, rare case. But yes. Human memory is more fragile than people think. In your friends' case, all I had to do was convince them they heard one word wrong."

She counted up all the hours they had spent together since the escape from the mansion. "So what have you done to me?"

A hurt expression flashed across his face. "Nothing."

She believed him. "And why not? Why not just make me forget everything? Repeat a new story until I believed it?"

Jackson shifted in his chair, the rickety wooden legs scraping against the stone floor. "It would be more complicated with you."

"But if you could have?" She realized that she wanted to erase her memory of the whole thing. She was angry because she didn't have the option.

"Erasing all traces of an event and replacing it with a new one is science fiction."

"You didn't answer my question." She squirmed under his direct gaze.

"Yes, I would have." There were no traces of apology in Jackson's tone.

The admission was strangely comforting. "To protect me," she whispered, more to herself than to him.

"Erasing a memory . . . it's not something I often wish for." Jackson's hand hovered over his leg, as if he might reach toward her.

Sara and Moss had started walking in Navy and Jackson's direction.

"So this thing I don't know, it's a very dangerous thing," Navy said. Dangerous as in deadly, he was trying to tell her.

He nodded.

"Okay." She slumped in her chair and stared straight ahead. A wide, white cloth was draped over the wooden altar at the front of the church. Embroidered in gold thread on either end of the cloth was a dove with an olive branch in its mouth. Candles with misshapen, burnt ends stood on top of the altar, the silver candelabra shining in the light of the stained glass windows.

"Do you still trust me?" he asked.

With my life. The answer came so easily it startled her. "Yes."

There was more to say, but Moss had arrived with Sara in tow.

"I can't memorize any more facts about Gothic churches. Say we have to leave now," Moss said to Jackson.

"I'll quiz you over lunch," Sara promised, kissing Moss on the cheek.

Even the overcast morning seemed too bright and busy after

the solemn church. Byron was just putting his phone back in his pocket, and he didn't look happy. Navy followed Sara to a small, nearly empty café, with green and white awnings. The lunch crowd wouldn't descend for another half hour or so. The menu was in Dutch, but there were enough words Navy could decipher.

Sara prattled on endlessly about Oude Kerk until even Navy was tempted to roll her eyes. When the guidebook came out again, Moss muttered something about the art on the wall being fascinating, then got up to examine it. Jackson and Byron made their escape too, to a different corner. They bent close and talked quietly, too low for Navy to hear. She wondered if it was about her.

"Finally." Sara huffed, then took a long drink of water. "I thought they'd never go away."

"You were doing that on purpose? Thank God. I nearly left too."

A mischievous smile took over Sara's face. "So he's cute, right?"

"Who's cute?" It was never good to give in too easily when Sara was trying to play matchmaker. Sara's elbow dug into Navy's side.

"Jackson. The one who's been giving you 'therapy' dinner dates."

Navy hadn't decided how she felt about Jackson. She couldn't deny that she would miss him. But she also knew any attraction to him was a dead end. William was already worried that Jackson had been lying about what Navy knew. Imagine what William would think if she and Jackson were involved. "After everything we've been through in the past three weeks, you're thinking about my love life?"

"Your lack thereof, actually."

"So there hasn't been anyone in a while. Work's been busy." Work was an easy crutch for Navy. Technical problems always had easier solutions than her personal ones.

Sara touched her arm gently. "It's not just that. There hasn't been anyone serious since . . . well, you know." Since Theo, the man who broke Navy's cheekbone, Sara meant. "And I think you and Jackson would be good together. You can just say you met online or something." All Sara and Moss knew was that the CIA had shown up to rescue them. Sara had no idea what games Navy would have to play with William tomorrow.

Navy forced a smile. "I just don't think it would work between us." The words hurt to say, even if she didn't mean them. "That's all."

<h1 style="text-align:center">CHAPTER 20</h1>

JACKSON WATCHED NAVY twist her hands into knots on the kitchen table while they waited for William. Byron and Erin waited with them. William had demanded that Jackson and Navy be in the kitchen at noon sharp. It was noon and they were still listening to him bang objects around in his quarters.

Last night, Jackson had practiced Navy's story with her for as long as he dared. Too much practice and she wouldn't seem genuine. Too little and William wouldn't be fooled.

Two weeks couldn't turn Navy into an agent—even if she could swing a pretty good right hook now.

William walked into the kitchen at three minutes after noon, just late enough to demonstrate his importance. He was wearing his jacket and gloves over his suit.

"Change of venue," he announced. "This interview will be at the mansion."

Navy looked at Jackson, more confused than scared. Having the interview at the mansion was a way to throw her off balance. There was nothing Jackson could do—William wouldn't tolerate being challenged in front of Navy. Jackson kept his expression blank, as if he hadn't noticed. The effort scraped at his chest. But Navy must have understood. A grim sort of determination set in her face before she furrowed her brow and softened the line of her jaw, just enough to convince William she was anxious. Erin had been coaching her in skills other than fighting.

"If you think it would help," Navy said.

"Erin," Jackson said, "could you take Navy to the garage and pull a car around for us?"

"Why don't you?" she asked, not looking away from William. Erin looked like she was about to jump over the table and strangle William.

To his credit, William didn't flinch. He was enjoying his power. Probably the first time he felt like he was in control.

"I want to talk over some details with William before we go."

"Fine," Erin snapped.

When Jackson could no longer hear their footsteps he dropped his mask.

"What the the hell do you think you're doing?"

"Lost that famous Jackson cool, Mr. Fletcher?"

"She's not ready for this," Jackson said.

"Good."

"We've been giving you reports every single day. Just like you asked," Byron said. "Is there something missing from them?"

"I don't trust you," William said. "Or you." He pointed a stubby finger at Jackson. "Or that third musketeer of yours. You three might be able to lie to me. But Navy can't. I have to be sure Navy doesn't know the name Jackie Pierce."

She had managed to lie well enough to her kidnappers, Jackson thought. She had managed to hide her enmity toward William after that first confrontation. But allowing William to underestimate Navy was her best chance right now. "This is a cruel thing you're doing. You know that, right?"

"I need to know if she's a liability."

Jackson hadn't lied yesterday. To save her from this interrogation, he would have erased Navy's memory if he could. Even if it made her recovery longer. Even if it meant she wouldn't remember anything about him. Jackson studied William again, looking for any signs of hesitation. There were none. Jackson was being forced to watch Navy suffer. He stood up and walked toward the garage. William stepped into his path.

"I'm ordering you not to coach her," William said.

As if I would ever follow an order from you. "Noted," Jackson said.

"Jackson." Byron's hand closed around Jackson's elbow, trying to pull him to the side.

Jackson uncurled his fists and stepped around William, out of Byron's grip, and walked toward the garage.

Navy was in the front passenger seat of a plain sedan, engine running. Erin was just getting out of the driver's seat.

"You'll drive," William said to Jackson.

Like his fucking chauffeur. Jackson climbed behind the wheel and readjusted the seat to his height.

"Whenever you're ready," William said from the backseat.

Jackson had the car in third before they left the garage.

A chill wind ferried wisps of clouds across the bright, clear sky. William watched Jackson and Navy carefully from the backseat. Navy was looking out her window. Her eyes were distant, like the night Jackson had found her.

Jackson turned the car off the highway and onto the gravel road that led to the estate. Navy's shoulders tensed and she hunched over, drawing her calves to the edge of the seat, as if she wanted to hug her knees to her chest. William, openly studying her, leaned forward. When William's phone buzzed and he was distracted, she caught Jackson's eyes and gave him a small smile, so short it could have been a flash of sun. It was gone by the time William looked back at her.

Jackson wondered how much time Erin had spent on Navy's acting skills. There was a delicate balance between letting enough emotion show and getting lost in the process.

When they reached the driveway, Navy's eyes widened. Her hands clenched the edge of the seat and her knuckles turned white. She started to rock, ever so slightly. William seemed almost happy at the visible evidence of her discomfort.

Jackson wanted to drive as fast and as far as he could from the set of Navy's nightmare. Instead, he shifted the car into park. "Navy?"

Navy stilled herself, almost under control again. She was staring at the mansion as if it would creep closer when she looked away.

William got out of the car and opened Navy's door.

Navy unfolded herself and stepped out. "Where do you want me to start?" she asked William in an unsteady voice.

"Did they talk about anything while they were in the van?"

This would be lie number one: not telling William that she had overheard them say she was related to the senator. "One of them was worried the halothane would wear off before we reached the house."

"And that's it?" William's eyes narrowed, studying Navy carefully. "You're sure?"

Navy widened her eyes just a little. If not for the hours they had spent together, Jackson would have been fooled too. "Yes. That's all I heard."

"How did they get you in the house?"

"All I remember is being carried up the stairs."

William's eyes narrowed to slits. "You don't know how you got in the house, but you remember going up the stairs?"

Jackson saw a dimple form in her right cheek, the cheek William couldn't see. When she looked back at William, her features were soft and her eyes had teared up. She had bitten the inside of her cheek to make her eyes tear. Another trick from Erin. "I was really tired and hadn't eaten. That, plus the halothane . . ." She shrugged to punctuate the sentence.

"Okay, let's go in."

William kept close to Navy as she walked toward the entrance. Jackson kept his distance. He couldn't appear protective. Jackson had an act to put on too. Navy traced the sharp lines of the glass front doors with her eyes. A flicker of a smile crossed William's face as he watched her reaction. Jackson took a deep breath through clenched teeth, imagining the line his fist would travel to connect with William's jaw. He reminded himself that attacking William wouldn't help Navy and stepped behind her instead. Just in case.

William pulled a key out of his pocket and opened the door, then stepped back and motioned for Navy to enter. Jackson tried to imagine what Navy must see as she stared at the grand sweeping staircase. Were the voices of her captors here? She hadn't moved.

William opened his mouth to speak; Navy's head jerked to face William. Whatever Navy's eyes said took him aback. Careful now, Jackson thought. Anger will give you away. She stepped across the entrance, her limbs moving as if she were walking through water. Once her feet rested on the marble, she stared down at her tennis shoes against the speckled white and black pattern. When she started to move again, her hand went to her stomach. A trick her mother had taught her, she had said. To help with her nerves. The fingers of her left hand trailed up the shining banister. It had been cleaned off after they dusted for prints.

Her eyes wandered from the ornate molding to the patterned wallpaper. William's steps were awkward and noisy compared to her trancelike walk up the stairs. Jackson, again, followed. Navy stopped on the first floor landing.

"I never saw anyone on this floor," she told William.

"You said you didn't see this floor when they carried you in."

"I saw it later, when the cart driver took me to see Sara and Moss."

"Let's keep things in order," he said crisply.

They climbed another flight of stairs to the second floor. Navy's lips were moving, almost imperceptibly. Counting, Jackson realized. She was counting the stairs to keep calm.

They turned a corner. Navy continued, walking and counting, until she reached a door, ten paces from the end of the hallway. "This was my room, where they kept me." She seemed to be addressing the door, the hallway, the carpet, but not William. She put her hand on the doorknob, jumping a little as if the metal had shocked her. The other hand she pressed flat against the door, pushing the door open.

Jackson had been surprised during his examination of the scene at how good Navy's description was. Most witnesses missed the small details or mixed them up badly. Her description had been accurate. A bed, two dressers, and an armoire. The rosettes on the wallpaper. The wall plate lying on the carpet by the side of the bed.

"Was there a guard outside the door? Did you hear conversations in the hallway?" William asked.

"I only heard them when they came to get me or brought me food."

"And you really didn't hear any conversations in the hallway?" William was giving himself away.

"No. I only ever saw two people up here, and I never heard them talking close to the door."

"Let's go to the office." As subtle as a bulldozer, Jackson thought.

Navy kept moving down the hall until she reached an open door. The lights were on. The papers on the desk had been scattered and rearranged since Jackson had seen them. He peeked over the edge of the desk and saw, as expected, the drawers hadn't been completely shut. The filing cabinet in the corner had scratches near the locks where someone who couldn't pick a lock had jimmied it open. The prayer mat that had been standing up in the corner was lying on the floor, partially unrolled. Someone had searched this room for Navy's secrets.

"Tell me what happened in here," William said.

Jackson saw Navy's eyes cataloging the same details. Her narrowed eyes told Jackson Navy had come to the same conclusion. "It wasn't this messy before," Navy said.

"Forensic techs probably rearranged everything." Yeah, or this is where you snuck off to this morning, Jackson thought.

"They showed me this piece of paper and told me I had to read it for them," Navy said. "In a video. They had a camcorder." Lie number two: William shouldn't know that the ransom recording mentioned Jackie Pierce or the senator.

"Did you read it?"

"Not right away. I told them I would cooperate if I could see my friends. So they took me downstairs." Navy turned toward the door. "Do you want to go downstairs?"

"I don't care about that. Tell me what happened after they brought you back up here."

"I read the piece of paper. They filmed it." She was remarkably calm. Her nerves had hardened into a steely resolve.

"What did the paper say?"

"That if the CIA didn't deliver the names of all the agents in Yemen in thirty-six hours, we would be killed." Lie number three. Well done. She had even remembered to substitute *we* for *I*, as if she didn't know she was singled out.

"That's it?"

"That's the last time I was in this room."

"Did you see what they did with the memory card?" William had been ransacking the office looking for the card Jackson had destroyed. William wanted to see the recording to verify the story.

"No, they took me back to my room after that."

"How about the piece of paper you read? Did you see what happened to that?"

"No."

William studied her and she held his eyes. Her micro-expressions were betraying her but William couldn't read them. She was trying to act scared but not too scared. Like a cooperative victim. But she was more angry than scared. It flashed in the tension of her eye muscles and the set of her lips. William nodded, satisfied.

Jackson was grateful for William's ignorance.

"Thank you for your help, Ms. Trent."

"Glad to."

The visit was not what Jackson would have prescribed for Navy. After a few more weeks, or months, maybe. But she had handled it well. She hadn't lost her temper with William. She hadn't broken down. She would be able to handle returning to her life. And eventually her life would seem almost normal again. Jackson tried to imagine her at the bar with friends or out to dinner on a Friday night. One pint of beer was her limit, she had said. A nice, dark beer that you could barely see through. Best had with a good, thick burger, and fries with the skin still on. After enough Friday nights Jackson would be a footnote to her life. It was the best he could hope for, the way things were supposed to be, but the thought made him uneasy.

CHAPTER 21

NAVY PUT HER bags in the narrow hallway outside the room she had shared with Erin for the past two weeks. Sara and Moss were waiting for Navy in the garage. In less than an hour she'd be at Schiphol again, another tourist heading home.

The imprint of her body was still on the thin mattress of her cot. She made the bed neatly and plumped the pillow. Erin returned, as promised, and sat with her while they waited for Byron and Jackson. Navy didn't know how she had survived yesterday's visit to the mansion. Sure, there were tricks Erin had taught her. How to bite your cheek to get your eyes to tear. How to make a lie more convincing by matching it to the emotion you were already feeling. She would need all those tricks again.

Byron arrived first, dressed as a cab driver. He would be driving Navy, Sara and Moss to the airport. "Why'd you ask us to come to your room? Something wrong?" he asked Erin.

"Better to wait for Jackson," Erin said.

Navy picked at the rough fabric of her blanket. She felt like a marathon runner who had mistaken the last mile marker for the finish line.

"You, uh, call your parents?" Byron asked Navy. "Might be nice to see them when you get home."

"I can't quite face them yet," Navy said. "I haven't even turned the new phone on. It's packed away."

Byron was about to say something more, but Jackson's arrival cut him off.

Erin's cot creaked when she pushed herself up to close the door.

"Listen for William?" Navy asked.

Erin leaned against the door, one ear cocked toward the hallway. Byron and Jackson exchanged a glance, then turned toward Erin.

"Erin?" Byron lifted his newsboy cap and scratched at his forehead.

"Someone searched through our room last night while we were at dinner," Erin said.

"Did you—"

Erin cut Byron off. "Yes, I checked for bugs."

"You think it was William," Byron said

Navy sighed. "I thought I had him fooled, but I guess he still suspects one of us is hiding something."

Jackson shook his head, looking frustrated and tired. "I could have read him wrong."

"I read him the same way," Erin said. "I think he's just following orders. The people above him haven't been convinced by his reports."

"He needs something more. And it has to come from me," Navy said. "William has to be sure I don't know the name Jackie Pierce. And he has to believe that I hate all of you as much as I hate him, so he doesn't think any of you are lying about what I know."

No one disagreed with Navy's statement.

Jackson was wearing the look he had when he was thinking. He was trying to find another way out, but he knew as well as she did there wasn't one.

"Just don't be surprised when my head starts to do a three

sixty. And it's important to me that you know— " Navy swallowed hard and dug her fingernails into her palm. The three people with her had iron control over their emotions and she was going to lose it. "It's important that you know, whatever I say later, I'm grateful for everything you've done." There, she had managed. And she wasn't crying; she had only teared up slightly.

Byron tipped his cap at her and left. Erin pointed toward the kitchen, where William's loud footsteps echoed. She looked from Jackson to Navy, then followed Byron. Erin left the door open. Navy and Jackson were alone for a precious few seconds.

"What happens to you if William figures out you destroyed the ransom tape?" Navy asked. "Or if he figures out you lied about what I know?"

"That's my problem, not yours." Jackson pressed a white business card into her hand. There was no name on it. Just a printed number with a long extension. "If you need me."

"Is this to protect me or the operation?"

"Both."

She was glad for the evasive answer. The question was too large to contemplate right now. "If I call, will it be dangerous for you?"

He shook his head, but she could tell he was lying. She wondered what other risks he had taken for her. But now was not the time. She needed to focus on her next performance. William turned the corner from the kitchen and could see them through the open door. She thought of the anger that had carried her through yesterday. She thought of the bile she had forced down when her stomach turned at the first stab of her knife. She had no choice then; she had no choice now. She would do what she had to do.

She walked into the hallway and Jackson followed. She looked at Jackson as if he were the hateful leader of her captors and stormed past him. The effort hurt. She pressed at the card in her pocket to remind herself of what was real. Part of her was triumphant when she saw William noting the fake argument. But she had to stay in character. She grabbed her backpack and swung it with too much force onto her shoulder. It landed heavily and she winced, glad she wasn't facing William. She picked up the other bag and carried it by her side—the same way she had carried her bags leaving her apartment for her dream adventure to Africa.

In the garage, Moss and Sara were standing next to a yellow taxi. The perfect cover for dropping people off at the airport. Erin loaded Moss' luggage in the trunk and gave Navy a slight nod. Navy's turn now. Navy couldn't even take a deep breath—that's what someone preparing to play a scene would do.

Navy pushed her bag into Erin's hands, just hard enough to make Erin stumble back. Was Erin impressed with her acting? Navy couldn't tell. Erin had a part to play too. Byron opened the back door for Moss and Sara, who climbed into the cab with confused expressions. The last time Sara and Moss had seen Navy with any of the agents was at breakfast yesterday, and everyone had been friendly.

Byron held a hand out to Navy, and she shook it curtly, throwing it away as quickly as she could. William followed suit, holding out his hand for Navy to shake. Byron had set the scene for her. Of course.

Navy refused William's hand and turned to get in the cab.

"Oh, come now. We can part as friends, can't we?"

William couldn't have given her a better opening. "Friends? Really?" Just when she thought she had reached the end of her anger she found more. "You show up in some sort of late, half-assed rescue attempt and then tell me I have to stay here and *help* you."

"We didn't force you to stay." William's face was red. Good, she had surprised him.

"You told me to cooperate or else. Same thing the kidnappers told me. What were you hoping to learn yesterday at the mansion anyway? I had told you everything I know." She looked at each agent in turn, almost stumbling when she met Jackson's eyes. This was the last time she would see him. "And in return you forced me to go back to that place. For what, exactly? So that I could confess I conspired with terrorists to get us kidnapped?"

William was trying to look angry, but she could see he was hiding a smile. Let him think he had broken her. Let him think he had won. "So what now, Ms. Trent?"

"I don't want to hear from any of you ever again. As far as I'm concerned, this whole thing has been one very bad dream." Her control was slipping. Tears stung her eyes.

"That would be best," William said.

Smug bastard, Navy thought. "Let's go," she said to Byron. "Unless you'd like to interrogate me again." She got into the cab and slammed the door so hard the sound rang in her ears.

Sara hugged Navy protectively and glared at the group outside the car. Don't look at any of them, Navy told herself. Especially not Jackson. But she did, in the rearview mirror, as Byron started the car. Jackson's green eyes, normally calm, were stormy and fractured. Was he acting hurt or had she actually hurt him? Did it matter? She swallowed the bitterness of her false ingratitude and pushed Sara away.

"I'm fine," Navy managed. "I promise."

Sara looked doubtful, but allowed Navy her space.

When they reached the airport, Sara gave Byron a handful of small bills to complete the taxi driver cover. Languages from around the globe met Navy's ears when she stepped out the door. Suitcases slapped on the ground. Hard plastic wheels bumped over cracks in the sidewalk. Children whined and were hushed by their parents. The lights in the terminal were too bright for the early morning. Sara and Moss emptied the trunk, then started with their bags toward the sliding doors.

Navy put a hand on each of her bags, but couldn't find the strength to lift them. She watched Byron drive away, the now-familiar face reduced to a set of eyes in the rearview mirror. He gave her a nod. It was the most he could do without attracting attention. Did it mean she had done well? What did she want from him? A friendly pat on the back? A wink and a nod? Forgiveness?

Yes, forgiveness. Byron would understand the charade in the garage. But who could forgive her for real sins? She hadn't killed for revenge, but she wanted to. Would she have gone room to room in the mansion with the machine gun if there had been more people to kill? Would she have twisted the knife in the guard's belly if there had been time? If she were smarter she could have found a way to get out that was less violent. If she were stronger she would have overpowered their captors at the airport. If, if, if. It was all in the past. She had no choice then; she had no choice now. She would do what she had to do. She pressed the white rectangle in her pocket again and picked up her bags.

CHAPTER 22

BYRON SIGNED HIS name on the final report for Operation Critical Mass and closed the folder with relief. In the week since Byron had been back from Amsterdam, he'd spent most of the time carefully organizing the final report to remove any questions about what Navy knew. William would have to approve the report. Then the file would be archived and Byron could call the whole mess done. Navy's trauma would haunt him for a while longer, and then it would fade. Like all ghosts. Byron had seen friends—good friends—go down in history as terrorists because they died while they were undercover. He had attended barbecues with the families of soldiers whose bodies would never come home. He had listened to countless retellings of fake stories to cover lifelong injuries: car accidents to explain spines cut by bullets, grease fires to explain burned arms. Navy's secrets weren't the most sensitive ones he kept.

When life in the field had become too much, Byron asked for a transfer from field work to desk work and told his wife it was an unexpected promotion. The long weeks away from home had started to gnaw at him. His daughter seemed like a new person every time he came home, going from infant to toddler during one trip, toddler to potty-trained in another. Jenna did her best to keep him present by showing photos of Byron to their daughter every night. But his heart couldn't take how she looked at him like a stranger every time he came home.

This was his life now, a drab office building, a long commute, a nice house in a quiet neighborhood with a good highschool for his daughter, now a senior. And he was grateful.

The phone on his desk rang. Byron glanced at his watch, heard his stomach growl for lunch. The extension was William's.

"Are you finished with your report?"

"Just this second."

"Come by my office for a minute, will you?"

As if it were a request. "Sure."

The file for Operation Critical Mass was open on William's desk. The sheet on top of the file looked like a warrant for a bug—with a recent date. Byron handed William the report. He signed it without reading it, then slipped it into the file.

"I have a new assignment for you."

"Related to the kidnapping?"

"Yes." William had seemed satisfied after Navy's performance. Her pretend hatred had relieved William's suspicions of Byron. Byron didn't know what he would have done if Navy's performance hadn't worked. Jackson and Erin were already on other assignments—he wouldn't be able to reach them for weeks. "We have a warrant to bug Navy's cell phone," William continued. "I need you to monitor the audio files uploaded from the bug."

Not just a tap from the cell phone company. A bug that would pick up any conversations within three feet. Had the bug picked up any of their conversations on base? Impossible. William wouldn't be this cavalier if he knew that Byron was hiding Navy's secrets. Unless no one had listened to the recordings yet.

"I really don't think she's anything to be concerned about," Byron said.

"Just a precaution." William held up his hands in mock defense, confident and relaxed. He had settled back into his element in Washington, acting as if everything in Amsterdam had gone so well because of his stellar leadership. "Not my call, really. It's not even a high priority. Just check it every week or two."

"What if the bug picked up any of our conversations on base?" Byron needed to know when the surveillance on Navy had started.

"The bug wasn't activated until she left Valkenburg. I insisted. It was installed the night before while she and Erin were out at dinner. On surprise orders from—" William stopped. "It was a last-minute request."

Byron felt sick. He tried to remember if he'd seen the outline a cell phone in her pocket when they talked just before the feigned altercation in the garage. No, it had been in the hallway. Because she hadn't been ready to face her parents yet. Byron and Jackson and Erin were probably safe—or as safe as they ever were. Byron was sure he wouldn't be the only one listening to the bug. Navy was a victim all over again.

Back at his desk and still hungry, Byron clicked on the icon that looked like a giant purple eye. IRIS, the interface for listening to bugs and wiretaps, had been designed when DOS was the primary operating system and hadn't been updated much since. Byron plugged in the authorization code William had given him. Each authorization code in IRIS was tied to an investigation and a clearance level. Files he wasn't cleared to see would be invisible to him.

Luckily, Navy's activities over the last few days made his assignment boring. She took a taxi home from the airport. Went grocery shopping. She went to work. Byron selected the last file.

The background noise was familiar to him: WAMU, the public radio station for the DC area. The foreground was two male voices. Navy's recordings were higher quality; the techs had had plenty of time to customize her phone. This mic wasn't as good, and the two men speaking weren't close to it. He had to strain to understand both of them, though one was closer than the other. Neither voice had been on any of the other recordings. This wasn't from Navy's bug. Occasionally, flaws in IRIS meant recordings meant for one investigation showed up in another. He would have to report the mistakenly filed recording. At least it meant he was done spying on Navy for the day.

"Give me an update on the Navy Trent situation," said the faraway voice.

Byron's finger paused over the stop button.

"She's being monitored, sir," said the closer voice. Someone's deputy. Someone Byron might have met in passing on his occasional trips to DC. But the recording was too faint to trigger any memories.

I have to find out who these men are. Voice recognition software wouldn't work on a recording with such low quality. Byron would have to rely on clues from their dialogue.

The far away voice got louder as the mic picked up soft footsteps. "By whom?"

"By the CIA, and one of our own.," said the deputy.

There was a knocking sound in the background. The deputy answered the door.

"Mr.—"

The recording cut off. Byron checked his headphones. Still connected. He looked at the screen. The recording had disappeared from the list.

CHAPTER 23

NAVY OPENED THE dashboard on the company's intrusion detection system. She was half-hoping to find a serious incident. A distraction might keep her from falling into the quicksand of her thoughts. A list in the corner showed her the most active external IP addresses in the firewall logs with a flag showing the country for each. Always a diverse list: Ukraine, Germany, Russia, China, Korea. Most of it was background noise. Any server on the internet was regularly scanned by attackers, most of whom were too much work to track down. Her job as a defender meant making the network as resilient as possible, then watching for inevitable failures.

One click took Navy to the firewall records for just the first IP address. They were all SSH connections; someone was trying to guess usernames and passwords. Probably. Budget constraints and general disorganization kept her from collecting all the information she could from the company's servers. If she had the logs from the targeted server, she could confirm that nothing had been compromised. Instead, Navy would have to guess based on the length of the connection. She typed in a command to calculate the mean and standard deviation of the connection times, to see how much variance there was.

Not the distraction she had hoped for, but it was something. She was trying to concentrate on just being Navy. Navy who sat at a desk in a cubicle looking for attackers on the network. Navy the information security engineer who had tried to go to Africa for a safari but ended up touring the marijuana museum in Amsterdam instead.

"I do not understand what you do." Amber had come up behind her. Amber was polished, as always, in a short, tight skirt and heels that cost half of one of Navy's paychecks. Apparently, winter weather didn't factor into Amber's wardrobe. Navy reminded herself that Amber was in a line of work where appearances mattered. She was responsible for the regular flow of venture capital that was carrying the company through the development of their next product—a high-end sneaker that promised to make running on the sidewalk as comfortable as bouncing on a trampoline.

"I'm looking at the variance in the SSH connection logs to determine if the . . ."

Amber's face went blank.

Navy was too tired to translate. "How's the new server working?"

"Reliable, so far. I hope you didn't waste any of your vacation thinking about it."

A rush of images came at Navy—a dusty canopy on a creaking bed frame, a broken mirror, the play of colors from a stained glass window on a stone floor. "No, we kept ourselves busy."

"Yeah, I heard. Bum deal about the tour getting cancelled at the last minute. I just wanted to thank you for getting the server up before you left. We only lost fifty percent of our sales. It could have been much worse"

"Glad things worked out."

"And accounting said it was your turn with this." Amber handed Navy a sheaf of papers.

"PCI compliance paperwork. Thanks, I think."

Amber turned and walked away, the pointy ends of her heels making small dents in the carpet with each step. At 4:59 Navy turned off her laptop, stowed the paperwork in a locked drawer, and picked up her backpack to go home.

"Happy hour?" Jarrod asked. The same Jarrod she'd left. Same cheerful, lopsided smile. Same long, smooth, brown hair tied back in a ponytail. Same scruffy beard that always seemed to resemble a five o'clock shadow. And yet he, like everything else, had seemed surreal since Navy got back.

"I'll pass."

"Oh, come on. You haven't been since you got back. It's Friday, most of the office is at Grumpy's already. If you don't show up soon, you'll lose your status as a regular."

"Next week," Navy promised.

"That's—"

"What I said last week, I know." She tried for a smile, but the corners of her mouth turned down instead of up. "But this time I mean it."

"You'll get your visit to Africa. Maybe they'll let you take unpaid vacation."

"Sure. Have fun at Grumpy's."

"Don't be a stranger."

Jarrod's concern made her want to hug him. Everyone had been very sweet since Navy had returned. She should find it encouraging that she was doing a reasonable impression of a person disappointed with missing out on a dream instead of the victim of a kidnapping.

Navy walked toward the elevators and the stairwell. Every day she had to make the choice between the stairs or the elevator. Enclosed places still made her nervous. But whether she preferred the brightly lit, claustrophobic square of the elevator to the dim stairwell where she could always run varied day by day. She forced herself to walk down one flight, then two. The parking lot was cold and damp with melted ice. Bits of gray ice and white chunks of salt crunched underneath her tennis shoes. Navy was holding her car keys too tight, looking around too much. No one was here to notice. On her drive home in the fading daylight, she felt conspicuous even though the other drivers ignored her.

Her phone rang just as she put the key in the front door of her apartment. It was Sara. The old Navy would have answered. Navy let the call go to voicemail and unlocked the door. The new high-security lock clicked open. Then, quickly, inside. She slid the deadbolt and chain in place. Her cell phone beeped to let her know she had a message.

Navy went from room to room, checking that the wooden sticks in her sliding windows were still in place, the windows still locked. The routine comforted her. Part of her wished she was at Valkenburg again. No windows—no way in to their section of the base except for the metal door. She'd liked the comforting weight of it, of knowing how much it could resist attack. Her apartment door was wooden and hollow at the core. A good axe could cut through in two or three blows. But that wasn't the point, was it? There was no man with an axe. Her kidnappers were dead or scattered. They didn't know who she was. William had been convinced—or at least she was pretty sure he had.

Failure was allowed in the small things, Navy had decided. Jackson had warned her what the first weeks home would feel like. But she hadn't expected how much effort pretending took. To accept Sara's comfort for how Jackson had betrayed Navy, when he had risked his reputation to protect her. To tell the story of her vacation to her parents, and leave out the most traumatic experience of Navy's life. To not jump in the grocery store when a cart bumped hers. To stand in a crowded line at the bank without pushing people away. Sometimes Navy piled up the couch cushions to give herself a target and practiced the boxing moves Erin had taught her.

She left the television off. She used to watch crime dramas but the violence was too real now. Every time she saw a dead body her hands smelled like blood and the healed, invisible cuts on her hands stung. Every time a gun fired she heard the shot as if it were in the room.

The rubber gasket of the freezer squeaked as she opened the door. The lasagna frozen dinner looked as unappealing as the meatloaf. Navy closed her eyes and grabbed the first thing her hand touched. While it was cooking, she paced the kitchen.

She didn't need to look at the card. Navy had the number memorized. She opened the freezer again and lifted up the automatic ice tray. Jackson's card was frosted and warped, but legible. The cold rectangle left a red mark on Navy's palms when she pressed it between her hands. The microwave dinged and she returned the card to its hiding place. Just who did she think was looking for it?

No one was watching her. She would eat dinner on the couch, like a normal person. She would fill the time until bed by watching television, like a normal person. If she acted normal long enough, one day she would be normal. She felt pressure on the back of her skull, the hair on her neck stood on end. More than usual. Her heart was beating fast. Navy went to the door. The deadbolt was still in place. The lock below it was still engaged. And below that, a white envelope on the carpet. One word was written in blue pen in unfamiliar handwriting on the outside of the envelope. Navy.

The plate fell out of her hands. Navy fumbled with the locks and opened the door, and looked both ways down the hallway. No one. She ran to the window overlooking the entrance to her building and the street next to it. No one. Not even a car leaving the garage.

Her fallen lasagna had left red drops on the carpet. Like the spray on the wall of the room with the camcorder. *Clean later.* She picked up the envelope. It was light and unsealed. A small object bulged at the center. Should she be worried about opening it? Should she even have picked it up? She considered dropping it and calling the number on Jackson's card.

A thumb drive and a note fell into her hand when she tipped the envelope. Navy opened the folded page. *William was going to kill you.*

CHAPTER 24

NAVY TURNED ON all the lights on the empty second floor of her office building to force the shadows to retreat, even though she only needed to visit the spare equipment room. Old laptops were stacked on the metal shelves like books, sorted by model. Navy chose a white plastic MacBook too old for anyone to miss and grabbed a matching power supply. She couldn't risk using a possibly infected thumb drive in her laptop at home.

On the neighboring set of shelves, there was a bulging CD binder. Navy flipped through the install CDs until she found a Mac OS X disk as old as the laptop and the developer tool's disk. Navy didn't want her home internet connection to show any sign of installing a new laptop. The rest of the tools she needed were at home.

"Navy?" Jarrod almost ran into her as she left the equipment room.

"Oh, hey. Why are you here early on a Saturday morning?"

Jarrod held up a scratched plastic square. "Forgot my cell phone. You aren't working on the weekend again, are you?"

"Pet project at home. I thought no one would miss one of the spare laptops."

"I thought maybe someone had called you in—all the lights on the floor are on."

"Must have been left on Friday."

"Well, I was going to call you." He sheepishly held up his phone again. "But since you're here. Carlie's having people over for dinner and a movie tonight. You want to come?"

Navy didn't. But Jarrod's face was eager and worried. And the thought of another night alone in her apartment listening for the soft swish of an envelope slipped under her door was too much. "Sure. When should I be there?"

"Good. I wasn't going to let you say no anyway."

If you cooperate, you have a chance at getting home. Navy's jaw tightened as she pushed the memory away.

"Seven. Don't bring anything. You know Carlie—she always makes enough food for an army."

"I'll be there."

On the drive home, her raw nerves left her feeling exposed. Did the person who gave her the thumb drive have good intentions or bad? Was the person who gave her the thumb drive watching her? Navy looked at the other drivers around her. A mother with a child screaming in back. A school bus full of dejected athletes towing a trailer. A middle-aged man driving with a much older woman as a passenger and the back seat crammed with her belongings.

Ordinary people with ordinary problems. Navy envied them,

After deadbolting the door, she checked her apartment twice, circling like a fish in a cramped bowl. Navy searched the channels on her TV for background noise to calm her nerves and settled on a children's animated movie, something with dancing animals that cheerfully broke into song every few minutes.

It took about half an hour to reinstall the laptop and reformat the drives. Then she powered the laptop off, flipped it over, and removed the battery. Using a piece of scratch paper, Navy sketched a diagram of the bottom of the laptop, marking the location of the screws. She placed each screw next to its mark on the diagram as she removed them. Navy kept removing parts until she could see the wireless card. It was only held on by two antenna connectors. These came off easily, and the card was freed.

Navy reassembled everything, minus the wireless card. The thumb drive might have software on it that would phone home to let the sender know she had plugged it in. A trap set to prove she knew the name Jackie Pierce. Even with forensics tools, the thumb drive was dangerous. Now the laptop could only connect to a network if she plugged in an ethernet cord. Was she being too careful? She didn't know what else to do. Navy wondered if the thumb drive was a message from Jackson. Or Byron. Or Erin.

No. They wouldn't have sent a message designed to make her panic.

She turned on the computer and loaded her forensic tools, so she could make an exact copy of the contents of the thumb drive without changing the drive itself, or allowing any programs on the drive to run. Navy tapped her fingers impatiently as the bit-by-bit copy chugged along. Two minutes passed, then three. Her tools were copying the entire thumb drive, including sectors marked as empty. Finally, the command finished. Navy's impatience turned into hesitation.

She could still call Jackson. She could call no one, throw away the drive and return the laptop on Monday. Would another thumb drive appear if Navy threw this one away? Was it a warning from a well-intentioned stranger that she couldn't afford to ignore? Would calling Jackson expose him to more risks than he'd already taken for her? They were all questions she couldn't answer.

Three o' clock. Four hours before Navy was supposed to be at Jarrod's house. She clicked on the copy she had made of the thumb drive's contents. One folder labeled "Operation Critical Mass." The name of Navy's rescue operation? Of Erin's original operation? Jackson had carefully censored her looks at his files.

There were no executables or programs inside the folder. Just a bunch of image files. For extra measure, Navy checked the file headers to confirm they were JPEGs. A virus scan on all of the files came up clean. Of course, virus scanners couldn't detect everything, and any file could contain malicious code. Or an exploit that would infect the computer. But that was why Navy was using a throwaway laptop that couldn't phone home. She opened the first image file—a picture of some sort of official document. The image was too clear and too straight to have been taken with a camera. A high-quality scan from someone who was not in a hurry. At the top of the document was the official presidential seal. There was only one sentence on the page.

I, President of the United States, hereby authorize Operation Critical Mass.

Navy was Alice, falling down a rabbit hole. The sweeping signature at the bottom of the document she recognized from news coverage: a majestic "M" followed by a scrawl and a dramatic "O." Michael Orway, the current president of the United States.

Navy opened the rest of the files in a slideshow. A vague description of an agent assigned to be an inside man, Roy. Roy had given false intelligence to some amateur terrorists about a well-connected senator's niece traveling through Amsterdam in February. The false intelligence was supposed to lead the terrorists to kidnap Erin and two other agents. There was a message Roy sent to the kidnappers with the date and time of her flight—except the font spacing was off. As if the words didn't fill the space correctly. Like the image of the document had been modified after it was scanned. The font spacing looked normal in all of the other documents.

She created a chronology based on the creation times of the documents. They were all created on the same day, two days ago. The first document was created at 14:03:29, the second at 14:04:54, the third another minute after and so on. All of the documents had been created about a minute apart, as if someone had scanned them in order.

But that didn't tell Navy which documents had been modified after they were scanned in. She created a second chronology based on the last modified time. The anomalies were so clear it frightened her. The first document was last modified at 14:03:29, the second at 14:04:54, and so on . . . until the tenth document. The message Roy had sent identifying the kidnap victims. That document had been scanned in at 14:15:23 and modified at 15:06:46. Other documents had been tampered with as well.

Navy flicked the thumb drive with her finger and it spun on the table. How much of the information should she trust?

She read the records of all of the communications sent to her kidnappers. Navy's flight information from Des Moines to Amsterdam. Navy had been described in detail. Sara and Moss had only been listed as "two American companions." Navy was referred to as a high-value target. Sara and Moss had been labeled expendable.

Navy recognized the photos of her kidnappers. They were cropped down to mug shots, but the perspective in the photographs looked more like the surveillance photos she'd seen in Jackson's files. Navy read the histories on each of her kidnappers, and some on people she had never seen in the mansion. Where they had been recruited, where they had been trained, their known associates.

There were pictures of Navy's driver's license and passport. The last batch of files were from after Navy and Sara and Moss had been kidnapped. A perfunctory report by the Amsterdam police of her mother's frantic call when Navy hadn't checked in. Reports from Jackson and Byron as they attempted to track down where the kidnappers were hiding. One note stuck out. *Delayed surveillance legislation complicated finding subjects.* Neither Jackson nor Byron had mentioned anything about politics to Navy. But then, they wouldn't, right? Navy skimmed Byron's final, typed report. Even in the clipped, formal sentences she could recognize Byron's voice. It was comforting in an odd way. *Subjects were found alive but injured. Received medical care at base.*

Navy pushed the laptop back, wrinkling the sketch she had made to keep track of the screws. She felt small compared to the questions circling in her head: new questions she hadn't thought to ask before, old ones she'd hoped to forget. Erin was supposed to play the senator's niece in Operation Critical Mass. Erin and her companions were supposed to neutralize their captors, then escape and use what they had observed to track the kidnapping ring in Amsterdam back to the other groups connected to it. But for some reason, Roy had identified Navy as the target instead. Jackson and Byron had been scrambling to find her. The memos on their investigations were in the file. Along with other memos—unsigned and in different handwriting—listing worries about what Navy, Sara, and Moss would know if they were rescued.

William was going to kill you.

Maybe she could compare the handwriting on the note to the memos on the thumb drive. She pulled the note out of the drawer in the kitchen and held it next to the screen. Not the same handwriting as the unsigned memos.

The next document Navy pulled up took the air out of the room. A message from William to Roy, ordering him to "clean things up." Then a message to her kidnappers from Roy. *Wrong package picked up at airport. Disposal requested.* That's how Navy's kidnappers had known she wasn't Jackie Pierce. Not from her phone. Not because Sara or Moss had used her real name. William had ordered the execution.

It explained the secrecy on the base. Why Jackson had told Navy to lie to William. Jackson and Byron had been trying to find her, but she wasn't supposed to be found. Navy's unlikely escape had presented William with a conundrum. Did he really want to have them killed? Was he forced by someone? His relief at seeing Navy safe had seemed real. Navy couldn't know for sure. She didn't know *anything* for sure.

Navy felt a flash of anger toward Jackson—toward Byron and Erin too. Erin for spending all that time with her in the gym and not breathing a word. Erin had probably been assigned to bunk with Navy just to find out what she knew. Byron had smiled affably through their morning excursions, never mentioning William's orders. And Jackson. Jackson who had coached her through her lies to William. Jackson who had forced Navy to stay at the base hospital long enough to get examined after she had insisted she was fine. Jackson who had found the best delicacies at the street markets for Navy. He had kept the truth from her.

No, Jackson had done his best to protect her. They all had.

Still, nothing Navy had seen in the files answered the biggest question. If Navy's kidnapping was a case of mistaken identity— like the files seemed to imply—why had the agency even allowed the possibility of a mistake? Why be so vague when describing the fictional niece's companions? Erin's party of three was one female and two males. A few more words from Roy and it would have been obvious that Navy's party of three wasn't the right target. And there was no record of any communication to the senator whose imaginary niece had been kidnapped. Even if Erin had been kidnapped as planned the operation would have been blown when the ransom tape arrived. It was as if the operation had been designed to fail. Or had been sabotaged. But what would the death of three Americans accomplish?

Six fifteen. Navy had fifteen minutes before she needed to leave for Jarrod's. She flipped through the rest of the images in the folder. Her sketches of the mansion she had drawn for Jackson. Autopsy photos, now familiar to her. William's daily, terse reports during her two weeks in Amsterdam. Personnel records on all the agents involved. Except the personnel records on Jackson, Byron, and Erin were more detailed than the rest.

Jackson had a brother in Lansing, Michigan. The brother was married with two children. Jackson volunteered at a refugee center. Went to a gym two blocks from his apartment. Byron had a wife and a teenage daughter, soon to leave for college. Byron's favorite lunch spot, the closest pizza place to the office. Erin's personnel record didn't list any family, but there was a list of known associates. Lists of people. Places. Why?

Insurance. Jackson, Erin and Byron were targets because they had helped her.

If I call, will it be dangerous for you? The question Navy had asked Jackson in Amsterdam. Now she understood exactly how dangerous.

And then the final image.

Recommend continued monitoring of subject Navy Trent to confirm the operation wasn't compromised.

She had reached the bottom of the rabbit hole.

Navy's phone rang, showing Jarrod's picture. It was six thirty. Her phone had been replaced at Valkenburg with a different model; William had claimed the kidnappers damaged her phone. Navy had put all of her contacts into the new phone. If William was monitoring her, he now had her entire contact list—all of her friend's and family's emails, phone numbers, and addresses. Had they tapped her cell phone? Her parent's land line? Or worse, a bug in the phone. The phone seemed possessed, vibrating against the table. She had another scene to play.

"Checking up on me, Jarrod?" Navy's smile wasn't real but Jarrod couldn't tell.

"Just making sure you're not thinking of backing out. Carlie's made a feast and we can't finish it without you."

There was no one she could confide in. Everyone she had known before Amsterdam couldn't help her. Everyone who had helped her in Amsterdam would be in danger if she called.

"I'm getting ready now," Navy said. "See you soon."

CHAPTER 25

BYRON HURRIED TOWARD the entrance to his office building. The first hints of a pale sun peered through the gray clouds just above the horizon. Earlier than he normally came in, but Byron needed time at his desk when the floor would be almost empty. He needed to get in touch with Jackson or Erin. Byron couldn't warn Navy without implicating himself. Any calls to her cell phone would be recorded on the bug. It was likely her email and internet connection were tapped as well. Someone had to visit Navy, but Byron couldn't leave DC without attracting attention. Jackson or Erin could visit Des Moines without arousing suspicion. Field agents fell off the radar for brief periods all the time.

The two SIGINT techs from the night shift were still in their glass cage, remarkably awake considering it was the last two hours of a twelve-hour shift. One of them looked up from his computer just long enough to give Byron a friendly wave. A whiteboard behind the techs was covered with doodles and acronyms. He remembered when he had been that naively dedicated, when he had thought his agency could do no wrong.

Byron checked all of his email addresses and his voicemail. No message from Erin or Jackson. Byron was relying on back channels they had set up years ago. He didn't have the clearance to find out how to contact Jackson or Erin while they were on their missions.

Time for his most distasteful task, listening to the conversations recorded on Navy's phone. Byron had put off the task for a week. The list of files to be reviewed spanned two pages, at least two hours' work.

Might as well get started. Byron felt as guilty as if he were reading Navy's journal. He listened to a conversation with her coworker, Jarrod, while at the office on a Saturday. A call later where she promised she was on her way to Jarrod and Carlie's house for dinner. A happy hour with coworkers at Grumpy's, the bar near the office. Navy was slowly settling back into her life. For the first few weeks, she hadn't gone out at all.

Byron found the calls from Sara hardest to listen to. She called often, always with the same question asked a hundred different ways. *Are you okay?* Given what Sara had to recover from, her attempts to keep Navy engaged were impressive. Navy's answers were always evasive. Their conversations circled around until Navy made excuses to hang up. A good thing for Byron's report, but probably not good for Navy's health.

"You have something?"

William. Looking grim, as if expecting bad news.

"Nothing interesting," Byron said. "Good for us, right?"

"Yes. Good." William looked more perplexed than relieved.

Byron decided to test if William had been listening to the recordings. "She even went to Sadie's for the office happy hour. Her friends were starting to wonder."

"Sure. Good." William hurried away. He hadn't corrected Byron on the name of the bar.

What was going on? William wasn't listening to the recordings, but he had been expecting that Byron would have an incident to report. Who had told William that Navy had said something incriminating? Who else was listening?

Byron tried to think of Navy as a suspect instead of a victim and replayed the recordings he had already listened to. Nothing. A pet project. A dinner invitation. A hike on a nice day. Who was William getting orders from?

Still a page of recordings left to review. At first Byron took the background conversations on the next recording to be Grumpy's, but he recognized the tinny sound of the lower quality mic. This was from the same bug he'd heard several weeks ago. With the deputy. *She's being monitored, sir. By the CIA, and one of our own.*

Byron reached for his notepad; the recording might disappear as quickly as the other one had.

"It's good to meet you," said the deputy. "You came highly recommended."

"Men with titles like yours don't normally contact me directly," the other stranger said.

Byron drew two boxes on the paper, one for each man. "The nature of your work in this matter would be highly sensitive. My boss prefers I handle it directly."

High-ranking? Byron wrote in one box. The deputy spoke in the language of a bureaucrat.

The stranger snorted. "Your boss? That's what you call the man in the big house?"

"That's what I call him here," the bureaucrat said in a steely voice. "I was told you knew how to be discreet."

In the long pause that followed, the dull thrum of a bass beat, the clink of glasses and the scraping of chairs were the only sounds. "If those are your orders," the stranger said. "I'm a soldier. The general says to follow you, I follow you."

A soldier, a general, and a bureaucrat. What could that sort of triad have to do with Navy? Byron added *Soldier* to his notes on the stranger.

"Did the general explain why I chose you?" the bureaucrat asked.

"No, enlighten me."

"You fought in Afghanistan, and you plan to go back."

"Lots of people fought there," the soldier said.

"But not everyone lost an entire squad in an off-the-books mission."

The recording got scratchy, like the bug was rubbing against fabric. Navy's recording had a similar sound when her cell phone was in her pocket. If the surveillance on Navy had been requested by the same party around the same time, it would explain how the recordings were ending up in the wrong place. Byron heard footfalls in the recording; he cursed his luck. One of them was walking away.

"Come back to the table," the bureaucrat said in a low whisper. "I'll explain."

"You'll explain quickly," the soldier said.

"I chose you because I think you are in a unique position to understand what's at stake here. Do you know why all those men in your squad died?"

"Because of some asshole with a cell phone."

"No. Because we couldn't find the asshole with the cell phone in time. CRYSTAL will solve all that. The Counterterrorism Response Yellowjacket Surveillance Threat Assessment Labeler."

"You can't expect me to take you seriously with an acronym like that."

"Then just think of it as a technological crystal ball. A system that vacuums up communications of all kinds, picks out what's important, finds networks of people, predicts behavior. All so we can target them in sting operations."

It was a pipe dream. Byron had heard the rumors around

headquarters about a new surveillance program. The lawyers were nervous. The majority of the analysts didn't like it. Despite what was often written about the CIA, most analysts did not favor Orwellian fantasies.

"We can finish what we started in Afghanistan," the bureaucrat continued. "We can prevent the next 9/11. But we can't admit it exists until we update the laws that govern surveillance."

"I like how you think," the soldier said. "But I still don't know what you want me to do."

"A civilian accidentally became involved in a CIA operation related to CRYSTAL. Unfortunately, she survived. We're afraid she knows more than she should. If she goes public, our legislative initiatives are at risk."

Byron paused the recording. CRYSTAL was already operational. It would explain the wild goose chases he'd been sent on in the last year. In Byron's twenty-odd years at the CIA, he'd seen the next big thing come and go several times. CRYSTAL would fail like the rest. Despite the billions spent on systems like it over the years, intelligence always came down to one thing: agents on the ground. Talented, smart agents who put themselves in the right places at the right times.

And how was CRYSTAL related to Amsterdam? The terrorist cell wasn't found by some magic machine; Jackson found them. Byron forced himself to concentrate on their conversation.

"Navy Trent is your target," the bureaucrat said. "I brought some photos and general background for you."

Byron heard pages being flipped. "Shouldn't be too hard to take care of a nerdy rock climber from the Corn Belt," the soldier said.

"Surveillance target," the bureaucrat clarified. "Follow her for a week. I want the names of anyone she talks to. Even parking attendants and waiters."

"I'd do a better job if you could tell me why you think she knows something."

"A little bird whispered in my ear that she may know something she shouldn't. We have to be sure."

"A little bird?" the soldier asked with a snort. Byron wondered if the same little bird had visited William. "If she was dead, you'd be sure."

"Even accidental deaths make people ask questions," the bureaucrat answered. "Just surveillance, until we say otherwise."

"Sure, Andy." There was a sneer in the soldier's voice.

Finally a name.

"Kindly explain your tone," Andy said.

"This is how it always is. You and your boss make plans from that lily-white office of yours and when you're too soft to do the job right, you have to call in a man like me."

"Be that as it may, I'm still the one giving you orders." In the pause, Byron imagined Andy leaning forward, trying to intimidate. "Surveillance only until you hear otherwise *from me*." The recording ended abruptly. Byron jotted down the date the recording was made, then turned a page to hide his notes.

Byron sent the email to the admins to tell them about the recording mistakenly filed with Navy's case. If he was going to stay in a position to help Navy, he had to be a model employee.

He needed a place to think. Byron took his notepad to an empty meeting room on a quiet part of the floor. His sparse notes mocked him. The recording was dated two weeks ago. Navy's shadow was supposed to last a week. That meant the soldier had already left Iowa, and Navy was still alive. No thanks to Byron.

Follow the trail, Byron told himself. He could search military records for all soldiers who were the sole survivors of IED attacks in Afghanistan. But since the soldier had been part of a covert operation, the search would be useless. Covert ops deaths were often recorded in entirely different countries. Andy was a dead end too. All he knew about Andy was that he had an impressive sounding title, knew a general, and worked for a man on a power trip. That wasn't unique in DC. And it wasn't enough to help Navy.

CHAPTER 26

NAVY FELT AS if she were becoming two different people. Outside her apartment, she smiled through work happy hours and joked with friends. Inside her apartment, she plotted and schemed and worried.

She dropped her work bag on the couch and her lunchtime purchases on the counter in the kitchen. Navy's current battlefield was a table holding the forensics laptop and a cell phone.

Eat dinner first, she told herself. She had skipped lunch. Navy was out of microwave dinners. She poured herself a glass of milk and opened a bag of chips. The new phone, identical to the one she was given in Amsterdam, was expensive. Navy had driven to a store an hour away to get it and paid in cash. The longest part of the transaction was convincing the salesman she didn't want to sign up for a contract.

She took a small knife from a drawer in the kitchen. The sides of the shrink wrap on the box peeled away like skin as Navy sliced around the edges of the box. Why was she staring at the box instead of opening it? She was hoping the whole exercise would turn out to be a ridiculous waste of time. That she would find nothing in her phone that wasn't in the purchased phone. Each new discovery she made pulled her further away from her old life.

The apartment was too quiet. The evening news. That would work for background noise.

"Unnamed administration officials said that the president was going to announce a surge of troops in Afghanistan, despite eroding support for the war," intoned a somber newscaster. "However, the president's press conference this afternoon didn't indicate any changes in proposed legislation. The president's spokesperson continued to emphasize that increased surveillance powers are necessary to protect national security. In other news, today a local dog owner has a lot to thank man's best friend for. After Perry's owner fell into a river, Perry alerted walkers on a nearby path who called in emergency services."

Navy sat with her back to the television. On her right, she put the phone she had been given in Amsterdam. On her left, the phone she had purchased over lunch. First, she removed the batteries. The battery compartments looked exactly the same, except for differences in the serial and IMEI numbers. Navy took her smallest screwdriver and removed the four screws on each phone that held the back plate on. She carefully pulled the back off the new phone. Inside was a green circuit board as long as her palm but only two-thirds as wide. Three gray squares, almost the size of postage stamps, one marked with Qualcomm, occupied the lower half of the circuit board. The metal brace that formed the battery case reflected the gray squares. On the upper half of the circuit board, four small gray squares and tiny hollow white squares dotted the geometric landscape. A pair of twisted wires, one red and one black, connected to a round speaker.

Now to examine the speaker on the phone she'd been given in Amsterdam.

At first, she thought she was imagining the extra black wire. But no, she could see three wires instead of two. The extra wire went into the speaker on the back of the phone.

Navy took a penlight out of her repair kit and shined the bright beam into the speaker. A bit of metal, about the size of the eraser on the end of a pencil, glinted under the light. She picked up the new phone and examined the speaker. There was only plastic and foam. Navy checked twice more to be sure. There was no extra wire on the purchased phone. The room was tilting, as if any second it might spin.

Navy put both phones back together. She felt violated as soon as she turned on her bugged phone. She wondered how the bug was transmitting to her watchers what it had recorded. The easiest way would be to use the cell phone itself by modifying the firmware.

Navy connected her phone to the forensics laptop and made a bit-by-bit copy of the memory and the firmware. Then she did the same for the new phone. Two hours later, when her eyes were gritty with exhaustion, she found the anomaly. There were honest differences between the two phones, of course. Her contacts and pictures were on her phone. And there were no call records on the new phone, just on Navy's. But there was ".tmp" directory under "Media" on her phone that wasn't on the purchased phone. She navigated through the menus on her phone. The screen that listed her pictures, videos, and ringtones didn't show the extra directory.

Inside the directory were MP3 files with long numeric names. The numbers looked familiar—a Unix timestamp. The name of one file was a timestamp for today at 11:37 a.m. Navy hit the play button. A syllable of Jarrod's voice came out of the laptop before she remembered that the bug in her phone was still listening. She hit the mute key on her keyboard.

Navy took the battery out of her cell phone and carried it into the bedroom. Back in the living room, she selected the file again. "I'm going to Mario's for lunch, you want?" Jarrod's voice in her apartment talking over the news anchor. Worlds mixing that shouldn't mix.

Her life's intimate details, neatly packaged for delivery to an office somewhere in DC.

She turned off the recording before her own voice came on. Frantically she thought back to where her phone had been the morning she left Valkenburg. In the hallway, in her backpack. And turned off. Navy had left the phone in the box until it was time to pack.

Don't panic. Think. Every conversation she had within the microphone's range was being recorded and sent somewhere. . . . Constantly transmitting data should eat up the phone's battery. But the battery wasn't dying sooner than it should.

If she were designing the program, how would she hide its activity? Upload at night. When Navy's phone was at home charging. Any delay between the recording and the upload time would give her time to react.

Navy needed to test her theory. She could buy a device that eavesdropped on cell phone transmissions, but even buying the hardware might raise a red flag. She went to the closet by the front door and dug around in the box of electronic rejects. There was an old pair of cheap computer speakers, the white plastic yellowed with age. Navy had stopped using them in her apartment because they crackled every time her cell phone was about to get a call. Beneath them was an old audio recorder left over from a college project. The mini-tapes could hold ten hours of audio. She set the speakers up next to her cell phone on the dresser, using an audio cable to pipe the sound from the headphone jack of the speakers to the audio recorder. Navy would run one test with her cell phone tonight, another test with the new phone tomorrow.

Based on the crackling in the speakers, Navy would be able to tell how often the phones were transmitting. Since she didn't check email or have her work calendar on her phone, any extra transmissions from her phone would indicate when Navy's conversations were being uploaded. It was a small victory, if it could be considered a victory at all. She thought back to the Chinese restaurant in Amsterdam and Jackson's careful distance from her. *Smart and lucky. That's how it goes most of the time.* Navy might be smart enough to find a way to survive this. But would she be lucky enough?

⌁

Navy opened the passenger door of Jarrod's car and stepped into the dark parking lot outside their office building. Hers was the only car left in the lot.

"Are you sure you don't want me to drop you off at your car?" Jarrod asked.

Sweet Jarrod. They'd been at an office happy hour. He was already late getting home to Carlie. "I have to get something from the office," Navy said. "I'll see you Monday."

"I can wait."

"Go." Navy used up her last smile. Two hours of pretending to be happy made her cheeks hurt. "Say hi to Carlie for me." Jarrod nodded uncertainly and drove away.

The parking lot seemed darker when Navy came back downstairs. She had only been in her office a few minutes, just long enough to grab a thumb drive with some work she needed to catch up on. Perhaps she should have accepted Jarrod's offer. No, it was her nerves. Her paranoia. No one knew she had the file on Operation Critical Mass but the people who gave it to her, whoever they were. And if they wanted to kill her, they could have easily done it when they visited her apartment a week ago.

Only twenty feet to her car, parked next to the electrical box the size of a refrigerator. She stepped out of the safety of the building lights. Ten feet. Her keys in hand. *You're being silly.* Two feet. Her keys in the door. Nothing—

The first punch slammed Navy's cheek into the car window. Up against the car, she had no room to maneuver. He punched her twice in the gut, doubling her over. *Fight*, Navy told herself. Like Erin taught you. She shoved her attacker away. Her bag flew off her shoulder and landed several feet away. The attacker barely moved. She saw his shape for the first time. A burly man in a ski mask. Not much taller but definitely heavier and stronger.

Navy tried a right hook, but he dodged her punch and grabbed her wrist. He squeezed it in a vise, then twisted, leaving her skin burning. He could have broken it. Navy cried out and pulled her arm back, cradling it against her stomach.

He pushed her against the car again and she stumbled. Her ankle bent; she crumpled to the ground. Sprained, not broken. Navy tried to get up to run, but he was too close, practically on top of her. He kicked her over and over with the toe of his leather boots. She hated the sound of her cries. She curled up in a ball and waited.

He could have taken her wallet, her bag, her laptop. She couldn't stop him. But he stayed, grunting, kicking until Navy was sure there wasn't a spot left on her that wasn't bruised.

When he stopped, he crouched next to her. Navy saw the moon glint off the eyelets on his laces. He ran his hands over her pockets, reached into them. No. Not that.

She would claw his eyes out. She would die before she let—

But his hands only brushed the thumb drive in her pocket and then moved away. He looked toward her bag and then back at her.

"We know you have the file," he said. He was yelling, even though he was only a foot away. "Keep your mouth shut or we'll kill you." He kept using that same loud voice. With the same focus on her bag.

He sprinted away. Navy could hear cars rushing by on the

highway, but no one would have seen her. She forced herself up. She picked up her bag. She should call the police. But this obviously wasn't a mugging. Navy couldn't tell the police why she'd been attacked. The prospect of adding one more lie to her growing list kept her from dialing 911.

Navy opened the car door and locked herself in. A sprained ankle. A bruised cheek. A ring on her wrist that felt like a second-degree sunburn. He could have done worse.

And the thumb drive in her pocket? He'd left it there. He knew about the file, but didn't know it was given to Navy on a thumb drive? Or he chose not to take what could have been a copy of everything she knew? Why didn't he search her bag? Why not just kill her?

And why yell toward her bag?

The bug. He had searched her pockets for her phone. Her attacker had wanted his threats to be audible on the bug. When he figured out her phone wasn't on her he knew he had to yell to have a chance at being heard. The attack was meant to make her a target for William. To make sure that William knew Navy had his secrets.

Navy hit the steering wheel with her fists to fight the tears streaming down her face. William's men would kill her for having the file on Operation Critical Mass. And the people who gave her the thumb drive were going to make sure William knew.

Breathe, Navy told herself. Think. *You're not dead yet.*

CHAPTER 27

ANOTHER PARKING LOT. But this one was bright with morning sun reflecting off unbroken snow. Navy pulled her balaclava down and stepped out of the car. A bitter wind tunneled down the gravel road and swirled into the tiny parking lot. Navy knew she and Sara would be alone. This was their favorite cross-country skiing spot because it was so often deserted.

Next, tinted ski goggles. The balaclava would cover the bruises and her cheeks and her neck. The ski goggles would cover her black eye. Her jacket, gloves, and snow pants would cover the rest of her. Sara would never know.

Navy's ego was just as bruised as her body. Last night's attack was fresh in her mind. How had she let someone surprise her like that? Why hadn't she fought back harder?

Sara's car appeared around the curve just as Navy was pulling the skis off the top of her car. As far as Sara knew, they were just getting together as friends. Navy felt like she was organizing an ambush.

"Navy!" Sara jumped out of her car and hugged her.

Pain. Navy gritted her teeth as Sara's arms pressed into the bruises. "I'm so glad you could come on such short notice."

Finally, Sara let go and stepped back. "Well, you've been such a hermit lately. Moss wanted to come, but you know he's a baby about the cold."

Navy had been counting on it. Sara might forgive her for the questions Navy had to ask; Moss would not. Navy willed her tone to be light. "I saw high winds, blustery snow, and ten below windchill and thought of this spot. We haven't been in a while."

The wind kicked up on cue, and the air sparkled with dry snow. Sara's cheeks and nose were already red. "Let me get my gear on before I freeze."

Navy clipped into her skis at the break in the woods, where the trail started. Sara, her face now covered too, clipped into her skis next to Navy. As she had hoped, the trail was untouched. The exertion would challenge her. Though Navy's body ached after a few minutes, her muscles appreciated the movement. A reminder she was still strong.

The curled, peeling bark of the river birches fluttered in the wind. Their trunks weren't large, but collectively the forest blocked the wind. Navy could feel it was warmer under their cover. The landscape was her protector and her refuge.

"You're right," Sara said. "It's been too long."

Navy understood. The only sound besides the wind was the soft swish their skis made as they broke trail. She tried to draw on that peace for her strength. To find stillness in the midst of her struggle.

"I've been thinking about Amsterdam," Navy said.

The rhythm of Sara's stride skipped, then recovered. "You never told me what happened to you upstairs."

For a second, Navy smelled the dusty room where she'd been kept. "They made me record the ransom note. That's all."

Sara shook her head, but said nothing.

"So in the basement . . ." Navy started.

Sara's skis inched ahead of Navy's, as if she were trying to get away. "I really don't want to talk about this."

At the hospital on base, Sara had given Navy an open invitation to talk. Navy was struck dumb by the change. *You have to ask her.* "I just—I need to understand what happened."

"It was bad luck," Sara said. "That's all. We made it through. I don't care about anything else."

A perfect winter day. A good friend. Navy cursed the person who had given her the thumb drive for ruining this too. "After I saw you for the first time. When I told you to call me—" Navy remembered that Sara shouldn't know the name Jackie. "When I told you it was a case of mistaken identity—"

Sara's ski poles stabbed through the thick crust on the snow with a crack. "You know everything that happened to me. *Everything.*"

The rape. The rape that was Navy's fault.

"But you won't tell me anything," Sara said. "You're still hung up on the way we met? You want to forget that you were ever vulnerable?" Sara huffed and the cloud condensed into crystals on her face mask. "I get it. I understand now. But I don't want to be the only one sharing."

The conversation was familiar to Navy. The give-and-take required by relationships was uncomfortable for her. For the first time, Navy wanted to tell Sara everything. Sara deserved to know. But Navy couldn't. Not without putting Sara in more danger.

"I haven't told you because I don't know," Navy said. Did lying hurt less with practice? She wondered how Jackson handled lying to the people he loved. "I just woke up in the bed upstairs; I think they drugged me."

"So they may have—"

"Probably. Or maybe not," Navy said. "I don't know. I don't remember much."

"Oh, honey." Sara leaned over and hugged her.

Navy couldn't decide what hurt more: her bruises or the calculated deception. "I'm just trying to understand. How did they figure out I wasn't their intended victim?" Had the kidnappers actually been told to "dispose" of Navy, Sara, and Moss like the file said? Or was there another explanation?

Sara looked angry again. "We never told them. If you're asking if it's our fault."

"No, no, no. Nothing is your fault." Navy felt the cold creeping in where her gloves met her coat. "What I mean is, did you overhear anything? Conversations in the hallway? Anything?"

"Nothing." Sara dug her poles in, preparing to move forward.

At least she wasn't turning around. "I'm sorry," Navy said. "I'm sorry . . . for keeping you in the dark. I'm sorry for everything. But I have to ask one more thing."

Sara didn't look at her. "Then ask."

"Has anyone contacted you? About what happened?"

"Don't tell me you're missing Jackson. After that creep dragged you back to the mansion?"

Navy hadn't meant for Sara to jump to that conclusion, but it was as good an explanation as any. "Not really."

"Forget about him. Forget about all of them. I wouldn't talk to them even if they did contact me. Because of what they did to you."

You're a good friend. "No more questions. I promise."

Sara pushed on ahead. Navy followed, glad to let the forest swallow their words.

CHAPTER 28

JACKSON STEPPED OFF the plane at the Des Moines airport, blinking at the gray winter morning. His delayed arrival in Washington wouldn't be noticed; it wasn't uncommon for operations to run long. Jackson had turned off his cell phone and removed the battery. He wouldn't turn on his work laptop until his short detour was over.

At the closed Chinese restaurant near his gate, he grabbed a pair of chopsticks from the metal cup on the counter. He followed the signs to baggage claim, walked past the carousels crowded with impatient people waiting for luggage, and out toward the rental car shuttles. A light backpack was all he carried.

The earnest attendant with bad acne tried very hard to sell Jackson on insurance and prepaid gas at Evergreen Car Rental. Sam Taylor, the alias Jackson was using, refused politely.

Jackson drove to the address in Navy's file and circled the block. Her apartment building had two entrances on opposite sides, and one entrance/exit for the garage. Good. He knew she drove to work; he would see her leave the garage. He parked on the street within view of the garage exit and fought a yawn—6:00 a.m. He never slept well on planes.

Navy's car left the underground garage at 8:01 a.m. Jackson

followed her through rush hour traffic for ten minutes, then she left the highway. At the edge of town she turned into the driveway of an office building. The sign listed at least twenty companies with hopeful names like NewGen and Genius Bits. Jackson kept one car between them as he followed Navy down the driveway. He parked at the edge of the lot, hoping he wouldn't spook her.

She parked as close to the entrance as she could. Navy didn't get out right away. She watched the car that had come in behind her. She watched Jackson's car. He had parked too far away for Navy to recognize him.

More cars came in. Jackson wondered what Navy was waiting for. When she did leave her car, Navy walked with hurried steps toward the entrance. She had a slight limp. Jackson took out his monocular and focused on the only exposed skin her winter coat and gloves allowed—her face. Her coworkers probably wouldn't notice, but it was obvious to him: she was covering up bruises. Jackson felt for the chopsticks lying on the front seat. He hadn't been sure he would make contact with Navy, but now he knew he would.

Unfortunately, Jackson couldn't just walk up to Navy. William might have her under surveillance. Including monitoring the security cameras Jackson could see mounted to the outside of the office building. If Jackson was seen talking to her and didn't report the contact, all of William's suspicions from Amsterdam would be confirmed. Jackson would pass Navy a note when she left for lunch. If she left for lunch.

Three and a half hours passed before she left the office again. Navy was talking to someone with a long ponytail and a knit cap, pulled low on his forehead. Her eyes flicked to Jackson's car again before she got in her own. He gave her a long lead, almost losing her in a maze of residential streets. Jackson didn't see anyone else tailing her.

Navy drove for about thirty minutes, eventually stopping at a neighborhood coffee shop. She had passed several before settling on this one. Jackson could see the tactical advantages. This coffee shop was busy enough that she wouldn't be alone, but not so large that someone following her could blend in. The parking lot was small and easily monitored from the tables inside. Jackson parked on the street a block away. Coffee would be good right about now, but he couldn't meet her in public.

A note would have to do. On the free map from the rental car agency, he sketched the outline of Oude Kerk and scrawled a note, *Water Works Park, footbridge. 1:00.* Jackson folded the paper, then slipped the chopsticks inside. He hoped that she remembered their dinner at the Chinese restaurant as vividly as he did. He walked to the parking lot, forcing himself not to turn toward the large windows in front of the coffee shop. Out of the corner of his eye, he saw Navy look up from her laptop.

Better move quickly. Jackson slipped the note under a wiper blade on Navy's car. She was closing her laptop and getting out of her chair. She had recognized him. If he just waited two minutes, she would be next to him. He could ask about the bruise on her face.

No. You'll see her later. Walk away.

❧

At Water Works Park, Jackson arrived with just enough time to get to the bridge and watch for anyone who might be following Navy. He was thankful the map he'd consulted on the plane had been accurate. The footbridge linked two fields on either side of a river. Anyone following Navy would have a hard time hiding. He leaned his forearms on the railing, watching both fields. The cold metal bit through the thin canvas of his coat. He wasn't dressed for a Midwestern winter. A light wind stirred the snow on the icy river and found the holes in his cotton gloves. Jackson checked his watch—five minutes after one. Maybe Jackson was wrong about Navy recognizing him earlier. Or Navy had decided the note was a hoax. No, he saw her red coat and white hat approaching from across the field.

Navy waited for an old man walking his poodle to cross the bridge before she leaned on the railing next to Jackson. "I wasn't sure it was you."

Jackson tugged at the whiskers on his chin. "Laziness as camouflage."

"You're shivering. Let's walk."

She led him toward a narrow trail in the woods. It was barely wide enough for them to walk side by side and the dense trees cut the wind. Jackson shoved his hands in his pockets to warm them up.

"Why did you come?" Navy asked.

"To make sure everything was all right. I would ask how you've been," Jackson said. "But I think I can guess." There were bags under Navy's eyes and her gaze was focused straight ahead, past the edge of the trees.

"I was attacked Friday night as I was leaving work." She touched her bruised cheek. "Was it your car I saw this morning? I thought maybe they were watching."

"Yes, it was me this morning." Twigs snapped under Jackson's feet. He was warm suddenly, ashamed of having left her unprotected. "Do you know why?"

Navy nodded and pressed her lips together—the same expression she had made during dinner that first night when she had been uncertain of how much to tell him. Jackson leaned toward her, but she walked faster so he had to scramble to keep up, even with her limp. "Navy, come on. Tell me what happened."

Navy stopped. She had run out of forest. A paved path was visible just beyond the edge of the woods. Two cyclists whirred by, riding into the fog of their own breath.

"I'm not sure I should." Navy paced the distance between him and a large oak.

"You don't trust me." Jackson's words sounded like an accusation. Not what he had intended.

"It's not that." Navy shook her head and the fibers of her white knit hat caught what little sunlight there was. "You took enough risks for me in Amsterdam."

"I didn't take any—"

"Don't lie to me," Navy said. "I'm having enough trouble figuring out what's real and what's not."

Jackson tried again. "You shouldn't worry about protecting me." He put a hand on her shoulder and turned her to face him. Underneath the foundation, Jackson could see the purple shadow of the bruises on her face. "Tell me what happened."

Navy brushed his hands away. "No privacy here," she said as two more cyclists whizzed by. "Follow me."

They walked back toward the bridge and into another wooded area. The path was a narrow rut in the dirt, not even wide enough for one person. Branches scratched at Jackson's shoulders. At the end of the dirt rut was a fire pit with discarded, dented beer cans. A fallen tree served as a bench. The splintered trunk was still tan where it had broken. Navy hopped onto the impromptu bench, and Jackson sat next to her. She moved away until they weren't touching.

"A thumb drive was slipped under my door a week ago. It has a bunch of scanned documents on it. About Operation Critical Mass."

Jackson inhaled sharply. What Navy had known before coming home was dangerous enough.

"Some of the scans have been altered. To tell one version of the story. A version of the story where us getting kidnapped was an accident. But it looks more like someone told Roy we were the targets. Like the operation was sabotaged."

Navy knew almost as much as Jackson did. Everything Jackson

had done to protect her in Amsterdam didn't matter. "Jesus, Navy. Why didn't you call?"

"Is it that sunny in DC?" Navy asked him, pointing to his sunburn. "Could you really have answered?"

"Yes."

"I didn't want to drag you in." Navy dug the tips of her fingers into the grooves of the bark. "I don't know what the endgame is yet." She was looking at him and through him at the same time. "I've been going through the documents every day since and I still can't figure out what's going on. I've asked Sara, and it doesn't sound like they've received anything."

"So why just you?" Jackson finished her thought.

"I think it's because I'm being monitored."

"What do you mean?"

"William ordered a bug on my cell phone. It records any conversations that the phone is close enough to hear. A high-end mic too, I checked it out. The built-in speaker phone mic wasn't sensitive enough for them."

"Is it—"

"With me? No. I left the phone at work. It uploads everything it records during the day at night. Two a.m., to be exact."

"They're probably tracking your location via the phone. And monitoring the Internet connection at your apartment too."

"Yeah, I know. This is my field, remember?" Navy said. "I've been spending a lot of time at coffee shops lately."

"There are other ways to track you."

"I'm taking precautions."

Jackson couldn't tell if Navy was angry at him or the situation. "You should have called me. Doing this kind of research is dangerous."

"I needed answers first," Navy said. "Some time to figure

things out." The leafless branches of the trees formed a stiff, brown web around them. "It feels like there are two architects here."

"Walk me through what you know." Jackson was hoping Navy hadn't seen the entire file. It was possible she didn't know as much as she thought she did.

"I know I'm supposed to think it was William's man who attacked me on Friday. Even though it wasn't."

"You're certain?"

"William ordered Roy to send the message that would have killed me, us, in Amsterdam," Navy said. "If William thought I had a thumb drive about Operation Critical Mass, he wouldn't have bothered with a warning."

"So you've seen the 'disposal requested' message. Are you sure no one else knows you have the thumb drive? You didn't say anything to anyone about the thumb drive before you knew about the bug? Google something from the tapped internet connection at your apartment?"

"No. The only people who know I have the thumb drive are the ones who gave it to me. And I think it's the same people who sabotaged the operation." Navy stared ahead.

"There's something you're not telling me," Jackson said.

"My attacker went through my pockets. I had a thumb drive with work stuff on it in my pocket. He didn't take it. And when he threatened me, he used a really loud voice. Like he needed someone else to hear."

Jackson was starting to see Navy's logic. "He looked for your phone and when he saw it wasn't on you he tried to threaten you loudly enough the bug would still pick it up." Jackson scanned the clearing again, listening for the telltale snap of a twig or the crackling of leaves. If the bug had picked up the attacker's threats and William knew Navy had the file, the hit on Navy was already in motion.

"Well, he didn't yell loud enough," Navy said.

"How do you know?"

"Two a.m., remember? I had time to get home before the recordings were uploaded. I listened to them to be sure. William doesn't know. Yet."

"You think the saboteurs gave you the thumb drive and arranged the attack to get you noticed by William's men."

Navy nodded slowly, still looking away. "The saboteurs don't need me to tell the world government secrets. Wikileaks or the *Times* or the *Washington Post* would work just as well. I think they want something bigger."

"You should have called me," he said angrily.

"And said what exactly?" Navy finally turned toward him. "Come rescue me?"

"This is bigger than you, Navy."

"And you," Navy countered. "If anyone knew you were here you'd have a target on your back just like I do."

"What are you going to do?" Jackson could tell she didn't want him to plan her rescue, even if he had a brilliant idea. He didn't.

"I don't know. If I don't go public, I'll get harassed by the saboteurs. If I make any noise about going public, I'll be targeted by William's men. There's still a lot to figure out anyway. What I have isn't the whole truth, just bits and pieces." Navy's legs swung in the empty space below the tree, heels kicking at the frozen bark. "And I still don't know the endgame except . . ."

"Except what?"

"Something Erin told me in Amsterdam. When she was coaching me for William's meeting. About how to lie well. If you really want to make a lie convincing—"

"Make it the truth." One of Erin's favorite phrases.

"I'm thinking that maybe I'm not supposed to make it out of this at all. I'm supposed to do something stupid, something that threatens to expose the operation. Have a meeting with a reporter with my bugged phone sitting on the desk." Navy kicked at the log harder, faster. "And then, after I'm gone, a few strategic leaks get people to start asking questions. It looks like the CIA messed up one of their ops and killed a civilian to cover it up."

Jackson wanted to tell her it wasn't true, but it was as good as any theory he had. "Let me help you. I can stay here for a while."

Navy shook her head. "Everything has to be business as usual. Unless there are any sleeper cells in Des Moines you need to bust?"

"Navy—"

"It's not that I want you to go." Snow melted into round droplets on the toes of Navy's tennis shoes. She watched the drips fall to the curled, brown leaves.

Jackson brushed his shoulder against Navy's coat and she accepted the invitation, laying her head against his chest, the fuzz of her hat catching in his scratchy beard. He put his arm around her.

Jackson couldn't think straight. Maybe it was the fatigue. Navy was still in danger, but he didn't know from whom or what and he didn't know how to help her, or if she would even let him. Jackson had come to Des Moines because he needed to see Navy was all right. He hadn't expected to find her abused and under siege.

"I can get you a gun. Unregistered."

"No guns."

Guns to him were simple, utilitarian. Like a fork or a spoon. Jackson wondered what she saw in the dull black barrel of a pistol. The head of the man she shot at close range with the machine gun, his eye socket blown out, his skull misshapen by the impact of the bullets? "Just a pistol. A few afternoons at the range—"

She shook her head against his shoulder. "No guns. Anyway, don't gun ranges keep records?"

"I know a few people."

"Of course you do."

Jackson squeezed Navy's shoulder a little tighter. She didn't pull away.

"I can't, Jackson."

"Okay, no guns."

The soft breath of the wind pushed against the trees. Leaves rattled on bare branches. The smaller trees creaked as they swayed, the upper branches scraping together like dry bones. Less than a mile away, the rush of people and their mundane lives moved along the highway. A cyclist called "On your left" to someone on the path. A child's eager footsteps clattered against the square beams of the footbridge. Jackson would seal up this little patch of forest if he could, make this place safe forever for Navy. But she was right. To protect her, he had to walk away.

She hopped off the log, barely wincing. Jackson's arm hung briefly in the space where she had been.

"The card I gave you is safe to use," he said. "I'll be in touch."

"Take care of yourself, Jackson."

Navy's red coat became smaller and smaller along the narrow path. Jackson kicked the log once with his heel, hard. The pain radiated up his ankle to his knee and back down to his toes. On the walk to the car, his anger kept him warm while he played his current role, a forgettable thirtysomething male out for a lunch-time walk in the park. Jackson smiled at a mother pushing a stroller holding a child bundled up against the cold. He stepped aside for two women as they crossed the bridge. The anger would pass. He would think of something. He would come back.

CHAPTER 29

BYRON JUMPED WHEN William slammed the report on Byron's desk. The edges of other papers cluttering his desk curled up then whispered flat.

"Your report on Navy is incomplete," William said.

William was close enough to kiss him.

"Incomplete!" William almost shouted. The chatter in the cubicles around them hushed. William lowered his voice and jabbed a manicured finger into the word "mugged" on Byron's report. "You said she was mugged."

"That's what it sounds like on the recording."

"There weren't any threats about keeping quiet? Like she knows something?"

"Her phone must have been in her backpack," Byron said. "You can't hear what the mugger is saying. Who told you someone threatened her?"

William turned white. "You better not be hiding things from me."

"Listen to it yourself if you don't believe me." Byron clicked on the file, wishing he could plug his ears. The recording started with a beep, the sound of a remote unlocking the door to Navy's car. Then her aborted yell and a loud thump, probably her backpack hitting the ground. The volume dropped off then. There were sounds of scuffling: Navy's higher-pitched grunts that he recognized from her practice sessions with Erin, and the lower pitched ones from Navy's attacker. He'd been in enough fights to imagine what was happening. She landed a few blows, but not enough. When she was overpowered, the sounds were reduced to the thick slap of leather boots against Navy's body. Then, a few muffled sounds in the deep timbre of a male voice. The words of Navy's attacker were unintelligible.

William's face was whiter than before. "You're right. There are no threats about keeping quiet. Why do they—" William must have realized he was thinking out loud in front of Byron and stopped midsentence with his mouth half-open. "Sorry to bother you."

Byron waited until William turned the corner before dropping the report in the shred pile. He tried to think about his daughter's high school graduation gift instead. Byron was deciding between music he didn't approve of or a gift card to a store he didn't approve of when the email icon jiggled.

Byron crossed his fingers, hoping it was not another reminder to turn off the coffee machine in the break room at the end of the day. Finally, a message from Jackson inviting him out to beers at the "usual place."

⁂

The "usual place" was code for a grimy neighborhood bar in DC that was dark even in the middle of the day. Most orders were taken at the bar and the limited food they offered was served with a frown. The only people at the bar around lunchtime were alcoholics draped over rickety wooden stools.

Byron walked toward the booths in back. From Byron's favorite corner booth, it was easy to keep an eye on the front door and the back door emergency exit that was usually propped open—despite the emergency exit only sign. The red vinyl seats were smudged and repaired with duct tape. He squeezed into the booth across from Erin.

"I ordered for us," she said.

"I've been trying to reach you for weeks," Byron said. "Where have you been?"

"Try the bat signal next time. I was on vacation."

"You don't take vacations."

"You're lucky I came at all," Erin said. "What's this all about? I thought this thing with Navy was settled."

Jackson slid into the booth next to Byron. "Very much unsettled."

"You should try sleeping," Erin said to Jackson. "I hear it's good for you."

The bartender walked over and set three almost-cold, less-than-full pints of beer on the table. "Fifteen bucks." The arm he held out had tattoos from his fingers up to the frayed sleeve of his T-shirt.

Jackson put a twenty on the face of the dragon in the bartender's palm. "No change," Jackson said. The bartender grumbled and walked away. "Byron, you called first. Fill us in."

"They put a bug on Navy," Byron said. "William has me monitoring it."

Erin's smirk slid off her face. "I thought William was convinced."

"He was," Byron said. "One of William's overlords requested the bug. I think they ordered a bug on someone else too, someone who's concerned about what Navy knows."

"That's a lot of unknowns," Erin said. "You've been trying to reach us for weeks and that's all you've managed to figure out?"

"I've tried. The only clues I have are two recordings that were filed under Navy's case by mistake."

Erin and Jackson looked at him blankly. Of course they

wouldn't know what he was talking about. They never had to work with these internal systems.

"Would it help if I made up some names for you?" Byron asked.

"Actually, yes," Erin said.

"In the first recording a man named Andy is talking to someone I haven't identified yet." He glanced at Erin. "We'll call him Mister. Andy tells Mister not to worry because there's a bug on Navy. Then Andy tells Mister that the CIA and 'one of our own' is watching it."

"So if Andy isn't with the CIA . . . then who?" said Erin.

"I don't know. I think he's a politician of some sort. In the other recording, Andy is talking to a third man, a soldier. Andy's nervous because 'a little bird' told him Navy knows something. So Andy tells the soldier to shadow Navy for a week, make note of everyone she talks to. Based on the date of the recording, the soldier would have completed his assignment the week before Navy was beaten up."

"She was beaten up?" Erin asked.

"Three days ago," Jackson said.

"You've seen Navy?" Erin and Byron asked in stereo.

"A little detour on the way home," Jackson said. "She has a twisted ankle and a few bruises." His face showed how worried he was, despite the casual words.

"I wish I knew more details." Byron stared at the phone numbers carved into the table. "I've been watching C-SPAN for two weeks, listening for anyone with a name close to Andy with the same voice. But the recording is low quality. And from what he said, he's a high-ranking aide of some sort. It's his boss that would be in the limelight."

"So our mysterious soldier goes down there, reports that Navy didn't talk to anyone and a week later she is attacked," Jackson said. "That doesn't make any sense."

"I don't think Andy ordered the attack," Byron said. "The way he talked, he wouldn't have settled for a few bruises if he thought Navy knew something."

What Byron left unsaid hung in the air between them. This wasn't the first time the three of them had worked together to save someone's life. But it was the first time they would have to conspire against their own agency. "I called you two because someone needs to warn Navy her cell phone is bugged. I can't get out of DC without looking suspicious."

"She already knows," Jackson said.

Erin raised her eyebrows. "Good thing she knows tech."

"In that case, I need help figuring out who's manipulating William," Byron said. "I've made some inquiries, but apparently I don't have the right friends."

"Someone is always manipulating William," Erin said.

"This is different," Byron said. "There's nothing in the recordings so far that says Navy knows the name Jackie Pierce or that the kidnappers thought she was a senator's niece. Or that Navy has tried to talk to anyone. But William keeps accusing me of hiding things. Today he comes by to tell me she was attacked by someone trying to keep her quiet, but there was nothing like that on the recording. The attack sounded like a mugging."

"Then Navy's right." Jackson said.

"What do you mean?" Byron asked.

"Someone sent her the file, or at least part of it." Jackson took a long swig of beer. "Probably the same people who sabotaged the operation so Navy was kidnapped in Amsterdam and organized the latest attack in Iowa."

"The saboteurs sent her the file and then attacked her for having it?" Erin asked.

"Navy said her attacker yelled when he told her to keep quiet or else. Even though he was close. She thinks the saboteurs wanted William to hear the threat on the recordings from the bug," Jackson said.

"It would explain why William was expecting to hear bad news this morning," Byron said. "Whoever sabotaged the operation wanted William to know that she has the file. How much does she have?"

"I didn't have time to see," Jackson said. "I offered to stay but Navy didn't seem interested. She didn't even want to tell me about the attack."

Byron would have to tread carefully with Jackson. Jackson clearly didn't know how much Navy cared about him.

"What *did* Navy tell you?" Erin asked.

"Navy knows the name of the operation. She knows that someone sent a message to the kidnappers directing them to pick up Navy and her friends. She knows that William, via Roy, sent the order to have them killed."

"This is an odd game." Erin spun the handle of her mug, leaving overlapping wet circles on the scarred table. "I thought everyone above William wanted things kept quiet."

"Navy thinks the saboteurs want to goad William into killing her. So the operation becomes public when the saboteurs can tie her death to the CIA. The saboteurs want Navy to be the leak."

Erin looked from Byron to Jackson and back. "There's no good play here. William was willing to have the kidnappers kill her in Amsterdam to keep this quiet."

Byron frowned. "And if Navy doesn't do what the saboteurs want, they'll keep pushing her until she does."

"We can buy her some time," Jackson said.

"How?" Byron asked.

"Spin your reports to give the saboteurs something to chew on.

Enough to make the saboteurs think she might go public but not so much that William's men will do anything right away."

"Buy her time for what?" Erin asked.

"I don't know." Jackson pushed his beer away and rubbed his eyes with the heels of his hands. "I need to go to my apartment and sleep for about three weeks. I'll think of something."

"Are you still in love with her?" Erin said.

Jackson scowled. "It's not about that."

"Isn't it?" she asked, serious now.

"She was picked out of a driver's license database because she looked like you and was traveling in a party of three. She doesn't deserve this."

"Yeah, it's not fair. What is?" Erin set her chin on her hands. "You need to be realistic."

Jackson's knuckles went white. "What are you saying?"

"I'm up for suicidal missions as much as the next soldier. I'm in. But you should be prepared. Navy isn't the first innocent person we've seen suffer."

"I won't back down on this."

"Even if it costs you your job?" Erin asked.

"Even then," Jackson said.

"You should have figured out by now why she doesn't want your help."

Byron wondered if it was wise to tell Jackson why Navy was being so stubborn. Knowing how Navy felt would only cloud Jackson's judgment more. "Erin, maybe you shouldn't—"

"Navy cares about you," Erin said. "She's trying to keep you out of it."

Relief, then regret flashed across Jackson's face. A sad country song crackled over the speakers. Byron watched one of the regulars stumble out the front door into the sunlight. The gray day seemed bright in comparison to the dingy interior of the bar. "Do you have a secure line to Navy?"

"I'm working on it," Jackson said. "Why?"

"Let her know I'm listening."

CHAPTER 30

NAVY FORCED HERSELF to take the detour from the garage to the mailboxes, even though she was impatient to get home to her apartment, where her projects waited. The flyer in her mailbox was addressed only to "Resident." A grainy black-and-white image of a butterfly took up most of the page. The text was grainy too—a copy of a copy of a copy: "Butterfly Mixed Martial Arts Studio". The famous Ali quote was underneath the name of the studio: *Float like a butterfly, sting like a bee.*

Navy had seen Jackson only two days ago. Was this what he meant by keeping in touch? The flyer could be from a friend of Jackson's. Or it could be from someone luring her to a place where she would be attacked again, this time at a place even more isolated. Everything was beginning to seem like a conspiracy.

The studio had classes in Shotokan karate, Tae Kwon Do, boxing, or self-defense. The first self-defense class was free. No guns, she'd told Jackson.

"All of the classes are full."

Navy looked up and recognized her neighbor from across the hall.

"I called the number yesterday," her neighbor said. "Popular place, I guess."

"Thanks," Navy said. She couldn't remember the woman's name. Navy wondered if the woman knew hers.

Navy dropped off her backpack and laptop bag in her apartment upstairs. She couldn't make the call from or near her bugged phone. She would have to go outside. She grabbed her extra phone—the one she'd bought to compare to hers—and a prepaid SIM card from a drawer. Only seven and already dark. Ever since her attack, being alone outside anywhere at night unnerved her. Navy walked a few yards away, but kept the building in sight. She circled slowly while she dialed the number on the flyer, to make sure no one was around.

"Butterfly Mixed Martial Arts Studio," said a gruff male voice.

"I was calling about your self-defense classes."

"Name?"

She hesitated. "Navy Trent."

"We have one spot left."

"Only one, huh?" Navy ran her tongue along the inside of her teeth.

"Tomorrow night. Seven sharp. Wear comfortable clothes."

"Someone told me the classes were full."

"A friend said I should save you a place. Said this would be a walk in the park for you."

So it was Jackson's doing. Unless someone else knew about her meeting with Jackson. At some point, she had to stop looking for conspiracies. More training in self-defense couldn't hurt. If nothing else, it was therapy. "I'll be there."

⁘

Butterfly Mixed Martial Arts Studio was a one-story brick building twenty minutes from Navy's apartment. The neighborhood around the studio was mostly industrial, lit in patches by street lamps. Hulking machinery rested behind tall chain-link fences. A backhoe loader curled up to rest, its scoop sitting on the ground. A excavator with a graceful neck and its jaws stopped mid-chew.

Navy had left her phone at her apartment with the TV on. She wasn't sure which would be more suspicious, carrying it with her to a martial arts studio or leaving it at her apartment all night. One of a million questions she would have asked Jackson if he could have stayed.

The entrance was marked with a plastic sign the size of a sheet of paper. The glossy surface made it almost illegible under the bright light mounted just above the door.

Navy tested the knob. The door opened. The studio was only marginally warmer than outside. The lobby was a small rectangle of carpet with a few mismatched chairs pushed against the concrete block walls.

Beyond the entryway was an area almost as big as a basketball court. Mats lined the floor. Metal shelves lined the walls. There were square pads with straps on the back, boxing gloves, teardrop-shaped punching bags, yoga mats, hand weights in all different sizes. In one corner, a bucket held long wooden sticks nearly her height. Just behind the mats was a row of offices. All but one was dark. A man with a pockmarked face and a crooked nose walked out of the lit office. She noticed the scars on his arms and hands as he came closer.

He reached out a hand to introduce himself. "Mark Spademan."

"Navy Trent." His grip was strong. If she had made the wrong choice in coming here, it didn't matter now. Navy would lose any fight with this man. "Is anyone else coming?"

"Just you. Unless you brought a friend?" He held up his cell phone.

"No, just me."

"Let's get started. Shoes off, please."

Navy didn't move.

"The training doesn't make you look like me, if that's what you're worried about," Mark said, a gruff joke.

"I'm a little overwhelmed, that's all."

"That's why we're starting with meditation."

"Meditation? Like New Age stuff? How is that self-defense?"

"Jackson said you weren't sleeping well," Mark said. "This will help."

"But I didn't tell—"

"Jackson does that."

Navy wasn't sleeping well, that was true. But she also wasn't sleeping enough. She had to work as usual. To keep her friends and family from worrying, she had to attend a few social events to keep up appearances. In the little time left over Navy had been sneaking away to coffee shops where she could research what she found in the documents. And she was still trying to decompile the firmware on her phone. It was slow going, but if she could get their code it might give her some clues. When Navy finally went to bed, wondering when the next attack would come kept her awake.

Mark dimmed the lights. He pulled a purple yoga mat from one of the shelves and tossed it to Navy. She hadn't panicked when she found the bug in her phone. She hadn't panicked when she was beaten in the parking lot. Now, in a place where Navy was safe, where she could almost feel Jackson's presence, she felt as if the world were about to crumble.

Fingers snapped loudly in front of her nose. When her eyes began to focus again, Navy saw a thumb with five short, dark hairs below the knuckle. "This will help," Mark said. "I promise."

"If you say so." Navy unrolled the mat. The bruises on her calves hurt when she sat down and crossed her legs, like she'd seen in photos in magazines.

"Beginners start by lying down," Mark said.

She reluctantly stretched out on her mat, trying to watch the door out of the corner of her eye. Mark went over to the entrance with fast, quiet strides. He clicked the heavy deadbolt shut.

"Better?" Mark asked when he was back by her side.

Navy nodded, tears pricking at her eyes.

"We're going to start with some breathing exercises. Close your eyes. Put your hand on your stomach. Fill your belly, then your chest. Breathe in until it almost hurts."

Navy's mom would be tickled to know the advice she had given Navy twenty years ago was being repeated in a clandestine self-defense class.

"Focus," he said firmly. "When you breathe out, empty your chest first and then push that hand down until it feels like there's nothing left."

As Navy repeated the exercise, her breaths grew longer and deeper. They began to feel like a tide washing up into her chest, the waves curling around her diaphragm. Navy's shoulder blades started to melt into the floor, the distance between the curve of her spine and the mat grew smaller. Her eyes stopped darting beneath her eyelids.

"Try to breathe in for six counts and out for seven."

Navy had adjusted to the tension in her muscles; for weeks she hadn't even felt it. Now she could feel a spring in every part of every limb uncoiling, releasing. Breathe in for one-two-three-four-five-six, out for one-two-three-four-five-six-seven.

"Wiggle your toes just a little bit. Do you feel that slight tingling sensation? Carry that up to your ankles, let your feet relax and turn out."

Navy's ankles, which she hadn't purposely been holding, relaxed and the outer edges of her feet touched the mat. Her body responded to each of his cues in turn, from her ankles up to her calves to her stomach to her chest to her arms. A tingling feeling spread over Navy's whole body, relaxing her neck and shoulders.

It wasn't the frantic energy that had kept her going the past few weeks. This energy was as calm as the surface of a lake on a windless day.

Mark was still while she continued to breathe long and deep. Navy couldn't say how long he let her rest—it could have been hours or minutes. She was simultaneously focused on everything inside her and everything outside of her. The cold in the gym, Navy's own fear, the mysteries she hadn't yet solved, the sound of Mark's breathing, the clattering of the duct system, the dull ache of her bruises. The distractions were all there, but somehow they were distant and bearable.

"Anytime you need to, you can return to this feeling you have now," Mark said. "It is yours. You carry it with you wherever you go."

Navy found herself smiling, the corners of her mouth turning up ever so slightly.

"Slowly roll to one side."

She didn't want to leave the peace she'd found. Reluctantly, Navy obeyed.

"Flutter your eyes open and sit up slowly."

Her focus made the room sharper and brighter. She saw how the metal posts on the shelves glimmered, even in the dim light. She saw the dust that moved slowly as the heat kicked on and felt the air moving against her skin. "That's . . . amazing."

"If you want to be able to defend yourself, you need to understand that fighting is not physical. It's mental. Your concentration is what carries you through."

"Do you meditate?" Navy asked.

"Every day. You should too."

"Anything for a good night's sleep."

"We'll do more meditation later. Second lesson about self-defense: Fighting is not about overpowering your opponent."

"Because I'm a woman."

Mark shrugged. "Being stronger isn't always an advantage in a fight. It can be a weakness."

"I don't understand."

"Jackson said you're into rock climbing."

"What does that have to do with fighting?"

"People with strong arms have bad technique because they cheat—they don't learn to climb with their leg muscles until they find a route they can't power through. Fighting is about good technique and focus. You can win if you don't panic or give up. Nothing more, nothing less."

"What about when you lose?"

"Sometimes you lose."

"That's it? Sometimes you lose. No Zen tricks? No guarantees?"

"You learn to not be afraid of losing."

"Even if it means being dead?"

Mark nodded. "I only pick fights that are worth losing."

Navy felt the burlap bag over her face for a second before she pushed the memory away. "What if a fight picks you?"

"You're here, aren't you? You already know the answer to that."

"How much has Jackson told you?"

"A big guy overpowered you in a parking lot. He'd like the story to end differently next time."

Navy pulled her legs into her chest, trying to hang on to the calm she had found a few minutes ago.

"Anything else you want to tell me about what happened?"

Navy shook her head. "Do we get to hit things now?"

Mark laughed. "Yes. But before that, Jackson has a message for you. He said to tell you, 'The good host is listening.'"

Byron was monitoring her bug. Jackson must have talked with Byron in DC. Byron might be able to spin the reports to keep her from getting attacked again, at least for a little while.

She wondered if Byron was the only one listening. Was Jackson trying to tell her she should help by giving Byron material to work with? Or just letting Navy know she had another way she could contact them? She must have looked at Mark with the question in her eyes because he just shook his head.

"If Jackson wanted me to understand the message he wouldn't have put it in code," Mark said. "But maybe you wouldn't tell me anything anyway."

"No. I wouldn't." Navy couldn't keep many secrets from Jackson; she had tried. But she wouldn't drag anyone else in.

"Jackson didn't say how long we would have. I'm planning on doing your lessons boot camp–style."

"I won't shave my head."

"A sense of humor helps," Mark said. "Every weeknight. Lessons start at six and end at nine. Buy a big bottle of ibuprofen—not aspirin—on your way home. You're going to need it. Also, don't plan on wearing short sleeves at work."

Navy was too exhausted to work on her projects when she got home. She might have one day, one week or six weeks before the next attack. She didn't know and it didn't matter. What she needed right now was rest. For the first time in weeks, when Navy's head hit the pillow she fell into a deep, dreamless sleep.

⁓

Jackson waited until exactly 10:01 p.m. EST, 9:01 p.m. CST, to dial the number at Mark's gym. Navy would have just left.

Mark answered with a grunt. "Been waiting by the phone?" he asked.

"How is she?" Jackson asked.

"Bruised and scared and recovering."

Jackson nodded, pushing crumbs from his sandwich around the counter.

"I assume you called for a reason," Mark said. He finished the sentence with a yawn.

"I need to track down whoever ordered her attack," Jackson said. "What did she tell you?"

"Less than you told me."

Jackson sighed. Without Navy's cooperation, finding her attacker would be difficult.

"Not that she'd tell me if she did, but I don't think she knows any more," Mark said.

"I need another favor. But you'll have to be quiet about it."

"Ask away."

"The person who attacked her must have followed her to pick out when she'd be vulnerable. He knew the cameras on the office building didn't cover the whole parking lot. But he might have appeared on surveillance video somewhere along the way."

"I suppose I could dig out an old uniform and lie my way into a few offices," Mark said. "Who should I be looking for?"

"I'll send you some pictures in a few days."

"You have a list of usual suspects already?"

"I can get a list of people in the area who do that sort of work for the agency and find out who was on assignment the night Navy was attacked," Jackson said.

Mark's sharp intake of breath hissed on the line. "So it's like that."

"Yeah, it's like that." Jackson unclenched his jaw. "But if word gets back here about what you're doing—"

"I'll keep an eye on her, Jackson," Mark promised.

Jackson didn't feel much better after he hung up the phone. It was Amsterdam all over again. What little help he could offer was likely to be too little too late. Except this time it wasn't just a civilian's life at risk. It was the life of a woman whom, under difference circumstances, he might have dared to love.

CHAPTER 31

THE CLOCK SAID 10:13 a.m. when Navy finally pushed herself out of bed. Her alarm must have gone off at seven, as usual, but it wasn't even buzzing now. Navy lay down on the bed again and stretched until the tips of her fingers pressed against the wall. Every inch of her ached, and Navy was happy for it. She wondered if it was the meditation or her exhausted muscles that allowed her to sleep.

After a quick shower, Navy emailed work to say she wasn't feeling well. Should she carry her bugged phone with her while she did her research at yet another coffee shop? Her watchers would probably see the email. She settled on leaving the phone in the kitchen. The hum of the fridge would easily identify the location. Hopefully, her watchers would assume she was sleeping in the bedroom recovering from her "illness."

Navy turned on her laptop in the bedroom and started the program she used to simulate her network activity at home. The program randomly chose from a list of innocuous sites and connected to them, clicking around in the articles for good measure. She had designed the program to vary the time spent on each article, as if some articles held her attention more than others.

Because Navy was supposed to be sick, she set the program to turn itself off after one hour.

She crept around her apartment to gather what she needed—keys, coat, the forensics laptop—and shut the door very slowly behind her.

Navy was careful to randomize the coffee shops she visited. She never visited the same place twice in a row. And never the same day at the same time. Her precautions left her with a blizzard of details to remember, but reduced the chance of someone recognizing her.

Today she chose the Victoria, named for the Victorian mansion it occupied. The wood floor showed rough scars where walls had been removed. The windows were dingy and the light meager. It felt like a cave, and fit her mood perfectly.

Navy ordered an Italian soda and took a table in the corner, where she could see the front door. She liked corner tables the best. The privacy kept people from looking over her shoulder at her screen.

Coffee shops required different precautions than at home. Before turning on her Wi-Fi, Navy generated a random MAC address and configured the Wi-Fi connection with that address. A MAC address was as close to a unique identifier as there was for any machine. The laptop could be traced from place to place if Navy didn't disguise it.

To hide her activity, she used a virtual private network and Tor. The VPN hid the fact she was using Tor from anyone who might be monitoring the Wi-Fi at the coffee shop. Tor was a protocol that would mix her traffic with a bunch of other people's traffic, bouncing Navy's web requests privately among a bunch of IP addresses. Even if her watchers did manage to figure out which MAC address she was using, and the coffee shop kept records good enough to tie that address to an IP address, using

Tor would make it difficult to determine what sites Navy had visited. Nothing was completely anonymous, of course. Tor was software, and software always had flaws. Sometimes Navy felt like she was doing the same thing she'd done in Amsterdam: playing a game to keep her mind busy so she could stay calm.

Navy turned her attention to the one mystery that all her questions seemed to hinge on—the order to kill the hostages.

Was the kill order a complete fabrication? Not likely. Jackson hadn't contradicted her when she had mentioned it. Jackson must have already known. And the metadata on all the images matched. All of the images had been created by a Canon scanner. In sequence.

Of course, images were just files that could be modified. But the only documents that showed signs of alteration were the documents that identified the kidnap victims.

Metadata and file modification times. That was all she had. And even those could be changed. But the saboteurs hadn't bothered to match the file creation times with the last modified times. They weren't expecting Navy to look that closely.

She felt her calm slipping away in the face of all her questions. She reminded herself that analyzing incidents was what she did at work every day. The stakes were higher this time, but the method was the same. Make up scenarios. See if the data fits.

Scenario: the kill order had been created after she had been kidnapped instead of Erin. There were many documents that fell into this category. Jackson's notes on his hurried, hamstrung investigation. The travel plans for Byron and Erin from DC to Amsterdam. Erin's assignment to bunk with Navy to find out what Navy knew.

Maybe the answer wasn't in the documents themselves. Maybe she had to read between the lines. On paper, the goal of the mission was to track down a known kidnapping ring and sleeper cell operating out of Amsterdam. The operation had been identified as "sensitive and difficult" in the planning stages. But of the three agents assigned to pose as kidnap victims, only Erin was experienced. The only thing Erin had in common with the other agents, Navy noticed, was that all three had no next of kin listed. Erin's parents had died when she was young, and she grew up in a series of foster homes. Some had been good to her; some had not. Navy had never imagined Erin as a victim. All of Erin's hard edges had been earned.

Of course, Erin wouldn't appreciate Navy's sympathy. Erin would tell Navy to stop feeling and start thinking. Maybe there was a clue in the false identities the agents had been given. But Navy had been over and over the files detailing the cover stories for Jackie Pierce, Ron Tucker, and Ted Swisher. The photos of their vacation to Montgomery could have been the photos from any twenty-something's vacation: bars and monuments and hanging out by the pool. The biographies were also unremarkable.

Navy googled the three aliases. Nothing interesting. Had the covers extended to Facebook and Twitter? She went to Google's real-time search.

Jackie Pierce had a Twitter account. And a Facebook page. Ron Tucker had a Facebook page and a blog. Ted Swisher had a Flickr stream. The profile photos were cartoon images, avatars. The photos on their public pages were high resolution but, again, unremarkable. A brick house with a well-tended lawn with the number of the house blocked by a tree trunk. A nondescript car with the plates cropped out of the frame. A picture of the capitol building in Montgomery in an album called "Trip to Capitol." Generic photos with no people in them. Navy did a quick comparison to confirm her theory. Sure enough, the photos were exact matches for images posted in Wikimedia. Untraceable images used to build fake profiles. *Why?*

The tweets and blog postings went back several months before the trip, but the electronic trails started on the same week. Curiouser and curiouser, she thought. There was a story in the tweets. Ron and Jackie were dating, hinting at being engaged. Ted was thinking of starting his own business. A great all-American story of three grad school students just about to start their lives. Navy's stomach growled and she pushed away her hunger.

Agents in the field wouldn't want to have photos posted online. That would explain why the images in Navy's files weren't posted. But it didn't explain why those images were created in the first place.

Navy risked opening the encrypted copy of the thumb drive she had hidden with steganography on her hard drive. And noticed something she hadn't noticed before. The shadows on Erin's face didn't quite match the direction of the sun. The line at her neck on several of the pictures was subtly adjusted to match a change in skin tone. Navy used an image error analysis program to confirm her suspicions. Erin had never posed for these photos. Her face had been added to someone else's vacation photos. Navy wondered if Erin even knew the photos existed.

The whole operation seemed Frankenstein-like: bits and pieces of incompatible parts pasted together to form a lumbering whole. Google's cache and the Wayback Machine showed even more social media trails. Trails that had been deleted from their public postings elsewhere. Someone was cleaning up. Navy saved what she had found while she waited for her thoughts to fully form.

Why lay such an elaborate trail for identities that would only be used for one mission? Why create a bunch of photos for a fake vacation?

Jackson would know the answers to these questions. Or at least Jackson could have told Navy if this was normal.

Don't call him. It would be suicide for both of you. Think.

Navy knew the photos had never been sent to the kidnappers. If the kidnappers had seen these pictures, they never would have believed Sara and Moss were among the targets. So the pictures weren't meant to be used before the kidnapping. After the kidnapping then? Why? Publishing the photos would have risked blowing the agents' covers for any future operations.

Think.

For a rescue operation then? A story to garner sympathy in case the CIA needed outside help retrieving their agents. No. Surely the CIA had arrangements with the military to help with covert operations. And the history laid down for Jackie Pierce read more like fodder for a news story.

Navy remembered another incongruity in the files. Mixed in with the planning details and the investigation were repeated references to how existing limits on surveillance complicated tracking the kidnappers from Afghanistan to Amsterdam.

The president had been traveling widely to speak in support of two bills he was trying to get though Congress: a funding bill to support the war in Afghanistan, and a bill requesting sweeping new surveillance powers for national security.

If three Americans were *killed* while on vacation it would be news for months. It would bolster support for a war that was rapidly becoming unpopular. There would be demands for retribution. The perfect opportunity to highlight the president's surveillance initiatives.

The facts kept leading Navy to one unbelievable conclusion. The death of three American agents had been arranged for political capital by their own government. Her own government.

If the kill order had remained a secret and the operation hadn't been sabotaged, those in the know would think a risky operation had gone south. To those outside the intelligence community, it would look like three Americans had died in a terrorist attack.

This was the secret William's men were trying to protect. That the United States government had intended to kill three of their own agents for propaganda. Had William known what kind of operation he was managing? It seemed too calculating, even for him. William's men: men working for William or manipulating William?

None of that explained the motives of the saboteurs, though. What was the advantage to the saboteurs if Navy had died instead of Erin?

Navy drank the rest of her Italian soda, now warm.

The answer was close, just under her consciousness. Go back to the one thing you know about the saboteurs, Navy thought. The saboteurs wanted Navy to tell a story. They wanted her to tell the world that she had been accidentally caught up in the operation, and that the government had chosen execution over rescue. *Disposal requested.*

It was the sort of news story that would demand the sacrificial offering of high-ranking employees. As high up as blame could go. The first document on the thumb drive was the mission authorization signed by President Orway. The saboteurs wanted to dethrone the president. They knew if Navy were kidnapped in Erin's place, William's men would have Navy executed, rather than risk exposing the operation. With Navy, Sara, and Moss dead, all the saboteurs had to do was make sure the kill order was leaked.

If you want a lie to be convincing, make it the truth.

The saboteurs didn't want her to figure out any of this. They wanted her to play a role: a hysterical American citizen shocked to find out her government had arranged for her death to cover up a botched CIA operation.

Navy closed her laptop and carried it to the counter. She was so hungry she felt nauseous. The plastic-wrapped sandwiches oozing limp lettuce did nothing for her appetite. She bought one anyway and forced down the dry bread and stale lunchmeat. Did politicians really trade in lives so carelessly? The death of three citizens to embarrass a president. The assassination of three agents to curry political favor for a policy change. Had the president really known, Navy wondered. It was a question she couldn't answer. No matter how long she stared at her computer.

The barista was watching her. Navy looked at the time. Of course the barista was watching her. She had been at the coffee shop for five hours. If Navy didn't leave now, she wouldn't have time to change and swallow dinner before her lesson at Butterfly Studio.

At home, Navy changed into clothes that still smelled of yesterday's sweat and made herself a peanut butter sandwich for the car ride. She turned the television on, and started the program on her laptop so it would look like she was at home browsing the *New York Times*. Then Navy left, her muscles already wishing for the sweet, numb release of exhaustion.

❦

Navy emailed work the next morning to say she still had a fever.

The coffee shop she chose had décor that was more modern than comfortable: gleaming metal tables and hard, black plastic chairs. The barista matched; he was dressed in a dark T-shirt and had ears ringed with silver piercings. Behind him, tall bottles of flavorings lined blue-lit shelves. He finished her mocha with precise swirls of caramel and a wink.

Navy chose a corner with a table small enough that no one would try to share it when things got busier. For once, she didn't pull out her laptop. She needed to think.

Should she disappear? Could she? No, the saboteurs would simply target Sara or Moss. They had been through enough.

Navy's healing bruises reminded her that she couldn't stay silent. The saboteurs would continue to push her to do something to catch the attention of William's men.

Navy couldn't simply go to a reporter with her story. That would be as good as suicide. A good reporter would take the time to verify facts, especially on something as explosive as this. Navy couldn't risk the story leaking before she was safe. She wanted desperately to talk to someone about everything she had found, but anyone she told would be at risk. Even Jackson.

If only Navy could tell the whole world at once. Let the crowd sort out if the president had authorized the assassination of three American agents. If everyone knew, there'd be no point in killing her. Yes, that just might work. Release the most important documents to the whole world. Navy could make herself more dangerous to Operation Critical Mass dead than alive.

Some things were better left secret. The identities of the undercover agents. Sara and Moss' involvement. A plan formed in her head.

Not just a plan. A machine. A conspiracy of one. An unstoppable chain reaction—even if every router in the United States were turned off. Even if they did get to Navy before she reached safety.

Two nights of deep rest had restored her. She pulled out her notebook. Navy's mind was clear. The details of her plan took form. Two trips to the capitol. A false trail to give her time to escape. A virus to reveal her secrets. A place to hide until the fallout cleared.

A finger of fear crept into Navy's heart. The deep bass beat thumping from the speakers rattled her ribs against her heart. Was the man with brown hair and square glasses at the counter sent to watch her? Had she given herself away already? Someone else might be at her apartment right now, going through her computer. In last night's meditation, Mark had said fear would come. He told her there was no sense in denying it. "Accept its presence," Mark said. "And let it strengthen your resolve." Breathe in for six counts, Navy reminded herself, and out for seven.

In for six counts and out for seven. And again. And again. When Navy came back to herself, the same song with the deep bass beat and a throaty female voice was playing. The man with brown hair was walking out the door, coffee in hand.

Navy filled more pages with doodles and words. Every device or programming idea she had ever read or dreamed about or seen in a magazine. She listed everything she would reveal. By lunchtime, her fingers were cramped, but a sketch had formed on the page. The beginnings of the machine she needed. She held the notebook against her chest as she walked to the counter to order whatever they served for food. The beef soup smelled heavenly. The edges of the room were sharp and the red, silver, and black décor more intense. As if Navy had just finished meditating.

"A fellow artist?" asked the cashier as he ladled bits of vegetable and beef into a ceramic bowl.

Navy looked at him, confused.

"Are you an artist? I saw you sketching all morning. I do metal sculpture—"

"Doodles," Navy said. Six months ago she would have smiled at this man. A little pleasant banter, perhaps even an exchange of phone numbers and a first date. "Nothing serious."

"Oh." He pushed the soup across the counter. Greasy liquid sloshed onto the plastic-wrapped squares of crackers. "Okay."

Another coffee shop Navy couldn't return to.

In between spoonfuls of soup, Navy translated her doodles into a list of materials with a timeline. Some details came clearly.

Some she left unsettled. It would take at least a few weeks to finish the plan and build all the components. Navy wasn't sure how many weeks the saboteurs would wait before they pushed her again. She couldn't afford to rush things; the delay was a risk she'd have to take. *Sometimes you lose.* She was beginning to understand what Mark meant, what Erin had been trying to tell her in Amsterdam. If the best she could do wasn't good enough, it didn't matter. Navy would fight anyway.

An alarm on her phone beeped. It was four in the afternoon already. Time to go home and prepare for training. Navy was already craving the stubborn resistance of the heavy bag.

❧

Erin was surprised to see Zack Harris through the peephole of her apartment door. With sprigs of baby's breath and a dozen roses in an opaque vase. True, they had been friends with benefits for many years. Well, more like colleagues with benefits, but he didn't normally bring roses. Zack knocked again and looked up and down the hall. Then, for a split second, down at his waist.

My, what a big belt buckle you have, Erin thought. Also out of character for Zack. She guessed Zack had a knife hidden at his waist. This was business, not pleasure. Erin let him in.

"Zack, good to see you. And you brought roses."

Was it guilt she saw in his expression? "Yes. I hope you like them," Zack said.

Erin was a little insulted that he thought roses would distract her from the fact he had come prepared to kill her. "They're lovely. I'll put fresh water in the vase."

"Allow me—"

"Don't be silly," Erin said. "Please, sit." It took two firm pulls before Zack gave the roses up. Looking down into the vase, she saw something metallic glinting among the stems in the bouquet.

Erin pretended not to notice the gun. "Do you want coffee? I just made a pot."

"Sure." He sat down at the very edge of the couch, where he could just peek into the kitchen.

Erin changed the water, then set the vase on the table by the entrance. Far enough away from the couch that Erin could reach Zack before he reached the gun. There was no graceful way to disable the gun while he was watching.

Erin returned to the kitchen. She had other weapons. Like her favorite sugar bowl. Half of the circle was painted in overlapping blue doves, and the other half in intricate, brown tree roots. With her back to her guest, she sprinkled a white powder over the sugar on the blue half of the bowl. She brought out a tray with two cups of coffee and the sugar.

"I wasn't expecting you," Erin said. "I thought you were out on assignment for another month."

"Oh, you know how it goes. They changed their mind and called me back." Zack rested his hand near his belt buckle, within easy striking distance of his knife.

"For another assignment?" Erin asked.

The shift of Zack's eyes was subtle but unmistakable. "No, I have a couple weeks off. I heard what happened in Amsterdam. Another William fuck-up."

Erin wondered how much ignorance she could claim. Navy's secrets were safe with Byron and Jackson. But after Roy came home he might have talked about their little conversation. Roy had probably talked. "That's not what Roy said."

"Roy said you called that tourist, Navy something, a friend."

Erin shrugged. "I was adding motivation to my character." Zack wouldn't be much harder to deal with than Roy. If Erin was careful.

"Kyle nearly had Roy thrown out of the agency when he

heard about everything Roy told you. Any guesses on why Kyle had the tourists kidnapped instead?"

So that's what Zack's visit was about. Not what Navy knew. What Erin knew. Erin hoped for the sake of her upholstery she could guess the right answer. Knife fights were always messy. "Make William look bad, I guess. Not that William needs much help."

Zack moved his hand away from his waist and laughed. "True."

Erin glanced at the clock. "Sugar?" Zack always took sugar.

"Please."

Erin added a spoonful from the brown half of the bowl for her and the blue half of the bowl for his.

Zack sipped his coffee and leaned closer. "So, uh, the usual then? I promise I'll be gone by midnight." Erin accepted his kiss and counted the seconds. When she reached sixty, his head became unsteady. Erin rested it gently back on the couch. The drug would give her five minutes at most before Zack passed out completely. The last thing he would remember was Erin offering him sugar.

Erin stroked her fingers through his hair and spoke in a soft voice. "Kyle sent you here, didn't he?"

Zack giggled. "Kyle. Yes."

"To kill me?"

"Only if you—" Zack giggled again. "If you knew."

Shit. Erin had given him too much of the drug. "If I knew what?" she asked.

"Gun in the roses." Zack closed his eyes and laughed so loud Erin had to cover his mouth. "I put a gun in the roses." And then he passed out.

Erin needed more information. She called Jackson. By the time Jackson arrived, the coffee tray had been replaced by a half-full bottle of tequila and two shot glasses. Zack was naked.

"Jesus, Erin. You couldn't cover him up? I might have to work with him someday."

Erin smiled at Jackson. "This way he'll think he had fun. Help me carry him to the bedroom."

Jackson took Zack's shoulders and kept his eyes on Erin.

"You want to tell me what's going on?" Jackson said, when they returned to the living room.

"Kyle sent Zack here to find out if I knew why Kyle sabotaged Operation Critical Mass."

"I wish we knew," Jackson said. "What's with the roses?"

Erin dug the wet gun out. "Sloppy tradecraft."

"He was going to kill you?"

"I told Zack I thought the sabotage was just to embarrass William. Then Zack changed his mind."

"Did Zack say anything useful before he passed out?"

"No. Have you managed to find out who paid to have Navy attacked?"

"No." Jackson rubbed at his eyes. "I have to talk to Navy again. Get her to tell us what she knows."

"Maybe I should talk to her instead," Erin said.

"Why?"

Because Navy is protecting you, Erin thought. "Fine. Do it your way. Let me know what you find out."

CHAPTER 32

BACKPACKS OF ALL sizes lined the wall in front of Navy like deflated balloons. She rubbed the nylon strap of a waistband on a green and blue pack, wishing she were preparing for her next camping adventure. Instead, she was purchasing a week's worth of dehydrated meals using her credit card, to start laying a trail for her trackers. When she disappeared and they started to scrutinize her credit card bills for clues, Navy hoped they would guess she had run away to the backcountry.

The beef stew rattled like croutons as she threw it into the cart. She tried not to wince when she heard the total at the register.

"Looks like it'll be a fun trip," the clerk said.

"No doubt." Navy forced a smile.

At Goodwill she chose a metal lunchbox with a picture of Wonder Woman heroically flying, fist clenched and arm outstretched. The costume aisle only had unrealistic wigs and clown makeup. Just the lunchbox today then. She paid cash.

Sparks was crowded on a Saturday afternoon. Geeks were rummaging through the bins to find that day's specials and consumers with confused expressions were being lectured by awkward salespeople. Sparks was more of a technician's supply store than a friendly neighborhood electronics store. Navy was glad to see everything she needed was in the pile of open box items. These items had to be purchased with cash, which meant she was on a budget. Drastically changing the amount of cash she took from her checking account might have attracted suspicion. She had withdrawn a little bit more than usual and had to make it stretch.

The FreeAgent Dockstar was on sale, luckily. The Dockstar would allow her to share files from a thumb drive wirelessly. A plastic bin buried in the back of a shelf in the clearance section had cheap USB drives she could buy by the handful. The drives were shaped like cartoon characters from a show she had never seen. No wonder they had ended up on overstock. The wireless router was the most expensive item. Navy pressed the wad of twenty-dollar bills in her pocket, hoping it would be enough.

The back seat of her car was crowded with her purchases by the time she was done. There wouldn't be much time for her projects tonight, however. Jarrod, Sara, and Moss had threatened to storm her apartment if she didn't come out to the bar with them. They said, again, that she was becoming a hermit.

Navy was. Her programming project had turned her into a shut-in. It was the linchpin of her plan: a mechanism that would be invisible until it revealed a few carefully chosen documents at a carefully chosen date and time. For the past two weeks when she wasn't eating, sleeping, working, or training, she had been hunched over her desk at home, swearing at code.

A piece of paper crunched under her feet when she stepped into her apartment. She hesitated before picking it up, wondering which "friend" had sent it. There had been no attacks since Jackson had visited her. No one following her that she had noticed. Whatever Byron was doing in Washington to keep the heat off appeared to be working. Navy picked up the creased piece of paper now marked with the dirty imprint of her shoe.

"Our mutual friend wants you to call." The word call was

underlined twice. Mark had told her every day at training that week to call Jackson and she kept putting it off. She couldn't lie to Jackson and she couldn't tell him the truth. She didn't want to know what kind of sacrifices he was willing to make. This was her fight, even though she hadn't chosen it. The last time they had met, she had thought the saboteurs were just trying to embarrass the CIA and that William's men were just trying to cover up a botched operation. Now she knew differently. The saboteurs were trying to embarrass the president and William's men were trying to hide a disinformation campaign targeting the United States populace. William might even have been taking orders from the White House.

Navy took the bugged phone to the bedroom and left it there, shutting the door behind her. In the kitchen, she took a new pre-paid cell phone out of its package. The keypad waited expectantly. She didn't need to see the card with Jackson's number on it. She dialed the first number and then the second. After the fifth number she held down her thumb on the delete button until the number had erased itself, the cursor blinking in annoyance. If she called Jackson, her will would break at the first syllable of his voice.

She burned the note from Mark and threw the ashes on top of the remains of last night's dinner: canned corn and canned green beans. She turned on her forensics laptop and opened up a terminal window.

Navy typed "make_reveal Song.mp3 +2min." That command instructed her program to create an mp3 file that would reveal the documents two minutes after the song had finished download-ing. She imported the song into iTunes and waited. Two minutes later a window popped up, showing a list of documents with small thumbnails as previews. Another small victory. The pro-gram would only matter if everything else worked.

A glance at her phone told her she had to hurry to make her

obligatory social plans for the evening. She installed DD-WRT on the new router she had purchased. The install went quickly, but not quickly enough. She still had to create the rest of the trojaned media files. And double-check the files revealed by the virus. And that was just the beginning of the list. But her friends would leave concerned messages on her voicemail if she didn't show up soon. Messages that her watchers would be able to hear. She turned off the laptop and left her half-finished project on the table.

CHAPTER 33

NAVY HAD NEVER seen a blue sedan in the gym parking lot before. Mark drove a truck. She knew because it was always the only other vehicle in the parking lot when she arrived. She got out of her car anyway. She wasn't afraid of dark parking lots anymore. She wasn't afraid of the stairwell at work. She knew she couldn't win every fight. She knew she was still in danger. But failure was a possibility she had accepted.

She took a deep breath of the early spring air. Beneath the car exhaust was the promising scent of thawing earth. In a few weeks green stalks would poke their way out of soft ground—wet with melting snow and ice. She would be on the run.

She opened the studio door and called out Mark's name. For a moment she thought the figure was a trick of the light as her eyes adjusted.

"Jackson."

"You didn't call," he said.

She couldn't tell if he was angry, hurt, or just annoyed. His face was flushed and his hair was tousled. The mats were wrinkled in places where bodies had fallen. He had been sparring with Mark.

"Didn't you get my note?" asked Mark.

She could have thought of a million excuses if Jackson weren't standing in front of her. "Yes, I saw it." She tried not to squirm under his studied gaze.

She took off her shoes and put them on the mat by the door. Her coat and gloves she threw on a chair. She was wearing her usual training outfit: black cotton pants that hugged her waist and were wide at the ankles and a tight T-shirt. With Mark, she never cared. Around Jackson, the outfit left her feeling naked.

"I'm ready to train," she told Mark. Jackson walked off the mats, crossed his arms, and leaned against the wall.

"Right hook," Mark said. He swung fast at her left cheek. Her nervousness faded as she focused. She raised a bent left arm in an arc from her waist to just above her head to deflect the punch as she stepped back, then countered with a jab to the stomach. Her fist stopped just short of Mark's abdomen.

"Left uppercut."

She swept the punch aside, leaving Mark open, and stepped forward to aim the point of her elbow at Mark's throat. Mark combined attacks, then stopped naming them entirely, challenging her to read the attacks in the movements of his eyes.

"Very good," Jackson said. He seemed genuinely impressed, but worry still creased his forehead. "Mark, I think that's all for training tonight. Navy and I need to talk."

Navy grabbed Mark's arm to keep him from leaving. "I'd rather train." She had promised herself that she wouldn't tell Jackson anything that might endanger him. An easy promise to make when she was alone in her apartment.

Jackson's eyes flicked to Mark, then back to Navy. "I need you to tell me everything. Now. My flight back is in three hours."

"I need a new sparring partner."

"What?"

"First person to get the air knocked out of them loses. You win, I tell you everything. I win, I tell you nothing."

He ran a hand through his hair. "You've been training for three weeks. I've been training for years. This isn't a fair fight."

"Five weeks, counting Amsterdam. And that's exactly the point."

Jackson shook his head, perplexed.

"This way, neither of us will hold back," Navy said.

"Navy." Every spark in his eyes matched hers.

"Take it or leave it."

"Fine."

She wondered if she'd made this deal because she wanted to lose this fight. Because she wanted proof he really wanted to know.

"I think you two need some gloves," Mark said. "And headgear."

Jackson threw the first punch, a left hook that came too close. They circled the mat warily, the plastic crackling under their bare feet. Navy stepped forward to attack. In a wink, Jackson had her in a headlock. She broke free, rolled on the ground, and came back to face him. Jackson gave nothing away in his eyes. She listened for the whoosh of air that preceded his blows instead of watching his eyes, and still his gloves glanced off her chin.

He kicked and she dodged, stepping past the kick and behind him, delivering a mock one-two punch to his kidneys with a brush of her gloves. His form wavered for a split second; she had surprised him. He snapped his leg toward her in a vicious back kick that stopped just short of where she was standing.

She was doing more dodging than attacking. He was faster than she was. By the time she had prepared her counterattack, he was already attacking again.

She would have to stop thinking. Silence the conscious mind and let the body be. There was no delay between thinking and acting. Her muscles knew what to do. Her muscles were her thoughts. She knew the arc of her punches, each millisecond captured and superimposed on all the others.

He caught her arm in the crook of his elbow, hard, and she felt the breeze of his attempt to kick her legs out from underneath her. She jumped, and the cotton of his jeans rubbed the bottom of her feet. Their mingling sweat made his grip tenuous and she freed her arm. But the effort distracted her and she left herself open. He grabbed her in a bear hug from behind. She used a jab of her hips to flip Jackson over. But Jackson landed on his feet, throwing another punch as he found his balance.

Her arms found a rhythm to match his and he was retreating. Her legs were pistons in an engine, firing in time, one limb reaching to fill the gap left by the other. She couldn't see Jackson anymore, only a collection of limbs attached to a chest. Navy matched him other blow for blow. He stumbled back and she saw her opening. She swept his legs out from underneath him and he fell, shocked, against the mat.

She used her teeth to yank on the strings of her gloves. Her heart was pounding so loud she couldn't hear her own breath. Jackson was panting, elbows bent to hold himself up.

"Mark, give us a minute, will you?" she asked.

Mark disappeared into his office.

She had won and she had lost.

She sat cross-legged in front of Jackson. He pulled off his gloves and threw them against the wall. They made a slap that echoed in the large room.

"Fair is fair," he said. "You won." He started to rise. She put a hand on his knee.

"Jackson, wait."

Their knees were touching. She could feel a current running between them, a ribbon connecting him to her and her to him. She hadn't hurt him physically; she had done worse. She took his clenched fist and separated the fingers, running her thumb across his short nails, his red knuckles.

"I know what the real purpose of Operation Critical Mass was. I know why the operation was sabotaged. And I know the story the saboteurs want me to tell. What I know isn't just dangerous, it's . . . radioactive. I can't back out of this fight. I don't have a choice."

"I can help you."

"By sacrificing yourself?"

"Taking risks is what I do, Navy." He grabbed her hands. "Please let me help you."

She closed her eyes to avoid his gaze. She felt dizzy. *Stay strong.* The chill on her skin was only the adrenaline fading, she told herself. "You are helping me. You sent Mark. And Byron's reports have kept me safe for the time being."

"This isn't a beginner's game."

"No. But it's my game."

"Navy—"

"I promise I'll call if there's something you can do. For now, just keep my attackers away for a little bit longer."

"Fine."

Jackson pulled his hands into his lap and pushed himself up. He strode out of the large room and down a hallway she hadn't noticed before. Come rescue me, that's all she had to say. But she wouldn't do it. Even if it meant he hated her.

CHAPTER 34

NAVY WAS IN the parking lot of Butterfly Mixed Martial Arts Studio at ten to six by habit. Only Mark's truck was in the parking lot.

The small duffel bag with her workout clothes bounced against her hip as she walked. When she entered, Mark was sitting at the desk in the entryway typing on his laptop. He waved her in, his expression no different from normal.

"Jackson left?"

Mark shut the laptop and nodded.

"Was he—is he all right?"

"I don't get involved in lovers' spats. Jackson is Jackson. He'll be fine." He pointed to a white box sitting on the corner of the desk. "He left you something."

The box was the kind that held a department store shirt. She weighed it in her hands; something heavy shifted inside. A scrap of paper taped to the top of the box read "Don't hate me." She pulled the thin cardboard lid up.

A pistol was nestled in a bed of bubble wrap. She dropped the package. A box of bullets popped open and three of them spilled onto the floor, rolling like misshapen gold marbles. Like the shells that had fallen at her feet in the basement of the mansion.

Her mind carried her back to her execution chamber, pulling on the pants of a man she had killed, feeling the pool of his blood go from warm to clammy. She saw the Brit's smirk while she stood over him. She felt her right hand curled in the shape of the machine gun's trigger. She wondered now if she had read the Brit all wrong. He hadn't been smiling because he thought he would get his pistol in time. He had been smiling because he could see what she had become—would become. They had made her a killer.

Jackson's anger last night wasn't because she had hurt him. He hadn't just been trying to protect her from her attackers; he'd been trying to keep her from becoming more like him.

"If you wanted Jackson to do your shooting, you should have read him in last night." Mark scooped up the three bullets from the floor using a slip of paper and dropped them into the box next to a pair of black gloves. "Fingerprints. That's what the gloves are for. It's easy to wipe off the outside of a gun in a pinch, but you also need to make sure your fingerprints aren't all over the magazine and shells."

These are the things she had asked to know by refusing Jackson's help. She followed Mark down the hallway. Beyond the office was a narrow, long room twenty feet wide and the length of the entire building. She set the box down on the chest-high counter at the front of the room. The walls of the room were covered in a puffy, shiny metal material.

"Soundproofing," Mark explained when he saw her touching the wall. He tossed her a pair of hard-shelled ear muffs. "Don't put them on yet."

She caught them and laid them next to the box. Navy stared at the gun. She would rather reach for a live snake than touch the handle. Mark's words came to her as if she were waking from a deep sleep, too slow and low to understand. Navy forced her mind away from the soundtrack of that night in Amsterdam play-ing over and over in her head.

"The magazine," he was saying, pulling a rectangular object out of the handle of the gun, "is what you load. But the gun might be loaded even if the magazine is empty." He pulled back the slide and angled the gun so she could see the light coming through the barrel. "That means it's not loaded."

He handed her the pair of gloves Jackson had bought. They were black leather like the ones Mark wore. They fit perfectly.

"Pick it up," Mark said, pointing at the gun. When she didn't move, he took her right wrist and gently but firmly pressed her hand on top of the cold metal. "Pick it up."

Her fingers closed around the handle, as if they knew what to do. She picked the gun up and turned her hand over, letting the gun rest flat on her palm. Just an object, she told herself. How she used it was what mattered. She stopped fighting the memories and let them come, then slide away. The less she fought, the less impact they had. She could acknowledge her suffering without letting it take possession of her. She pointed the gun at the targets at the far end of the room. The gun rested naturally in her grip. The trigger gave easily when she pulled. It was hard to believe such a small motion could propel death.

Mark turned her hand over so the gun lay flat again and pointed to a small lever just above the trigger. "The safety."

In her head, she heard the *flick, flick* of Cart Driver's nervous hand playing with the safety on his machine gun. She remembered the tip of her finger, wet with someone else's blood, searching for the safety on the machine gun she had held. *Acknowledge. Release.*

"Push the safety up," Mark said.

She flicked the lever and tried to pull the trigger, now locked into place. She flicked the safety down and tried again. The trigger clicked. He took the gun from her. "Make sure the safety is engaged every time you pick up the weapon," Mark said.

"Next, to load the magazine, push this plate down and put the bullets in here." A spring-loaded plate held the bullets flush against the top of the magazine. She pressed gold ovals into the gray metal box. "Now put the magazine back into the gun."

She checked the safety, then slipped the magazine into the hollow of the gun's handle.

"Show me how you check to see if there's a bullet in the chamber."

She pulled the slide back and looked down the barrel. It was empty.

"Again."

"But I just—"

"Check again."

She pulled the slide back and peered into the dark barrel, blocked by a bullet.

"If you pull the slide all the way back, a bullet is loaded into the chamber. If you're just seeing if it's loaded, pull the slide halfway back."

The loaded gun shook a little, suddenly too heavy to hold. There was too much to remember. Mark repeated the lesson several times—the safety, how to check the chamber, how to load the gun—until her hands were steady.

"Now we can start target practice." Mark reached for a switch on the wall. A motor whirred and a yellow paper target moved closer to Navy. "To shoot, use the sight, that little fork halfway down the barrel."

She fingered the small piece of metal with a groove cut in the center. It felt sharp, even through her gloves.

"See that little nub on the end of the barrel?"

"Yes."

"Line up that nub between the fork on the barrel to aim at your target."

The target had the outline of a torso. She aimed for the heart. The target changed from an outline to a man. The driver of the cart. And his eager hands. She pulled the trigger and jumped when nothing happened. The safety was still on.

"Hearing protection first," Mark said. She put the headphones on, and Mark put a matching pair on. Except his had a switch on the side and a microphone that hovered near his mouth. He pushed the switch up.

"Now release the safety and try again." His voice echoed in her ear.

Lining up the sight with the target was like fitting two puzzle pieces together. But her first shot went wild, not even landing on the target. Even with the bulky headphones, the shot left her ears ringing.

"You're missing because of recoil. You're anticipating the shot."

Her second shot nicked the edge of the target.

"Breathe out and pull the trigger slowly so you don't know when the shot will come."

She hit the target's kidney. She willed the bullet to follow her directions, but it was only by calming her mind, focusing on the target, and controlling her breathing that her shots drifted closer to the mark. Only minutes later, she could reliably hit the upper chest of the target.

"That's enough for tonight. We need to get back to the rest of your training."

She took off the headphones. The sound of the shots hung in the room and the smell of gunpowder stung her nose. She put the safety on and pulled the magazine out. "Do I leave the gun here?" she asked Mark.

"It's yours. Do what you want."

Erin followed Navy to a run-down drive-in restaurant several miles from her apartment. Most of the speakers at the parking spots were marked out of order and blue spray paint decorated one of the exterior walls. The patrons ranged from scruffy to dangerous. An off-duty police officer stood by the ordering window, thumbs hooked into his waistband. Navy was at one of the uneven covered picnic tables near him.

Navy nearly choked on her hot dog when Erin sat down across from her.

"Give me your phone," Erin said.

Navy only hesitated for a second. Good. That meant Navy trusted her. Erin took the battery out of the phone and dropped it into Navy's bag.

"Miss me?" Erin asked.

Navy stared down at her bag. "They'll hear your voice on the recordings—they'll know—"

"Relax. William knows I'm here. I told him I wanted to check up on you."

"And he doesn't want to hear our conversation?"

Erin smiled. "Oh, he does. Very much. But he doesn't want anyone else to hear our conversation."

Navy took a sip of her soda. "I thought he didn't trust you."

"He doesn't have much choice. He's running out of friends." Erin ate a fry and made a face. "Those are awful."

"Yeah, nothing here is good."

A muscle car roared into the parking lot with the bass turned up so loud the table vibrated. Erin scanned the crowd again and saw a bag of white powder being exchanged in a dark corner of the parking lot. The off-duty officer was busy watching the jostling crowd in line at the window. "So if it's not the ambience and it's not the food, what attracts you to this charming place?"

Navy tilted her head toward the cop behind her. "The help. Some nights I can't stand my apartment. Pathetic, right?"

It wasn't a bad survival strategy. Navy was probably safer here than at her apartment, Erin thought. It was hard to stage a crime scene with a cop watching. Erin shook her head. "No."

"If you're here to talk me into working with Jackson, you can save your breath," Navy said. "I won't change my mind."

"You owe me a shot," Erin said.

Navy pushed away her half-eaten hot dog. "I can pretend to listen."

"Jackson was here because something happened in DC. A colleague of mine dropped by for a visit."

"I'm glad you got a chance to catch up."

"Don't be cute. He came by because he thought I knew something. About why the operation was sabotaged. And he was going to kill me for knowing."

Navy's eyes widened for a split second before her expression hardened. "So you want me to make you more of a target? That's not much of a pitch."

"I'm trained for this. You're not."

"You need some new material. That's exactly what Jackson said."

"Navy—"

Navy stood up and grabbed her bag. Her mouth was set in a flat line and her eyes glistened under the fluorescent bulbs. Erin had miscalculated. She had expected learning about the attack would scare Navy into cooperating. Instead, it had hardened Navy's resolve. Her refusal to cooperate was about more than wanting to protect Jackson.

Erin blocked Navy's path. "What happened to Sara and Moss was not your fault. What's happening to us right now is not your fault. You need to work with us so we can protect you. So we can protect ourselves."

"Get out of my way," Navy hissed.

Erin shook her head.

Navy sidestepped closer to the off-duty officer. Already he was glancing their way. "I'll make a scene," Navy said. It was the same voice she'd used with William when he'd threatened her. "I'll start a fight with you. And when they arrest me I'll make a signed statement. About everything. Even the three of you can't keep that quiet."

Erin studied Navy's stony face and knew she wasn't bluffing. "All right, Navy," she said. "If that's what you want."

Navy pushed past Erin and got into her car. The driver's door slammed shut so loud even the unruly crowd paused. The crowd turned their curious eyes to Erin and she hurried away.

CHAPTER 35

NAVY WALKED AROUND the floor of her office twice to make sure she was alone. Then she let herself into the storeroom. She found herself hoping the FBI would storm in, that shadowy CIA agents had known about her plan the whole time. If she were caught, she would be in a hopeless situation with a quick end. Some days it seemed preferable to the interminable waiting and preparation fighting back required.

Her main weapon was a few pieces of electronics gear assembled inside the Wonder Woman lunch box she now put in the corner cluttered with rejected laptop bags.

Navy had built what was known as a pirate box, a self-contained mobile communication and file-sharing device. Most pirate boxes were just meant to share files with whomever was within range of the wireless signal. Hers was designed to seed P2P networks with the infected files she had put on a thumb drive.

Unless they were closely inspected, the files on the thumb drive would look just like music, image, or video files. She had chosen the collection of files carefully: a range of independent records, classical music, freely shared movies, and Wikimedia images. Popular enough that they would be downloaded widely. Legal, so that no one would be trying to track down the cell phone modem in the pirate box to serve a takedown notice. Diverse enough that it would be difficult to trace the infection to a group of people who listened to one type of music or watched one genre of movies.

She took the cartoon figure thumb drive out of her pocket and squeezed it in her fist until she could feel the shape imprinted on her palm. This was the point of no return. Better test the pirate box again. She had already tested it five times that morning. She opened up her laptop and used Tor to connect to the P2P client installed on the hardware in the Wonder Woman lunch box.

Everything worked.

The files on the thumb drive had all been infected with benign viruses she had written. The viruses were designed for three of the most popular operating systems: OS X, Windows, and Ubuntu. Once the file was opened, the virus installed itself, then rewrote the infected file to remove any traces of its existence. If the virus was unable to complete installation, it would simply rewrite the file, then delete itself. On the day she had chosen, her virus would activate and decrypt a small set of documents. One of the documents was a letter from her. The others were carefully chosen lower-quality copies of some of what she had been given — documents she was reasonably sure were unaltered. They were only enough to fan the flames. Enough to make sure that killing her wouldn't make the story go away. After the documents had been decrypted and saved, the virus would erase itself to avoid detection.

When she disappeared in a few weeks, she would have to replace the expensive cell phone modem in the lunch box. If she used it again, someone might connect her with the files on the pirate box.

Zero files shared on the pirate box, the screen on her laptop reported. No files would be shared until she plugged the USB drive in. The USB connector in the cartoon figure's neck hovered near the port inside the lunch box.

She could still back out. She could call Jackson, let down her hair, and he would climb up to rescue her. Even if it was suicide for him. No, she would rescue herself. Or die trying.

She pushed the drive in. The number on her screen flickered and changed: 193 files shared. Already someone had connected to her pirate box and was downloading a Beethoven symphony. She closed her laptop before she could change her mind. She rearranged the laptop bags so they hid the Wonder Woman lunchbox.

The countdown to her disappearance had started. And Navy still had more work to do.

The hardware store parking lot was crowded with couples pushing carts overfilled with home improvement supplies. Next to the automatic doors, a couple argued about how to fit eight-foot pieces of drywall into a van that was one foot too short.

She paid cash for a short piece of lumber and two door locks. At the next hardware store, she bought two more locks of a different kind. By lunchtime, she had ten different locks in her backseat. The lock-picking kit had been more difficult to find. It was only available in few local stores—too few for her comfort. Too easy to trace even if she did pay cash. So she had asked around in chat rooms, under a new handle, until she found a guy who was willing to sell his lock-picking kit. Not untraceable, but less traceable than showing her picture to a few store owners.

When she got back to her apartment, she hid her cell phone under a pile of dirty clothes in her closet for the afternoon while she drilled, cut, and installed the locks on the board she had purchased. She had downloaded a bunch of lock-picking directions to her forensics laptop. She couldn't visit lock-picking sites from her laptop at home.

She started with the cheapest lock, one that wasn't even

installed on her test door, a Master padlock. The directions for picking a padlock seemed simple enough. Use the tension wrench to torque the lock, then insert the hook-shaped pick. Push against each pin until you reach its shear point. It took half an hour before she could feel the shear point of the first pin. She was so excited to get one pin in place she forgot to keep the torque on the tension wrench. The first pin slipped down again.

Three hours later she was ready to throw the padlock through the window of her apartment. She set it down instead and stood up to stretch. She sat down cross-legged in her favorite spot to meditate, where the afternoon sun cast warm rectangles of light on the carpet. Even with her eyes closed, she could see the bright yellow rays reflecting off the snow two floors below. Breathe in for one-two-three-four-five-six. Breathe out for one-two-three-four-five-six-seven. It took several minutes before her heartbeat slowed and the stress melted from her shoulders. She found her place, the place Mark had guided her to during their first session.

She felt like she was floating and yet being grounded at the same time. The boundaries of her self were more tenuous and at the same time more real. She took the calm energy and sent it to the tips of her limbs, each muscle, to her mind. Ten minutes later she was back at the table patiently failing, over and over again. Pushing each pin up was like pressing the trigger on her gun. She had to move slowly and breathe out. That way when the pin reached its shear point she didn't jump or lose focus.

Her phone beeped, reminding her that she had evening plans to attend. She had spent all afternoon picking one cheap, easy lock. She was looking forward to the restaurant anyway. Soon she would leave on a dangerous trip and she didn't know if she would be able to return. She wanted to see her friends, to collect the moments she had left. Good moments were like good luck charms. If she kept the good moments close, they made the bad ones easier to manage.

CHAPTER 36

NAVY'S LIMBS WERE already beaded with sweat, despite the cold gym. A familiar feeling.

Her training and shooting sessions at the gym were beginning to feel like the most normal parts of her life.

Her shooting was improving rapidly. She could see the bullet, the target, her finger on the trigger, all in slow motion. All working exactly as she intended. Mark was holding back less and less when they sparred. Bruises peppered her arms and legs. They hurt, but the pain didn't matter. She was stronger, faster, smarter after every fight.

"Today you're going to learn some advanced fall techniques," Mark told her.

"Shouldn't you be teaching me how to stay up?"

"You're no match for a fresh, experienced fighter. Jackson was tired."

Her bruises stung along with her ego. "Oh."

"Let me show you. Attack me."

She stepped forward with a combination kick-punch, and before she knew it she felt the full force of the mat against her back. She shook it off and stood up, arms tensed like Mark told her not to, cheeks burning with the shame of losing so easily.

"Again."

She hesitated but obeyed. Again she was flipped in a microsecond, the impact of the ground against her elbow leaving a ball of pain in her shoulder. An electric fear bounced around in her chest, snaked up her spine. Mark was right.

Again, again, Mark said. Every time she came at him she had barely set up her attack before he threw her. A new bruise formed at the base of her spine. She tried again, desperately windmilling her arms, and again the mat crinkled against her back. She tried until tears sprung to her eyes and her legs refused to let her stand.

"What did I tell you the first day?" he barked at her.

"To only pick fights worth losing." Red dots were scattered around her vision. She wanted to throw herself at Mark and scratch his eyes out.

"Not that. You win fights here." He pointed to his forehead. "Until you learn to fall, you will be afraid of losing. What happened to your form?"

"I stopped thinking."

"No, you were panicking."

"But I wasn't—"

"Panic isn't always about running for the exits. If your fear prevents you from focusing, you're panicking. Got it?"

A dark cloud rolled inside her. Navy was afraid. She thought she had left that sort of fear in Amsterdam, that she had mastered it.

He grabbed her arm roughly and pulled her up. She was as limp as a rag doll. "Are you giving up?"

She shook her head.

"Then we're going to learn how to fall."

She choked back the knot in her throat. "Okay."

He clapped once and it echoed in the studio. He brought

his hands apart again and slowly lowered his right hand until his palms touched silently. "What's the difference?"

"You're controlling the fall."

"Exactly. You can do something similar when you're thrown. It's just a different set of muscles."

She learned to twist to avoid landing on her ribs. To roll forward from a crouch if she needed to absorb the energy of the fall. To tuck her arms in so she never landed on her elbows. She was finding ways to control her body she hadn't imagined possible.

When Mark said training was over for the night, Navy went straight for her bottle of ibuprofen. She swallowed two tablets with a long drink of water.

"I won't see you until Tuesday," Navy said.

"How much longer do we have after you get back?" Mark asked. She shook her head.

"I'll have to tell Jackson, you know."

"I wouldn't expect anything less." The cold air felt good on her warm skin when she opened the door.

"Stay safe, Navy."

"Yeah, you too."

On the ride home she called Jackson. It went directly to a canned voicemail message. She realized she was disappointed to not hear his voice.

"I thought I'd come up to DC for the cherry blossoms this weekend," she said. "I'll be at the Hyatt. There is one favor, if you don't mind." She flipped the phone shut and shifted in her seat, wincing. No matter how she arranged herself in the driver's seat, something hurt.

What she had conquered tonight was small in comparison to the challenge of not telling Jackson everything when she saw him in a few days.

She tried to remember how she had felt in the park, sitting

on the log next to him, his arm draped around her shoulders. Safe and protected and invisible for a moment. Before she had broken the spell and walked away.

CHAPTER 37

JACKSON SMILED AT the night desk clerk at the Hyatt and swayed a little as he walked toward the elevators—just another drunk guest headed back to his room after a late business dinner. The elevator arrived as Jackson saw Erin following another guest through the back door. He got in without waiting for her.

When he got off on the second floor, Jackson glanced both ways down the hall to make sure no one would see him enter Navy's room. The door opened before he knocked; she had been watching for him. Navy was wearing a black tank top that was ratty at the edges. Jackson was surprised again by how much her body had changed since they were in Amsterdam. Her arms were ropes of muscle.

Jackson pulled a cell phone out of his pocket and held it up. She picked up what looked like a plush silver brick from the bed.

He turned the object over in his hand until he recognized it—the same soundproofing Mark used at his indoor gun range was wrapped around her cell phone. She took the phone from him and slipped it in a drawer.

"As long as we speak normally, the mic won't pick up anything," Navy said.

Before Jackson could think of what he wanted to say, there

was a light knock on the door. Navy looked through the peephole and let Erin and Byron in. Neither of them greeted her.

"You can talk," Navy said. "The bug won't pick up your voices at a normal volume. I wrapped my phone in pieces of a QBS blanket. Then I tested it."

"Tested it?" Byron asked.

"I found out which directory stores the recorded files. I listened to them to see how much it could hear."

Byron looked shocked.

"I tinker for a living."

"Oh, right."

"I even poked a little hole for the antenna so it stays connected to the network and no one thinks I'm hiding anything."

"Clever," Erin said. She flopped down on the bed. Jackson chose the chair next to the desk. Byron leaned against the wall by the door.

Navy's loose pajama pants decorated with pink skulls and crossbones pooled at her feet. "I have tap water and anything from the mini-bar. Anybody want?"

"Tequila," Erin said.

Navy opened the mini-bar and tossed a small bottle of amber liquid to Erin. For herself, she padded to the bathroom sink and filled a plastic cup. Her arms and shoulders were spotted with bruises—some fresh, some yellow, some almost healed.

"Everything all right in Des Moines?" Byron asked, pointing to her injuries.

"Oh, yes." She held out her arm in the weak light and studied the bruises. "This does look bad, doesn't it? It's all from training."

"I'm sorry about the attack. If I'd known . . .," Byron said.

"How would you have known?"

"You should have called us." Byron used the same tone Jackson had heard him use when his daughter arrived home after curfew. He took a seat on the edge of the bed, tapping one loafered foot on the carpet.

Navy's eyes flicked to Jackson. "So I've been told," she said.

Jackson tipped his chair back, trying to keep his expression from matching the thoughts running around in his head. Had he made the right decision in leaving her the gun? He was sure she hadn't been happy to see it. "How's the marksmanship training?"

"Mark says I'm good enough to defend myself from twenty yards." Remarkably, her answer was unperturbed.

Erin drained the tequila in one gulp and licked her lips. "Like Mexico in a bottle."

"Minus the worm," Navy said, with a small smile, as she sat down next to Erin.

"I did some digging into your attack," Jackson said. "Tried to follow the money trail. The trail disappeared somewhere in the Cayman Islands."

"Not surprising," Navy said.

"That means it wasn't your average thug," Byron told her.

It was a long shot, but Jackson had to try. "Are you sure you still want to do this alone?"

"What would you do?" she asked him.

A fair question. Someone had to go into the line of fire. Would he let someone else take his place? "You'll be a target the second William knows you're going public," Jackson said. "It would be easier for us to protect you if you work with us."

"You don't know what I know."

"Then tell me," he snapped.

Navy shook her head.

"Stop being an idiot," Erin said. "You know who's manipulating William. And you know why the operation was sabotaged. If you tell us, we can help you."

"I'm sorry," Navy said. "I can't."

Erin threw the tequila bottle into the trash can across the room. "You asked for a favor. Tell us what you need."

"What I know has to be revealed, at least part of it." Navy crossed and uncrossed her legs. "The names of the undercover agents might be compromised. You need to warn Roy and the others."

Erin gasped. "You have the names—"

"Yes. I'm going to do my best to keep your names from getting out. But people will be digging."

Jackson wondered how Navy could find compassion for the man who had ordered her execution.

"You know that Roy—" Byron started.

"Sent the message to have us killed. Yes, I know. It doesn't matter. He was following orders. I won't endanger more people than I have to."

"That's the one favor? Warning Roy?" Jackson asked.

"No." Navy pulled a duffel bag close. In the pocket on the end she had sewn a false panel. She took three small plastic cartoon figures out and held them in a tight fist. For the first time that night, nervousness crossed her face. She tossed one figure to each of the agents.

"These are thumb drives. A copy of everything I was given and everything I've found out since is in a self-decrypting archive. The file won't open until April 22. After I disappear."

Jackson weighed the thumb drive, still warm from Navy's hand, on his palm. "What are we supposed to do with it?"

Navy picked at a stray thread on the comforter. "Blackmail them into releasing me if I don't escape. Punish them if I don't make it. I don't know. I would understand if you just went home and destroyed the thumb drive."

"What if I set my clock to April 22?" Byron asked.

"Try it." Navy smiled impishly. "It won't work."

Erin turned to Jackson. "Why are you letting her do this?"

"Letting her?" Jackson's laugh was short and guttural.

"She doesn't have to tell us anything." Erin had her back to Navy, as if Navy weren't in the room. "There's three of us and one of her. We can hide her even if she doesn't want to hide."

Navy leaned away from Erin, shocked and touched at the same time.

"The saboteurs would find her," Jackson said. "And if they didn't find her, they'd go after Sara and Moss. Unless Navy wants to tell us who the saboteurs are or who William's working for, we can't help her."

"I don't have a choice, Erin," Navy said. "You see that, right?"

"We could help you with more than this errand boy crap," Erin said.

"And what about your brother's family in Lansing, Jackson?" Navy asked. The front two legs of Jackson's chair hit the floor. "Or your wife and daughter, Byron?"

"Who's threatening my daughter?"

She pointed to the drawer with the phone to remind him to keep his voice down. "They will. If it doesn't end with me. What I have includes files on all of you. And everyone close to you. Someone already suspects that one of you managed to get your hands on the real set of messages sent to the kidnappers."

"Who's 'they,' Navy?" Jackson asked.

"It doesn't matter. You understand now. I have to do this alone."

"No one likes a martyr," snapped Erin.

"I'm not a martyr. I have a plan, that's all I can tell you. You've already done more than you should have."

"What do we do until April 22?" asked Byron.

"Just keep spinning your reports if you can. For a little bit longer. You'll know when to stop."

Byron frowned, but nodded.

A blaring TV turned off next door. Footsteps ran down the

hall above them. The four of them were poised to listen—a pack of wolves looking for a threat. Navy had become part of the pack, even though Jackson had tried to keep her out.

"You should go," she told them.

Erin left first, then Byron a few minutes later. Jackson checked his watch. Five minutes and then he should go too. It wasn't long enough. But it was too long to sit with a room full of silence between them. He crossed the room, watching to see if Navy would shy away. She moved over to give him space to sit next to her. He slipped his arm over her shoulders. She drew her legs to her chest and leaned against him. He was reassured by the weight of her head on his collarbone. "Will you be coming back to Washington?"

"You'll see," she said, her voice muffled and drowsy.

"Are you scared?"

"Terrified," she said matter-of-factly.

Mark had told him Navy would have made an excellent agent. He was right. Despite Jackson's best efforts, she was already becoming one.

"You should go," she said. But she didn't move her head from where it rested on his shoulder.

He kissed the top of her head and felt the warm rectangle of skin from the part of her hair. "I'd disappear with you, if you'd let me," he said.

She sat up and pushed a piece of paper into his hands. "This is an email address I'll be checking once things heat up. Now, go."

He heard the dead bolt click after she closed the door. A baby started to cry at the end of the hall. A door opened and a man in a robe shuffled to the ice machine without looking up. Jackson took the stairs and left the hotel through the back door. How long had he been alone with Navy? He wondered if attachment was clouding his judgment and hers.

The metro station was filled with workers from second shift

jobs, mostly. He watched the shadows in the station, searched beneath the exhaustion of his fellow passengers' faces for anything more sinister. This was the real cost of his job—a constant wariness, always needing to watch for the next attack. He tried to close his eyes as he rested his head against the side of the subway car but there were too many people around for him to relax. Instead, he focused on a lone spider walking along the ceiling of the car while the track sped, rattled, and squeaked underneath him.

CHAPTER 38

NAVY'S GROCERY LIST was the same as a bachelor's. Her cart contained premade pasta dinners and frozen meals. The only things from the produce aisle were bananas and apples. There was no time in her schedule to cook.

Her last stop was the health and beauty aisle. She chose the largest deodorant she could find: men's, eight inches tall, and decorated with black and green lightning bolts.

She would have to use her credit card. Hopefully the men's deodorant wouldn't raise any red flags. Her cash was being spent on burn phones, money orders for private detective fees, and saving up for the reserves she would need when she disappeared. In her head she kept a list of used cell phone donation locations. Maybe it would throw people off her trail if the phones were in use when she disappeared.. Maybe they weren't watching for that yet. Maybe they knew everything and were just waiting to pick her up.

The checkout girl scanned the purchases, looking up at Navy with pity. Navy mentally crossed off the grocery store from the list of places she could visit.

She drove to an empty parking lot behind a dying strip mall. She left the car running, but turned down the heat so her frozen lasagna wouldn't turn to mush. From a directory on her laptop, she opened a list of all the private investigators in Cedar Rapids, Iowa. It took three tries to find one answering the phone on a Saturday morning.

"Trusted Investigations, Derek Mollan." The man's voice was gruff and impatient.

"I have a friend who's . . . well, he's in a little trouble . . . I'm worried about him and I was wondering if you could help."

"Can I get your name?" he asked.

"May Potter."

"What would you like me to do?"

"I'd pay a fee for your time, of course. I just need you to call his office on weekdays, drive by the house on weekends. Monitor the police scanner for his name. If it looks like he's in trouble, call his lawyer."

"You mean the kind of trouble where he lands in jail."

"Yes, that kind."

"It would help if you could tell me a little bit more about what his problem is."

Navy wondered whether her father would prefer a gambling addiction or being caught up in a car accident insurance scam. "It's probably nothing, he thinks it's nothing. But he says his bookie has been pressuring him about his gambling debt. I'm afraid his bookie might force Peter to do something illegal."

"You have a lawyer in mind?"

"Yes. The lawyer will have information that will be useful if he's arrested."

She made similar calls for one other family member in a different city, using a different list of private investigators, then pulled the battery out of the phone and tossed it on the backseat. One more phone to donate. If she had used one phone to hire all the private detectives, the entire network of protection she built for her friends and family could be wrapped by tracing the calls made from that number. Her fingers were frozen and she had used up two more phones by the time she finished making her calls for the day.

On the drive home, she took a mental inventory of what she would need for her next project: a simple robot. Her pack rat tendencies were finally paying off. She could go straight home and start working.

∾

The men's deodorant gel oozed like worms out of the narrow openings in the top of the container. She ran the water to rinse the stubborn gel down the bathroom sink, using a butter knife to break up the mess until it disappeared. Then she rinsed the now-empty deodorant container until the water ran clear. She left the container to dry on the counter while she gathered the rest of the materials she needed.

From her collection of electronics hobby equipment in the closet she collected a servo motor, a microcontroller, and an AAA battery holder. She checked her watch; she had an hour or so before her lunch plans. Hopefully she would have enough time to finish programming the new software she needed for her pirate box. Right now, the pirate box was seeding P2P networks. When she went on the run, it would be her failsafe. Even if she didn't make it, her secrets would come out.

She cleared the table of her notes on the DC Metro and bus stations to make room for the new project. First, she turned on her soldering iron so it could warm up. Using her rotary tool, she drilled a hole in the top of the deodorant container just large enough for the wooden dowel from the craft store that she had cut down to three inches in length. Navy attached the dowel to the plate on the plate inside the deodorant container that pushed the gel up as the knob on the bottom turned. The servo motor was mounted near the bottom of the container on the inside. She used a rubber O-ring as a belt to attach the axle of the motor to the knob. She tested it by manually turning the motor before she reassembled the container.

Now, the battery and the microcontroller. Navy used Velcro to attach the battery holder and the microcontroller to the inside of the container, near the motor. She touched the solder to the soldering iron briefly and smelled the acrid smell of the rosin core. She worked quickly to connect the wires according to her schematic. Holding the soldering iron against the wires for too long could melt the insulation on them. When the wires had cooled, she inserted a battery.

The final step of her project would be programming the microcontroller to wait for the exact amount of time before activating the motor, but for now she could test manually by giving the microcontroller directions via the serial port.

She hooked up her laptop and brought up the Arduino application. A few keystrokes pushed a new program to the micro controller. The motor whirred, which pushed the plastic plate inside the deodorant toward the top. The wooden dowel jerkily emerged from the top of the deodorant, and retreated when the motor went in reverse. She took the battery out of her cell phone and balanced the case over the battery. She held the container upside down over the power button on and triggered the motor again. The dowel pressed down with enough force to push the battery back in, turning on the phone. She tested it again, allowing herself a little smile. Another small victory that would give her a fighting chance. Now she had have a robot capable of making it look like she was miles away from her actual location.

She gathered up her transit notes and hid them with her new toy underneath the false bottom she had fashioned for the kitchen towel drawer. She kept a Wi-Fi-connected pedometer in the drawer as well. Everytime the drawer opened, the pedometer recorded steps and logged them to an online account. The account was configured to send her congratulatory text messages every time activity was detected.

The lunch crowd at Sara's favorite Mexican grill was in full swing when Navy arrived. "Navy!" Sara waved excitedly. A waitress rushed by bearing a tray full of fajitas sizzling on steaming plates next to heaping bowls of cheese and sour cream.

Sara had a daquiri with sugar on the rim and Moss was nursing a Corona with a lemon wedge sticking out the top. Carrie was sipping a large coke with two maraschino cherries floating at the top.

"You're late, again," Sara teased Navy. "Your beer is getting warm."

A glass bottle with a lemon wedge was waiting at her spot. "I slept in," Navy lied. She leaned over to hug Sara.

"Gentle! Are you weight training now?"

Navy remembered the bruises covering her arms. In a couple weeks it would be too warm to wear long sleeves. But by then she would be gone.

"Pilates," she lied again. "There's a place that opened up near work." She tried to take mental snapshots of her friends as she sipped her beer. White teeth in open laughing mouths against the bright Mexican décor as Sara told her latest story. Sara and Moss holding hands on top of the table, finally seeming comfortable and unscarred. They talked about the new training Carrie was getting for her EMT certification, the trip to Glacier National Park Sara and Moss were planning, the winter that had seemed endless but was now receding. It was all comfortingly normal and completely foreign.

Navy excused herself before dessert to return to her cave.

On her way home, Navy mentally checked and rechecked her lists. She was right on schedule. She sketched out her escape plan, minute by minute. She wrote the new software for her pirate box. She finished programming her deodorant robot. But she hesitated before finishing her next task. The blog entry had taken her hours to compose, but it was less than one hundred words. When she made her move in a couple of days, William's men would think she wanted to make a deal.

Okay, so I don't normally do these things but I thought this one was interesting. It's called Five Things. Name five things you think would be interesting but you'll never get to do. Find sunken treasure. Spend fifteen minutes with the president. Live in a treehouse. Make the perfect curry sauce. Win an Olympic medal.

When she looked up, it was almost midnight. Exhaustion didn't creep up on her anymore. She worked until her energy plummeted, as if she were falling off a cliff. And then she worked a little more. And then she slept.

The garage of Navy's apartment building was deserted early on Sunday morning. Exactly as she had hoped. Even using the smallest knife from her kitchen, it was hard to fit her hand and the knife under the driver's seat. The blade scratched against springs in the upholstery as she dug out a hole large enough for the deodorant robot. Bits of yellow foam and fluff fell on the floor. She slipped the robot into the hole and secured it to the metal frame using zip ties. With some difficulty and swearing she was able to reach the switch she'd installed on the bottom for testing. The dowel emerged from the case, pressed firmly into the floor, and retreated again.

She cleared the debris from floorboards using a small hand vacuum. If they found the robot, they would know that she had deliberately thrown them off her trail. She went back up to her apartment, emptied the vacuum. For the first time in weeks, there weren't any projects littering her bedroom, living room, and kitchen table.

She was delaying her next task. Everything had been put in motion when she installed the pirate box at work, but now she would be trying to attract attention.

Instinctively, she reached for her latest burn phone, but then closed her fingers around her bugged cell phone. She needed to be outside. The scrubby brown lawn still had small patches of snow. A breeze made her feel cold even in the sun, but the air cooled her nerves. She closed her eyes and tried to feel the warmth, the open space, the world surrounding her.

She dialed the number for the CIA switchboard and an impersonal secretary's voice answered. As she had expected.

"I'd like to speak to William Grand," she said. Asking for William would be a sign she wanted to talk. The saboteurs wouldn't kill her while William's men might do it for them. For a few days, she would be safer than she had in weeks. Her eyes were still closed. If she opened them, she knew she would hang up. She would run away, forget her plan. Everything she had done would be for nothing.

"I can't connect you unless you have an extension."

"I need to speak to William Grand. About some information I was given. By a friend. It's very important." If she hinted that she was working with someone, William's men wouldn't kill her until they knew whom. She hoped.

"I'm sorry. It's policy. I can't connect you unless you have an extension."

"Thanks anyway."

She hung up and pressed a hand to her stomach, reminding herself to breathe. The boulder she had started rolling downhill was pressing against her back, pushing her to go faster than she wanted to go.

Navy stashed the bugged cell phone inside the soundproof sleeve in her bag and pulled the burn phone out of her pocket.

"Butterfly Mixed Martial Arts Studio," Mark answered.

"I need to cancel my class registration." She bit her lip, but tears pricked her eyes anyway.

"Can I ask why?" If she didn't know Mark, she would have thought she heard concern in his voice.

"Your classes are getting a little bit too crowded." *I'm going to be tailed soon.*

"Well, that's a shame," he said carefully. "I hope you found the classes useful."

"Very," she managed over the lump in her throat.

"Feel free to call us back up if you need a refresher course."

"Sure. Thanks."

She couldn't go back anytime soon. Leading a tail to the gym would expose Mark, and maybe even Jackson. One more place that was offlimits. She stood on the lawn longer than she should have, long enough that she had to shove her hands in her pockets to keep them warm. The thought of going back to her apartment made her feel claustrophobic, as if bit by bit the rest of the world were falling away, until her self-imposed prison would be the only safe place.

CHAPTER 39

"SHIT," BYRON MUTTERED under his breath. He listened to the call again, wondering if he could find a way to downplay it, knowing he couldn't. Navy didn't want him to hide this, even if he could. This was Navy's play, and she had started the final act.

William was at Byron's desk two hours later.

"What's going on here?" William demanded. Byron's report was wrinkled in William's fist.

"I don't know," Byron said. "You know as much as I do, just what was in the transcript."

"You said she didn't know anything."

What did Navy want him to say? The cubicles around Byron had gone quiet. "As far as I know, she doesn't."

"In my office. Now."

William asked him the same questions over and over again until Byron's patience wore thin.

"I don't know why she wants to talk to you," Byron hissed through closed teeth. "Maybe you should call and ask her."

"How can we get her up here without attracting too much attention?"

Something clicked in Byron's memory. He cursed Navy for

setting up the inevitable. "Easily, I think. Bring up her blog. She posted a wish list a few days ago."

Byron knew what it said without looking. He'd been puzzling over the entry last week. Now he understood. It was Navy's signal she wanted to meet. Calling the CIA switchboard to ask for William had just been a way to get their attention. *Okay, so I don't normally do these chain letter things but I thought this one was interesting. It's called Five Things. Name five things you think would be interesting but you'll never get to do. Find sunken treasure. Spend fifteen minutes with the president . . .*

"So we can trick her into coming into Washington with an invite to the White House? Find out who she's working with?"

Dumbass, Byron thought. William still thought Navy was the one being manipulated. "That would probably work."

"I'll arrange it." William dismissed him with a wave of his hand.

For the rest of the afternoon, Byron fidgeted at his desk until he could sneak away. Jackson and Erin had been inventing work in DC for themselves, waiting for Navy to make her move. They didn't have to wait anymore.

Byron met Jackson and Erin in the same corner booth in the back of the same grimy bar.

"She did what?" Jackson slammed his beer on the table. Liquid sloshed out, dripping down his hand and gathering into a puddle around the bottom of his glass.

"It's smart," Erin said. "Navy's betting William's men won't kill her as long as they think she's trying to deal. And the saboteurs won't bother to kill her as long as there's a chance William's men will do it for them. And since she mentioned 'a friend,' William's men are going to be distracted by looking for a contact that doesn't exist."

"It's risky," Jackson said.

"There's nothing we can do. William called her an hour ago to invite her to DC. She accepted." Byron looked down at the beer he hadn't touched; he had no appetite for it. "It's how she wants it."

"What happens now?" Erin glanced at Jackson's stormy face, visibly worried.

"We'll see how convincing Navy's performance in Amsterdam was," Byron said. "If William thinks she still hates us, he'll assign one of us to bring her in. My guess is she asked to speak to William to keep us in the clear."

The stormy expression on Jackson's face worried Byron. Byron had never seen Jackson this upset. Byron reached across the table to touch Jackson's shoulder. Jackson exploded out of the booth.

"Do you still think I want her to do this?" Jackson looked at Erin.

Byron saw the guilt plainly in Jackson's defeated, tense posture. When they had met with Navy in the hotel room, Erin had accused Jackson of not trying hard enough and Jackson, apparently, agreed.

"I'm sorry, Jackson." Erin paused until she could see that Jackson heard her apology. "You need to keep your voice down."

"I need to go to Des Moines."

Byron blocked Jackson's path. "You need to stay here. William is setting up tails for her right now. She doesn't have the training to lose them. You'll get made." Jackson took a step toward the door, running into Byron's hand. "If you're made, you'll be useless to her."

"Sit down, Jackson. Finish your drink." Erin's smile would have looked genuine to anyone who didn't know her. She was trying to mask their argument from curious stares looking their way. "We have options." Then softer. "There have to be options."

⚜

Jackson spent as little time in DC as possible. The winters were raw and snowy and the summers were miserably hot and humid.

It was a city designed for bureaucrats who spent most of their time in meetings making decisions based on how they thought the polls were going to swing tomorrow. Meetings in rooms almost exactly like the one he was in now.

Sitting around the lacquered blond wood table were Byron, Erin, Jackson, William, and a man Jackson hadn't met before.

"Everyone, I'd like you to meet Curt Holiander," William said. "He's our liaison to the president's office."

Jackson had never met a presidential aide with boxer's ear, eyes like a lizard's, and a suit that cost two of Jackson's paychecks. The suit was cut to downplay the muscles that flexed in Curt's thick upper arms.

"I'll take it from here, William," Curt said.

Jackson saw Byron stiffen at the sound of Curt's voice. By the time Curt's eyes swung back to Byron, his posture was relaxed again.

"William has briefed me on everything so far, and I've read all your reports," Curt continued. "Is there anything else I should know?"

The words were innocuous, but Curt's tone was more combative than curious.

"All right, then," Curt said. "It's clear that Navy Trent called the switchboard just to get our attention, and the note on her blog means she wants to meet the president."

"Obviously, Navy thinks she knows something about the attack in Amsterdam and wants to discuss it with the president," William said, as if he had figured all that out on his own.

Curt's eyes narrowed. "Right. We'd like to keep this quiet, of course. Since the three of you were already involved in Amsterdam, we need your help. Jackson and Byron, you'll tail Navy when she comes into DC for the meeting we've arranged. She must have a contact, someone who leaked information to her. We need to know who that is. Erin, we need you for a separate mission."

Erin raised her eyebrows and exchanged looks with Jackson and Byron.

"Between you and me," Curt said firmly. Curt unconsciously clenched his fist and released it, stretching his fingers like Jackson did after a fight. Erin nodded.

"So when do we bring her in?" Jackson asked. He kept his voice businesslike, pushing away the memory of his fingers skimming over the bruises on her arm.

"You won't. You're just going to tail her when she gets closer to the city. Three days from now. She's going to meet the president."

"The—the president?" William stuttered in surprise. "Are you sure that's wise?"

Curt shot William a look that made him wither. "We think the quickest way to find out what she knows is to let her think we're playing along."

We? Jackson wondered, a thousand gears spinning in his mind. This wasn't intra-agency jockeying and politics, as he had suspected. The players weren't the saboteurs and William's men. It was the saboteurs and whoever was manipulating William. And if the president was willing to dirty his hands by meeting with Navy, that meant the White House was involved.

"What, where, and when?" Byron asked. Jackson admired Byron. He looked for all the world like a loyal soldier. Obedience was the best play to make with a man like Curt. Appearing submissive would buy Curt's favor and keep him from getting suspicious.

"She's at a hotel in Toledo right now. We've been tracking her phone. We asked her not to talk to anyone about her trip, and her bug says she hasn't. She's on track to arrive sometime tomorrow night. Much earlier than she needs to. She must be planning to meet the leak when she comes to DC. Jackson and Byron, you'll start trailing her when she gets into the city. In the meantime, you need to get fitted for tuxedos from wardrobe. She's meeting the president at a formal occasion at the White House. One of those bullshit diplomatic functions."

"There are some forms we need to deal with," William said.

"Forms?" Curt asked.

"When you detain a U.S. citizen, there's extra paperwork," William said. "I can file it for you."

"There's no need," Curt said. "I'll take care of it."

Jackson was surprised by the queasy expression on William's face. As if it hadn't occurred to William, until this moment, that Navy Trent would be denied the civility of formalities.

"But the paperwork's all finished," William said. "I'll just—"

"You'll do nothing," Curt snapped. "Erin, stay for a minute. The rest of you are dismissed."

Two pieces of paper stuck out of Curt's leather binder. Jackson could see the end of a bar code on a boarding pass. Curt was going to send Erin away without giving her the chance to tell anyone else where she was going. Jackson filed out with Byron, who was calm, and William, who looked close to hyperventilating.

When William disappeared into his office, Byron pulled Jackson into the nearest empty cube. "Curt is the soldier," he said softly.

"The soldier?"

"From the recording. The one Andy sent to Des Moines to shadow Navy."

"That's not surprising," Jackson whispered.

Byron shook his head. "He's not just any soldier. He's an assassin."

Jackson was about to ask for details when the conference room door opened.

"Heads down," Byron said. "I sent Suzy on a mission."

Erin walked out with Curt close behind her. Curt was

watching her carefully. Jackson had known Erin long enough to see that she was worried about something.

"Erin!" Suzy, one of the administrative assistants, stopped Erin and Curt before they got to the elevator. "Before you run away again, I have to ask you about your expense report." Suzy was wise enough to know she was being played, and good enough not to show it.

Curt looked annoyed about the delay. He looked up to see if Jackson and Byron were watching.

"This dinner," Suzy pointed to something in the sheaf of papers in her hand. "It's too expensive. I can only reimburse you up to thirty dollars."

"Oh, okay. That's the place you wanted to go to, right?" Erin had emphasized the words purposefully. "Well, it's fantastic."

The place Jackson wanted to go—Des Moines. They were sending Erin to Des Moines. The words on the page Jackson was pretending to read swam in front of him. William had asked Navy to keep quiet about her trip. Erin was a decoy. Erin's assignment was to be seen far from away from DC by as many people and on as many cameras as she could. Curt was planning to make Navy disappear in DC and he didn't want the trail to lead back to the capital.

CHAPTER 40

NAVY FOLLOWED THE signs to a neighborhood on the outskirts of Cleveland. She stopped for lunch at a greasy pizza joint, lingering over the tasteless pizza and watery pop to watch for tails. She hadn't seen any since Des Moines. She knew William's men were tracking her cell phone signal; hopefully, they had figured they didn't need to follow her during the trip. She took the battery out of her phone, dropped the battery in one coat pocket and her phone in the other, then dropped some bills on the table. When she was ready to broadcast her location again, she would put her phone under the seat of her car, where the robot could turn it on.

At the secondhand clothes shop, she pretended to study the retro pink skirt with flounces along the bottom edge. She was watching for tails in the reflection of the dirty glass. She wanted to wait longer to find out for sure, but William's men would get suspicious as soon as her phone dropped off the network. She had to get back on the road. In the car she wrapped her cell phone in the soundproofing material, this time plugging the hole normally left open for the antenna. Just in case. The closer she got to DC, the more paranoid she was becoming.

She drove five miles above the speed limit, as fast as she dared to go without risking getting pulled over. The ridges on the steering wheel dug painfully into her hands. Go through the list, she reminded herself. She had swept the outside of the car for GPS trackers before leaving Des Moines. She had installed homemade tamper detection mechanisms on the hood and trunk of her car. The car had no onboard GPS. The GPS she normally carried in the car she had left at home. If they were tracking her with another device she had no way of knowing.

She drove for ten minutes longer, then pulled into a rest stop. When the only other visitors, a family of four, climbed back into their van and left, she reached into the glove compartment for the white reflective tape. She used small strips of the tape to cover up the 8 on her front and back license plate until it looked like a 3. It wouldn't fool anyone if closely inspected, but it might fool the toll road cameras. To hide her face, she pulled a baseball cap low on her forehead.

The highway seemed different when she merged back into the flow of traffic. When people changed lanes around her, she watched to see if they were going to block her in. When no one changed lanes, she watched to see if the other drivers were watching her. She grew suspicious of the truckers. She couldn't watch them as well; they could easily look down into her car. She wondered what she was expecting exactly—a shotgun pointed at her head? No, if they wanted to kill her before she got to Washington it would have happened in Des Moines.

By early afternoon she reached the entrance for Chesapeake and Ohio Canal National Historical Park, an hour outside DC. Just before she reached the ranger's station, she pulled over to the side of the road. She took the bits of reflective tape off the front and back license plates. She had stopped at a post office en route with the altered plates. If they found her car with the altered plates, they might be able to trace her movements back to the post office. They'd know eventually. But she needed to give her packages a head start.

This is where she would lead them by turning on her cell phone. The point was to be seen. She parked next to the ranger's station and sat for two minutes, hands glued to the wheel, before she worked up the courage to get out. Just follow the plan. If the plan wasn't good enough, it didn't matter now.

"I need a parking pass for five days and a camping permit for four nights," she told the ranger inside, hoping her smile looked genuine. "I'll be backpacking."

The ranger printed out her permits and neatly folded a map to go with them. "A little muddy now, but the weather looks fine. Here you go."

"Any recommendations for trails?"

"Feel like you're in good shape?"

She smiled her most charming smile, with a little bit of flirt, as if she were just a backpacker on an adventure, not a soon-to-be fugitive starting a wild goose chase. "I'd like to think so."

"I like Billy Goat Trail Section A. You'll need good boots— it's strenuous—but you can't beat the view."

"Can you reach any of the islands on foot?"

"There's a bridge to Bear Island. Watch for bicycles, it's busy on the weekends."

"Thanks." She slipped the map into her back pocket.

In the parking lot at the trailhead, she carefully packed her supplies. Everything for camping in the woods and her trip to DC had to fit in her backpack. More importantly, she had to leave nothing behind that might leave clues to where she had been. Even a gas receipt would give her away.

Once she was sure the car was clean, she kneeled next to the driver's seat and unwrapped her phone. Gently, she positioned the phone over the battery underneath her robot. Her nerves quickened her breath. Her robot would work, she told herself. William wouldn't find her until she wanted him to. Or he would and it didn't matter. Her packages had been sent. Her virus had been spread.

She shouldered her backpack and welcomed the weight. A physical force to work against, rather than the shadowy forces that had been stalking her for months. The trees closed in behind her and the parking lot disappeared. She pretended that she was just a backpacker on an early spring hike. A very fast early spring hike. She needed to cover as much ground as she could on the north end of the park before dusk.

When the sun hung low and the trees turned dark under the blue-gray sky she pitched her tent at a flat spot near the trail. Dinner was a freeze-dried meal she rehydrated with boiling water. She should have lain awake to see if she had been followed, but she was lulled quickly to sleep by the wind whispering through the branches. Her alarm woke her at dawn.

Breakfast was oatmeal, a power bar, and some gulps of water. She would need the energy today. Training with Mark had given her stamina, and that would help. But she would still be pushing herself. She walked the Gold Mine Loop trail and every trail she could reach before lunch. She stopped for a short time for a granola bar, nuts, and more water. Then she turned south. She had only the early morning to mark trails before she left for the long bus ride to D.C tomorrow.

CHAPTER 41

JACKSON ANSWERED HIS phone before the first ring finished. He hadn't really been sleeping anyway.

"Yeah."

It was early dawn, judging by the wan light that peeked through his blinds. Tonight he was supposed to begin trailing Navy. He didn't have a plan to stop Curt yet and he didn't know where Curt was planning to take Navy or when she would be spirited away.

"Meeting," Curt's voice barked. "Main office. Now."

The phone clicked before Curt finished the last syllable.

In the car, the news reported that a flight from Maryland to Des Moines had to turn back due to a domestic disturbance. Erin had always been good at thinking on her feet. Any delay she could add would make the false trail in Des Moines seem less credible. If he couldn't get to Navy in time. He pushed down on the gas pedal, weaving between drowsy early morning commuters. He was going too fast; he was tired too. But he hurried anyway. If Curt was unhappy, that was probably good news for Navy. Unless someone else had reached her first.

Jackson found Byron waiting for him in the hallway that led to the conference room.

"I thought I'd let William stew in there for a while," Byron said. "Curt's pissed about something."

"I think William is going to have a heart attack before this is all over." Jackson followed Byron into the claustrophobic conference room. The room was so tiny the back of his chair hit the wall when he pulled it out to sit down.

"We've lost her." Curt's suit was gone. He was dressed in a wrinkled business shirt and khakis. The ends of the shirt hung out of the waistband. The bags under his eyes told Jackson that Curt had been up all night.

"Lost her?" Jackson asked, trying to hide his relief.

"Her phone went off the network in Cleveland. Her license plate hasn't appeared on any of the toll road cameras. We didn't have eyes on her for the drive because we were tracking her with the bug and GPS on her phone. We figured she would come straight to Washington."

"All of her closest friends are in Des Moines," Byron offered. "She doesn't have anyone to hide with."

"What about her social network contacts? Any blog posts? Comments on her blog from people in the Cleveland area?"

"No."

"Could the meeting with her contact be outside of DC?" Jackson asked. Her fictional contact.

"We have eyes on everyone who had access to the detailed mission material. They're all in DC."

That explained why Curt didn't have enough men to tail Navy on the way to DC. He had moved anyone he had covering her in Des Moines to cover all of her potential contacts as well, and he couldn't involve too many people without attracting suspicion. Jackson wondered if this was part of Navy's plan. Was she betting on them being shorthanded? He was impressed. Again.

He hadn't expected she would be able to escape her surveillance even for a little while.

"I don't think she'll miss her date tomorrow," Byron said. "Maybe we should just wait for her to show up."

Curt planted two broad hands on the table, sweeping everyone with a glare. William shifted in his seat nervously. "I need to know what she's doing," Curt said.

"If we call out the cavalry we'll attract too much attention," Jackson said. He pretended to think for a long minute. "Though . . ."

"What?" snapped Curt.

"Byron and I could monitor the lines of her friends and family. If you had a list of numbers. She might be calling someone for help."

"I'll have it sent to you. Get on it. If you hear anything, call me immediately."

Each department and agency collected and stored data a little differently. The list of numbers might give Jackson a clue that could point him toward who had been watching Navy. Jackson followed Byron out of the room. William hadn't been excused. Navy's disappearance would be his fault somehow, and Jackson didn't feel an ounce of pity for him.

❧

The Potomac River ran high and smooth. Navy stretched her aching legs on an outcrop of gray rock streaked with bands of white. The roar of a plane passing overhead drowned out the rustling of the breeze that pushed the first leaves of the season against each other. In the distance, she could hear the rush of traffic on the Clara Barton Parkway. She spread her arms out, laid her back against the rounded rock, as if to make a snow angel. The chill felt good on her sore muscles. When her hands grew too cold, she sat up and rubbed them together, held them out to the morning sun, willing its rays to warm them. Everything she had prepared would be tested tonight. The plan would work or it wouldn't. She would leave DC unharmed or she wouldn't. For every risk she had prepared for, there were a thousand outside her control.

She crossed her legs loosely, cupping her hands over her knees. She closed her eyes to feel the wind, the sun, her own heartbeat keeping time with the slowly rushing water, the horns from the traffic, the restless branches.

But she wanted to be anywhere else. In her apartment in Des Moines preparing to go to a normal day at work. In Amsterdam with Jackson, seeing the sights this time as two tourists and not a psychologist and a patient. At her parent's house in Cedar Rapids, sipping tea and discussing her mother's spring gardening plans. *Acknowledge. Release.* She had no choice; she would do what she had to do.

She emptied her backpack onto the rock. Everything but the tent went into a smaller pack. The tent she returned to the larger pack. She didn't need the tent anymore, and she needed it to weigh the larger pack down.

She gave the larger pack a light shove. Years of memories rolled down the rock, into the lazy currents of the Potomac. She had carried that gear up mountains and paddled it across lakes. She had slept in that tent through snowstorms and thunderstorms. She scraped at the rock with her fingernails to keep from rushing down to the water to save her tent and her backpack. The water slowly closed over the fabric, air bubbles drifting to the surface. As the top of her backpack disappeared, she took a desperate breath, as if she too were drowning.

Her watch beeped insistently. She turned back to the path, her smaller pack heavy on her shoulders. While she walked she checked her mental list to make sure she had everything: a rolled-up ball gown and nylons crammed inside the pirate box, uncomfortable dress shoes that took up too much room, costume supplies, the remainder of her dehydrated meals, camp stove, collapsible water bottles, collapsed red duffel bag, lock picking kit, an emergency radio that could be powered by hand, sleeping bag, ID and credit cards, a roll of cash, and five folded sheets of paper that felt radioactive in her hands.

She walked from the campground and then along the noisy road, gathering curious stares from drivers on MacArthur Boulevard during the one-mile hike to reach the bus stop. Three buses and two hours later she reached DC. At the Foggy Bottom Metro station she rented a bike locker. She took the pirate box out of her backpack and crouched on the ground. Using her body, she shielded the pirate box from any cameras and onlookers as she connected the battery. Out of the corner of her eye she could see the students from George Washington deliberately looking past her. Understandable. A woman in dirty clothes with unwashed hair kneeling on the ground and digging through an overstuffed backpack? To them, she must look homeless.

Like you practiced, she told herself. Take the dress and shoes and makeup for the ball and put them into a plastic shopping bag. Take the backpack and put the whole thing inside the more visible red duffel bag. Every detail would matter later.

A short walk from the campus took her to an overpriced hotel within view of the White House. The doorman wrinkled his nose as she entered. She smelled like public transit, campground, and two days of hard hiking. When the desk clerk swiped her credit card, she almost expected red lights and sirens to go off. William's men would find her soon, and she probably wouldn't even know they were there.

CHAPTER 42

JACKSON WAS HAVING a hard time looking busy while doing nothing. The only activity on the lines Jackson and Byron were monitoring was a few telemarketing calls. Jackson had known Navy was too smart to call anyone she knew. What he had counted on was being able to sneak away to press a few old friends for some information. Unfortunately, Curt had been by every fifteen minutes without fail. When Byron had complained about not getting lunch, Curt brought two greasy hamburgers with limp fries and watery sodas.

Curt's familiar footsteps stormed down the hallway to the tiny room that smelled like sweat and beef.

"She just checked in to the Hay-Adams Hotel," Curt said. "Byron, go to the White House. Jackson, tail her from the hotel."

Curt was separating Jackson and Byron. Why? And why had Navy showed up again? She could have stayed far away from Curt. No, that was wishful thinking. Eventually, Curt would have given up trying to keep things quiet and started a national manhunt. Jackson felt like he was buckled into a roller coaster, being pushed forward, upside down, falling over a horizon he couldn't see.

"You have to trust her plan," Byron said quietly as Curt stormed away. "She made it this far, didn't she?"

Jackson left the office and drove to the Hay-Adams Hotel. Jackson flashed his badge and showed the hotel clerk a photo of Navy. The clerk confirmed that Navy had checked in thirty minutes ago.

Jackson chose a bench where he could watch the front doors. When the slats on the bench started to cut into his thighs, Jackson changed position leaning against a nearby tree, and when his shoulder started to hurt, he found a new bench. At dusk, two hours after they had arrived at the hotel, Navy emerged from the front doors in a long blue gown with sparkling shoulder straps. She must have been cold, but she didn't show it. The gown was tight on top and loose from the waist down, swirling all the way to her ankles. She didn't have a princess' grace in heels, but his breath caught in his throat anyway. Her long hair had been cut into a bob that framed her chin. She must have seen him, but she gave no sign. Everyone saw her. A lone woman dressed in a ball gown crossing the street with purposeful steps. Not staring at her would have made him stand out. Women in fancy dresses left the Hay-Adams all the time. But they had limos and escorts.

Jackson gave Navy a small lead before following. It was a silly exercise. She was heading toward her meeting, of course. She wasn't trying to hide. A small purse that matched her dress swung by a flimsy strap from her hand in time to her measured, careful steps. The sharp clicks of her dress shoes counted down her entrance to the lion's den.

Jackson saw Curt spot Navy as the guard at the East Wing entrance examined her invitation and the contents of her purse. When Navy was inside and being led toward the party, Curt looked at Jackson and pointed toward a side hallway where Byron was supposed to be waiting with their tuxes.

Jackson was reluctant to leave Navy alone with Curt, but he had no choice. A tuxedo would have made him too obvious in front of the Hay-Adams hotel, but not wearing one inside the president's home would make him stick out like a sore thumb. Jackson and Byron dressed quickly. In the immaculate bathroom next to their dressing room, they clipped cufflinks onto their sleeves and pulled at black satin bow ties. Two boutonnieres of pink carnations sat next to the sink. Jackson opened the plastic box and ran his hand over the petals. He was not surprised to find a small metallic bug buried in the center of the flower. The other boutonniere had one as well.

Byron frowned when Jackson silently pointed out the bugs. Jackson pulled up the stopper on the sink and turned on the water. He held a boutonniere over the sink, looking Byron in the eye. "Need some help with that tie?" Jackson asked, for the benefit of their eavesdroppers.

"Sure," Byron said. "Thanks."

Jackson dropped Byron's carnation and bug into the sink. He brushed the other boutonniere into the sink, as if he had knocked it in. He let them soak until he was sure the bugs were shorted out and then drained the sink.

"He didn't give us earpieces," Jackson said. "Curt doesn't want us to be in contact with his team."

"Curt doesn't trust us," Byron said. "This isn't good."

"Shake off that stupid flower and let's go. He's suspicious enough, we don't want to be late."

Brightly lit chandeliers cast a shimmering glow over the ballroom. Tea lights flickered in the center of fresh flower center-pieces. A string quartet played in the corner. A few brave couples were already dancing in the center of the room. Curt's tuxedo was generously cut in the back. Jackson guessed it was to hide a gun. A reedy man with a humorless smile and perfectly white teeth was conferring with Curt. It was Andrew Harrow, the president's chief of staff.

Curt tipped his head to the left and Jackson finally spotted Navy through a break in the crowd. Jackson took a step toward her and stopped. He had to wait for Curt's orders. Curt detached himself from the chief of staff and put himself in between Jackson and Byron.

"Go," Curt said to Jackson. "Rattle her a little bit. It'll make things easier later. I'll come get her in a few minutes." Easier to make her disappear, Curt meant.

Jackson knew this might be his only chance to talk with Navy. She was leaning on the wall next to the bar and sipping something golden and bubbly from a long-stemmed glass. A tilt of her head betrayed her surprise when she saw him.

He should have been watching the whole room, looking to see if other people had been sent to watch her. But he couldn't focus on anything but her unnatural calm. In the microseconds where her composure slipped, he saw she was terrified—and completely under control.

He didn't remember walking toward her, but he must have because now she was in front of him. He felt her gaze move from his scuffed black shoes, the freshly pressed suit, the straight lines of the pleated white tuxedo shirt. He was suddenly jealous of the other guests at the ball who were simply dancing, simply drinking, simply attending a fancy occasion.

"Care to dance?" he asked.

"With whom am I dancing?" She was smiling slightly.

"Jim Marshal, defense contractor."

She nodded slowly and took the hand he offered her. "What firm do you work for?" They walked to the center of the floor, now crowded with couples.

"Frankly, I don't know anymore." He fit his hand to the small of her back. "The name keeps changing."

Jackson scanned the room as they moved across the floor, trying to pick out enemies and friends.

"Who were you talking to?" she asked softly, inches from his ear.

"Curt Holiander." He held her tighter. Curt would be taking her to the meeting with the president. "Be careful with him. Is your plan working out?"

"Did they lose me in Cleveland?" she asked, just as quietly. She smiled politely at a diplomat with a shock of white hair who looked her up and down.

"Up until the hotel."

"Then, yes." He lifted her arm and she twirled around the tip of his finger, her skirt brushing the ankles of other men's tuxedos. "What are we supposed to be tonight?"

"Enemies," he said. The word felt harsh in his mouth, too large and thorny to swallow. "My orders are to make you nervous."

"You didn't know?"

He shook his head, lost.

"You've always made me nervous."

The rest of the world fell away. He tried to act as if his hand didn't fit perfectly against the silky curve of her dress, that his thumb didn't rest easily in the hollow between her fingers and her palm, that their hips weren't swaying in time.

"In your plan," he said, "what happens now?"

"You let me go." Her eyes were following the path of someone behind him. He turned and saw Curt pushing his way through the couples on the dance floor. Curt was agile, aggressive. He would be mean in a fight.

"The president is ready to see you now," Curt said. Navy's grip on Jackson's shoulder tightened for a second before she composed herself. Curt grabbed Navy, tearing her hand away from Jackson's. Her lips brushed Jackson's cheek, but it wasn't a kiss.

Curt was pulling her away. Jackson pressed his sweating palm against the stiff fabric of the tuxedo pants to keep from reaching for her. She was two feet away, three feet away, and then at the edge of dance floor. He could only catch glimpses of her between the rest of the dancers.

She followed Curt out a pair of double doors in the ballroom, her back straight, her purse over one shoulder and held firmly at her side. She didn't look back. Byron stepped into Jackson's line of vision and waved him off the dance floor. Jackson was making a one-man scene, standing in the middle of the dance floor like a castaway tossed to shore.

❧

Navy was led into a room with white walls and elaborate furniture upholstered in orange brocade. The president sat in one of the chairs by the fireplace. She had seen him on CNN, of course. And in campaign ads a few years ago. In person, he seemed like any man who had money enough for an exquisitely coordinated wardrobe and fancy furniture. When she turned to see if Curt had gone, the bare, impassive doors were already shut behind her. Two men with white wires coming out of their ears stood on either side of the doorway. She wondered if they were supposed to protect the president or to keep her in the room.

"Ms. Trent." The president rose from his chair and held out his hand. His fingers were narrow and there was no trace of dirt underneath the nails. She felt like she was reaching out to shake the hand of a wax statue.

She kept the handshake for a second longer than she should have. She wanted to study the face of the man who had aided terrorists in the name of patriotism. The face was both handsome and forgettable. His features did not boast of any particular ancestry. The olive skin could have been Italian or Latin American.

His eyes were chameleonlike, a different color from every angle. "Mr. President."

"Please, sit." He sat down in his chair.

Still standing, she brushed her fingertips against the dark polished wood of the chair across from him. She had planned every detail of her approach and every detail of her escape. Now she found herself mute.

"I believe you called this meeting?" he said.

Was he mocking her? She decided it didn't matter. She had come to make an announcement, not have a discussion. "Not exactly. I would have been content just to come home after Amsterdam. It's important you know that."

He crossed his legs, one ankle on his knee again, and spread his fingers across his lap.

"Someone gave me some information," she said. "Information I wasn't allowed to ignore."

"I read the file. Tragic business."

"A funny thing to say considering someone in your government had me kidnapped."

His affable smile dropped and his eyes narrowed. "What else do you know?"

"That's not important."

"Isn't that why you're here?"

"No. I'm here to give you a message."

The two men at the door shifted their weight and turned toward her.

"Relax, boys." She dangled her purse in front of her. "I'm going to get some sheets of paper out of my purse. Slowly." She handed the folded sheets to the president.

He inhaled sharply as he started to read, then flipped through the rest with wild eyes. "I won't say whether I voted for you," she continued. "But I believed you. Straight talk, honest politics. Integrity. Change. All that."

"Whatever you think I did—"

She held up her hand, enjoying the fact that she temporarily had the power to make the president of the United States stop speaking. "Don't bother. I won't believe you. I don't know whom to believe anymore. I decided to let the crowd sort it out."

He shook his head, still clutching the sheets of paper.

"The documents you have in front of you will be revealed to the world in forty-eight hours, regardless of what happens to me. Or what happens to anyone I know. You can't stop it. I can't stop it. I came to tell you because I thought you should have a chance to clear your name. In case I'm wrong."

He gave a curt nod to the men by the door and one of them whispered something into the mic at his wrist. "This is blackmail," the president said evenly.

"It's not blackmail. I don't have a price."

"Name anything and I can get it for you."

"Weren't you listening? The leak is done. It's in motion. I can't stop it."

"You don't have the clearances to understand what you have."

"Then you didn't organize an operation specifically designed to kill three American operatives to get support for the war in Afghanistan and your precious new surveillance powers?" She looked carefully at his face. She wanted to see if he was guilty or innocent. But his slight, practiced smile gave nothing away. "Whatever you choose to do in the next forty-eight hours, don't lie."

"Okay, I'm curious. How could you keep me from lying? Assuming you're right."

"What you have in your hands is only a small portion of what I have. There will be a second set of documents revealed. If anything you say contradicts what's in there, you lose all of your credibility."

She walked to the door. As she expected, the two guards stepped in front of her.

"I've arranged for protection for my friends and family. If anything happens to any of them, the documents will be released early. Don't bother bringing them in. They don't know anything."

The guards didn't move.

"You probably want me to leave. I have a very important meeting to make. If I'm not there in time, you'll be the only story on the morning news."

"If what you say is true—that no matter what I do to you all this becomes public anyway—why would I let you leave?"

"Because you thought I came here to make a deal and you aren't prepared for the reckoning. Because you think I'll lead you to the person I'm working with. Because you think you can capture me and force me to tell you how to make sure your secrets stay secret."

"Do you think you're smarter than I am, Ms. Trent?" For the first time, she believed the president had arranged for the death of three American agents for political convenience.

Her next words weren't the words of the Navy who had been kidnapped. Nor the words of the woman who had killed four men. They were the words of the woman who had formed to protect the woman left behind, beaten and afraid, in a dark parking lot. "I don't know," she said. "Why don't we find out?"

She couldn't look back. She was afraid her face would betray her fear. The president's signal, whatever it was, was silent. The two men stepped out of her way, one whispering urgently into his wrist.

Time to run.

⸙

"She's been in there a long time," Jackson said. Curt was watching Jackson and Byron closely from across the room.

"It's only been ten minutes. Curt doesn't look happy. She must be all right." Byron smiled as if Jackson had commented on the tablecloths or the flower arrangements.

Jackson took a sip of whatever he'd ordered to keep his hands busy. Curt pressed a finger to his ear—someone was talking to him through the earpiece—and his face took on the complexion of a mottled apple.

"Well, something's changed," Byron said.

Anything that made Curt angry was probably good for Navy.

Curt waved them over. "Get back to headquarters. Now."

"What about—" Byron asked.

Curt's eye narrowed to slits. "We're letting her go. And you can't tail her in those penguin suits." Curt stomped away.

"I'll meet you at headquarters," Jackson told Byron.

"Don't do anything stupid," Byron said.

Jackson loitered outside the entrance, hands shoved in his pockets. He didn't have a plan. The only thing he knew was that he had to see Navy leave, to know she was all right. At least for a little bit longer. A door opened and a woman's heels clicked against the hard steps. She was moving as quickly as she could in the uncomfortable shoes. Two figures moved in the shadows of the building. He wondered what she had done to buy her freedom. They were letting her go, but they weren't going to let her disappear again.

He fell into step beside her and she refused to look at him, continuing to stare straight ahead.

"You need to go," she said under her breath. "Now." She was fearless and afraid, completely in control of her long strides, as she watched her tails in the shadows.

There were two figures behind her and now two more in the shadows twenty yards in front of her, ready to box them in. Her freedom was conditional. "You're not the person I'm supposed to meet," she said. "If you don't leave, it will be very dangerous for both of us."

"Navy . . ." Jackson whispered. He saw her as she was the first night they met, when she was tired and bruised and still willing to fight. He saw her as she was in the gym learning from Erin, hitting the bag until her arms refused to lift anymore. And this Navy, standing like a statue, her dress shimmering under a pale moon. She wore a heavy sadness with grace.

"It has to be like when I left Amsterdam," she said. She turned toward him with a fierce expression that made him stumble. The shutters fell from her eyes and he saw her desperation, heard it in the banshee-like scream that echoed off the concrete. "Leave me alone!"

He stepped back, the hard soles of his shoes catching on a crack in the sidewalk. Her tails continued to follow her as she hurried away, like black roses attached to an invisible train on her dress. Heavy footsteps ran toward him. Curt.

"I told you to go back to headquarters."

"I was on my way. Why are we letting her go?" Jackson asked. She was getting smaller, starting to blend in with the darkness.

"Little bitch had a trick up her sleeve."

Jackson held his tongue. He kept his face turned toward Navy, unsure whether his expression would give him away, even in the dark.

"It is a waste," Curt said, watching Navy. "She won't be so pretty when I'm done with her."

The knife sheathed at Jackson's ankle itched. His mind was already planning the motions. Three moves and two strokes with the knife and he could have Curt bleeding like a stuck pig.

"We have work to do," Curt said. "Let's go."

For a second, Jackson hated Navy for arranging things so he had to stand and watch, helpless, while she walked into danger.

Was this how she had felt in Amsterdam? Trapped by what he wouldn't tell her? Her refusal to share anything with him may have protected him in the beginning, but now he was a pawn in someone else's game.

CHAPTER 43

PART OF NAVY wished that the president had called her bluff. She'd be a captive again, in very dangerous company. But she would have been done running. One block to the Foggy Bottom Metro Station on the George Washington University Campus.

Navy timed her steps so she had to stop at the crosswalk. All she carried was a purse with three items: the key to the bike storage locker she had rented, the invitation to the president's fancy event, and a compact with foundation powder that had cracked into five hard chunks from hiking. She pulled out the compact, angling the mirror discreetly to see how many were behind her. Three men, one woman. She hadn't expected them to send a woman.

The light changed and she tucked the compact back in her purse. She continued across the street, forcing herself to keep an even pace. There was no point in trying to outrun them. She would need that energy later.

The bike locker opened easily. Her stash appeared to be undisturbed. She disconnected the battery pack from the pirate box. The light on the cell phone modem faded from a bright green to black. The batteries went into the duffel bag. She disconnected the thumb drive from the pirate box, keeping it in her hand.

She slung the bright red duffel bag over her shoulder, knowing it would make her visible in the crowd. Just as she intended.

Keep following the plan, she told herself. Navy crossed the street again, and walked to the beer and burger place she'd picked out on her earlier trip to DC. The bag bounced on her shoulder, jostled by the line of people waiting to order. She went straight to the bathrooms. Three stalls and they were all busy. The crowd that would hide her was also going to delay her.

Someone finished and left. Navy set the duffel bag on the toilet and pulled the dress up over her head. Her tail would be here soon. Navy pulled her pack out of the duffel bag and hung it on the bathroom door. The dress she rolled into a ball and stuck into the duffel bag. The jeans were a relief after the panty hose and dress shoes. The sweatshirt would hide her figure.

A pair of shoes appeared in the stall next to her, conservative brown loafers. Most of the students wore sneakers or Doc Martins. Her tail?

The wig itched on her scalp when she pinned it into place. The colored contacts stung her eyes when she put them in; she hadn't had time to wait for the hand sanitizer to dry completely. Now she was a brown-eyed redhead. The bathroom had emptied except for the stall next to her. Now Navy was sure it was her tail.

Even with her disguise, it would be foolish to run. She had to keep them from seeing her disguise until she could blend in with the crowd. Duct tape. She always brought some for camping. She found the small roll next to her burn phone in the outside pocket of her pack. Another person entered. She waited for the toilet to flush to cover the sound of the ripping duct tape. She forced herself to relax her tense muscles. Tension would just slow her down. She opened her door, saw the lock on the stall next to her turning to open too. She turned the circle on the lock to close the stall and pressed the strip of duct tape over the metal circle that controlled the lock, pretending to stumble against the door. The person in the stall gasped. No one seemed to notice.

Something clattered to the floor as she straightened: her burn phone. Navy watched as it spun into an occupied stall. She didn't dare waste the time to find it—she didn't know how long her tail would be fumbling with the lock.

A few seconds, that's all she needed. To get out of the bathroom and onto the street.

At the Foggy Bottom Metro Station, she squeezed onto the escalators with the river of people. Even the mild descent left her feeling lightheaded. The ceilings and walls wavered, ready to close in on her, until there was nowhere to run. She shook her head to clear the feeling. The station was crowded. Just as she wanted. She had lost her trackers in Cleveland. Just as she wanted. A few more lucky breaks and she just might come out of the whole thing alive.

She pushed her way out of the bathroom and followed the crowd to a northbound train. She had left the red duffel in the stall. She had different hair, different eyes, and a different outfit. She hoped that was enough. In her pack, the butt of her gun pushed against her back on the crowded train. The contact lenses felt dry, and she blinked often to keep her eyes moist. What would a normal passenger do? Grab a handhold and look around bored. She grabbed the grimy rail above the full seats and pretended not to notice that four figures were pushing people out of their way to reach the trains.

She rode the trains randomly until she had lost her tails. At an overpriced tourist shop she used cash to buy a new sweatshirt. She changed again, stowing the sweatshirt she had been wearing in her pack. In a fast food restaurant bathroom, she filled her collapsible water bottles at the tap. She chose the longest possible route on the Metro to Union Station, arriving in time to catch the 1:00 a.m. bus to Baltimore.

As she settled on the bus, Navy saw a reflection in the window and smiled politely at the stranger before realizing it was her own face. In the cars below her window, parents drove sleeping children home. Groups of college kids danced to music so loud she could hear it through the bus windows. Tired second shift workers held on to their steering wheels like zombies.

By the time the bus reached downtown Baltimore around 2:00 a.m., the contacts felt like sandpaper. She shouldered her pack, the blunt handle of the gun bouncing against her spine, and walked east toward Patterson Park. Patterson Park was everything her research had told her to expect. A neighborhood with some nice streets and some blighted streets. The real estate bust had hit hard here. Which is exactly why she had picked this area in advance. The neighbors were up in arms over the developers and landlords who had abandoned their properties to crack dealers and drug addicts. A good place to hide.

She walked down the street as if she knew where she were going. Dogs barked from the few occupied homes. Curtains parted and then closed as she passed. Eventually, she found a block that had only boarded-up houses. She chose the house where the garbage had blown into a pile on the wooden porch. Hopefully it had been abandoned long enough that anything of value was gone.

The alley was darker than the street; she had to pick the lock at the back door entirely by touch. Even so, she could tell the lock was new and the doorjamb was scarred. She relocked the door from the inside.

Something scurried across the kitchen when she set down her pack. She stood in the eerie silence until her eyes adjusted to the dim interior. Once, it had been a nice place to live. The drywall in the kitchen had been torn out to steal the copper pipes for scrap. Electric wires stuck out of holes where outlets had been. Even the kitchen faucet had been stolen. Good.

She walked through the upper floor of her temporary home. There was evidence of past tenants: a soiled mattress nibbled by rodents and a pile of dirty clothes in the corner. There was a toilet she could use if she didn't mind not being able to flush. But no signs that anyone had been there recently.

She took the stairs to the basement and unrolled her sleeping mat on the concrete floor. The air stunk like mildew. She would count herself lucky if the house stayed empty for two more days. As she settled in her sleeping bag, she checked her watch. In ten minutes, her deodorant robot would push the battery back into place and turn her phone on.

CHAPTER 44

CURT SLAMMED THE Wonder Woman lunch box down on the table in front of Byron, Jackson, and a very nervous IT person. Jackson stifled a yawn. They had been out for hours looking for Navy. He had seen every bored hotel night desk clerk within half an hour of the capitol.

"Okay, I'll bite," Jackson said. "What is it?"

"I don't know." Curt's face had been as dark as a thundercloud since Navy lost her tails at the Metro station. "Can you tell me?"

Had Jackson given something away? Or had someone suspected that he was working with Navy ever since Amsterdam? If Curt had anything firmer than innuendo to accuse Jackson with, Curt would have. "I don't know," Jackson said evenly.

Curt pushed the box toward the technician. "Then you tell me."

The technician dug inside the box, then smiled. "Neat work." Then he looked at Curt's face and sobered. "It's a pirate box."

"A what?"

"A pirate box. It's a wireless router plus a Dockstar and a thumb drive. They're designed to share files with anyone within range of the signal. But this one is a little different. It's designed to share files, but it also has a connection to the Internet. See the cell phone modem? Was the modem powered off when you found it?"

"Yes. What does it do?"

The technician took the Dockstar out of the box. "This lets you share files on a thumb drive with other computers. But the thumb drive is missing?" He connected the Dockstar to his laptop, fumbling with the cables. Curt leaned in, blocking Jackson's view. "It looks like . . . it was programmed to send whatever was on the thumb drive to a list of email addresses at midnight. Mostly reporters' email addresses. All over the world. But you found it at 10:30. The emails never got sent. Oh, there's a README. It says 'Do you believe me now?'"

Curt cracked his knuckles and swore under his breath. "Then she wasn't lying."

"Wasn't lying about what?" Byron asked.

When Curt turned on him angrily, Byron held up his hands in submission. "Look, I'd be happy to be off this case. But if you want me to be useful, you need to fill me in," Byron said.

Smooth, Jackson thought. On most operations, Jackson could keep his cool. He was known for it. On this operation he was having trouble not strangling Curt every time they were in a room together.

"Navy told the president she had a meeting to make," Curt said. "And if she didn't make it, everything she knew would become public. We thought she meant a person. So we weren't going to pick her up until we saw her meet with her contact."

Jackson hid a smile. It explained why she had been so eager for him to walk away. And so confident that they would let her go. "What about her phone?" he asked.

"Her phone is still off the network. When you were dancing with her, did she have it on her?"

For a split second, Jackson felt Navy's lips brushing his cheek. "It could have been in that purse she had."

Curt's phone vibrated. When he read the message his eyes widened. "Her phone is back on the network. At Ohio Canal National Park. How the fuck did she get all the way out there?"

She knew they were tracking her phone, Jackson thought. She knew better than to turn it on.

"Do you want us to go?" Byron said.

"I'll get the ranger out of bed. You and Jackson will go interview him. I'll meet you there."

Jackson finally let his nerves show when he was alone in the car with Byron. "She wouldn't turn that phone on unless she was desperate," Jackson said.

"Or someone else already tracked her down and wants to make sure she's found." Byron winced, realizing what he had implied. "I'm sorry. We don't know—"

"Just keep driving," Jackson said. He couldn't find the energy to apologize, even though he knew he should.

Byron pressed down on the accelerator. Jackson had twenty minutes to think about all the ways he would make Curt suffer if Jackson and Byron found Navy's body.

The ranger was waiting in the parking lot. He shuffled his feet and tugged on his green coat. The night was black and cold.

"I remember her," the ranger said when Jackson showed him Navy's photo. "She seemed fine. She bought a five-day car permit and four nights of camping. Is she in some sort of trouble?"

"She was supposed to check in with her boyfriend," Jackson said, flipping the fake police badge closed. "It's probably nothing, but the father's connected . . . you know how it goes."

"Well, she had a backpack full of gear. She asked which trails were good. Seemed like she knew what she was doing."

"What trails did you recommend?" Byron asked. He had a notebook open and was pretending to jot down the ranger's answers casually.

"Ummmm . . . Billy Goat Section A and the Bear Island loop. I saw her at the campground yesterday morning, digging around in her car. I hope she's okay."

"I'm sure everything's fine. Thanks for your help."

"Let's check out her car," Jackson said to Byron. His eyes adjusted to the darkness quickly as he walked down the short road to the campground. Clouds blocked the stars. The black dome of the sky made the park feel small and oppressive. The few tents in the campground were far enough away that Jackson could jimmy the lock on Navy's car without attracting attention.

The overhead lights in the car came on. Her cell phone wasn't on any of the seats. He took a penlight out of his back pocket and crouched to search. "It's here, under the driver's seat," Jackson said. He grabbed the phone and stood up.

"The ranger said she had a pack," Byron said. "But there's nothing in the car." He opened the trunk, then looked at Jackson and shook his head.

The glove compartment had a few maps and her insurance card. There were no clues to say where Navy was or what had happened to her.

"Do you think she was taken from here?" Byron frowned.

Jackson pointed at the speaker on Navy's phone and held a finger to his lips. "Well, if she was trying to call someone before she dropped the phone she didn't manage to. There are no outgoing calls for the past two days."

Jackson and Byron walked back to the main entrance in silence. Had someone taken Navy? She wouldn't have turned her phone on unless she had no choice. Or . . . she wanted to throw them off her trail. But how could she have inserted the battery and turned on the phone remotely?

The ranger was repeating his story to Curt. Another car was

behind Curt's. The shadow of a dog's head was visible against the backseat window. Curt had brought in a tracker.

"Her phone," Curt demanded.

Jackson was glad to be rid of it. He wouldn't be able to talk normally until they were out of its range.

Curt handed Jackson a gallon-sized plastic bag with a ball of blue fabric. Navy's dress. A sequin had fallen off and was lodged in the corner.

"Give that to the handler."

"Shouldn't we wait until first light?" Jackson squinted at the dark forest between them and the river.

"We don't have time."

The German shepherd snarled and barked when Jackson knocked on the driver's window. He hoped Navy wasn't out there. The window rolled down. The handler had a tense, square jaw. His eyes were in shadow. His right hand was holding a cell phone up to his ear. "What."

"Your exemplar." Jackson passed the dress into the dark cave of the car. The handler started rolling up the window before Jackson pulled his arm out.

"Charmer," said Byron as they walked away, toward the campground. "I wonder who took her."

"No one took her," Jackson said. He knew he sounded like he was in denial. "There's no sign of a struggle, and she wouldn't go without a fight."

"There's no way she could have put the battery back in remotely. You have to admit that."

Jackson's shoes crunched in the gravel as he stopped. "The ranger's station had a box outside where you could fill out permits and pay."

Byron nodded slowly. "Yes. Most parks do."

"So she didn't have to go inside to talk to the ranger," Jackson said.

"Unless—"

"She's laying a false trail. Has Curt seen the car yet?" Jackson asked.

"Nope, he's still scaring the ranger."

"Watch for him." Jackson reached under the driver's seat and felt for anything out of place. He wondered what he was expecting to find. Not expecting, he thought. Hoping. Anything to give him some hint that Navy hadn't been abducted. A hard object brushed the top of his hand. He reached up to tug on it.

"Incoming," Byron said.

Jackson took a knife out of his pocket and sliced at the spots that had the most resistance. Something fell into his hand. He shoved it quickly into the pocket of his cargo pants.

"Is her camping gear in the car?" Curt asked.

"Nope," Byron said.

"Then she must be out there."

"Ranger said the easiest place for her to hide would be along one of the wooded trails," Byron said. "Like the inner mine loop."

"You two check it out. I want to look through the car."

Jackson and Byron scrambled along the path, feeling their way through rough terrain in the dark. When the sound of brushing tree branches and owls replaced people's voices, Jackson stopped. Byron turned on his flashlight so Jackson could examine the plastic object Jackson had pulled out of his pocket. It was a large stick of deodorant. But heavier. And the cap was missing. Jackson angled the deodorant so Byron's flashlight shone into the holes on top. All the deodorant had been replaced with plastic pieces and wiring. He tried to twist the circle on the bottom but it wouldn't turn. There was a switch next to the circle on the bottom. He flipped it on. A rod extended from the case then disappeared again. "It's a robot," he said, grinning wildly. "A robot that could have turned her cell phone on."

"Son of a bitch. Her odds are better than I thought."

"She chose a good spot to fake her disappearance. They'll have to check anywhere she could reach by crossing the river too. That, plus a hundred acres should keep them busy for a while." He kept his hand wrapped around the device in his pocket as they stumbled down the trail, killing time. She was alive. Navy was alive. And if Jackson just played along, she would have plenty of time to get ahead of Curt.

"Did you figure out anything based on the phone list he sent us?" Byron asked.

"Someone inside the CIA pulled it. That's about it. You?"

"My contacts clammed up." Byron shook his head, clearly worried. "I couldn't open the files she gave us. Have you tried?"

"A few hundred times. We're going to have to be more paranoid than usual."

"I can't figure out which side Curt is working for."

"He does have some scary friends," Jackson said. The sound of a dog barking came from the direction of the parking lot. "I'd rather not be in the woods with that thing."

"Let's keep moving," Byron said. "We need Curt to think we're searching for Navy." Byron glanced sideways at Jackson. "Funny how she seems to have everyone twisted around her little finger."

"Oh, shut it," Jackson muttered.

CHAPTER 45

THE BASEMENT IN Navy's temporary home was dark and moldy. Small slivers of daylight escaped past the edges of the plywood that covered the windows.

She had imagined the biggest challenge while hiding would be her nerves. Instead, she found it was difficult to stay awake. She drifted off to sleep midthought. Her naps were shallow and unsatisfying. She tensed every time a car drove by or she heard voices in the alley. Things scurried in the corners and inside the walls. She zipped up her sleeping bag all the way to her chin and sweated inside. Even then, her skin twitched with the imagined tickles of insect legs.

She had a headlamp, but light didn't make the room more comforting anyway. The concrete block walls were covered with graffiti. A spray of brown water covered the far wall in a sticky arc. Blackened spoons and used-up lighters gathered in the corners. Eighteen hours ago she had been in an expensive hotel room waiting for her hair to dry, getting dressed for the president's formal ball. Now her hair was stringy, oily, and matted from being stuffed underneath the wig.

Her pack seemed cavernous when she lit the inside with her headlamp. She dug in the bottom, past a cell phone modem, her small roll of duct tape, and a net book. The emergency radio was buried underneath her spare sweatshirt. She was tempted to bring out the cell phone modem, connect it to the net book, plug back into the world. Maybe Jackson had emailed her. But it was too early to risk exposure. She spun the handle on the side of the radio until she could hear static on the speakers. It didn't take long to find the local news.

She was more grateful than she wanted to admit when the news interrupted the damp silence.

"A flight from Maryland to Des Moines was diverted today because of a domestic disturbance. The Transportation Security Administration released a statement saying the incident began when a wife discovered her husband's mistress was also on the plane. In other news the administration is warning that the latest weapon in the terrorist's arsenal might be information, not bombs. Recent terrorist chatter indicates that there may be a plot to discredit the president just when he is about to take up the issue of extending the surveillance powers in the Patriot Act."

Navy pulled her legs to her chest, holding them tightly. She had expected a nationwide manhunt to start after they failed to bring her in quietly, to be labeled as an enemy of the state. The manhunt would have provided the context for the set of documents revealed by her virus. The secrets she knew plus the threat of capture by her government would prove she was being targeted for political reasons. She had hoped to make herself too high-profile to kill quietly. Instead William's men—the president's men—wanted her existence to be a secret a little bit longer.

She rocked back and forth feeling her old friend, panic, close in as the sound from the radio faded.

Mark's gruff face popped into her mind; she could almost felt his meaty hand on her forearm pulling her up from the mat. She unfolded her legs and sat cross-legged, let her knees hover over the dirty floor. Her lungs were stiff, locked in place by the same fear that churned in her stomach. The first breaths of her meditation were shaky and uncertain. There could be assassins stalking her through the streets of Baltimore. Opponents who were stronger, faster, and more experienced than she was. The president's men might have found a scrap of evidence in her apartment that would give up her secrets. Stop the computer virus she had written. The thoughts wouldn't be pushed away. She focused on her breath instead and eventually she could take one full breath. Then two. Breathe in for six counts, out for seven.

It wasn't the sun-drenched square of carpet in her apartment. But it was enough for now. Her fingertips brushed the textured handle of her gun sitting next to her. She cranked the radio again. As the news switched to the morning call-in show, her eyelids grew heavy. An hour later she woke up in silence. She slept the rest of the day and night in spurts, cranking the radio until her wrist hurt, waking when the sound faded.

Erin took a long shower in the impersonal hotel room she had been told to check into. Her second flight to Des Moines had gone off without a hitch, and she hadn't thought of any other ideas for delaying her mission. Erin was supposed to pretend to be Navy fleeing to Canada. Erin had been given a duplicate of Navy's passport to use when crossing the border and soon there would be a car waiting in the parking lot that matched the registered make, model and color of Navy's.

But Erin knew she would think of something to frustrate Curt's plan. Or tell Curt to fuck off. Navy's decision to go it alone made it hard for Erin to protect Navy, but Erin wasn't going to help Curt cover up Navy's disappearance. If Curt succeeded in murdering Navy, Erin would see that he paid for it. Curt had almost reached through her cell phone to throttle her when he learned her flight had to turn back. He had the nerve to accuse her of creating the disturbance on purpose.

She had, but Curt had no way of knowing that. The love triangle she had noticed while waiting to board had been a stroke of luck. Sure, the napkin with the lipstick print hadn't actually belonged to the mistress. But the husband had looked for the mistress when he found the napkin. A slight kick to the wife's seat had been enough to get her to look up from her magazine to notice the lipstick and her husband's roving eyes. From there the whole situation had blossomed quite nicely.

If Curt weren't so suspicious, she would simply fake a bad cold and stay in the room for three days. April 22 was tomorrow. That was the date their archives would open. Hopefully, her mission would be irrelevant by then.

Or they could have already captured Navy in DC. Curt wouldn't have told Erin and she was under strict orders not to contact Jackson or Byron. Or anyone. Curt had taken her cellphone before she left and she suspected Curt had eyes on her for the whole trip. Her stomach growled and she considered dinner.

A good soldier would walk to a restaurant. A good soldier would make herself memorable. She browsed the room service menu and settled on the fourteen dollar hamburger with crinkle-cut fries. She ignored the knock on the door when her meal arrived. A good soldier would have answered the door to create another witness. The tray bumped into the bottom of the door as it was set down, then the footsteps headed toward the elevator. She padded over to the door to get her food but someone was there. Kyle Pierson. William's rival had followed her all the way to Des Moines. Kyle looked up and down the hall, at her door, and then walked away. *What did he want?*

She devoured her food while watching whatever old movies

were on USA. Some action adventure movie supposedly featuring spies. More like comedy. Spies didn't drive fancy sports cars. They drove late model cars that were common in the area, cars that didn't attract attention. And she could count on one hand the number of times she'd needed to enter a club full of scantily clad women for an assignment. Most of her assignments involved boring hotel rooms. Or hot, dry, dusty tents in some corner of a military camp.

Four hours later her stomach was doing flip-flops. She recognized the distinctive sudden nausea of food poisoning. When her stomach had emptied its contents into the toilet, she collapsed on the bed. She took a sip of water from the plastic cup she'd filled from the tap. But even water wouldn't stay down.

Fuckin' great, she thought. Now Curt would accuse her of faking an illness. He might figure out that she was working with Jackson and Byron to protect Navy. And it was Kyle's fault. There were ways she could have helped Navy without being a target herself. Erin would have some scores to settle when she got home. The door to the room next to hers opened and heavy suitcases landed on the bed. Surveillance equipment. She hoped her watchers enjoyed the show.

✎

Jackson was trying very hard to look worried instead of relieved. He and Byron were in the parking lot with Curt listening to the tracker deliver the results of his latest search.

"What do you mean you can't find her?" Curt was livid. Again. They had been searching the park all day.

The German shepherd was finally showing signs of being tired. The dog jumped obediently into the car when his handler gave the signal. "There are trails with her scent everywhere," the handler said.

"Then why can't you find her?" Curt asked.

"She's been on almost every trail in this park. Either she's moving very quickly ahead of me or . . ."

"Or what."

"Or these are old trails. Trails she took while scouting for a place to hole up . . . or trails she left for us to find." Curt looked angrier with every word.

"We could search this park for days," the handler said. "If she's even still here. Get her to come to you. This is a dead end."

The logical next step for Curt was to threaten someone Navy cared about and force her to show herself. Jackson hoped that Navy's plan to protect her friends and family was as solid as her escape plan.

"Fine. Take your mutt and get out of here." Curt said.

Part of Jackson was glad to see the handler and his vicious dog leave. But he wanted to buy Navy more time. Was she safely hidden or still on the run? He checked his watch. Eight hours before the date changed to April 22. Eight hours before he could open the files Navy had given him.

"I have a feeling we're going to be on a plane soon," Byron said.

Curt's back was facing them, his cell phone pressed up against his ear. "Have the father arrested. For what? I don't care. Just have him at the station when I get there." Curt shoved his phone in his pocket and turned around. "You two are coming to Cedar Falls with me."

Jackson felt the high from knowing Navy was alive fading. What if her family wasn't as protected as she thought? "Are you sure threatening her father is wise?" Jackson asked.

Curt's expression was about as friendly as Jackson had expected.

"Navy wasn't bluffing about the meeting with her pretend contact," Jackson said. "What if she's not bluffing about having protection for her family? What if arresting her father means the material is leaked early?"

Both of Curt's hands had formed into white-knuckled fists. "I have the resources of the United States government. She's one fucking girl. She can't hide from me."

✦

The private plane Jackson, Byron, and Curt took to Cedar Rapids, Iowa, was dingy but functional. The kind of plane that looked like it had been used to smuggle valuable objects over borders. Jackson closed his eyes when they took off. It was hard to be civil around Curt, and he needed the sleep. Jackson awoke when the landing gear hit the tarmac.

A car was waiting at the airfield. Curt tossed the keys to Byron and climbed in the backseat with a thick manila folder. He pored over the files as they pulled onto the gravel road leading out of the small airfield. Jackson caught a glimpse of a tax return.

"Anything we can use against Navy's father?" Byron asked.

"He's a Boy Scout," Curt said. "Even his itemized deductions are itemized correctly."

At the police station an eerily familiar voice filled the lobby. The officer behind the counter was young, inexperienced, and completely intimidated by the woman who was currently berating him. Navy's mother. "Tell me why you have arrested my husband. Now."

The frantic voice on the recording with the police in Amsterdam had led Jackson to imagine someone weaker. When Navy's mother turned to see who had entered the police station, Jackson saw the same heart-shaped face and determined jawline. Her brown hair was shoulder length and gray at the roots. Her tan face was mapped with laugh lines at her eyes and worry lines on her forehead.

A man in gray slacks and a long-sleeved shirt fraying at the cuffs looked Curt over, then stood up and walked to Navy's mother. "I believe I can help, ma'am."

"Who are you?" she demanded.

The officer behind the desk sat down, relieved.

"A friend," said the man in slacks. "I think I can settle this for you." He placed his palm on Navy's mother's elbow and led her to a seat. "If you'll just wait here for a minute."

Curt had noticed the man in gray slacks too. Curt went straight to him. "Why are you helping her? Who are you?"

"Derek Mollan, private investigator. You must be the bookie."

"The what?" Curt stiffened and clenched his fists. By Jackson's count, he and Byron had Curt had been up for at least twenty-four hours straight.

"She said to look out for the scary-looking guy who would show up after the arrest."

"Who said?"

"Friend of the family." Derek smiled. Ex–law enforcement or military, Jackson figured. Whatever his history, Derek had been in enough dicey situations that even Curt's aggressive stance didn't intimidate him. "Mind if we talk for a minute?"

"Talk quickly."

"This friend of the family was concerned that you might do something that would get Mr. Trent arrested."

Curt's neck and face bloomed crimson.

"I have a courier headed to a reporter's office with information that might be embarrassing to you. A package very much like this one." He pulled a tan envelope lined with bubble wrap out of his worn leather briefcase and handed it to Curt.

Curt opened the sealed envelope and a book slid into his hand. The title of the book was *Critical Mass*. Jackson bit his own cheek to keep from smiling. Curt opened up the front cover, read a quick scrawl of handwriting, and threw the book to the floor. The smack made everyone in the room jump.

"I can make a call and tell the courier to cancel the order," Derek said calmly. "Of course, that will depend on me seeing Mr. Trent leave police custody within the next ten minutes."

"Who sent you?" Curt demanded, as if there was any question.

Derek took a tactical step back. Enough room to give himself space to fight, but not so much that Curt could mistake it for retreat. "That's not important. I'll just wait here until I see Mr. Trent leave. Or not. It's really up to you."

Curt turned his back on Derek and directed his next demand to the officer behind the desk. "Let me in." The officer pressed a button and a harsh buzzing sound signaled the door was opening. Jackson waited until the solid metal door closed and locked behind Curt to pick up the book on the floor. The note written inside the front cover said "Do you believe me now?" He could hear her saying it as if she was in the room.

Byron looked over Jackson's shoulder. "Clever."

Within five minutes, a harried middle-aged man was led out into the lobby. Navy's mother ran to him and hugged him. Derek Mollan watched the couple leave, then made a call on his cell phone. Jackson and Byron followed Curt to the car. This time Curt took the driver's seat.

Five miles down the road, they stopped at a gas station. "I'm going to get coffee," Curt said. Jackson watched through the grimy windows as Curt walked past the coffee machine and into one of the aisles. He made a call on his cell phone, pacing as he talked.

"We need to figure out what his endgame is," Byron said.

"You said he was an assassin. What else can you remember from the recording?"

"He was a soldier in Afghanistan. The sole survivor of an IED attack on his squad during a covert op. I couldn't find him through the official casualty reports. The attack is why Curt was chosen for this.”

“Because he has combat skills?”

Byron kept a careful eye on Curt as they talked. “Because he has the motivation. Andy gave him this little speech about some fancy new surveillance system that could find terrorists before they strike, said that if Navy went public with the details of Operation Critical Mass, the president couldn’t get the legislation passed to authorize the new surveillance system.”

Jackson frowned. “The operation in Amsterdam was all based on old-fashioned intelligence. There’s something we’re missing.” He saw Curt ending his phone call. “He nearly blew his cover at the party when he got the order to let Navy go. He slips up when he gets angry.”

“He hates you already. I nominate you.”

“You’re a good friend, Byron.”

“Anytime.”

When Curt got back into the driver’s seat, his hands were empty.

“How’s the coffee?” Jackson asked.

“Changed my mind. We’re flying back to DC. I want you two looking over Navy’s financial records and the forensics report from her laptops. Nobody disappears without leaving any clues.” Curt started the car, then pressed his foot down on the gas impatiently before shifting out of park and cutting off a driver pulling out of the gas station.

“Looking for her is a waste of time,” Jackson said. “She wasn’t lying when she said she had a meeting to make. She wasn’t lying when she said she had arranged protection for her family. What if she’s telling the truth about finding her not preventing the information about Operation Critical Mass from leaking?”

“Cowards will say anything to save their own skin,” Curt said.

Jackson could almost hear Curt's teeth grinding over the sound of the engine. They were traveling at eighty miles an hour. Jackson couldn't push Curt much further without risking an accident. "And if we do find her before the deadline? And the information is leaked anyway?"

"Then we punish her."

He skipped past the image of Navy being tortured at Curt's hands. "You're wasting my time with a revenge mission?"

"No. You're wasting my time with these questions."

What Jackson wanted to do was find a quiet rest stop on the highway where he could have some quality time with Curt. But Curt was just the messenger. It was Curt's superior Jackson needed to find. In the meantime, he would have to email Navy and hope she was able to check the address she'd given him. If she expected to be safe once her secrets were revealed, she was wrong.

CHAPTER 46

ERIN NIBBLED AT a saltine cracker and took a sip of lukewarm water from the plastic cup on the nightstand. It had been six hours since she last threw up. She hoped the worst of it was over. Kyle certainly had access to worse poisons than E. coli. Curt hadn't called. Her friends next door were probably keeping him updated. A brown circle of grilled meat topped with bright green lettuce and a juicy tomato slice filled the television screen. Her stomach turned and she changed the channel.

A CNN anchor shuffled papers in front of a bank of monitors. "Explosive documents were revealed this morning about a CIA operation in Amsterdam that may have resulted in the accidental kidnapping of three American citizens. The documents were revealed by what appears to be a computer virus, though experts haven't yet managed to isolate a copy of the virus for analysis. We have Jennifer Ward on Capitol Hill with the latest about what is now being called the Amsterdam Operation."

Erin was sure Jennifer Ward wasn't the only journalist outside the White House gates. She could imagine the line of vans, one from each of the major stations, each roof bristling like a porcupine with antennas and the dish for the satellite feed. The correspondent's carefully arranged short red hair was framed by a gray morning sky. "It's getting complicated quickly, Mike. The White House released a statement yesterday warning about a terrorist plot to use disinformation against the United States government, but inside sources are telling us the documents are genuine. Reporters at several national newspapers, including our sister paper, have received additional material from a woman named Navy Trent that contradicts the White House's statements. I'm afraid it will be awhile before this is all sorted out. In the meantime, officials are looking for Navy Trent. The White House claims she's in hiding while critics contend Navy Trent may have been targeted as an enemy combatant under the Authorization of Military Force put in place shortly after 9/11."

Erin pressed the mute button. The scene switched from the White House to generic shots of Amsterdam and then some low-resolution pictures of Navy, probably from Facebook. Then higher resolution images of documents from the file on Operation Critical Mass. So far, it was only the most innocuous documents from the file—if anything in that file could be called innocuous. One document that discussed plans to target and track the kidnapping ring. A few pictures of the terrorists killed at the mansion, with snippets of their dossiers. And some of the messages sent to the kidnappers. Any lines that named a specific agent or Sara or Moss had been redacted. By Navy or the station, Erin wondered.

The connection to Sara and Moss would be out soon enough. The agent names might, with luck, stay secret. Erin scowled. Choosing what to reveal was a delicate business. Navy's life wasn't the only one at stake.

She finished the first cracker and nibbled at a second. When her stomach didn't protest, she took a long drag of water to soothe her parched throat. Yes, the worst of her nausea was over.

Her cell phone rang.

"Erin."

"I assume you've seen the news," Curt said.

"Haven't been able to do much but watch TV."

"I need you back in DC. Take the first plane you can. Be quiet about it. No more tricks."

She didn't bother to explain that the vomiting and diarrhea weren't her fault. Curt wouldn't believe her. And telling Curt about Kyle's involvement would only help Curt. For the moment, letting Kyle work against Curt would help Navy. Erin wondered if Kyle was the one who had leaked Operation Critical Mass to Navy in the first place. If Kyle was working with the saboteurs, and the saboteurs wanted Navy's disappearance to be tied to the leak, it would explain why Kyle didn't want Erin's ruse to succeed.

She dug in her travel medicine kit for pink tablets and swallowed two of them. In a compartment underneath the medicine, she always kept a small flip phone with the battery removed. She couldn't use the cellphone safely in the hotel room. Her surveillance would be able to detect that a cellphone signal was coming from her room. At the airport, she would find a quiet place to send a message to Jackson and Byron. She changed out of the clothes she'd been wearing for two days. A quick shower washed the acrid scent from her hair. Once she put on fresh clothes, she almost felt human again.

"Front desk," said a bored voice when Erin dialed zero.

"I need a cab in fifteen minutes."

When she swung her duffel bag into the backseat, the cab driver did a double take. "Navy Trent?"

Erin sighed. "No. I need to go to the airport." She gave the driver enough bills to cover the fare plus a generous tip, then laid back and closed her eyes

The cab driver didn't take the hint. "Can you believe what's on the news?"

"Crazy." The thought of dealing with William, who was

probably pissing his pants, and Curt, who seemed to be unraveling toward homicidal, made her head ache.

⁊

Navy stood in the center of the dank basement refuge. She was alive, the information had been revealed as she intended. It was time to come back to the world. Probably.

The set of documents revealed by the virus only proved there was a kidnapping plot that had gone wrong in Amsterdam. The second set was more sensitive and had been sent only to reporters. They contained proof that the operation had been authorized by the president and that the operation had been deliberately sabotaged. She left out any editorial bits. If she was right, the reporters would come to the same conclusions she had. She would let the crowd sort it out.

She plugged the cell phone modem into the net book and turned it on. The signal bars wavered. She held the net book up to a boarded up window while the messages on her temporary email account slowly downloaded. There were about fifty, most of them spam. She had purposely subscribed the email address to some dodgy lists so Jackson's message wouldn't be the only one. If he'd sent her anything. She had to sort through them all now to figure out. The message would be in code. Just in case she wasn't the only one reading the email account.

Her finger twitched, pressing the down arrow before she finished reading each message. She had to go back and reread several of them. Viagra spam, penny spam, a few chain letters, suspicious links to pornography sites and . . . a sunscreen ad.

"Not safe in the sun!" read the subject line. "Your high SPF sunscreen will not protect you! Solar flares are keeping radiation at an all time high for the next three days! Stay inside until your order arrives!" The text was followed by an odd link that was all numbers. It was the same length as the number Jackson had given her on the card in Amsterdam. A new phone number.

She had lost her burn phone at the metro station. To call Jackson, she would have to venture outside. A siren screamed by the house. Ten minutes ago the basement had felt like a prison, now it felt like a sanctuary. Should she just stay hidden? No, she had to keep moving. She had used the cell phone modem from here. And she had to call Jackson.

She didn't let herself consider that she was only taking the risk of calling because she was desperate for the sound of a familiar voice.

There was enough in one of her water bottles to scrub the worst of the dirt off her face and dig at the dark moons underneath her nails. The badly rumpled wig was only marginally better than her dirty hair and it scratched at her scalp.

She shouldered her pack and walked slowly upstairs. Her eyes blinked to adjust to the dim first floor, bright compared to the basement. No one was in the alley when she stepped out of the back door. After two days of intense darkness, even the gray daylight assaulted her eyes.

In the parking lot of the first gas station she found, she dropped the cell phone modem into the garbage can by the pumps. Keeping it would have been too much of a temptation.

She turned randomly through the neighborhood until she reached another gas station with grimy windows reinforced by silver wire. The prepaid cell phones were next to some cookies well past their sell-by dates. She bought a phone and a candy bar with cash. The radio story in the background was punctuated by her name. The White House had switched their story. Now they were claiming that she was part of the conspiracy to discredit the president. She didn't have time to hear the end of the story. She wondered if the media would see through it.

A small square of green grass euphemistically called a park looked like her best bet. A little bit exposed, but she would be able to see anyone coming. She couldn't make the call from her next hiding place, wherever that would be. Discarded fast food wrappers surrounded the singular bench. She used the mirror from her makeup compact to scan for anyone behind her. There were only pedestrians, hauling small plastic bags full of what passed for groceries from the gas station. The phone had been on the shelf for too long and the battery was already low.

The number Jackson gave her rang once, twice, and when she was about to hang up Jackson answered. Her eyes closed involuntarily at the sound of his voice. She missed him.

"Signal's weak," he said. "One minute." The signal was fine. In the background she could hear him walking through a hallway, down a set of stairs, and then out a door. "Okay, we can talk now. Are you safe?"

"For now. The battery's low. If I get cut off. What's going on?"

"Our friend feels like revenge."

"Great." It was a risk she couldn't have worked around.

"Can you stay hidden for three more days?"

"I think so. What are you going to do?"

"We'll think of something."

"Don't—"

"You can't say you don't need me." His voice was focused now, relaxed. He could protect her, like he had always wanted. "Let me worry about it."

"I don't have a way to contact you."

"Keep this phone. I have the number now. Take the battery out until you're ready to check in."

"J—"

"No names," he said brusquely.

"Keep an eye on my twin for me."

"Why?"

She searched carefully for the right words. "I think next week's horoscope will upset her."

"Stay safe." When he hung up, she felt a twinge in her chest.

Using the compact, she scanned the area behind her. Then she pretended to study the robins pecking in the weed-choked lawn to see if she had any watchers in front of her. If they were there, she couldn't tell. She consulted her mental map of Baltimore for other blighted areas with empty houses for her to hide in. The bus map and schedule crinkled in her pocket. Her purchase at the gas station had given her exact change for one more ride.

CHAPTER 47

EVERYTHING ABOUT THE hotel room said cheap to Jackson. The garbage can in the corner still had used condoms from the last occupants. Fraying threads hung from the comforters. The walls were so thin, Jackson could hear the click of a lamp turning on in the next room. He took a seat on the bed and the mattress sagged underneath him, releasing a musty smell.

Byron arrived several minutes later in disguise, hunched over and shaking like a junkie. His worn hooded sweatshirt had rips at the elbows and streaks of dirt across the sleeves. He straightened after the door had closed. Erin came in soon after. She looked tired and her face was pale.

"How was the toilet at the Marriott in Des Moines?" Jackson asked Erin softly. The three of them clustered together to keep their voices low enough for the thin walls.

"Lovely."

"Not your most subtle tactic," Byron said. "The domestic argument was nice, though."

"I didn't give myself food poisoning," she snapped. "Not that I didn't get blamed anyway."

Jackson wondered again who Curt was working for, and who was working against Curt. "Did you see who poisoned you?"

"Kyle. Same person who sabotaged the operation in Amsterdam."

Kyle was in the opposition party. He would have an interest in embarrassing the president. His position at the CIA would have given him the access.

"The operation was sabotaged so it would become public." Now Jackson was beginning to see the crosshairs Navy had been forced into. "Kyle was planning on Navy, Sara, and Moss dying in Amsterdam and using their deaths as a way to embarrass the president."

Byron rubbed his temples. "So Kyle sabotages the operation knowing William would have Navy executed instead of risking exposure."

"Roy said William was forced to order the execution," Erin said. "By someone named Andrew. Could that be the Andy that hired Curt?"

"And now Curt's going after Navy regardless of any tactical advantage," Byron said. "We have to get him to back off."

"I talked to Navy this afternoon," Jackson said. "She's going to lay low for three more days. We have some time to figure things out."

Erin's eyes lit up. "I could—"

"I'd prefer to have Curt walk away voluntarily. Navy's going to be in enough trouble after this is all over."

"Spoilsport."

"If we can find Andy, Curt's master, maybe we can get Curt muzzled." It wasn't much of plan, but it was the only one Jackson had.

"We can open those files now," Byron said. "That might give us some clues."

The ten o'clock news turned on in the next room, almost as loud as if it had been the TV in their room.

"The Amsterdam story, as it is being called, has taken a new turn this evening," an announcer's voice said.

Erin picked up the remote and hit the power button. The television didn't turn on. She got up and went to the TV, flipping through the channels until the sound matched the neighboring room.

"The president's initial attempts to distance himself from the operation have been fruitless. New documents released today by a *New York Times* reporter indicate that the Amsterdam Operation was authorized by the president himself. Internal sources confirm this. Even the agents who were supposed to allow themselves to be kidnapped didn't know its true purpose."

Jackson looked at Erin, wondering if this was the horoscope Navy had warned him about.

"A rescue for the kidnapped agents was never in the plans," the announcer continued. "The records seem to indicate that the death of the agents was intended to be part of a propaganda effort to shore up softening support for the war in Afghanistan and the president's surveillance initiatives. Navy Trent is still nowhere to be found and some are calling on the White House to prove that she hasn't been harmed."

Jackson saw a blur out of the corner of his eye and leapt toward the door. He caught Erin just as her fingers grazed the door knob. He wrapped his other arm around her waist to keep her from breaking free, wincing at the kick she delivered to his shin.

"Let me go!" she yelled, still kicking. Sadly, that kind of outburst wouldn't attract much attention in this neighborhood.

Byron stepped between Erin and the door and put his finger to his mouth. He held out his hand and lowered it slowly, a firm order to stand down. A commercial for strawberry yogurt interrupted the newscast. Two more commercials passed before Jackson felt comfortable letting Erin go. He sat her down on the bed.

"I'm going to kill them," she whispered. Her hands were balled into fists and pressed into the mattress. "Every single one of them."

"Keep your head on straight," Byron said. "It's suicide and you know it."

"You weren't on the chopping block. Don't tell me to calm down."

"You want your revenge?" Jackson wanted his revenge too.

Erin's eyes were burning with rage, intense in her pale face. "Yes."

"Then be smart. Work with us." She wouldn't be talked down to protect herself, but she might be convinced for their sake. "We need you."

She unclenched her fists. "Okay," she said finally. "We'll see how things go."

Byron sat down on the bed next to her. "William's our lever."

"He doesn't have any power," Jackson said.

"But he's growing a conscience," Byron said. "I think we can get him to tell us who controls Curt, who this Andrew person is. We find Andy and his team and let them know Curt is going to make it worse for everyone if they don't pull their assassin back in."

"And then?" Erin asked.

"Navy might have taken care of it already." Jackson pointed to the television. Pictures of a few senators, a general, and the head of the agency, each one neatly labeled with name and title. "Let it play out."

"You're just going to try and talk me out of killing them later," Erin said.

"Probably."

"Why didn't Navy tell us?" Erin was staring at the television where reporters crowding the press room of the White House were waving their recorders and yelling questions over each other. The spokesman at the podium was sweating at the temples.

"Not William's men," Jackson said, thinking out loud. "The *president's* men." In Des Moines, after they sparred, Navy had said what she knew was radioactive.

"What are you talking about?" Erin asked.

Jackson suddenly understood why Navy had been distant. "Navy thinks the president ordered her execution in Amsterdam because he was afraid of what she might have overheard during the kidnapping. She didn't want to add us to his list of enemies."

He felt a rush of sadness for her, wherever she was hiding. Becoming famous had been her best shot, and it wasn't enough.

The picture on the screen was replaced by a document Jackson didn't recognize, one not from the operations file he had seen. "Sources inside the White House have told us the surveillance powers bill relates to CRYSTAL, a previously undisclosed national security program said to be the personal project of the president and his chief of staff, Andrew Harrow."

Byron punched the mattress. "Andy. That was the person in the recordings."

"We need eyes on Curt," Jackson said. "Can you find him? Since he likes you so much."

"I always get stuck with the pyschos," Byron said.

"Erin, you and I are going to find William."

"I'd rather find Curt."

"Go with Jackson," Byron said. "With the mood you're in, William will believe you're going to kill him."

Three days, maybe sooner, until Jackson could call Navy and tell her everything was all right. He held on to that thought, pressing the pocket holding his burn phone. Except it wasn't there.

"My burn phone—" Jackson said. He stood up and shoved his hands into both front pockets, then the back pockets. He checked his coat. He kneeled by his pack and searched through it, the sound of the zippers loud in his ears.

"The phone Navy called you on?" Byron asked.

"Curt. Damn it. He bumped into me on my way out of the building. He picked my pocket and I didn't even notice."

"He can get the number Navy called you from."

"And an approximate location," Jackson finished the thought.

"She must have been disguised at the Metro station. They don't even know what she looks like," Erin said.

"They were running the surveillance video from the Metro station through facial recognition. Even with different hair and eye color they can match the bone structure. With a description and the cell tower she called from. . . ." Jackson felt the sting of his failure. "Curt suspected the whole time. He was just waiting for us to do something to lead him to her."

"Save your guilt for later," Byron said. "We need to change our plans. You have the number Navy called you on?"

Jackson recited it from memory.

"I'll go to ops and get the last known location for Navy. And any hits from the facial recognition software. Erin, it's probably better if you come with me, since the people Jackson needs to see nearly killed you," Byron said. "Jackson, you need to arrange a meeting with Andrew. Get him to call off Curt and get protection for Navy. Now that the story's broken, there's no advantage to killing her. You can make them see that."

"Oh, is that all?" Jackson said.

"Stop wallowing and do your job."

The words were harsh. And exactly what Jackson needed. He swung his pack over his shoulder. "I need that location and description as soon as you have it."

Jackson was up to eighty on the highway before he noticed. He forced himself to slow down. It would take Byron some time to get back to headquarters. There was no point in arriving at the White House without his bargaining chip.

His phone buzzed with Byron's answers just as he parked his car illegally near the White House gate. Navy had asked for an invitation; he didn't need one. It was dark, but the Secret Service would be watching the grounds. Jackson walked up to the gate and waited for a guard to confront him.

"If you're on the list for a tour, you'll have to wait until morning," the guard said.

Jackson held his hands up, showing he was unarmed. "My name is Jackson Fletcher. I have a message for the president. From Curt Holiander. I think the president will want to see me."

Ten minutes later, Jackson was escorted to a meeting room in the bowels of the West Wing. Andrew Harrow sat at the head of a long table that could seat at least twenty. He wasn't surprised to see William. Aside from Andrew and William, the rest of the chairs were empty. Judging by their disarray and the papers left behind, Jackson guessed the other occupants of the room had been told to leave in a hurry.

"I hope you don't mind delivering your message to me," Andrew said.

"I hope you don't mind a little white lie," Jackson said. "I needed an invite."

Andrew's eyes narrowed. "You're wasting my time. We have a situation to deal with."

"Let me guess. You've figured out that killing Navy Trent isn't going to help your case. But the man you sent to kill her, Curt Holiander, has disappeared and you don't know how to find him."

"That's a fair summary."

"I can find Curt for you. But I'll need some promises first."

Andrew leaned his chair back and tapped a pen on the table.

"Her protection. From here on out."

"That's not hard. As you said, she's arranged things so we'd rather have her alive."

"I need a team to find her and bring in Curt. And a second team to track down anyone else in the operation who's still at large."

"Done."

An aide stuck his head in the room. "Andrew, we have another situation brewing. In the legislature."

Andrew frowned, then looked at William. "William, you can make the arrangements. Jackson, I trust you can handle it from there." Without waiting for Jackson's answer, Andrew hurried out of the rom.

"If there's anything else I can do," William said. "I want to help."

Jackson studied William's slumping, portly figure. Could he trust William? Erin had said that William had been forced to give the kill order. Jackson needed all the allies he could get. "Make a list of everyone you know that might be holding a grudge against Navy. Make sure we bring them all in. I have to concentrate on finding Navy before Curt does."

CHAPTER 48

BY EARLY AFTERNOON, Navy had found a second basement that was very much like the first. The hours passed oppressively. When night fell, she allowed herself to try sleep. She needed it. But every time her eyes closed the walls leaned in toward her. The cracks in the dirty concrete oozed the scent of decay. At 2:06 a.m., she was still sitting upright in her sleeping bag holding a gun loaded with two bullets. Those had been Mark's instructions. With her range, she would only be able to reliably get off two shots before an attacker would be close enough to wrestle the gun away from her and use it to shoot her.

Wood splintered upstairs. A board being torn off one of the windows, or the door being kicked in. The hinges on the front door protested as it opened. A pair of heavy boots landed on the floor just above her. She pulled her mat and sleeping bag under the stairs. Maybe it was a junkie, or someone searching for the last of the copper pipes. She released the safety on her gun and leaned against the wall, reminding herself to breathe. The boots clomped up to the second floor, methodically searching each room, and then back down to the first floor. Someone looking to strip the house would be moving slower. Someone looking for a place to get high would have stopped in the first empty room.

She checked the safety again to make sure it was released.

The door at the top of the stairs opened and the dim light of a streetlamp illuminated her hideout. Boots landed heavily on the wooden steps, shaking debris onto her hair. Breathe slowly, she reminded herself. Whoever it was didn't know she was here. A panting breath would give her away. A speeding heart would take her closer to panic. The intruder searched the other half of the basement, and then returned to the bottom of the basement steps.

Her gun would be useless if she let the intruder get too close. She stepped out from under the stairs into the dim light to face him, pointing the gun at his chest. Her hands were not shaking.

Curt was no longer wearing a tuxedo, like at the White House. His loose army green T-shirt stretched over a barrel chest. His arms were twice the size of hers. The length of his right bicep was covered with the tattoo of a battlefield cross. A crowbar was swinging from one hand, a gun pointed at her in the other. "Loverboy led me to you."

The phone call Jackson answered. Somehow Curt had traced it.

"My death won't change anything," she said. "You must know that by now." From Mark's lectures, she knew a shoot-out was unlikely to end in her favor. There were no good places to get shot, just bad ones and worse ones.

"I don't care." The crowbar spun in his hand once, twice. "You don't understand what you've done."

"I defended myself."

"You killed my men!" Wood splintered as Curt buried the hook of the crowbar in the stair frame. Curt re-aimed his gun at her chest.

She could have shot him while he was distracted; she had wasted the opportunity. "The men in the mansion, they were yours."

"No, my unit in Afghanistan. Killed by the bomb that

CRYSTAL could have prevented." The wildness in his eyes did not make his gun any less steady. He pulled the crowbar free without looking away from her.

"You led a unit in Afghanistan."

He smiled. "Now you understand."

The mad hatter's eyes were replaced by cold calculation. He would take her life because it was here to be taken, because the real enemy would be forever beyond his grasp.

"I didn't kill them."

"As good as. You made our secrets public. Our enemies will use that against us. More soldiers will die because of what you did."

The accusation had occurred to her. It wasn't enough to say someone else would have done the revealing for her; an action could be both immoral and inevitable. "I revealed the plot of a corrupt president who wanted to hijack the democratic process to build a false justification for a surveillance state."

"Fancy words from a traitor."

She tried to summon Jackson's patience, Erin's courage. Instead, she found a simmering rage, a tainted jury within her that demanded she match Curt, pain for pain. "I won't go quietly. I might even take you with me."

He laughed and dropped his gun on the floor. "Little girls shouldn't play with guns." Then he was one stride closer to her, with the crowbar in striking position.

She shot him twice as he took the second stride. Curt flinched but didn't fall.

Two circles of blood appeared on his shirt. One shot in the ribs and one shot in the stomach. A little higher and she could have stopped Curt's heart. Still, Curt should have been on the floor, bleeding out. Instead he advanced on her, the crowbar whistling in his hand.

She circled away from the wall to give herself room to maneuver, crouching forward to keep her balance. Air hissed in and out of a hole in Curt's chest as he swung the crowbar. She dodged down and to the right; it whistled past her ear, glancing off her shoulder. The jarring pain made her drop the gun and it clattered on the floor.

She didn't need to beat him; she just needed to outlive him. She weaved in between his blows. The shadows of his arms left swirls in the air. Navy circled the entire room before his movements slowed. When he stumbled, she saw her opening. She aimed her heel at his stomach wound and slammed an elbow into the wrist holding the crowbar.

He dropped the crowbar but caught her by the shoulders, squeezing his meaty thumbs into the tender spot just below where arm meets collarbone. She kicked at his groin. He fell back briefly, but not for long enough. Her arms still swung dumbly at her sides. He picked her up and threw her against the concrete like a rag doll.

She heard the smack of her skull before she felt it and rolled up to her feet before the pain registered. Curt was flagging, but he was still strong. The corners of his mouth turned up in a vicious smile. His rage was her advantage. He was focused only on her; he knew he didn't need any weapons. He had forgotten about the crowbar lying on the floor. Use that, she thought. Give him an opening he can't resist. She waited until she had circled back to the crowbar and turned as if preparing for a back kick.

His arms closed around her faster than she expected. She flipped him easily enough, grabbing the crowbar as he hit the floor. He was dazed, but not still. His hands were reaching for her throat. She turned the blade on the crowbar parallel to his ribs and plunged it into his heart. His eyes widened in surprise. Blood bubbled up through the wound at the end of the crowbar like liquid rust. His eyes took on a glassy look. There was one last hissing breath and the basement was quiet again.

Her whole body shook, and she fell to her knees. A pool of blood spreading from his body soaked her jeans and she scrambled backwards, landing hard against the concrete wall. Then the pool reached the toes of her shoes and she scrambled again, crab-walking along the wall.

She tried to take a deep breath but she could only manage short gulps of air that didn't satisfy her speeding heart. Jackson. She had to call Jackson. She took the phone from her pack and pressed the battery into it. The battery was almost dead. The phone rang before Navy could dial.

She was ashamed of the sob that escaped when she heard Jackson's voice.

"Navy, are you okay?"

"I had to kill him." *I had to kill him.*

"Tell me where you are."

The answer floated up in her mind. She was surprised it was still there. "Basement. 1352 Ashland. Balt—"

"Yes, Baltimore. We know. We'll be there in a few minutes. Are you injured?"

She didn't know. She couldn't feel any pain. "Nothing serious, I think." She pressed the phone against her cheek and huddled in the corner farthest from Curt's body. "Just . . . keep talking. Don't hang up." But the battery died and the phone went silent.

Several cars approached outside and doors slammed. Was it Jackson? Friends of Curt? She looked at her gun across the room, imagined trying to fumble two more bullets into the magazine. She couldn't. She had nothing left. If it was Jackson, she was saved. If it wasn't, she was done.

❧

Jackson dialed Navy's number again but the call went straight to voicemail. Thin patches of weeds stuck up through the cracks in the sidewalk in front of 1352 Ashland. The long grass and weeds strained the garbage from the wind that moved across the lawn, plastic bags with holes in the bottom, beer bottles coated with dirt, and open sheets of newspaper waving in the breeze.

The front door was open, splintered at the lock, swinging in the humid dawn air.

He motioned for the plain clothes Secret Service men to stay outside. Broken glass crunched under his feet when he walked into the house. The window by the front door had been broken before it was boarded over. Curt wasn't the first to break in.

He found the stairs to the basement and called Navy's name. She didn't answer.

"Navy? It's me. I'm coming down."

He reached the bottom of the creaking stairs and waited for his eyes to adjust to the pale dawn reaching through the front door. Curt's body was close to a wall at the center of an oval pool of blood. A long metallic object stuck out of his chest. Navy's gun was in one corner and Navy was across the room, pressing herself against the wall as if she could disappear into it, hugging her knees tightly to her chest. A pistol he didn't recognize—must be Curt's—was at the bottom of the stairs.

"I had to kill him," she repeated when he kneeled down next to her. Once again, he had arrived too late.

The concrete floor pressed against his knees painfully. He untangled her hands, running his fingers lightly across hers. She was shaking but her skin was warm. Not shock then. Adrenaline.

"I need to check for broken bones." He forced himself to concentrate on the practical.

She let her feet slide down until her legs were stretched out in front of her and her arms went limp. He ran his hands down her legs. Her jeans were crusty with the dirt from the basement, but nothing was out of place or swollen. He cupped a palm around each side of her chest, feeling for the telltale creak of broken ribs. This was not how he had imagined their first intimate touch. She was still shaking, breathing unevenly, her mind caught in the fight. She winced when he felt her shoulders but it was only a bruise. He could feel the straight line of the collarbone underneath her skin.

Her limp arms hung at the right angles, and nothing felt out of place. A nasty bump was forming at the base of her skull, the size of a hardboiled egg. "There's a paramedic waiting, but it looks like nothing's broken."

She held out her arms and twisted them in the dim light, examined the scabs forming at her knuckles. "I should be in pain."

"It's the adrenaline." He should bring Navy up to the paramedic. But he wanted to be alone with her. They would be caught in a whirlwind once they went upstairs. William was waiting to ask her questions Jackson was sure she wouldn't answer. The Secret Service men tasked to protect her had been told to not let her out of their sight. The media would find her soon if they hadn't already.

"It was my fault," he said. "Curt found you because I messed up."

"You mean Curt saw you answer the phone?"

"He picked my pocket. I was so worried about you I—"

"You had to answer."

Heavy footsteps thumped on the floor upstairs. Navy tensed and looked at Jackson.

"Friends," he said. "The vice president sent the Secret Service to protect you."

"The vice president?"

"President Orway resigned last night. He would have been impeached otherwise."

Navy shook her head. "So he really did do it."

"Yeah. What did you mean about next week's horoscope?

The detail about planning to let the operatives be killed broke last night."

"Oh, faster than I expected then. Is Erin okay?"

Jackson shrugged. "We'll see. We've managed to keep her from doing anything stupid so far. We left her in DC because William insisted on coming."

"I have to see him again?"

"Couldn't be helped. He was actually useful tonight."

"That's . . . odd."

He took a pair of latex gloves out of his pocket and walked over to Navy's gun. He picked it up by the barrel with two gloved fingers. A whiff of gunpowder floated up to his nose. He carried the gun over to Curt's body and flicked the safety up. He leaned over the pool of blood and wrapped Curt's fingers around the handle, pressing one finger to the stuck trigger. When he was sure there were enough fingerprints on it, he removed the gun from Curt's hand, released the safety, and dropped the gun on the floor a few feet from Curt's body. If the gun had Curt's and Navy's fingerprints on it, the techs would assume it belonged to Curt. Jackson had made sure the gun was untraceable when he gave it to her. The gloves snapped off and he stuffed them into the pocket of his cargo pants.

"Are you ready for me to call the paramedic down?"

She shook her head. "I can walk upstairs."

"The paramedic really should—"

Navy pushed herself up using the wall. "I can smell his blood," she said. "Let's go upstairs." Navy pulled her pack from the shadows. From her wince, he knew the strap had landed on her bruised collarbone when she swung it onto her shoulder. "I think the adrenaline's wearing off."

"Here, let me," he said. The pack was heavier than Jackson

expected. A box of bullets rattled near the bottom. "The pain will be worse tomorrow. Then it should get better."

"Agent Fletcher?" The voice belonged to the leader of the Secret Service team. Navy stopped moving.

"One minute," Jackson answered.

"What happens now?" Navy asked.

"After the paramedic checks you out, the Secret Service will take you to a high-security hotel in DC. The kind diplomats stay at. They need a few hours to finish rounding up everyone."

"And then?"

"I don't know, Navy."

She bit her lip and looked toward the stretched rectangle of light at the bottom of the stairs. "This might be too much to ask, but I really would appreciate it if —" She closed her eyes and took a deep breath. "I mean, maybe if you could —"

"You want me to stay with you?"

"Yes," she whispered. Her eyes were open now.

"Is this Navy Trent asking for my help?" She pushed him lightly on the shoulder and he caught her hand, pulling her close. There was barely a speck of dust between them. "Of course I'll stay with you."

She fell against him, wrapping her arms around his neck. Her warm breath touched the place where the artery in his neck pulsed. He was surprised to feel her full weight, her trust, against his chest. She was so exhausted she was barely standing. He kissed the top of her head and put his free arm around her waist. The silhouettes at the bottom of the stairs moved impatiently.

"Jackson, Navy, get your asses up here." It was Byron's voice, gruff and weary.

She hugged Jackson tighter, then stepped away, blinking, into the light, stronger and yellower as the sun rose. He followed her, his hand at the small of her back. Navy studied the crowd at the top of the stairs warily. There were ten plain clothes Secret Service men, white wires stuck in their ears, plus Byron. She stepped toward Byron and the crowd parted for her.

The paramedic had brought a stretcher into the wrecked living room. She walked toward it slowly, looking back to make sure Jackson followed. "Have a seat," the paramedic said.

Navy sat hesitantly on the edge of the stretcher.

"Lie back, please." Her body stiffened as the paramedic's gloved hands got closer and he paused, reconsidering. "Try to relax. No one's going to hurt you."

She nodded and took a few shaky breaths. The paramedic repeated Jackson's examination to check for broken bones, then held a stethoscope to her chest, lungs, and stomach to listen for internal bleeding.

"Lucky girl," he whispered under his breath. "Everything seems fine," he told Navy. "But we have a team waiting at the hospital for you. We should get some X-rays and—"

She shot up to a sitting position. "No." Her eyes jumped to Jackson and he took her hand. She hadn't reacted well to the doctor in Amsterdam either.

The paramedic looked at Jackson for help. "She could have a concussion. Or other internal injuries. She should go to the hospital."

The paramedic was right, of course. But after all she had been through, Jackson didn't want to force her to do anything. "I have some field medicine training," he said. "I can stay with her tonight—if you'll let me know what to watch for."

"She should go to the hospital."

"I won't go," she said. When the paramedic reached for her with a well-meaning touch, she jumped off the stretcher, nearly landing on Jackson's foot. "Don't touch me again."

"If she says she's not going, she's not going," Jackson said.

The paramedic shook his head. "Fine. That's a nasty bump

on her head, watch for signs of a concussion. And any signs of blood loss due to internal bleeding: low blood pressure, weakness, shortness of breath. If she needs pain medication, no aspirin."

The plain clothes men dispersed into the three SUVs with tinted windows that were parked on the street. Byron led Jackson and Navy to the middle SUV. Jackson wished the Secret Service had sent a plainer SUV. William had requested one that was more like a limo, with two rows of seats facing each other to allow for business meetings in transit. William waited in one of the seats that faced backward. Byron nudged William over so he could sit.

Jackson and Navy took the other row of seats.

The SUV growled to life and turned into the street to follow the lead car. The third car pulled in behind them. They headed south on the deserted streets. Navy tried to sit up to stare out the window, but her drooping eyelids and yawns betrayed her. She rested against Jackson, her head on his shoulder.

Byron noticed and hid a smile. A block later, William took out a pen and a notebook and looked expectantly at Navy. "I've been sent to debrief you."

"No," she said simply.

"No what?"

"No debriefing."

"I didn't know about the real purpose of Operation Critical Mass. You can trust me."

Navy smiled and shook her head, the gesture slight against Jackson's shoulder. "Who did you think Curt was when you first met him?"

"A liaison from the White House, like he said."

"You didn't notice his boxer's ear? The scars on his hands?"

The pen poised above his notebook wavered. "No," he said.

"You seem like an okay guy, William. But maybe you should look into selling insurance or something."

Jackson coughed to cover his laugh. Byron grinned and turned away to look out the window so William couldn't see his expression.

William puffed himself up and held the pen straight again. "I have the authority of the president of the United States."

"If I told you how I got that information, how I escaped in DC, how I managed to reveal all of it—what do you think the people above you would do with that information?"

William didn't answer.

"Go ahead and ask me again—if you think they'd use the information well. I still won't tell you a thing, but you'll know what kind of man you are." She said it all with her eyes closed, curled into Jackson's shoulder, as calm and relaxed as a cat on a windowsill. When she fell asleep a few minutes later, William was still trying to answer her challenge, staring down at the pen and paper in his lap as if the pen would spell out the answer.

CHAPTER 49

EVERY SINGLE ONE of her bruises greeted Navy when she woke up, despite the soft bed that cradled her as gently as a cloud. Jackson was right. The next day was worse. The smell of the floors of the cold, dark basements surrounded her. It wasn't her imagination. She'd been so tired when they reached the hotel, she'd crawled into bed in her filthy clothes.

She sat up and fingered the down comforter. The duvet cover alone probably cost more than her bed at home. Lush gold curtains blocked most of the light. A gust from the vent stirred them. She tensed, half-expecting Curt to emerge from behind the fabric. No, Curt was dead. She had killed him.

Dead, dead, dead. She saw his eyes just after his heart had stopped, glassy and wide with surprise. She wondered what had kept her nightmares away. A pillow rested on top of a neatly folded blanket on the floor next to the bed. Was that where Jackson had slept? Where was Jackson?

Her pack was by the nightstand. Its grimy exterior was out of place next to the polished furniture. A set of fresh clothes sat on the nightstand, next to the alarm clock. She had slept past lunch. Beyond the door into the larger suite of the hotel room, she could hear the rustling of people, but no voices to identify them. She wasn't sure she wanted to see anyone yet.

In the bathroom she dropped her crusty clothes on the cream tiles. Every motion hurt. Her jeans fell into stiff, creased triangles. Dirt sprinkled into the thick mat by the shower. Her hair hung in oily, knotted clumps. She took a deep breath and faced the mirror, naked. Her injuries were worse than any bruising Mark had given her in training. On her shoulders, where Curt had dug his fingers in, were small spots the shade of a river at midnight. There were two fist-shaped bruises on her stomach and the long stripe of the crowbar against her collarbone. Even her hands were injured. Several knuckles had scabbed over and dirt had gathered in scratches on her palms. She turned around and craned her neck to see the rest of the damage.

Nothing visible, but she could feel a tender spot just below the base of her spine. She pressed her fingers to it and winced. A bruise so deep it hadn't even reached the surface. She lifted her hair to feel the possible concussion the paramedic had warned Jackson about. The swelling was the size of a plum. She was glad she couldn't see what color it was.

The shower head was large and flat, like a sunflower. She welcomed the hot needles of water that pounded the dirt off her shoulders, neck, and arms. Brown rivulets of water snaked down the drain. It reminded her of the woods and her pack, sunk at the bottom of the Potomac River.

When her skin was red she reluctantly abandoned the shower, digging her toes into the plush mat. Her toenails were filthy. Her fingernails too. A manicure set was next to the bottles of shampoo. She scraped at her nails until they were spotless. She threw the old clothes into the waste basket.

The new clothes fit perfectly: a snug but comfortable pair of jeans, and a tight red T-shirt with cropped sleeves. She felt almost human again. She pressed on the gold handle of the door to her room and opened it slowly.

Two Secret Service men guarding the front door looked up, nodded at her briefly, then went back to their posts. Erin was attacking a grapefruit at the small breakfast table. The table was framed by transparent silky drapes. Fruit and cut bagels were laid out on a platter.

Erin's body went stiff as a board when Navy hugged her.

"I don't do hugs," Erin said, muffled by Navy's shoulder.

"I'm just glad you're here," Navy said. And not getting arrested for assassination, she thought.

Navy unwrapped the cloth napkin from the silverware but didn't bother with the plate. She speared pineapple chunks and strawberries and grapes and cubes of melon until her mouth was full.

"Blame Jackson and Byron," Erin said sourly. "They've been keeping me busy. Congrats, by the way."

Navy's mouth was stuffed with a bite of an onion bagel smeared with cream cheese. "Hmmm?"

"You survived a fight with Curt."

She wondered how much she should say in front of her Secret Service protectors. "Well, he was shot twice and he still managed to give me a pretty good bruising. I could probably use a few more lessons."

"Anytime," Erin said.

The offer seemed genuine. Did Erin consider her a friend? Navy never would have imagined that someday she'd be accepting the congratulations of a CIA assassin over breakfast.

There was a knock on the door. One of the Secret Service agents looked through the peephole, then opened the door. Byron entered, followed by Jackson. An unfamiliar emotion relaxed Navy's shoulders. Safety, she realized. She felt safer when Jackson was around.

The agent returned to his post. The movement revealed a gun holstered at his waist and another at his ankle.

Jackson walked through the maze of ornate furniture and dropped a newspaper next to her plate. He brushed a hand across her shoulders, his warm fingers coming to rest just above the bruise on her collarbone. She wasn't sure if the headline or his touch made her shiver.

Two large pictures dominated the page above the fold. One was President Orway at a press conference, looking haggard and beaten. The second was the curved tables of the Senate, every seat filled with a suit. "Midnight Resignation," the headline read.

"I thought you might like to see your handiwork," Jackson said.

She unfolded the front page and scanned the rest of the headlines. Every line on the front page was related to the Amsterdam story. Her name was in half of the headlines. Was this what she had wanted?

"Maybe there'll be an earthquake somewhere tomorrow," she said hopefully.

"What did you expect?" Erin asked.

Navy's eyes flicked to the Secret Service men by the door, then back to the headlines. "I didn't think much past survival."

Jackson dug in his pocket until he pulled out a tiny square of plastic. The SIM card from her phone. "Secret Service has a new phone for you downstairs. Your mom is calling the White House switchboard every five minutes."

"Can't I call from here?"

"Not enough time. We have a busy afternoon."

"Are my parents all right? And Sara and Moss?" Navy asked. "I mean, did everyone stay . . . protected?"

"We had to visit the police station in Cedar Rapids," Byron said. "But everyone's fine."

"Well, I'm off," Erin said. "Now that your escort has arrived."

"No, you're not." Byron stepped between Erin and the door. "We have errands."

"I don't need babysitting."

"Yes, you do."

"I was kind of hoping to sit here and eat ice cream all day," Navy said as the door shut behind Byron and Erin.

Jackson took the seat Erin had left. "The former vice president, now president, has arranged for one of his media people to meet with you. They want you to do interviews. They'll probably give you some coaching on what not to say. Be prepared for flash photography downstairs. It's leaked that you're here."

"Why is the president so eager for me to talk?"

"To distance himself from the former president. Have people hear how you were rescued and protected by the Secret Service under his orders. The photographers are probably here because of him, to make sure there are pictures of you under his protection."

She picked up a pen from the table and jotted a question in the margins of the front page of the paper. She pushed the paper toward him.

Bullets in my pack?

"I guess it's time to get a phone then," she said.

"I know a place on the way," he said, answering her note while he talked.

Took them out last night.

She went through a mental inventory of what was left in her pack. The camp stove, the lock-picking kit, her net book, a couple dehydrated meals and some cash. The net book she shouldn't leave here. It was encrypted, but with enough time the encryption could be broken and traced back to the email account she had used.

Jackson checked his watch.

"I need to grab a couple things from the room," she said. "Are you sure we can't stay here eating ice cream all day?"

His wide smile made her heart flip. She realized she had never seen him this relaxed. "You have five minutes."

She put the net book in her back pocket. Her roll of cash had dwindled to almost nothing. She peeled a few tens off and stuck those in her front pocket. Her ID and credit cards went in the other front pocket.

Jackson took Navy's arm as they walked toward the elevator, Secret Service in tow. At the elevator, Jackson left, to avoid the cameras.

"I'll meet you at the car," he said.

The Secret Service agents had to clear a path through the crowd of photographers and reporters downstairs. The bright flashes were punctuated with reporters' questions. Had she escaped or been kidnapped? Was she happy about the president's resignation? She tried to keep her face neutral.

An agent handed her a shrink-wrapped box as soon as she sat down in the car. Did the seal on the box mean the phone hadn't been tampered with? Navy decided that it didn't matter for this call. She put her SIM card in and turned it on. It rang before Navy even had a chance to dial her voicemail.

"Are you okay?" her parents asked together.

"I'm fine," she promised.

"You're sure?" her mom insisted.

"Just fine. I was checked out by a paramedic and everything." Navy left out what the paramedic had actually said.

"In that case . . . what the hell were you doing? We've been worried sick. You just disappear, no note, no call. And then the news? You told me you ended up in spending three weeks in Amsterdam because . . ."

Navy held the phone away from her ear and let her mom

vent. The lecture Navy was getting was everything she expected and deserved. She had wanted to tell parents not to worry, but she knew that her parents had been under the same electronic surveillance she had been.

"Are you done, Mom? I'm fine."

"You couldn't have sent an email? Left a voicemail for us?"

"No, I really couldn't. You and Dad are all right?"

"He was arrested. Did you arrange for that PI at the police station?"

"Yes."

"So you know that scary-looking man that showed up at the station?"

She saw Curt's wide eyes after she had flipped him, her hand flat on his chest to hold him down. How the blade of the crowbar tore the green fabric of his shirt, split the skin of his chest. "Sort of. We've got a busy day. I just wanted to let you know I was all right. Can I call you back later?"

"We? Who's with you?"

She looked up at Jackson, sitting beside her. He had been with her almost every minute since he had pulled her out of the basement in Baltimore, exactly as he'd promised. "A friend. I have to go. I'm so glad you're both safe." She hung up the phone before there were any other questions.

"I think we could use her in interrogations," Jackson said.

She laughed. It was good to laugh, to be above ground again. To feel safe. She reached for Jackson's hand without thinking.

The press mob was stopped at the tall black gates at the White House. Navy and Jackson were taken through a back door into the White House. Before last week, she'd never even taken the official tour. Now, she was here for the second time in a week. At least she was in jeans this time. She could see her ghost in the hallway, the worried face of a woman in a blue gown, trying to walk but wanting to run. An agent led Navy and Jackson to an office in the West Wing.

"Dan Foornis," the man behind the desk said. He was wearing a well-cut blue suit. His nails were manicured and his limbs were spindly.

"Navy Trent," she said, returning the handshake.

"First, I've been told to pass on a message about your apartment," Dan said.

Her apartment?

"We searched it while you were . . . gone. I'm sure you understand that, from our perspective, it seemed necessary."

Navy had expected her apartment would be searched. Was Dan expecting her to collegially agree on the topic of the violation of her privacy?

"The search was extensive and you may find some things out of place when you return home." He slid an envelope to her. "This is the paperwork necessary to file for compensation if there was any damage. Also, a list of the items that will be returned to you in due time."

"Thank you," Navy said, then wondered what she was thanking him for exactly.

"My main job is to coordinate your media appearances. There's the *Today* show, of course. And *Good Morning America*. You might consider *The View*. That's for the morning and midday crowd. After we get that settled we can talk evening news and the taped shows—like *48 Hours* and *Dateline*." He pulled out a spreadsheet divided into seven columns with times listed vertically and "Navy Trent Media Schedule" written at the top.

"What if I don't want to do any of them?" she asked.

Dan paused, pen hovering over the page. "Well, that'll make scheduling easier." He set the pen down and pushed the page away from him. "It makes no difference to me, of course, but avoiding the media is just going to extend the circus."

She studied Dan for a moment, then looked at Jackson to see if Dan was telling the truth. Jackson gave her a slight nod.

"I'll do one taped interview. That's it. You choose." She wondered why she felt the need to be difficult. To test them? To see what they would threaten her with if she didn't cooperate? She had to wonder if exchanging one suit for another at the top was really going to make a difference.

"I'm not here to force you into anything," Dan said. "I'm here as a courtesy. They're going to call you anyway, and hopefully, I can make things easier for you."

"Like an publicist."

"That's a good way to think of it."

"I'd like to tell the story once and then forget it ever happened."

"I'll make the arrangements." Dan looked at the list of shows he had jotted down on his notebook. "But first."

And there it was. The tone she knew well now, a bureaucrat about to make a threat.

"The president conveys his deepest apologies to you for your treatment by his predecessor. He understands that you thought you were doing the right thing, and that your actions were well intentioned. This is a trying time for the country."

Navy waited.

"He wanted me to ask for your consideration in the event there are other issues you're concerned about."

"You mean he wants to know if I have any other secrets I plan to reveal."

"Yes."

She didn't owe this messenger an explanation. But she also didn't want to be seen as a threat. "I didn't ask for these secrets. I haven't saved any. I just want to get on my life."

"Okay, Ms. Trent. The president will be glad to hear that."

The president's feelings didn't concern her. "Is that all?"

"We'll be in touch about your media appearance. You can see yourselves out."

Jackson raised one eyebrow as they got up. "Welcome to DC."

Navy followed Jackson toward the garage where the car waited. As they turned the corner, Navy saw a man with a face she knew only from the papers. Andrew Harrow, the president's chief of staff. Ex–chief of staff, to be precise. The man who had sent Curt to kill her.

Andrew lifted the cardboard box perched on his hip, the tip of a glass award wavered and clinked against something else. The remains of a career, packed into one box. A career that she had ended. "Guess you got what you wanted," Andrew said.

"No." She shook her head. "Not what I wanted." She felt Jackson hovering behind her.

"You have no idea what you've done. How many people you've killed."

Again, she shook her head. Nothing was ever that simple. She had known in the abstract that some people would consider her a traitor. A man like Curt she could fight. This man's hatred would fester.

"CRYSTAL would have saved lives. Crippled terrorism. I was here on 9/11, you know. Not so far from the Pentagon. I promised myself it would never happen again. Because of you, I can't keep my promise. Lots of good people work on CRYSTAL. I'm a good person."

"No, you're not," she heard herself say.

"We were protecting United States citizens. People like you don't understand what we were trying to do."

"I do, and that's the scary part."

For a split second, Andrew's sneer was replaced by confusion. "Then why—"

"You're blinded by your good intentions. You don't see the ways CRYSTAL can be abused. Imagine how different Watergate would have been if Nixon had the machinery you're asking for. Or if Hoover had CRYSTAL to watch Martin Luther King? Democracy can't function inside a surveillance state."

"Whatever you have to tell yourself."

She jumped when he pushed past her. She hoped none of the people pretending not to watch could see her shaking. A light touch on her shoulder pushed her forward.

"Well done," Jackson whispered.

"Tell me it's going to get easier."

He grinned. "Nothing you can't handle."

CHAPTER 50

BY THE TIME Jackson returned to the hotel with Navy, night had fallen. Her Secret Service detail had been pulled. Everyone involved in Operation Critical Mass had been accounted for. For the first time in months, Navy wasn't in immediate danger.

The ride in the elevator up to Navy's room was the first time they'd been alone since Jacskon had found her in the basement. He was surprised and disappointed to find Byron and Erin waiting for them in the room. Tomorrow, he had to leave for his next assignment. That left one night, tonight, to find out what he meant to her.

She had looked to him for comfort. She had looked to him for protection. She had cared enough to try to protect him. But did she want from him now that the moment of crisis had passed?

Erin lounged in one of the fancy stuffed chairs, her back to Byron. "Byron said we had to come back here to make sure you two were safe," Erin said. "You look fine."

Jackson looked at his watch. Erin's handler should have called an hour ago with her next assignment. She should be on her way to Afghanistan. Jackson knew because he and Byron had arranged the assignment to keep Erin out of the country until she had cooled down.

"How many meetings did they force you into?" Byron asked Navy.

"Just the one with some media agent." Navy hung her coat on the fancy coat rack. "And then we ran into Andrew Harrow on his way out the door."

"Sounds like a pleasant afternoon," Byron said.

There was a tentative knock on the door. Erin's handler? No, he wouldn't want Navy to see him. Jackson motioned for Navy to move away from the door and then looked through the peephole. William. Great. Jackson glanced at Erin. Navy noticed his concern and walked farther into the room, blocking Erin's view of the door. Navy couldn't have known why, but somehow she had known what he wanted. Navy knew Erin was unpredictable around William, especially now.

Jackson opened the door for William. There were bags under William's eyes, and his tie was loose and crooked. He was holding a piece of paper in one hand.

"Jackson. Byron." William nodded in greeting.

Erin was getting up when Navy turned toward her. "If you do anything stupid, I promise to give you a big hug," Navy said.

Erin glared at Navy, but sat down.

"I'll be quick," William promised. He looked at Erin apprehensively, shifting his weight from foot to foot. There was something different about him, Jackson thought. He seemed remorseful, humble. "I just need to talk to Navy for a second."

"So talk," Navy said. She took a seat on one of the couches.

William hesitantly approached. "I've been instructed to convince you to take a job in my department." He handed her a piece of paper with the official seal of the United States government centered at the top. "I don't expect you to take it. Two days ago I would have tried to talk you into it. Scared you into accepting the position. But, frankly, I don't know who this job offer is coming from. Or what they're up to."

Navy tilted her head to study William. "I might have been a bit harsh on the ride back from Baltimore."

William waved the apology away. "There's a deadline on the offer. If I don't hear from you in two weeks, I'll assume the answer is no."

Erin's expression had changed from angry to dumbstruck.

Judging by the nervous tic in William's foot, William still considered Erin a threat. "I'm sure you need some time to think," William said. "So." William left without finishing his sentence.

"What did you say to him?" Erin asked, once the door had closed.

"I don't remember exactly," Navy said. "I was kind of out of it."

"You told him he should consider being an insurance salesman," Byron said.

Navy winced. "Oh."

"So all these years we've been stepping around William like a land mine and all we needed to do was tell him he was incompetent?" Erin swung her legs over the edge of the chair. "I wish I'd thought of that."

"What did they offer you?" Jackson asked.

"Cybersecurity analyst," Navy read from the page.

"Not a bad gig," Byron said. "Give me a few days to check it out. See if someone's playing an angle."

Jackson liked the thought of Navy in DC—closer to him. Someone to come home for.

"You've made a few enemies," Jackson said. "It would be easier to keep an eye on you if you were here in DC."

"You think I need babysitting?" she asked. She looked up from the document, smiling. Was it possible she felt the same way he did?

Before Jackson could answer, Erin's phone rang. Jackson prepared himself.

Erin took the news from her handler as well as expected.

"I've been reassigned," she said in a chilly voice. "To monitor and respond to insurgent communications in Afghanistan for the next two months. From an underground bunker in the middle of nowhere."

"I can give you a ride to the airport," Byron offered.

"This is your fault!" Erin yelled at Byron and Jackson.

"And I know you would do the same for either of us," Jackson said. "Two months should be enough time for you to . . . get some perspective."

Erin walked out and slammed the door. It reopened a second later. "Are you driving me to the airport or not?" she asked Byron.

"At your service, ma'am." Byron waved at Jackson and Navy on his way out.

Jackson sat on the couch opposite Navy, leaning over to take the job offer from her. The letter was written on standard letterhead, the kind any recruit might get. "I wasn't entirely kidding about enemies," he said. "I don't know what to make of this."

"Whoever it is and whatever they're planning, it won't happen tonight," Navy said.

She stood up and took the job offer from him and wrapped her other arm around his neck, lowering herself to straddle his lap. She let go of the page and it fluttered, crackled, twisted to the floor. Her arms closed around him. The job could be a ploy to keep her close to Washington so she would be an easier target. It could be an offer of protection to make sure that the Amsterdam story wouldn't be reignited by an attack on her. It could be an attempt to find out her methods by watching her work. But his overwhelming thoughts were for the curve of Navy's hips, the slope of her shoulders, and the pads of her fingers against his spine. He moved his hands to her waist and pulled her against him until her hips rested against his stomach. They were two circles, one bound within the other. He could feel her strength, despite her recent ordeal, in the grip of her hands behind his neck. He could feel the beat of her heart in the vibration of her ribs, where his hands were clasped at her back.

"Navy—"

"You don't need to make any promises, Jackson."

He had committed himself to her months ago, when he had visited Des Moines. He couldn't walk away after tonight anymore than he could have then. "But—"

"The past few months I've done nothing but strategize and plan and *think*. Give me tonight."

He couldn't refuse her. He pressed his palm to her cheek; his thumb brushed her warm, flushed earlobe and he pulled her face to his.

The kiss made his heart pound in a deep, fast rhythm that drowned out everything else. She unclasped her hands from his neck, shrugged out of the long-sleeved shirt, and let it fall on top of the job offer. Her arms were covered with bruises.

"Jesus, Navy. Does it hurt?"

"Does it matter?"

"It does to me."

She looked down at her arms and touched the bruises one by one with a blank expression. "I survived."

"Maybe we shouldn't—"

"I want to."

He reached under the hem of the tight undershirt, felt the handfuls of cotton, and lifted the shirt slowly, revealing her stomach, her ribs. She bit her lip, suddenly shy under his intense investigation, and raised her arms over her head to let him undress her. Curt had given her all these injuries. Jackson's fury must have shown in his expression because she shrunk away from him, crossing her arms protectively over her stomach.

"No," he said. "Let me see."

Ovals the size of Curt's fists decorated her ribs and the taut skin of her stomach. Lines from the crowbar made x's along her shoulders.

His hands hovered over the bruises. "I should have been there."

She put a finger under his chin and tilted his head up. "Helping a civilian reveal state secrets? You would have lost everything. I wouldn't be here with you now."

He wished he could tell her that she was wrong. Instead, he wrapped his arms around her waist. When their next kiss ended, her face hovered inches above his. A smile danced on her lips. He brushed her hair away from her face and tucked it behind her ear, letting his fingers trail across her cheeks.

"I was so close to losing you," he said softly.

"I know." Her eyes were open now, searching his face.

He pressed his forehead to hers, the tip of his nose brushing hers. "The odds were against you."

She traced the collar of his shirt with her fingers and his heart sped up. "Why do people bet even when they think they're not going to win? You're the psychologist. You tell me if there's a fancy term for that." She kissed him again and the room seemed to spin.

"Can't seem to recall right now."

"Funny that."

He was being drawn into a whirlpool, warm and dark and enveloping. He didn't deserve to hold Navy; he had failed her in a hundred ways. He hadn't known she would be attacked in Des Moines. He should have won their sparring match. He should have been there to take Curt's blows instead of her. But her passion overwhelmed him and soon those thoughts too fell away. There was nothing in the world but the places where their bodies touched.

᪥

Navy woke up with her hand on Jackson's chest, her head nestled against his shoulder. He was sleeping soundly. The slit between the curtains showed no sign of dawn. She closed her eyes but they only moved restlessly beneath her eyelids. She disentangled herself from Jackson and slipped out of bed. Her bruises protested every movement. In bed with Jackson, she had felt no pain. It made her wonder what a night with him would be like when they didn't need to be so tentative. She pushed the thought away. Part of her attraction to him was that she knew he had to leave soon.

She picked up Jackson's shirt from the floor and pulled it over her head. His shirt swallowed her, a size too wide at the shoulders and the hem falling six inches past her hips.

Her job offer was still facedown on the floor next to the couch. She picked up the room service menu. Everything sounded good.

"Late dinner or early breakfast?" Jackson asked. He was framed in the doorway to the bedroom, wearing only his boxers.

She looked away, startled.

"You have my shirt." He didn't seem displeased.

She twirled. His gaze pulled her closer and pushed her away at the same time. "I think I look better in it."

"I agree."

She tried to focus on the menu. Her dizziness was only because they hadn't eaten dinner, she told herself.

"How does pizza and ice cream on the government's tab sound? That should make up for trying to have me killed. Twice."

"Only if you add onion rings." He walked toward her.

She picked up the handset of the phone on the end table and edged away, putting the table between them. A courteous voice answered. Her order would be delivered to the room in thirty minutes.

Jackson sat on the couch facing the door. He shifted to make space for her, but she took the seat across from him instead. Hurt flickered across his face.

"What do you think the job offer means?" she asked.

"I don't know," he said.

"Maybe you arranged for the job to keep me here." She tried to make it sound like a joke, but it fell flat.

"I can't say I'd mind."

She dropped her eyes to his chest, sparsely covered with dark hair, and then to the floor. "Am I more protected if I take the job?"

His tone became all business. "It's kind of like joining a gang without the initiation rites. You get friends."

"And enemies too."

"Some. That doesn't matter so much for a desk job."

"Do I need protection? Is there another Curt somewhere?"

He looked troubled. "Any enemies you have left are likely around Washington anyway. But protection wouldn't be a bad idea." He stood up and moved to sit next to her. She couldn't move away, she was right against the edge of the couch. "We should talk," he said. "About us."

"If I don't take the job, you're here and I'm in Iowa."

"I could just as easily have an empty apartment in Des Moines."

Jackson was lonely. In all the time she'd spent with him, she'd never noticed. "You don't know what I'm like normally. I'm not an easy person to be with," she said.

"I'm not either. " She didn't say anything and he continued. "I love my job. I'm gone a lot. I won't be able to tell you where I went or what I did. You can't count on me for holidays, birthdays, or anniversaries. I get injured often. There's always a chance that I won't come home and you might never know why."

Home. He meant the place where she was.

"I don't trust people easily," she said. "I don't like to be needed. I don't like to need other people. I have a temper and a sharp tongue. I spend a lot of time alone and I like it that way."

He took her hands and kissed each knuckle one by one. She wanted to curl up in his lap and never move again. She wanted to run away. Her heart thumped in her chest. Fear. All the things she had conquered and still panic could find her. She thought of what Mark had told her and let the voice in her head scream, simply holding herself still. Gradually her panic went from a scream to a yell to a whisper and then it was gone entirely.

"I'm game," he whispered, his breath warm in her ear. "If you are."

She raised her hand to his chest. His tight hug pressed into her bruises but she didn't care.

The nightmare that had started in Amsterdam was finally starting to recede. She could appreciate how the glittering city lights pierced the windows. She could listen to the traffic humming by below without anticipating a threat. She relaxed, resting her forehead on his shoulder. With a finger, she followed the line of the scar that traveled in a swoop from his collarbone to his sternum. Pressure was building in her lungs, around her heart. Like her chest was opening to release a deep sadness she didn't know she had been carrying.

"This isn't so bad, is it?" he said into her hair.

The elevator down the hall dinged. Footsteps approached the room. There was a short knock on the door. "Room service." Neither of them was dressed to answer. Navy pulled Jackson's shirt off, enjoying how his eyes widened at the sight of her figure, and draped the shirt over his face.

"You better get that," she said. By the time he put the shirt on, she had gathered her clothes and retreated to the bedroom. "Make sure they don't forget the barbecue sauce for the onion rings."

✧

For the second time, Jackson woke up next to Navy. Something he could get used to. And would have to live without for a while.

He'd been putting his next operation off for weeks, hoping to be around when Navy made her move. He hadn't talked to his handler for the past two days, but he knew Kevin had his own sources. As if on cue, his phone rang. Kevin. Navy stirred, and he sent the call to voicemail, hoping to let her sleep. She woke anyway, with a questioning look.

"My brother," he said.

"This early? It's five a.m."

He shrugged. "He's a morning person." The lie immediately made him feel guilty. She knew he was leaving soon. They had talked about it in as much depth as he could.

His phone rang again and he sent the call to voicemail.

"It's not your brother, is it?" Navy said.

"My next operation."

"How long— Sorry, I forgot." She leaned against him, nudging her shoulder under his arm until she could rest her head on him. "You know where to find me when you get back."

"What if something happens while I'm gone?"

She tapped him on the nose playfully. "We're not going to work if you keep treating me like a damsel in distress."

"I know . . . I just." He shook his head at his own stubbornness. How could he expect Navy to open up to him if he didn't do the same? "If you got hurt again, because I wasn't there to help, I don't what I'd do."

"You think you're the only one who's going to be worried

while you're gone?" Her hand on his chest softened the words. "It's not like you're going to visit Disneyland."

"That's different."

"Not so different. You have things you need to do there; I have things I need to do here."

"It's not that simple. I have training—"

"You were trained to shoot a gun. I was trained to write code. My code protected both of us."

Jackson hadn't ever considered code to be a weapon. But she was right.

"I think we need to set a few ground rules."

Jackson tried to cover his worry with a smile. "Rules?"

"First rule: don't try to lock me in a tower for my own protection."

He grinned. "Fair enough. Do I get to make any rules?"

"Of course."

"Remember that you have friends. Ask for help when you need it."

"You know that's not easy for me."

"Navy, I'm serious," Jackson said. "No more going it alone. You have friends. Use them."

Navy stared out the window, her face impassive.

"Promise me or I'll tell your mother to keep an eye on you."

"You wouldn't."

"I would. Scout's honor."

His phone rang again, rattling loudly against the nightstand.

"You should probably answer that," she said.

"First, promise."

He saw apprehension in her knit forehead, hesitation in her downturned mouth. He could tell her next words came with difficulty. "I promise."

He answered his phone. "Jackson."

"We're outside her hotel in the blue sedan," his handler said. "Are you ready?"

Jackson looked at the small black duffel bag waiting next to the bed. "Yeah. Be there in ten minutes." The drill was familiar to him now. Car to plane to another plane to another car and then on to a dry, dusty ride on pockmarked roads. It was good work even if it wasn't honest work.

"You're leaving this morning?" she asked.

He nodded. "What are you going to do about the job offer?"

"I'm not sure I want to go home. Doesn't feel like my life anymore."

They sat in comfortable silence for as long as he dared. He knew his handler was downstairs, impatiently tapping his fingers on the steering wheel. "Fill me in when I get back?"

"For sure." She tipped his chin down and gently brushed her lips against his. The kiss was no less intense than last night. It made him think twice about leaving. "That was just a reminder," she said. "To make sure you come home."

Home. Jackson liked the sound of that.

CHAPTER 51

NOT EVEN TWO weeks, Navy told herself as she stared at her apartment door. She hadn't been gone that long.

So open the door.

Instinctually, she reached for her keys where she had always kept them. Even the familiar gesture felt foreign. She unlocked the door and, before she could think too much, pushed it open. The doorknob hit her wrist as the door bounced back.

Navy pushed more gently this time, and the door opened halfway. She slipped sideways into her apartment and nearly tripped over her blender. Or what was left of it, anyway.

Her apartment had been trashed. The front door was partially blocked by the contents of the coat closet. Her collection of hobby electronics equipment spilled out over her shoes. Half of the robotics components were broken. The kitchen was in a similar state. Everything she owned had been pulled out and thrown on the floor.

If there was any damage? Navy wished she could fly back to DC and tell Dan Foornis what she thought of his bureaucratic doublespeak.

"Navy?"

Navy turned to see Sara in the hallway. "I thought our plans were for tomorrow?"

Sara edged her way into Navy's apartment and hugged her.

Navy hugged Sara back. "It's good to see you. But you didn't have to miss work for me."

"You disappear, make international news, nearly die, text me that you're coming back and expect that I'm not going to—" Sara had let go of Navy and was finally noticing the mess. "Who did this?"

"Some three-letter agency," Navy said. "Or C—" Curt or Curt's men, Navy had been about to say. But the name would mean nothing to Sara and it was probably better Sara never heard it.

"Even your couch? Seriously?" Sara held up a cushion, slashed in several places.

The damage was beyond necessary. *They didn't think I was coming back.*

"I guess I'll have to redecorate," Navy said.

Sara threw the cushion down. "Enough. Would you stop?"

Navy shook her head. "Stop what?"

"You're angry about this. I can tell. So be angry. You don't need to hide your feelings around me."

"I—" Navy wondered when hiding her thoughts from Sara had become reflexive. "You're right. I'm sorry."

Sara carefully traced a path to the kitchen and rescued two mugs from the floor. "I get it," she said as she rinsed them out with soapy water. "You had secrets you had to keep. Maybe you can't even tell me everything now."

"Are you . . . making tea?" Navy asked.

"Well, you didn't offer," Sara said. "And we have a lot to talk about."

Navy found a blanket to drape over the ruined couch. By that time, Sara had two mugs of tea ready. Navy curled up on one end of the couch, Sara on the other.

"Were you and Moss threatened while I was gone?" Navy asked. "I was worried."

"We were contacted. It was weird."

"Weird? Not scary?" Navy cupped her mug to let the warmth relax her.

"Did you know the press meets with the government when there are stories about classified information?" Sara leaned in. "Apparently, some government bigwig went around to every major news outlet and promised full cooperation on the story, if our names were left out of it."

"So you were safe. And you'll be safe." Navy knew the motive behind cooperating had more to do with good PR for the current administration than any concern for her friends. But she was still relieved. "Thank God."

"Yeah, we just got this call. Dan someone?"

Dan Foornis, Navy suspected.

"Anyway, he called us before the story even broke. Told us that if our names were mentioned or if any reporters came to see us, we should call him."

Navy wished she had been less rude to Dan when they had met. Then remembered that, once again, she was hiding her thoughts from Sara. "I met him and I wasn't very nice to him. Now I feel bad."

"So we're safe and nothing has happened here worth mentioning and I want to hear all about you."

Navy smiled. "Nothing worth mentioning?"

"Quit dodging my questions. What happens now for you? Everything goes back to normal?"

"It could, I guess. Well, maybe. I haven't even called work. We depend on venture capital funding. If my scandal offends one of our investors . . . I don't want to cause problems."

"Finding another job shouldn't be a problem," Sara said.

"Actually, I've been offered one." Navy sipped her tea. "A job with the government."

"The one you just screwed over?"

The likely reason she had been offered the job, to guarantee her protection, was a secret she should keep. "Security is a funny business. It used to be common for people to get hired by the companies they broke into."

"Used to be?" Sara asked.

"You were right. There are a few things I can't explain." Navy rested her cup on her leg. "I think I might take the job. Even if I have to move." Her next thought was uncomfortable, not because of secrets this time. Because it might hurt Sara's feelings. "I'm different. I'm not sure I can stay here and go back to my old life."

"I understand. I feel different too. I went to the car wash the other day and nearly had a panic attack when the car was surrounded by brushes. "

"I hate going to the grocery store when it's crowded because I don't like to get stuck in an aisle." Navy shook her head. "It's silly, I know. Like someone's going to jump out from behind the cornflakes and attack me."

Sara nodded. "The worse part is the way people look at you if you give any sign of being upset. Like you're crazy."

"Because they don't understand. Except for you and Moss, no one here understands."

"Part of me wishes our names had come out," Sara said. "For a week now, the Amsterdam story is all anyone wants to talk about. I worked so hard to get to the point where I could go a day without thinking about that damn basement."

"If you were okay with going back to your old life, I should be. How did you make it work?"

"You said I understand what you've been through, but I'm not sure. I didn't ever hold a gun. I didn't shoot anyone. I have this memory of your face after everyone else was dead. Your face was . . . blank. Completely. Almost like you weren't really in the room with us."

Navy shifted uncomfortably. "That's how I felt."

"Maybe the support you need isn't here right now. Maybe the people you need are your friends who have experiences closer to yours. The friends who helped you survive the past couple months. Like Jackson and Erin and Byron."

The last time Sara had seen Navy with Jackson and Erin and Byron, Navy had been screaming at them in a garage in Amsterdam. "How do you—"

"Do you remember that morning we went skiing together? And you asked if anyone had contacted me?"

"I'm so sorry I couldn't tell you the truth," Navy said.

Sara frowned slightly. "It's my turn to apologize. I was so angry at you. I knew you were hiding things from me . . . and when I called Jackson a creep you seemed so surprised. Like you thought Jackson was a good guy. I thought it was Theo all over again."

"You thought I was trapped in an abusive relationship again." Navy tried to not be insulted. "You know I'm better than that now."

"What was I supposed to think? You disappeared from your social life for weeks at a time. Even when you showed up, you were distant. Moss told me the only thing I could do was be supportive so you'd talk to me when you were ready. And then you disappeared. And I read the story in the newspaper. How you were given a thumb drive with all the information on it." Sara took a deep breath.

Navy grieved, again, for the months of friendship lost to the secrets she had to keep.

"Anyway, the news stories got me thinking about that morning again. And I realized that you were actually asking if I had received a mysterious thumb drive too. And I went back over every conversation we've had since we escaped. How in the hospital at base you apologized as if it was your fault we were abducted. Because, even then, you knew that you had been targeted for a reason."

"I suspected," Navy said. "Jackson told me not to say anything."

"Moss and I spent the past week dissecting everything we thought we knew about what happened in Amsterdam. Why was Jackson so concerned with what we told William? Why did someone else magically appear in the kitchen when either Moss or I were about to be alone with William? Why did you seem so close to Jackson, Byron and Erin our last dinner together and then magically angry at them the next morning? Why did you tell me you didn't think a relationship with Jackson wouldn't work when you both clearly cared for each other?"

"Sara—"

"Let me finish. So we realized Jackson, Erin, and Byron were protecting us from William. But in order for that to work, William had to think you weren't getting special treatment. William had to think you hated everyone there except for us. Which is why you threw that little performance our last morning in Amsterdam. To convince William you weren't a threat. That we weren't a threat."

"I wish I could have been here to explain."

Sara looked down at her cup. "I still want to be angry at you. I keep trying to think of a way you could have done things differently, where we weren't kept in the dark."

"Maybe there was. But I couldn't think of one."

"I couldn't either." Sara laughed. "Look at us. We should be happy."

"Forget about should." Navy heard Byron's voice echoing in her head. "It takes time to adjust."

"I can't imagine how lonely you must have been."

"Lonely and guilty," Navy said. "But it doesn't matter now. I have to think about what happens next."

"Take a few days. With what you've been through, you deserve it." Sara squeezed her knee. "I'm sure you'll figure it out."

Navy finished her tea and looked around the hopeless mess in her apartment. She picked up the portable speaker that had nearly rolled underneath the couch. She flipped open a small door on the bottom. The memory card was still inside. Navy weighed the speaker in her hands. She wondered if her old job wanted her back. If she wanted to go back. She wondered how it would feel to see Jackson when he returned, if their feelings for each other would have changed. She wondered what she would tell her parents about everything that had happened to her, starting in Amsterdam. She knew that all of those questions would be answered in time.

"Do you remember what we used to do on Saturdays at the shelter?" Navy asked.

Sara looked surprised. Navy rarely referred to the time she had spent in the shelter unless Sara brought it up first.

"We would turn on Aretha Franklin and sing at the top of our lungs while I helped you clean."

"Because you were avoiding the group therapy sessions at the neighboring church."

Navy turned up the volume on the speaker. "Sorry, it's hard to hear you over the music."

Sara shook her head and grinned. "Fine," she yelled. "Have it your way."

Navy dug in the cabinet under the kitchen sink until she found her trash bags. She took one for herself, then handed one to Sara. Then she opened the windows to the let the late spring air in, not caring how far their off-key voices carried.

ACKNOWLEDGEMENTS

This book has had a long road to publication, and I'm grateful for that. In the years since I began writing it, I've changed so much the first drafts feel like they were written by a stranger. On the long journey of writing and rewriting and editing, I've been lucky to have help from many people. My agent offered me encouragement even though the book never found a publishing house. Cheryl Batson, a climber, heavily corrected my climbing chapter. She and other MN Rovers have given me invaluable experience outdoors. My friends and family, particularly Bridget Kromhout and Chris Gales, gave me honest critiques. Fellow writers (Carol Ervin, Lindy Moon, Katherine Lato, and Sky, among others) shaped multiple first drafts. My editor, Dara Syrkin, pushed my characters out of their comfort zones.

Secretly, I wish I could get everyone together in a room and raise a toast to them for all their kind efforts. But we're all too scattered for that to happen. So I'll raise my own glass in private, and hope I can pay their kindness forward.